Acclaim for **Ian Rankin's**

EXIT MUSIC

"Crime at its most culturally provocative. . . . Art, drugs, porn, real estate, surveillance cameras, and, of course, political influence all figure into the action. For Inspector Rebus, as for the Edinburgh he carries around with him like a diseased heart, 'underworld' and 'overworld' are one and the same, transparently corrupt."   —*Harper's*

"Rebus is as gruffly mischievous as ever, and *Exit Music* ends in a cliffhanger scene with his arch-enemy that will have readers gasping. . . . Rankin's work is crime fiction at its most consuming, cerebral best."
—*The New Yorker*

"A fine ending to a superlative series."
—ADAM WOOG, *Seattle Times*

"Neither age nor impending leisure has mellowed Rebus, who's as prickly as ever. . . . After seventeen books, I've grown awfully fond of the old grouch; like the rest of his fans, I'm going to miss him terribly."
—TINA JORDAN, *Entertainment Weekly*

"In the Rebus novels Ian Rankin has provided a portrait of his chosen city that's as rich, detailed, and loving as any that any crime writer working today has given us of any city in the world. . . . This has been one of the best police procedural series ever written."
—PATRICK ANDERSON, *Washington Post*

ALSO BY IAN RANKIN

THE INSPECTOR REBUS SERIES

OTHER NOVELS

IAN RANKIN
EXIT MUSIC

LITTLE, BROWN AND COMPANY

NEW YORK BOSTON LONDON

Extract from "Hotel Room, 12th Floor" taken from *The Poems of Norman MacCaig*, Third edition © 2005 by Birlinn Ltd. Reproduced by kind permission of Birlinn Ltd. on behalf of the Estate of Norman MacCaig. Extract from *Be Near Me* © 2007 by Andrew O'Hagan. Reproduced by kind permission of Harcourt.

Little, Brown and Company
Hachette Book Group
237 Park Avenue, New York, NY 10017
Visit our website at www.HachetteBookGroup.com

Little, Brown and Company is a division of Hachette Book Group, Inc. The Little, Brown name and logo are trademarks of Hachette Book Group, Inc.

Printed in the United States of America

Originally published in 2007 in Great Britain by Orion
First United States edition: September 2008
First Mass Market edition: December 2009

10 9 8 7 6 5 4 3 2 1

*The frontier is never
somewhere else. And no stockades
can keep the midnight out.*

Norman MacCaig, "Hotel Room, 12th Floor"

*My father always said a policeman's knock is
unmistakable, and so it is, the rap on the paintwork
a very public command, feasting on the hearer's
capacity for guilt.*

Andrew O'Hagan, *Be Near Me*

DAY ONE

Wednesday 15 November 2006

1

The girl screamed once, only the once, but it was enough. By the time the middle-aged couple arrived at the foot of Raeburn Wynd, she was kneeling on the ground, hands over her face, shoulders heaving with sobs. The man studied the corpse for a moment, then tried shielding his wife's eyes, but she had already turned away. He took out his phone and called the emergency number. It was ten minutes before the police car arrived, during which time the girl tried to leave, the man explaining calmly that she should wait, his hand rubbing her shoulder. His wife was seated curbside, despite the nighttime chill. November in Edinburgh, not quite cold enough for a frost but heading that way. King's Stables Road wasn't the busiest of thoroughfares. A No Entry sign prevented vehicles using it as a route from the Grassmarket to Lothian Road. At night it could be a lonely spot, with not much more than a multistory car park on one side, Castle Rock and a cemetery on the other. The street lighting seemed underpowered, and pedestrians kept their wits about them. The middle-aged couple had been to a carol service in St. Cuthbert's Church, helping raise money for the city's children's hospital. The woman had bought a holly wreath, which now lay on the ground to the left of the corpse. Her husband couldn't help thinking: a minute either way and we might not have heard, might be heading home in the car, the wreath on the back seat and Classic FM on the radio.

"I want to go home," the girl was complaining between sobs. She was standing, knees grazed. Her skirt was too short, the man felt, and her denim jacket was unlikely to keep out the cold. She looked familiar to him. He had considered — briefly considered — lending her his coat. Instead, he reminded her again that she needed to stay put. Suddenly their faces turned blue. The police car was arriving, lights flashing.

"Here they come," the man said, placing his arm around her shoulders as if to comfort her, removing it again when he saw his wife was watching.

Even after the patrol car drew to a halt, its roof light stayed on, engine left running. Two uniformed officers emerged, not bothering with their caps. One of them carried a large black torch. Raeburn Wynd was steep and led to a series of mews conversions above garages that would once have housed the monarch's carriages and horses. It would be treacherous when icy.

"Maybe he slipped and banged his head," the man offered. "Or he was sleeping rough, or had had a few too many . . ."

"Thank you, sir," one of the officers said, meaning the opposite. His colleague had switched the torch on, and the middle-aged man realized that there was blood on the ground, blood on the slumped body's hands and clothes. The face and hair were clotted with it.

"Or someone smashed him to a pulp," the first officer commented. "Unless, of course, he slipped repeatedly against a cheese grater."

His young colleague winced. He'd been crouching

down, the better to shine light onto the body, but he rose to his feet again. "Whose is the wreath?" he asked.

"My wife's," the man stated, wondering afterwards why he hadn't just said "mine."

"Jack Palance," Detective Inspector John Rebus said.

"I keep telling you, I don't know him."

"Big film star."

"So name me a film."

"His obituary's in the *Scotsman*."

"Then you should be clued up enough to tell me what I've seen him in." Detective Sergeant Siobhan Clarke got out of the car and slammed shut the door.

"He was the bad guy in a lot of Westerns," Rebus persisted.

Clarke showed her warrant card to one of the uniforms and took a proffered torch from the younger of the two. The Scene of Crime Unit was on its way. Spectators had started gathering, drawn to the scene by the patrol car's blue beacon. Rebus and Clarke had been working late at Gayfield Square police station, hammering out a theory—but no prime suspect—in an unsolved investigation. Both had been glad of the break provided by the summons. They'd arrived in Rebus's wheezing Saab 900, from the boot of which he was now fetching polythene overshoes and latex gloves. It took him half a dozen noisy attempts to slam shut the lid.

"Need to trade it in," he muttered.

"Who'd want it?" Clarke asked, pulling on the gloves. Then, when he didn't answer: "Were those hiking boots I glimpsed?"

"As old as the car," Rebus stated, heading towards the corpse. The two detectives fell silent, studying the figure and its surroundings.

"Someone's done a job on him," Rebus eventually commented. He turned towards the younger constable. "What's your name, son?"

"Goodyear, sir . . . Todd Goodyear."

"Todd?"

"Mum's maiden name, sir," Goodyear explained.

"Ever heard of Jack Palance, Todd?"

"Wasn't he in *Shane*?"

"You're wasted in uniform."

Goodyear's colleague chuckled. "Give young Todd here half a chance, and it's *you* he'll be grilling rather than any suspects."

"How's that?" Clarke asked.

The constable— at least fifteen years older than his partner and maybe three times the girth— nodded towards Goodyear. "I'm not good enough for Todd," he explained. "Got his eyes set on CID."

Goodyear ignored this. He had his notebook in his hand. "Want us to start taking details?" he asked. Rebus looked towards the pavement. A middle-aged couple were seated curbside, holding hands. Then there was the teenage girl, arms wrapped around herself as she shivered against a wall. Beyond her the crowd of onlookers was starting to shuffle forward again, warnings forgotten.

"Best thing you can do," Rebus offered, "is hold that lot back till we can secure the scene. Doctor should be here in a couple of minutes."

"He's not got a pulse," Goodyear said. "I checked."

Rebus glowered at him.

"Told you they wouldn't like it," Goodyear's partner said with another chuckle.

"Contaminates the locus," Clarke told the young constable, showing him her gloved hands and overshoes. He looked embarrassed.

"Doctor still has to confirm death," Rebus added. "Meantime, you can start persuading that rabble to get themselves home."

"Glorified bouncers, that's us," the older cop told his partner as they moved off.

"Which would make this the VIP enclosure," Clarke said quietly. She was checking the corpse again. "He's well enough dressed, probably not homeless."

"Want to look for ID?"

She took a couple of steps forward and crouched beside the body, pressing a gloved hand against the man's trouser and jacket pockets. "Can't feel anything," she said.

"Not even sympathy?"

She glanced up at Rebus. "Does the suit of armor come off when you collect the gold watch?"

Rebus managed to mouth the word "ouch." Reason they'd been staying late at the office so often — Rebus only ten days from retirement, wanting loose ends tied.

"A mugging gone wrong?" Clarke suggested into the silence.

Rebus just shrugged, meaning he didn't think so. He asked Clarke to shine the torch down the body: black leather jacket, an open-necked patterned shirt that had probably started out blue, faded denims held up with a black leather belt, black suede shoes. As far as Rebus could tell, the man's face was lined, the hair graying. Early fifties? Around five feet nine or ten. No jewelry, no wristwatch. Bringing Rebus's personal body count to . . . what? Maybe thirty or forty over the course of his three-decades-plus on the force. Another ten days, and this poor wretch would have been somebody else's problem—and still could be. For weeks now he'd been feeling Siobhan Clarke's tension: part of her, maybe the best part of her, wanted Rebus gone. It was the only way she could start to prove herself. Her eyes were on him now, as if she knew what he was thinking. He offered a sly smile.

"I'm not dead yet," he said, as the Scene of Crime van slowed to a halt on the roadway.

The duty doctor had duly declared death. The SOCOs had taped off Raeburn Wynd at top and bottom. Lights had been erected, a sheet pinned up so that onlookers no longer had a view of anything except the shadows on the other side. Rebus and Clarke were suited up in the same white hooded disposable overalls as the SOCOs. A camera team had just arrived, and the mortuary van was standing by. Beakers of tea had materialized from somewhere, wisps of steam rising from them. In the distance: sirens headed elsewhere; drunken yelps from nearby Princes Street; maybe even the hooting of an owl from the churchyard. Preliminary statements had been taken from the teenage girl and the middle-aged couple, and Rebus was flicking through these, flanked by the two constables, the elder of whom, he now knew, was called Bill Dyson.

"Rumor is," Dyson said, "you've finally got your jotters."

"Weekend after next," Rebus confirmed. "Can't be too far away yourself."

"Seven months and counting. Nice wee taxi job lined up for afterwards. Don't know how Todd will cope without me."

"I'll try to maintain my composure," Goodyear drawled.

"That's one thing you're good at," Dyson was saying, as Rebus went back to his reading. The girl who had found the body was called Nancy Sievewright. She was seventeen and on her way home from a friend's house. The friend lived in Great Stuart Street and Nancy in Blair Street, just off the Cowgate. She had already left school and was unemployed, though hoping to get into college some day to study as a dental assistant. Goodyear had done the interview, and Rebus was impressed: neat handwriting and plenty of detail. Turning to Dyson's notebook was like turning from hope to despair — a mess of hastily scrawled hieroglyphs. Those seven months couldn't pass quickly enough for PC Bill Dyson. Through guesswork, Rebus reckoned the middle-aged couple were Roger and Elizabeth Anderson and that they lived in Frogston Road West, on the southern edge of the city. There was a phone number, but no hint of their ages or occupations. Instead, Rebus could make out the words "just passing" and "called it in." He handed the notebooks back without comment. All three would be interviewed again later. Rebus checked his watch, wondering when the pathologist would arrive. Not much else to be done in the meantime.

"Tell them they can go."

"Girl's still a bit shaky," Goodyear said. "Reckon we should drop her home?"

Rebus nodded and turned his attention to Dyson. "How about the other two?"

"Their car's parked in the Grassmarket."

"Spot of late-night shopping?"

Dyson shook his head. "Carol concert at St. Cuthbert's."

"A conversation we could have saved ourselves," Rebus told him, "if you'd bothered to write any of it down." As his eyes drilled into the constable's, he could sense the question Dyson wanted to ask: *What would be the bloody point of that?* Luckily, the old-timer knew better than to utter anything of the kind out loud . . . not until the other old-timer was well out of earshot.

Rebus caught up with Clarke at the Scene of Crime van, where she was quizzing the team leader. His name was Thomas Banks — "Tam" to those who knew him. He gave a nod of greeting and asked if his name was on the guest list for Rebus's retirement do.

"How come you're all so keen to witness my demise?"

"Don't be surprised," Tam said, "if the suits from HQ come with stakes and mallets, just to be on the safe side." He winked towards Clarke. "Siobhan here tells me you've wangled it so your last shift's a Saturday. Is that so we're all at home watching telly while you take the long walk?"

"Just the way it fell, Tam," Rebus assured him. "Any tea going?"

"You turned your nose up at it," Tam chided him.

"That was half an hour ago."

"No second chances here, John."

"I was asking," Clarke interrupted, "if Tam's team had anything for us."

"I'm guessing he said to be patient."

"That's about the size of it," Tam confirmed, checking a text message on his mobile phone. "Stabbing outside a pub at Haymarket," he informed them.

"Busy night," Clarke offered. Then, to Rebus: "Doctor reckons our man was bludgeoned and maybe even kicked to death. He's betting blunt force trauma at the autopsy."

"He's not going to get any odds from me," Rebus told her.

"Nor me," Tam added, rubbing a finger across the bridge of his nose. He turned to Rebus: "Know who that young copper was?" He nodded towards the patrol car. Todd Goodyear was helping Nancy Sievewright into the back seat, Bill Dyson drumming his fingers against the steering wheel.

"Never seen him before," Rebus admitted.

"You maybe knew his granddad, though . . ." Tam left it at that, wanting Rebus to do the work. It didn't take long.

"Not Harry Goodyear?"

Tam was nodding in confirmation, leaving Clarke to ask who Harry Goodyear was.

"Ancient history," Rebus informed her.

Which, typically, left her none the wiser.

2

Rebus was giving Clarke a lift home when the call came in on her mobile.

They did a U-turn and headed for the Cowgate, home to the city's mortuary. There was an unmarked white van sitting by the loading bay. Rebus parked next to it and led the way. The night shift consisted of just two men. One was in his forties and had the look — to Rebus's eyes — of an ex-con. A faded blue tattoo crept out of the neck of his overalls and halfway up his throat. It took Rebus a moment to place it as some sort of snake. The other man was a lot younger, bespectacled and gawky.

"I take it you're the poet," Rebus guessed.

"Lord Byron, we call him," the older man rasped.

"That's how I recognized him," the young attendant told Rebus. "I was at a reading he gave just yesterday . . ." He glanced at his watch. "Day before yesterday," he corrected himself, reminding Rebus that it was past midnight. "He was wearing the exact same clothes."

"Hard to ID him from his face," Clarke interrupted, playing devil's advocate.

The young man nodded agreement. "All the same . . . the hair, that jacket, and the belt . . ."

"So what's his name?" Rebus asked.

"Todorov. Alexander Todorov. He's Russian. I've got one of his books in the staff room. He signed it for me."

"That'll be worth a few quid." The other attendant sounded suddenly interested.

"Can you fetch it?" Rebus asked. The young man nodded and shuffled past, heading for the corridor. Rebus studied the rows of refrigerated doors. "Which one's he in?"

"Number three." The attendant rapped his knuckles against the door in question. There was a label on it, but no name as yet. "I wouldn't bet on Lord Byron being wrong—he's got brains."

"How long has he been here?"

"Couple of months. Real name's Chris Simpson."

Clarke had a question of her own. "Any idea how soon the autopsy will get done?"

"Soon as the pathologists get their arses down here."

Rebus had picked up a copy of the day's *Evening News*. "Looking bad for Hearts," the attendant told him. "Pressley's lost the captaincy and there's a caretaker coach."

"Music to DS Clarke's ears," Rebus told the man. He held the paper up so she could see the front page. A Sikh teenager had been attacked in Pilrig Park and his hair lopped off.

"Not our patch, thank God," she said. At the sound of footsteps, all three of them turned, but it was only Chris Simpson returning with the slim hardback book. Rebus took charge of it and turned to the back cover. The poet's unsmiling face stared back at him. Rebus showed it to Clarke, who shrugged.

"Looks like the same leather jacket," Rebus commented. "But he's got some sort of chain round his neck."

"He was wearing it at the reading," Simpson confirmed.

"And the guy you brought in tonight?"

"No chain—I had a quick look. Maybe they took it . . . whoever mugged him, I mean."

"Or maybe it's not him. How long was Todorov staying in town?"

"He's here on some sort of scholarship. Hasn't lived in Russia for a while—calls himself an exile."

Rebus was turning the pages of the book. It was called *Astapovo Blues*. The poems were in English and called things like "Raskolnikov," "Leonid," and "Mind Gulag." "What does the title mean?" he asked Simpson.

"It's the place where Tolstoy died."

The other attendant chuckled. "Told you he had a brain on him."

Rebus handed the book to Clarke, who flicked to the title page. Todorov had written an inscription, telling "Dear Chris" to "keep the faith, as I have and have not." "What did he mean?" she asked.

"I said I was trying to be a poet. He told me that meant I already was. I think he's saying he kept faith with poetry, but not with Russia." The young man was starting to blush.

"Where was this?" Rebus asked.

"The Scottish Poetry Library—just off the Canongate."

"Was anyone with him? A wife maybe, or someone from the publisher?"

Simpson told them he couldn't be sure. "He's famous, you know. There was talk of the Nobel Prize."

Clarke had closed the book. "There's always the Russian consulate," she suggested. Rebus gave a slow nod. They could hear a car drawing up outside.

"That'll be at least one of them," the other attendant said. "Best get the lab ready, Lord Byron."

Simpson had reached out a hand for his book, but Clarke waved it at him.

"Mind if I hang on to it, Mr. Simpson? Promise I won't put it on eBay."

The young man seemed reluctant but was being prodded into action by his colleague. Clarke sealed the deal by slipping the book into her coat pocket. Rebus had turned to face the outer door, which was being hauled open by a puffy-eyed Professor Gates. Only a couple of steps behind him was Dr. Curt—the two pathologists had worked together so frequently that they often seemed to Rebus a single unit. Hard to imagine that outside of work they could ever lead separate, distinguishable lives.

"Ah, John," Gates said, proffering a hand as chilled as the room. "The night's grown bitter. And here's DS Clarke, too—looking forward, no doubt, to stepping out from the mentor's shadow."

Clarke prickled but kept her mouth shut—no point in arguing that, as far as she was concerned, she'd long ago left Rebus's shadow. Rebus himself offered a smile of support before shaking hands with the ashen-faced Curt. There had been a cancer scare eleven months back, and some of the man's energy had failed to return, though he'd given up the cigarettes for good.

"How are you, John?" Curt was asking. Rebus felt maybe that should have been *his* question, but he offered a reassuring nod.

"I'm guessing box two," Gates was saying, turning to his associate. "Deal or no deal?"

"It's number three actually," Clarke told him. "We think he may be a Russian poet."

"Not Todorov?" Curt asked, one eyebrow raised. Clarke showed him the book, and the eyebrow went a little higher.

"Wouldn't have taken you for a poetry lover, Doc," Rebus commented.

"Are we in the midst of a diplomatic incident?" Gates snorted. "Should we be checking for poisoned umbrella tips?"

"Looks like he was mugged by a psycho," Rebus explained. "Unless there's a poison out there that strips the skin away from your face."

"Necrotizing fasciitis," Curt muttered.

"Arising from *Streptococcus pyogenes,*" Gates added. "Not that I think we've ever seen it." To Rebus's ears, he sounded genuinely disappointed.

Blunt force trauma: the police doctor had been spot on. Rebus sat in his living room, not bothering to switch on any lights, and smoked a cigarette. Having banned nicotine from workplaces and pubs, the government was now looking at banning it from the home, too. Rebus wondered how they'd go about enforcing *that.* A John Hiatt album was on the CD player, volume kept low. The track was called "Lift Up Every Stone." All his time on the force, he hadn't done anything else. But Hiatt was using stones to build a wall, while Rebus just peered beneath them at the tiny dark things scuttling around. He wondered if the lyric was a poem, and what the Russian poet would have made of Rebus's riff on it. They'd tried phoning the consulate, but no one had answered, not even a machine, so they'd decided to call it a night. Siobhan had been dozing off during the autopsy, much to Gates's irritation. Rebus's fault: he'd been keeping her late at the office, trying to get her interested in all those cold cases, all the ones still niggling him, hoping that maybe they would keep his memory warm . . .

Rebus had dropped her home and then driven through the silent pre-dawn streets to Marchmont, an eventual parking space, and his second-floor tenement flat. The living room had a bay window, and that was where his chair was. He was promising himself he'd make it as far as the bedroom, but there was a spare duvet behind the sofa just in case. He had a bottle of whisky, too — eighteen-year-old Highland Park, bought the previous weekend and with a couple of good hits left in it. Ciggies and booze and a little night music. At one time, they would have provided enough consolation, but he wondered if they would sustain him once the job was behind him. What else did he have?

A daughter down in England, living with a college lecturer.

An ex-wife who'd moved to Italy.

The pub.

He couldn't see himself driving cabs or doing precognitions for defense lawyers. Couldn't see himself "starting afresh" as others had done — retiring to Marbella or Florida or Bulgaria. Some had sunk their pensions into property, letting flats to students — a chief inspector he knew had made a mint that way, but Rebus didn't want the hassle. He'd be nagging the students all the time about cigarette burns in the carpet or the washing-up not being done.

Sports? None.

Hobbies and pastimes? Just what he was doing right now.

"Bit maudlin tonight, are we, John?" he asked himself out loud. Then gave a little chuckle, knowing he could maudle for Scotland, gold-medal a nap at the Grump Olympics. At least he wasn't being sewn together again and slid back into drawer number three. He'd gone through a list in his mind — offenders he knew who'd go overboard on a beating. Most were in jail or under sedation on the psycho ward. Gates himself had said it — "There's a fury here."

"Or furies plural," Curt had added.

True, they could be looking for more than one attacker. The victim had been whacked on the back of the head with enough force to fracture the skull. Hammer, cosh, or baseball bat — or anything else resembling them. Rebus was guessing that this had been the first blow. The victim would have been poleaxed, meaning he posed no threat to his attacker. So why then the prolonged beating to the face? As Gates had speculated, no ordinary mugger would have bothered. They'd have emptied the pockets and fled. A ring had been removed from one finger, and there was a line on the left-hand wrist, indicating that the victim had been wearing a watch. A slight nick on the back of the neck showed that the chain might have been snapped off.

"Nothing left at the scene?" Curt had asked, reaching for the chest cutters.

Rebus had shaken his head.

Say the victim had put up some sort of struggle . . . maybe he'd pushed a button too many. Or could there be a racism angle, his accent giving him away?

"The condemned ate a hearty meal," Gates had eventually remarked, opening the stomach. "Prawn bhuna, if I'm not mistaken, washed down with lager. And do you detect a whiff of brandy or whisky, Dr. Curt?"

"Unmistakably."

And so it had progressed, with Siobhan Clarke fighting to stay awake and Rebus seated next to her, watching as the pathologists went about their business.

No grazes on the knuckles or shreds of skin under the fingernails—nothing to suggest that the victim had been able to defend himself. The clothing was chainstore stuff and would be sent to the forensic lab. With the blood washed off, the face more clearly resembled the one on the poetry book. During one of her short naps, Rebus had removed the volume from Siobhan Clarke's pocket and found a potted biography of Todorov on the flyleaf. Born 1960 in the Zhdanov district of Moscow, former literature lecturer, winner of numerous awards and prizes, author of six poetry collections for adults and one for children.

Seated now in his chair by the window, Rebus tried to think of Indian restaurants near King's Stables Road. Tomorrow, he would try looking in the phone book.

"No, John," he told himself, "it's already tomorrow."

He'd picked up an *Evening News* at the all-night petrol station, so he could check the headlines again. The Marmion trial was continuing at the Crown Court—pub shooting in Gracemount, one dead, one lucky to be alive. The Sikh teenager had escaped with bumps and bruises, but hair was sacred to his religion, something the attackers must have known or guessed.

And Jack Palance was dead. Rebus didn't know what he'd been like in real life, but he'd always played tough

guys in his films. Rebus poured another Highland Park
and raised his glass in a toast.

"Here's to the hard men," he said, knocking the drink
back in one.

Siobhan Clarke got to the end of the phone book's listing for restaurants. She'd underlined half a dozen pos-
sibles, though really all the Indian restaurants were
possible—Edinburgh was a small city and easy to get
around. But they would start with the ones closest to
the locus and work their way outwards. She had logged
on to her laptop and searched the Web for mentions of
Todorov—there were thousands of hits. He even featured in Wikipedia. Some of the stuff she found was
written in Russian. A few essays came from the USA,
where the poet featured on various college syllabuses.
There were also reviews of *Astapovo Blues*, so she knew
now that the poems were about Russian authors of the
past, but also critiques of the current political scene in
Todorov's home country—not that Mother Russia had
actually been his home, not for the past decade. He'd
been right to term himself an exile, and his views on
post-glasnost Russia had earned him a good deal of Po-
litburo anger and derision. In one interview, he'd been
asked if he considered himself a dissident. "A construc-
tive dissident," he had replied.

Clarke took another gulp of lukewarm coffee. This
is your case, girl, she told herself. Rebus would soon be
gone. She was trying not to think about it too much. All
these years they'd worked together, to the point where
they could almost read each other's mind. She knew she
would miss him, but knew, too, that she had to start
planning for a future without him. Oh, they would meet

for drinks and the occasional dinner. She'd share gossip and tidbits with him. Maybe he would nag her about those cold cases, the ones he was trying to dump on her . . .

BBC News 24 was playing on the TV but with the sound turned off. She'd made a couple of calls to check that no one as yet had reported the poet missing. Not much else to be done, so eventually she turned off the TV and computer both, and went through to the bathroom. The lightbulb needed changing, so she undressed in the dark, brushed her teeth, and found she was rinsing the brush under the hot tap instead of the cold. With her bedside light on, a pale pink scarf draped over it, she plumped up the pillows and raised her knees so she could rest *Astapovo Blues* against them. It was only forty-odd pages, but had still cost Chris Simpson a tenner.

Keep the faith, as I have and have not . . .

The first poem in the collection ended with the lines:

> *As the country bled and wept, wept and bled,*
> *He averted his eyes,*
> *Ensuring he would not have to testify.*

Flicking back to the title page, she saw that the collection had been translated from the Russian by Todorov himself, "with the assistance of Scarlett Colwell." Clarke settled back and turned to the second poem. By the third of its four stanzas, she was asleep.

DAY TWO

Thursday 16 November 2006

3

The Scottish Poetry Library was located down one of the innumerable pends and wynds leading off the Canongate. Rebus and Clarke managed to miss it and ended up at the Parliament and the Palace of Holyrood. Driving more slowly back uphill, they missed it again.

"There's nowhere to park anyway," Clarke complained. They were in her car this morning, and therefore dependent on Rebus to spot Crighton's Close.

"I think it was back there," he said, craning his neck. "Pull up onto the pavement and we'll take a look."

Clarke left the hazard lights on when she locked the car and folded her wing mirror in so it wouldn't get sideswiped. "If I get a ticket, you're paying," she warned Rebus.

"Police business, Shiv. We'll appeal it."

The Poetry Library was a modern building cleverly concealed amidst the tenements. A member of the staff sat behind the counter and beamed a smile in their direction. The smile evaporated when Rebus showed her his warrant card.

"Poetry reading a couple of nights back — Alexander Todorov."

"Oh yes," she said, "quite marvelous. We have some of his books for sale."

"Was he in Edinburgh on his own? Any family, that sort of thing . . . ?"

The woman's eyes narrowed, and she clutched a hand to her cardigan. "Has something happened?"

It was Clarke who answered. "I'm afraid Mr. Todorov was attacked last night."

"Gracious," the librarian gasped, "is he . . . ?"

"As a doornail," Rebus supplied. "We need to speak to next of kin, or at the very least someone who can identify him."

"Alexander was here as a guest of PEN and the university. He's been in the city a couple of months . . ." The librarian's voice was trembling, along with the rest of her.

"PEN?"

"It's a writers' group . . . very big on human rights."

"So where was he staying?"

"The university provided a flat in Buccleuch Place."

"Family? A wife maybe . . . ?"

But the woman shook her head. "I think his wife died. I don't recall them having any children—a blessing, I suppose."

Rebus was thoughtful for a moment. "So who organized his event here? Was it the university, the consulate . . . ?"

"It was Scarlett Colwell."

"His translator?" Clarke asked, gaining a nod of confirmation.

"Scarlett works in the Russian department." The librarian started sifting through the slips of paper on her desk. "I've got her number here somewhere. . . . What a terrible thing to have happened. I can't tell you how upsetting it is."

"No trouble at the reading itself?" Rebus asked, trying to make the question seem casual.

"Trouble?" When she saw he wasn't about to elucidate, she shook her head. "It all went swimmingly. Terrific use of metaphor and rhythm . . . even when he recited in Russian, you could feel the passion." She was lost for a moment in reminiscence. Then, with a sigh: "Alexander was happy to sign books afterwards."

"You make it sound," Clarke pointed out, "as if that might not always have been the case."

"Alexander Todorov was a poet, a very *considerable* poet." As if this explained everything. "Ah, here it is." She held up the piece of paper but seemed unwilling to relinquish it. Instead, Clarke entered the number into her own mobile before thanking the librarian for taking the trouble.

Rebus was looking around. "Where exactly did the performance happen?"

"Upstairs. We had an audience of over seventy."

"I don't suppose anyone filmed it, did they?"

"Filmed it?"

"For posterity."

"Why do you ask?"

Rebus gave a shrug by way of reply.

"There was a sound recording," the woman admitted. "Someone from a music studio."

Clarke had her notebook out. "Name?" she asked.

"Abigail Thomas." The librarian realized her mistake. "Oh, you mean the name of the recordist? Charlie something . . ." Abigail Thomas screwed shut her eyes with the effort, then opened them wide. "Charles Riordan. He has his own studio in Leith."

"Thank you, Ms. Thomas," Rebus said. Then: "Can you think of anyone we should contact?"

"You could talk to PEN."

"There wasn't anyone here that night from the consulate?"

"I wouldn't have thought so."

"Oh?"

"Alexander was quite vocal in his opposition to the current situation in Russia. He was on the *Question Time* panel a few weeks back."

"The TV show?" Clarke asked. "I watch that sometimes."

"So his English was pretty good, then," Rebus surmised.

"When he wanted it to be," the librarian said with a wry smile. "If he didn't like the point you were making, the ability seemed suddenly to desert him."

"He sounds quite a character," Rebus had to admit. He saw that a small pile of Todorov's books had been given their own display on a table near the stairs. "Are these for sale?" he asked.

"Indeed they are. Would you like to buy one?"

"Would they happen to be signed?" He watched her nod. "In that case, make it half a dozen." He was reaching into his jacket for his wallet as the librarian rose from her seat to fetch them. Feeling Clarke's eyes on him, he mouthed something to her.

Something very like "eBay."

The car had not received a ticket, but there were dirty looks from the line of motorists attempting to squeeze past. Rebus threw the bag of books onto the back seat. "Should we warn her we're coming?"

"Might be wise," Clarke agreed, punching the keys on her phone and holding it to her ear. "Tell me, do you even *know* how to sell something on eBay?"

"I can learn," Rebus said. Then: "Tell her we'll meet her at his flat, just in case he's lying in a stupor there and we've got a looky-likey in the mortuary." He stuck a fist to his mouth, stifling a yawn.

"Get any sleep?" Clarke asked.

"Probably the same as you," he told her.

Clarke's call had connected her to the university switchboard. She asked for Scarlett Colwell and was put through.

"Miss Colwell?" A pause. "Sorry, *Doctor* Colwell." She rolled her eyes for Rebus's benefit.

"Ask her if she can fix my gout," he whispered. Clarke thumped his shoulder as she began to give Dr. Scarlett Colwell the bad news.

Two minutes later, they were heading for Buccleuch Place, a six-story Georgian block that faced the more modern (and far uglier) university edifices. One tower in particular had been voted the building most people in Edinburgh wanted to see condemned. The tower, perhaps sensing this hostility, had begun to self-destruct, great chunks of cladding falling from it at irregular intervals.

"You never studied here, did you?" Rebus asked, as Clarke's car rumbled across the setts.

"No," she said, nosing into a parking space. "Did you?"

Rebus gave a snort. "I'm a dinosaur, Shiv — back in the Bronze Age they let you become a detective without a diploma and a mortarboard."

"Weren't the dinosaurs extinct by the Bronze Age?"

"Not having been to college, that's just the sort of thing

I wouldn't know. Reckon there's any chance of grabbing ourselves a coffee while we're here?"

"You mean in the flat?" Clarke watched him nod. "You'd drink a dead man's coffee?"

"I've drunk a damn sight worse."

"You know, I actually believe that." Clarke was out of the car now, Rebus following. "Must be her over there."

She was standing at the top of some steps and had already unlocked the front door. She gave a little wave, which Rebus and Clarke acknowledged—Clarke because it was the right thing to do, and Rebus because Scarlett Colwell was a looker. Her hair fell in long auburn waves, her eyes were dark, her figure curvy. She wore a hugging green miniskirt, black tights, and brown calf-length boots. Her Little Red Riding Hood coat reached only as far as her waist. A gust of wind caused her to push the hair back from her eyes, and Rebus felt as if he were walking into a Cadbury's Flake advert. He saw that her mascara was a bit blurry, evidence that she'd shed a few tears since receiving the news, but she was business-like as the introductions were made.

They followed her up four flights of tenement stairs to the top-floor landing, where she produced another key, unlocking the door to Alexander Todorov's flat, Rebus arriving, having paused for breath on the landing below, just as the door swung open. There wasn't much to the apartment: a short, narrow hallway led to the living room with a kitchenette off it. There was a cramped shower room and separate toilet, and a single bedroom with views towards the Meadows. Being in the eaves of the building, the ceilings angled sharply downwards. Rebus wondered if the poet had ever sat up sharply in bed and thumped the crown of his head. The whole flat felt not so much empty as utterly desolate, as though marked by the departure of its most recent resident.

"We're really sorry about this," Siobhan Clarke was saying as the three of them stood in the living room. Rebus was looking around him: a wastepaper bin full of crumpled poems, an empty cognac bottle lying next to the battered sofa, an Edinburgh bus map pinned to one wall above a foldaway dining table on which sat an electric typewriter. No sign of a computer or a TV or a music system, just a portable radio whose aerial had been snapped off. Books scattered everywhere, some English, some Russian, plus a few other languages. A Greek dictionary sat on the arm of the sofa.. There were empty lager cans on a shelf meant for knickknacks. Invitations on the mantelpiece to parties from the previous month. They had passed a telephone on the floor in the hallway. Rebus asked if the poet had owned such a thing as a mobile. When Colwell shook her head, hair bouncing and swaying, Rebus knew he wanted to ask another question she could answer in the same way. Clarke's clearing of the throat warned him against it.

"And no computer either?" he asked anyway.

"He was welcome to use the one in my office," Colwell said. "But Alexander mistrusted technology."

"You knew him fairly well?"

"I was his translator. When the scholarship was announced, I petitioned hard on his behalf."

"So where was he before Edinburgh?"

"Paris for a time . . . Cologne before that . . . Stanford, Melbourne, Ottawa . . ." She managed a smile. "He was very proud of the stamps in his passport."

"Speaking of which," Clarke interrupted, "his pockets had been emptied—any idea what he would usually carry around with him?"

"A notebook and pen . . . some money, I suppose . . ."

"Any credit cards?"

"He had a cash card. I think he'd opened an account with First Albannach. Should be some statements around here somewhere." She looked about her. "You say he was mugged?"

"Some sort of attack, certainly."

"What kind of man was he, Dr. Colwell?" Rebus asked. "If someone confronted him in the street, would he put up a struggle, fight them back?"

"Oh, I'd think so. He was physically robust. Liked good wine and a good argument."

"Did he have a temper?"

"Not especially."

"But you said he liked to argue."

"In the sense that he enjoyed debate," Colwell corrected herself.

"When did you last see him?"

"At the Poetry Library. He was headed to the pub afterwards, but I wanted to get home—essays to mark before we break for Christmas."

"So who did he go to the pub with?"

"There were a few local poets in the audience: Ron Butlin, Andrew Greig . . . I'd guess Abigail Thomas would be there, too, if only to pay for the drinks—Alexander wasn't brilliant with money."

Rebus and Clarke shared a look: they'd have to talk to the librarian again. Rebus gave a little cough, playing for time before asking his next question. "Would you be willing to identify the body, Dr. Colwell?"

The blood drained from Scarlett Colwell's face.

"You seem to have known him better than most," Rebus argued, "unless there's a next of kin we can approach."

But she had already made up her mind. "It's all right, I'll do it."

"We can take you there now," Clarke told her, "if that's okay with you."

Colwell nodded slowly, eyes staring into space. Rebus caught Clarke's attention. "Get on to the station," he said, "see if Hawes and Tibbet can come give this place a look-see — passport, cash card, notebook. . . . If they're not here, someone's either got them or dumped them."

"Not forgetting his set of keys," Clarke added.

"Good point." Rebus's eyes scanned the room again. "Hard to say if this place has been turned over or not — unless you know better, Dr. Colwell?"

Colwell shook her head again and had to remove a strand of hair from over one eye. "It was always pretty much like this."

"So no need for Forensics," Rebus told Clarke. "Just Hawes and Tibbet." Clarke was nodding as she reached for her phone. Rebus had missed something Colwell had said.

"I've a tutorial in an hour," she repeated.

"We'll have you back in plenty of time," he assured her, not particularly caring one way or the other. He held out a hand towards Clarke. "Keys."

"Pardon?"

"You're staying here to let Hawes and Tibbet in. I'll drive Dr. Colwell to the mortuary."

Clarke tried staring him out, but eventually relented.

"Get one of them to bring you to the Cowgate afterwards," Rebus said, hoping to sugar the pill.

4

The identification was immediate, even though most of the body was kept in its shroud, concealing the work done by the pathologists. Colwell laid her forehead against Rebus's shoulder for a moment and allowed a single tear to escape from either eye. Rebus regretted not having a clean handkerchief on him, but she reached into her shoulder bag for one, dabbing her eyes and then blowing her nose. Professor Gates was in the room with them, dressed in a three-piece suit that had fitted him beautifully four or five years back. He held his hands in front of him, head bowed, respecting the formalities.

"It's Alexander," Colwell was eventually able to say.

"You're sure of that?" Rebus felt obliged to press.

"Positive."

"Perhaps," Gates piped up, raising his head, "Dr. Colwell would like a cup of tea before the paperwork?"

"Just a couple of forms," Rebus explained quietly. Colwell nodded slowly, and the three of them went to the pathologist's private office. It was a claustrophobic space with no natural light and the smell of damp wafting in from the shower cubicle next door. The day shift was on, and Rebus didn't recognize the man who brought the tea. Gates called him Kevin, told him to close the door again on his way out, then opened the folder on his desk.

"By the way," he said, "was Mr. Todorov any sort of car enthusiast?"

"I don't think he'd have known the engine from the boot," Colwell said with a hint of a smile. "He once got me to change the bulb in his desk lamp."

Gates smiled back at her, then turned his attention to Rebus. "Forensics asked if he maybe worked as a mechanic. There was some oil on the hem of the jacket and the trouser knees."

Rebus thought back to the crime scene. "Could have been some on the ground," he admitted.

"King's Stables Road," the pathologist added. "A lot of the stables were turned into garages, weren't they?"

Rebus nodded and glanced towards Colwell, gauging her reaction.

"It's all right," she told him. "I'm not going to start blubbing again."

"Who was it spoke to you?" Rebus asked Gates.

"Ray Duff."

"Ray's no slouch," Rebus said. In fact, Rebus knew damned well that Ray Duff was the best forensic scientist they had.

"What's the betting he's at the locus right now," Gates said, "checking for oil?"

Rebus nodded and lifted the mug of tea to his lips.

"Now that we know the victim really is Alexander," Colwell said into the silence, "do I need to keep quiet about it? I mean, is it something you want to keep from the media?"

Gates gave a loud snort. "Dr. Colwell, we wouldn't stand a chance of keeping it from the Fourth Estate. Lothian and Borders Police leaks like the proverbial sieve—as does this very building." He lifted his head towards the door. "Isn't that right, Kevin?" he called. They could hear feet beginning to shuffle back down the corridor. Gates gave a satisfied smile and picked up his ringing telephone.

Rebus knew it would be Siobhan Clarke, waiting in reception . . .

After dropping Colwell back at the university, Rebus treated Clarke to lunch. When he'd made the offer, she'd stared at him and asked if anything was wrong. He'd shaken his head, and she'd said he must be after a favor, then.

"Who knows how often we'll get the chance, once I'm retired," he'd explained.

They went to an upstairs bistro on West Nicolson Street, where the dish of the day was venison pie. It came with chips and garden peas, over all of which Rebus dumped a quarter of a bottle of HP sauce. He was limiting himself to a half-pint of Deuchar's and had managed four drags on a cigarette before stepping over the threshold. Between mouthfuls of pie crust, he told her about Ray Duff and asked if everything was okay at Todorov's flat.

"Reckon young Colin has a thing going for Phyllida?" Clarke mused. Detective Constables Phyllida Hawes and Colin Tibbet shared the CID suite at Gayfield Square with Rebus and Clarke. Until recently, all four had worked under the baleful gaze of Detective Inspector Derek Starr, but Starr, seeking the further advancement that he saw as his right, was on secondment to police headquarters on Fettes Avenue. The rumor was that once Rebus walked into the sunset, Clarke would take his place, promoted inspector. It was a rumor Clarke herself was trying not to listen to.

"Why do you ask?" Rebus lifted his glass, noting that it was already almost empty.

"They just seem very comfortable with one another."

Rebus stared at her, trying for a look of pained surprise. "And we're not?"

"We're fine," she answered with a smile. "But I think they've been on a couple of dates—not that they want anyone to know."

"You reckon they're snuggling up just now in the dead man's bed?"

Clarke wrinkled her nose at the suggestion. Then, half a minute later: "I'm just wondering how to handle it."

"You mean once I'm out of the way and you're in charge?" Rebus put down his fork and gave her a glare.

"*You're* the one who wants all the loose ends tied up," she complained.

"Maybe so, but I've never thought of myself as an agony aunt." He lifted his glass again, only to find that he'd finished it.

"Do you want coffee?" she asked, making it sound like a peace offering. He shook his head and started patting his pockets.

"What I need is a proper smoke." He found the packet and rose to his feet. "You get yourself a coffee while I'm outside."

"What about this afternoon?"

He thought for a moment. "We'll get more done if we divvy it up—you go see the librarian again, I'll hit King's Stables Road."

"Fine," she said, not bothering to disguise the fact that it wasn't really fine at all. Rebus stood his ground for a moment, as if about to muster some words, then waved the cigarette in her direction and headed for the door.

"And thanks for the lunch," she said, as soon as he was out of earshot.

Rebus thought he knew why they could barely hold a five-minute conversation without starting to snipe at each other. It was bound to be a tense time, him leaving the field of battle, her on the cusp of promotion. They'd worked together so long — been friends almost as long. . . . Bound to be a tense time.

Everyone assumed that they'd slept together at some point down the line, but no way either of them would have let it happen. How could they have worked as partners afterwards? It would have been all or nothing, and they both loved the job too much to let anything else get in the way. The one thing he'd made her promise was that there'd be no surprise parties his last week at work. Their boss at Gayfield Square had even offered to host something, but Rebus had thanked him with a shake of the head.

"You're the longest-serving officer in CID," DCI Macrae had persisted.

"Then it's the folk who've put up with me who deserve the medal," Rebus had retorted.

The cordon was still in place at the bottom of Raeburn Wynd, but one of the locals ducked beneath the blue-and-white-striped tape, resistant to the idea that anywhere in Edinburgh could be off limits to him. Or so Rebus surmised by the hand gesture the man made when warned by Ray Duff that he was contaminating a crime scene. Duff was shaking his head, more in sorrow than anything else, when Rebus approached.

"Gates reckoned this is where I'd find you," Rebus said. Duff rolled his eyes.

"And now *you're* walking all over my locus."

Rebus answered with a twitch of the mouth. Duff was crouching beside his forensics kit, a toughened red plastic toolbox bought from B&Q. Its myriad drawers opened concertina-style, but Duff was in the process of closing them.

"Thought you'd be putting your feet up," Duff commented.

"No you didn't."

Duff laughed. "True enough."

"Any joy?" Rebus asked.

Duff snapped shut the box and lifted it with him as he got to his feet. "I wandered as far as the top of the lane, checking all the garages along the way. Thing is, if he'd been attacked up there, we'd have traces of blood on the roadway." He stamped his foot to reinforce the point.

"And?"

"The blood's elsewhere, John." He gestured for Rebus to follow and took a left along King's Stables Road. "See anything?"

Rebus looked hard at the pavement and noticed the trail of splashes. There were intervals between them. The blood had lost most of its color but was still recognizable. "How come we didn't spot this last night?"

Duff shrugged. His car was parked curbside, and he unlocked it long enough to stow his box of tricks.

"How far have you followed it?" Rebus asked.

"I was just about to get started when you arrived."

"Then let's go."

They began walking, eyes on the sporadic series of drips. "You going to join SCRU?" Duff asked.

"Think they'd want me?" SCRU was the Serious Crime Review Unit. It consisted of three retired detectives, whose job was to look at unsolveds.

"Did you hear about that result we got last week?" Duff said. "DNA from a sweated fingerprint. Sort of thing that can be useful on cold cases. DNA boost means we can decipher DNA multiples."

"Shame I can't decipher what you're saying."

Duff chuckled. "World's changing, John. Faster than most of us can keep up with."

"You're saying I should embrace the scrap heap?"

Duff just shrugged. They'd covered a hundred yards or so and were standing at the exit to a multistory car park. There were two barriers; drivers could choose either one. Once you'd paid for your ticket, you slid it into a slot and the barrier would rise.

"Have you ID'd the victim?" Duff asked, looking around as he tried to pick up the trail again.

"A Russian poet."

"Did he drive a car?"

"He couldn't change his own lightbulbs, Ray."

"Thing about car parks, John . . . there's always a bit of oil left lying around."

Rebus had noticed that there were intercoms fixed alongside either barrier. He pressed a button and waited. After a few moments, a voice crackled from the loudspeaker.

"What is it?"

"Wonder if you can help me—"

"You after directions or something? Look, chief, this

is a car park. All we do here is park cars." It took Rebus only a second to work things out.

"You can see me," he said. Yes: a CCTV camera high up in one corner, pointing at the exit. Rebus gave it a wave.

"Have you got a problem with your car?" the voice was asking.

"I'm a cop," Rebus answered. "Want to have a word with you."

"What about?"

"Where are you?"

"Next floor up," the voice admitted eventually. "Is this to do with that prang I had?"

"That depends — did you happen to hit a guy and kill him?"

"Christ, no."

"Might be okay, then. We'll be there in a minute." Rebus moved away from the barrier towards where Ray Duff was down on all fours, peering beneath a parked BMW.

"Not keen on these new Beamers," Duff said, sensing Rebus behind him.

"Found something?"

"I think there's blood under here . . . quite a bit of it. If you were asking me, I'd say this is trail's end."

Rebus walked around the vehicle. There was a ticket on the dashboard, showing that it had entered the car park at 11:00 that morning.

"Next car along," Duff was saying, "is there something underneath it?"

Rebus did a circuit of the big Lexus but couldn't see anything. Nothing else for it but to get down on hands and knees himself. A bit of string or wire. He reached a hand beneath the car, fingertips scrabbling at it, eventually drawing it out. Hauled himself back to his feet and held it dangling by thumb and forefinger.

A plain silver neck chain.

"Ray," he said, "better go fetch your kit."

5

Clarke decided it wasn't worth visiting the librarian, so called her from Todorov's flat while Hawes and Tibbet started the search. Clarke had barely punched in the number for the Poetry Library when Hawes arrived back from the bedroom, waving the dead man's passport.

"Under a corner of the mattress," Hawes said. "First place I looked."

Clarke just nodded and moved into the hallway for a bit more privacy.

"Miss Thomas?" she said into her phone. "It's Detective Sergeant Clarke here, sorry to trouble you again so soon . . ."

Three minutes later she was back in the living room with just a couple of names: yes, Abigail Thomas had accompanied Todorov to the pub after his recital, but she'd stayed for only the one, and knew that the poet wouldn't be satisfied until he'd sampled another four or five watering holes.

"I reckoned he was in safe hands with Mr. Riordan," she'd told Clarke.

"The sound engineer?"

"Yes."

"No one else was there? None of the other poets?"

"Just the three of us, and, as I say, I didn't stay long . . ."

Colin Tibbet meantime had finished rummaging through desk drawers and kitchen cupboards and was tilting the sofa to see if anything other than dust might be hidden there. Clarke lifted a book from the floor. It was another copy of *Astapovo Blues*. She'd managed a couple of minutes' research on Count Tolstoy, so knew that he'd died in a railway siding, shunning the wife who had refused to join his pared-to-the-bone lifestyle. This helped her make more sense of the collection's final poem, "Codex Coda," with its refrain of "a cold, cleansed death." Todorov, she saw, had not quite finished with any of the poems in the book — there were penciled amendments throughout. She reached into his waste bin and uncrumpled one of the discarded sheets.

> *City noise invisible*
> *Havoc-crying air*
> *Congested as a*

The rest of the sheet consisted of doodled punctuation marks. There was a folder on his desk, but nothing inside it. A book of *Killer Sudokus*, all of them finished. Pens and pencils and an unused calligraphy set, complete with instructions. She walked over to the wall and stood in front of the Edinburgh bus map, traced a line from King's Stables Road to Buccleuch Place. There were a dozen routes he could have chosen. Maybe he was on a pub crawl, or a little bit lost. No reason to assume he'd been heading home. He could have left his flat and crossed George Square, made for Candlemaker Row and wandered down its steep brae into the Grassmarket. Plenty of pubs there, and King's Stables Road only a right-hand fork away. . . . Her phone rang. Caller ID: Rebus.

"Phyl found his passport," she told him.

"And I just found his neck chain, lying on the floor of the multistory."

"So he was killed there and dumped in the lane?"

"Trail of blood says so."

"Or he staggered that far and then keeled over."

"Another possibility," Rebus seemed to concede. "Thing is, though, what was he doing in the car park in the first place? Are you at his flat?"

"I was just about to leave."

"Before you do, add car keys or a driving license to the search list. And ask Scarlett Colwell if Todorov had access to a vehicle. I'm pretty sure she'll say no, but all the same . . ."

"No sign of any abandoned cars in the multistory?"

"Good point, Shiv, I'll have someone check. Talk to you later." The phone went dead, and she managed a little smile, hadn't heard Rebus so fired up in several months. Not for the first time, she wondered what the hell he would do with himself when the work was done.

Answer: bug her, most likely — phone calls daily, wanting to know everything about her caseload.

Clarke got through to Dr. Colwell on the mobile, Colwell having forgotten to turn her own off.

"Sorry," Clarke apologized, "are you in the middle of your tutorial?"

"I had to send them away."

"I can understand. Maybe you should shut up shop for the day. You've had quite a shock."

"And do what exactly? My boyfriend's in London, I've got the whole flat to myself."

"There must be a friend you could call." Clarke looked up as Hawes walked back into the room, but this time all Hawes did was offer a shrug: no notebook, keys, or cash card. Tibbet had done no better and was sitting on the chair, frowning over one of the poems in *Astapovo Blues*. "Anyway," Clarke rattled on, "reason I'm phoning is to ask if Alexander owned a car."

"He didn't."

"Could he drive?"

"I've no idea. I certainly wouldn't have ventured into any vehicle with him behind the wheel."

Clarke was nodding towards the route map — stood to reason Todorov would take buses. "Thanks anyway," she said.

"Did you talk to Abi Thomas?" Colwell asked abruptly.

"She went to the pub with him."

"I'll bet she did."

"But only stayed for one."

"Oh yes?"

"You sound as if you don't believe her, Dr. Colwell."

"Abi Thomas got hot flushes just reading Alexander's poems . . . imagine how she felt squeezed in next to him at a corner table in some seedy bar."

"Well, thanks for your help —" But Clarke was talking into a dead phone. She stared at it, then became aware of two pairs of eyes on her: Hawes and Tibbet.

"I don't think we're going to find anything else here, Siobhan," Hawes piped up, while her partner clucked his agreement. He was an inch shorter than her and several inches less smart, but knew enough to let her argue their case.

"Back to base?" Clarke suggested, to enthusiastic

nods. "Okay," she agreed, "but take one more recon first—and this time we're after car keys or anything else that might suggest the deceased would have need of a car-parking space." Having said which, she relieved Tibbet of his book and swapped places with him, settling back to see if there was anything she'd missed in "Codex Coda."

The SOCOs tried pushing the BMW aside, with no success at all. They then debated jacking it up, or maneuvering a hoist in so they could lift it. The rest of the parking level had become a buzz of activity, as a line of cops in white overalls shuffled along in formation on their knees, checking that the ground held no further clues. Todd Goodyear was among them and greeted Rebus with a nod. Photos and video were being taken, and another team was outside, tracing the route from car park to lane. The SOCOs were trying not to look too shamefaced, knowing they should have spotted the blood trail on the night itself. They gave Ray Duff dirty looks whenever his back was turned.

Such was the scene that greeted the BMW's owner when she returned, briefcase and shopping bags in hand. Todd Goodyear was told to get to his feet and take a brief statement from her.

"Bloody brief," Tam Banks stressed, keen for his team to start work on the evidence beneath her car.

Rebus was standing alongside the car park's security guard. The man had just returned from a check of the other levels. His name was Joe Wills and the uniform he was wearing had probably been tailored with someone else in mind. He'd already explained that it would be hard to tell an abandoned car from any of the others.

"You're open twenty-four hours?" Rebus had asked.

Wills had shaken his head. "Close at eleven."

"And you don't look to see if any cars are left?"

Wills had offered a shrug that went beyond the casual. Not much job satisfaction, Rebus had guessed.

Now Wills was explaining that he still couldn't say whether any of the current bays had been occupied overnight.

"We do a number plate check once a fortnight," he said.

"So a stolen car, to give an example, could sit here fourteen days before you'd have an inkling?"

"That's the policy." The man looked to Rebus like a drinker: gray stubble, hair in need of a wash, eyes red-rimmed. There was probably a bottle of something hidden away in his control room, to be added to the daily round of teas and coffees.

"What sort of shifts do you work?"

"Seven till three or three till eleven. I seem to prefer the mornings. Five days on, two off; there's other guys usually do the weekends."

Rebus checked his watch: twenty minutes till the changeover.

"Your colleague will be starting soon—is that the same one who'd have been here last night?"

Wills nodded. "Name's Gary."

"You haven't spoken to him since yesterday?"

Wills shrugged. "Here's what I know about Gary: lives in Shandon, supports Hearts, and has a looker of a missus."

"That's a start," Rebus muttered. Then: "Let's go look at your CCTV."

"What for?" The man's eyes were glassy as he met Rebus's glare.

"To see if the tapes caught anything." From the look on Wills's face, Rebus knew what was coming next, a single word forming echo and question both.

"Tapes . . . ?"

They walked back up the exit slope anyway. Wills's lair was a small booth with greasy windows and a radio playing. Five flickering black-and-white screens, plus a sixth that was blank.

"Top story," Wills explained. "It's playing up."

Rebus studied the remaining five. The pictures were blurry; he couldn't pick out any individual license plates. The figures from the floor below were indistinct, too. "What the hell use is this?" he couldn't help asking.

"Bosses seem to think it gives the clients a sense of security."

"Bloody false at best, as the poor sod in the mortuary can testify." Rebus turned away from the screens.

"One of the cameras used to point pretty much at that spot," Wills said. "But they get moved around . . ."

"And you don't keep any recordings?"

"Machine packed in a month back." Wills nodded towards a dusty space below the monitors. "Not that we bothered much. All the bosses were interested in was when anyone tried conning their way out without paying. System's pretty foolproof, didn't happen often." Wills thought of something. "There's a set of stairs between the top story and the pavement. We had a punter attacked there last year."

"Oh?"

"I said at the time they should get CCTV into the stairwell, but nothing ever happened."

"At least you tried."

"Don't know why I bother . . . job's on the way out anyway. They're replacing us with just the one guy on a motorbike, scooting between half a dozen car parks."

Rebus was looking around the cramped space. Kettle and mugs, a few tattered paperbacks and magazines, plus the radio—these were all on the work surface opposite the monitors. He guessed that for most of the time, the guards would be facing away from the screens. Why the hell not? Minimum wage, bosses only a distant threat, no job security. One or two buzzes on the intercom per day, people who'd lost their tickets or didn't have change. There was a rack of CDs, bands whose names Rebus vaguely recognized: Kaiser Chiefs, Razorlight, Killers, Strokes, White Stripes . . .

"No CD player," he commented.

"They're Gary's," Wills explained. "He brings one of those little machines with him."

"With headphones?" Rebus guessed, watching as Wills nodded. "Just wonderful," he muttered. "You were working here last year, Mr. Wills?"

"Been here three years next month."

"And your colleague?"

"Eight, maybe nine months. I tried his shift but couldn't hack it. I like my afternoons and evenings free."

"The better to do some drinking?" Rebus cajoled. Wills's face hardened, encouraging Rebus to press on. "Ever been in trouble, Mr. Wills?"

"How do you mean?"

"Police trouble."

Wills made show of scratching dandruff from his scalp. "Long time ago," he eventually said. "The bosses know about it."

"Fighting, was it?"

"Thieving," Wills corrected him. "But that was twenty years back."

"What about your car? You said you'd had a prang?"

But Wills was peering through the window. "Here's Gary now." A pale-colored car had drawn to a halt outside the cabin, its driver locking it after him.

The door burst open. "Hell's going on downstairs, Joe?" The guard called Gary wasn't yet quite in uniform. Rebus guessed the jacket was in his carrier bag, along with a sandwich box. He was a few years younger than Wills, a lot leaner, and half a foot taller. He dumped two newspapers onto the worktop but couldn't get any farther into the room—with Rebus there, space was at a premium. The man was shrugging out of his coat: crisp white shirt beneath, but no tie—probably a clip-on tucked into a pocket somewhere.

"I'm Detective Inspector Rebus," Rebus told him. "Last night, a man was severely beaten."

"On Level Zero," Wills added.

"Is he dead?" the new arrival asked, wide-eyed. Wills made a cut-throat gesture with accompanying sound effect. "Bloody hell. Does the Reaper know?"

Wills shook his head and saw that Rebus needed an explanation. "It's what we call one of the bosses," he said. "She's the only one we ever see. Wears a long black coat with a pointy hood."

Hence the name. Rebus nodded his understanding. "I'll need to take a statement," he told the new arrival. Wills seemed suddenly keen to leave, gathering up his bits and pieces and stuffing them into his own supermarket carrier.

"Happened on your watch, Gary," he said with a tut. "The Reaper won't be happy."

"Now there's a turn-up for the books." Gary had moved out of the cabin, giving Wills room to make his exit. Rebus came out, too, needing the oxygen.

"We'll talk again," he warned the departing figure. Wills waved without looking back. Rebus turned his attention to Gary. Lanky, he'd have called him, and round-shouldered as if awkwardly aware of his height. A long face with a square jaw and well-defined cheekbones, plus a mop of dark hair. Rebus almost said it out loud: *you should be on a stage in a band, not stuck in a dead-end job.* But maybe Gary didn't see it that way. Good-looking, though, which explained the "looker of a missus." Then again, Rebus couldn't tell just how high or low Joe Wills's standards might be . . .

Twenty minutes got him nothing except a retread: full name, Gary Walsh; maisonette in Shandon; nine months on the job; tried taxi driving before that but didn't like the night shift; had seen and heard nothing unusual the previous evening.

"What happens at eleven?" Rebus had asked.

"We shut up shop—metal shutters come down at the entrance and exit."

"Nobody can get in or out?" Walsh had shaken his head. "You check no one's locked in?" A nod. "Were any cars left on Level Zero?"

"Not that I remember."

"You always park next to the cabin?"

"That's right."

"But when you drive out, you exit on Level Zero?" A nod from the guard. "And you didn't see anything?"

"Didn't hear anything either."

"There would have been blood on the ground."

A shrug.

"You like your music, Mr. Walsh."

"Love it."

"Lie back in your chair, feet up, headphones on, eyes shut. . . . Some security guard you make."

Rebus had stared at the monitors again, ignoring Walsh's glower. There were two covering Level Zero. One was fixed on the exit barriers, the other trained on the far corner. You'd have had better luck with a camera phone.

"Sorry I can't be more help," Walsh had said, not bothering to sound sympathetic. "Who was he, anyway?"

"A Russian poet called Todorov."

Walsh thought for a moment. "I never read poetry."

"Join the club," Rebus had told him. "Bit of a waiting list, mind . . ."

6

CR Studios took up the top floor of a converted warehouse just off Constitution Street. Charles Riordan's hand, when Clarke shook it, was pudgy and moist, seeming to leave a residue on her palm which rubbing couldn't remove. There were rings on his right hand, but not the left, and a chunky gold watch loose around his wrist. Clarke noted sweat stains at the armpits of Riordan's mauve shirt. He'd rolled his sleeves up, showing arms matted with curled black hairs. The way he moved, she could tell he always wanted to appear busy. There was a receptionist at a desk just inside the door, and some sort of engineer pushing buttons at a control desk, eyes fixed to a screen showing what Clarke guessed were sound waves.

"The Kingdom of Noise," Riordan announced.

"Impressive," Clarke allowed. Through a window, she could see two separate booths, but no sign of anyone in them. "Bit tight for a band, though."

"We can accommodate singer-songwriters," Riordan said. "One man and his guitar—that sort of thing. But really we're for the spoken word—radio commercials, audiobooks, TV voice-overs . . ."

A pretty specialized kingdom, Clarke couldn't help thinking. She asked if there was an office where they could talk, but Riordan just stretched out his arms.

A specialized *small* kingdom.

"Well," she began, "as I said on the phone—"

"I know!" Riordan burst out. "I can't believe he's dead!"

Neither receptionist nor engineer batted an eyelid; Riordan had obviously told them the minute he'd come off the phone.

"We're trying to account for Mr. Todorov's last movements." Clarke had opened her notebook for effect. "I believe you had a few drinks with him, the night before last."

"I saw him more recently than that, sweetheart." Riordan couldn't help making it sound like a boast. He'd been wearing sunglasses, but now slipped them off, showing large, dark-rimmed eyes. "I treated him to a curry."

"Yesterday evening?" Clarke watched the man nod. "Where was this?"

"West Maitland Street. We'd had a couple of beers near Haymarket. He'd been through to Glasgow for the day."

"Any idea why?"

"Just wanted to see the place. He was trying to figure out the difference between the two cities, in case it helped explain the country—and bloody good luck to him! I've been here most of my life and still can't make sense of it." Riordan shook his head slowly. "He *did* try explaining it to me—his theory about us—but it went in one ear and out the other."

Clarke noticed the receptionist and engineer share a look, and assumed this was nothing new as far as they were concerned.

"So he spent the day in Glasgow," she recapped. "What time did you meet up?"

"Around eight. He'd been waiting till rush hour was past, meant he got a cheap ticket. Met him off the train, and we hit a couple of pubs. Weren't the first drinks he'd had that day."

"He was drunk?"

"He was *voluble*. Thing about Alex was, when he drank he got more intellectual. Which was a bugger, because if you were drinking with him you soon started to lose the plot."

"What happened after the curry?"

"Not much. I had to be heading home, he said he was getting thirstier. If I know him, he would have gone on to Mather's."

"On Queensferry Street?"

"But he's just as likely to have wandered into the Caledonian Hotel."

Leaving Todorov at the west end of Princes Street, not a stone's throw from King's Stables Road.

"What time was this?"

"Must've been around ten."

"I'm told by the Scottish Poetry Library that you recorded Mr. Todorov's recital the previous night."

"That's right. I've done a lot of poets."

"Charlie's done a lot of *everything*," the engineer added. Riordan laughed nervously.

"He means my little project . . . I'm putting together a sort of soundscape of Edinburgh. From poetry readings to pub chatter, street noise, the Water of Leith at sunrise, football crowds, traffic on Princes Street, the beach at Portobello, dogs being walked in the Hermitage . . . hundreds of hours of the stuff."

"Thousands more like," the engineer corrected him.

Clarke tried not to be deflected. "Had you met Mr. Todorov before?"

"I taped another performance of his at a café."

"Which one?"

Riordan shrugged. "It was for a bookshop called Word Power."

Clarke had seen it that very afternoon, opposite the pub where she'd had lunch with Rebus. She remembered a line in one of Todorov's poems — *Nothing connects* — and thought again how wrong he was.

"How long ago was that?"

"Three weeks back. We had a drink that night, too."

Clarke tapped her pen against her notebook. "Do you have a receipt for the restaurant?"

"Probably." Riordan reached into his pocket and brought out a wallet.

"First sighting this year," the engineer said, eliciting a laugh from the receptionist. She'd clamped a pen between her teeth and was playing with it. Clarke decided the two of them were an item, whether their employer knew it or not. Riordan had pulled out a mass of receipts.

"Reminds me," he muttered, "need to get some stuff to the accountant. . . . Ah, here it is." He handed it over. "Mind if I ask why you want it?"

"Shows the time you got the bill, sir. Nine forty-eight — much as you said." Clarke slipped the piece of paper into the back of her notebook.

"One question you haven't asked," Riordan said teasingly. "Why did we meet up at all?"

"All right, then . . . why did you?"

"Alex wanted a copy of his gig. Seemed to him it had gone well."

Clarke thought back to Todorov's flat. "Did he ask for any particular format?"

"I burned it onto a CD."

"He didn't have a CD player."

Riordan gave a shrug. "Plenty of people do."

True enough, but the CD itself hadn't turned up, most likely taken with the other stuff . . .

"Could you make another copy for me, Mr. Riordan?" Clarke asked.

"How would that help?"

"I'm not sure, but I'd like to hear him in full flow, as it were."

"The master's back at my home studio. I could get it burnt by tomorrow."

"I'm based at Gayfield Square — any chance someone could pop it in?"

"I'll have one of the children do it," Riordan agreed, eyes taking in the engineer and receptionist.

"Thanks for your help," Clarke said.

When smoking had been banned, back in March, Rebus had foreseen disaster for places like the Oxford Bar — traditional pubs catering to basic needs: a pint, a cigarette, horse racing on TV, and a hotline to the local turf accountant. Yet most of his haunts had survived, albeit with reduced takings. True to form, however, the smokers had formed a stubborn little gang that would congregate outside, trading stories and gossip. Tonight, the talk was the usual mix: someone was giving his views on a recently opened tapas bar, while the woman alongside wanted to know what the quietest time was to visit Ikea; a pipe smoker was arguing for full-scale independence, while his English-sounding neighbor teased that the south would be glad of the breakup—"and no bloody alimony!"

"North Sea oil's the only alimony we'll need," the pipe smoker said.

"It's already running out. Twenty years, and you'll be back with the begging bowl."

"In twenty years we'll be Norway."

"Either that or Albania."

"Thing is," another smoker interrupted, "if Labour lost its Scottish seats at Westminster, it'd never get elected again south of the border."

"Fair point," the Englishman said.

"Just after opening or just before closing?" the woman was asking.

"Bits of squid and tomato," her neighbor stated. "Not bad once you got the taste . . ."

Rebus stubbed out his cigarette and headed indoors. The round of drinks was waiting for him, along with his change. Colin Tibbet had emerged from the back room to help out.

"You can take your tie off, you know," Rebus teased him. "We're not in the office."

Tibbet smiled but said nothing. Rebus pocketed the change and hefted the two glasses. He liked that Phyllida Hawes drank pints. Tibbet was on orange juice, Clarke sticking to white wine. They'd taken the table at the far end. Clarke had her notebook out. Hawes raised her fresh glass in a silent toast to Rebus. He scraped himself back into the chair.

"Drinks took longer than I thought," he offered by way of apology.

"Managed a quick smoke, though," Clarke chided him. He decided to ignore her.

"So what have we got?" he asked instead.

Well, they had a timeline for Todorov's last two or three hours of life. They had a growing list of items missing — presumed removed — from the deceased. They had a new locus, the car park.

"Is there anything," Colin Tibbet piped up, "to suggest that we're dealing with something other than a particularly brutal mugging?"

"Not really," Clarke offered, but she met John Rebus's eyes and he gave a slow blink of acknowledgment. It didn't feel right; Clarke could sense it, too. It just didn't feel right. His phone, which he'd laid on the tabletop, started to vibrate, sending tremors across the surface of the pint glass next to it. He picked it up and moved away, either for a better signal or to escape the hubbub. They weren't alone in the back room: a group of three tourists sat bewildered in one corner, showing too much interest in the various artifacts and adverts on the walls. Two men in business suits were hunched over another table, arguing near silently about something. The TV was on, tuned to a quiz show.

"We should enter a team of four," Tibbet said. Hawes asked what he meant. "HQ is having a pub quiz, week before Christmas," he explained.

"By then," Clarke reminded him, "we'll be a team of three."

"Heard anything about the promotion?" Hawes asked her. Clarke just shook her head. "Taking their time," Hawes added, twisting the knife. Rebus was coming back.

"Curiouser and curiouser," he said, sitting down again. "That was Howdenhall with a bit of news. Tests show our

Russian poet had ejaculated at some point during the day. Stained underpants, apparently."

"Maybe he got lucky in Glasgow," Clarke speculated.

"Maybe," Rebus agreed.

"Him and this sound recordist?" Hawes offered.

"Todorov had a wife," Clarke said.

"You can never tell with poets, though," Rebus added. "Could've been some time after the curry, of course."

"Any time up until the minute he was attacked." Clarke and Rebus shared another look.

Tibbet was shifting in his chair. "Or it could have been . . . you know." He cleared his throat, cheeks reddening.

"What?" Clarke asked.

"You know," Tibbet repeated.

"I think Colin means masturbation," Hawes interjected. Tibbet's look was a study in gratitude.

"John?" It was the barman. Rebus turned towards him. "Thought you'd want to see this." He held up a newspaper. It was the day's final printing of the *Evening News*. The headline was "DEATH OF A POET" and beneath it, in bold lettering, "The maverick who dared to say *nyet!*" There was an archive photo of Alexander Todorov. He stood in Princes Street Gardens, the Castle louring behind him. A tartan scarf was wrapped around his neck; probably his first day in Scotland. A man with only two months to live.

"Cat's out of the bag," Rebus said, taking the proffered newspaper. Then, to anyone around the table who might know: "Does that count as metaphor?"

DAY THREE

Friday 17 November 2006

7

There was a funny smell in the CID office at Gayfield Square police station. You often noticed it at the height of summer, but this year it seemed determined to linger. It would disappear for a matter of days or weeks, then one morning would announce its creeping reappearance. There had been regular complaints and the Scottish Police Federation had threatened a walkout. Floors had been lifted and drains tested, traps set for vermin, but no answers.

"Smells like death," the seasoned officers would comment. Rebus knew what they meant: every now and again, a body would be discovered decomposing in the armchair of a sixties semi, or a floater would be pulled from Leith docks. There was a special room set aside for them at the mortuary, and the attendants had placed a radio on the floor, which could be switched on when desired: "Helps take our minds off the pong."

At Gayfield Square, the answer was to open all available windows, which sent the temperature plummeting. The office of Detective Chief Inspector James Macrae—separated by a glass door from the CID suite—was like a walk-in fridge. This morning, Macrae had shown foresight by hauling an electric heater into work from his Blackhall home. Rebus had seen somewhere that Blackhall boasted the wealthiest resi-

dents in the city. It had sounded an unlikely setting—
bungalows and more bungalows. Homes in Barnton and
the New Town fetched millions. Then again, maybe that
explained why the people who lived there weren't as rich
as those in Bungalowland.

Macrae had plugged the heater in and switched it on,
but it stayed on his side of the desk and radiated warmth
only so far. Phyllida Hawes had already shuffled so close
to it that she was almost seated on Macrae's lap, something the DCI noted with a scowl.

"Right," he barked, clenching his hands together as
if in angry prayer, "progress report." But before Rebus
could begin, Macrae sensed a problem. "Colin, shut the
door, will you? Let's keep what heat there is to ourselves."

"Not much room, sir," Tibbet commented. He was
standing in the doorway, and what he said was true: with
Macrae, Rebus, Clarke, and Hawes inside, space in the
DCI's den was limited.

"Then go back to your desk," Macrae replied. "I'm
sure Phyllida can report on your behalf."

But Tibbet didn't want that happening: if Clarke was
promoted to DI, there'd be a vacancy for detective sergeant, making Hawes and him rivals as well as partners.
He sucked in his stomach and managed to get the door
closed.

"Progress report," Macrae repeated. But then his
phone rang and he lifted it with a growl. Rebus wondered
about his boss's blood pressure. His own was nothing to
boast about, but Macrae's face was typically puce, and
though a couple of years younger than Rebus, his hair
had almost gone. As Rebus's own doctor had conceded

during his last checkup, "You've had a lucky run, John, but luck always runs out."

Macrae made only a few grunts before putting the phone back down. His eyes were on Rebus. "Someone from the Russian consulate at the front desk."

"Wondered when they'd turn up," Rebus said. "Siobhan and I should take this, sir. Meantime, Phyl and Colin can tell you all you need to know — we had a powwow last night."

Macrae nodded his agreement, and Rebus turned to Clarke.

"One of the interview rooms?" she suggested.

"Just what I was thinking." They moved out of the DCI's office and through the CID suite. The wall boards were still blank. Later today, photos from the crime scene would go up, along with lists of names, jobs to be done, and schedules of hours. At some murder scenes, you would set up a temporary HQ, work from there. But Rebus didn't see the point this time round. They would put up posters at the car park exit, appealing for information, and maybe get Hawes and Tibbet or a few of the uniforms to stick leaflets on windscreens. But this large, cold room would be their base. Clarke was looking back over her shoulder towards Macrae's office. Hawes and Tibbet seemed to be in competition to see who could offer the best tidbits to the boss.

"Anyone," Rebus commented, "would think there's a DS slot going begging. Who's your money on?"

"Phyl's got more years in," Clarke answered. "She's got to be favorite. If Colin gets it, I think she'll walk."

Rebus nodded his agreement. "Which interview room?" he asked.

"I like Three."

"Why so?"

"Table's all greasy and scabby, graffiti scratched on the walls. . . . It's the sort of place you go when you've done something."

Rebus smiled at her thinking. Even for the pure at heart, IR3 was a troubling experience.

"Spot on," he said.

The consular official was called Nikolai Stahov. He introduced himself with a self-effacing smile. He was young-looking and shiny-faced with a parting in his light-brown hair which made him seem even more boyish. But he was six feet tall and broad-shouldered, and wore a three-quarter-length black woolen coat, complete with belt and the collar turned up. From one pocket peeked a pair of black leather gloves — mittens, actually, Rebus realized, smooth and rounded where there should have been fingers. *Did your mum dress you?* he wanted to ask. But he shook Stahov's hand instead.

"We're sorry about Mr. Todorov," Clarke said, reaching out her own hand towards the Russian. She got a little bow along with the shake.

"My consulate," Stahov said, "wishes to be assured that everything possible is being done to capture and prosecute the perpetrator."

Rebus nodded slowly. "We thought we'd be more comfortable in one of our interview rooms . . ."

They led the young Russian down the corridor, stopping at the third door. It was unlocked. Rebus pulled it open and gestured for Clarke and Stahov to go in. Then he slid the panel across the door, changing its message from Vacant to In Use.

"Take a seat," he said. Stahov was studying his surroundings as he lowered himself onto the chair. He was about to place his hands on the tabletop, but thought better of it and rested them on his lap instead. Clarke had taken the seat opposite, Rebus content to lean against the wall, arms folded. "So what can you tell us about Alexander Todorov?" he asked.

"Inspector, I came here for reassurances and from a sense of protocol. You must know that as a diplomat, I am not obliged to answer any of your questions."

"Because you've got immunity," Rebus acknowledged. "We just assumed you'd want to assist us in any way possible. It *is* one of your countrymen who's been killed, and rather a notable one at that." He tried to sound aggrieved.

"Of course, of course, that's unquestionable." Stahov kept turning his head, trying to talk to both of them at the same time.

"Good," Clarke told him. "Then you won't mind us asking how big a thorn Todorov was proving to be?"

"Thorn?" It was hard to tell if Stahov's English was really defeating him.

"How awkward was it for you," Clarke rephrased the question, "having a noted dissident poet living in Edinburgh?"

"It wasn't awkward at all."

"You welcomed him?" Clarke pretended to guess. "Was there any kind of party at the consulate? He'd been talked about for the Nobel. . . . That must have given you great satisfaction?"

"In today's Russia, the Nobel Prize isn't such a big deal."

"Mr. Todorov had given a couple of public performances recently . . . did you happen to go see him?"

"I had other engagements."

"Did anyone from the consulate—"

But Stahov felt the need to interrupt. "I don't see what bearing any of this could have on your inquiries. In fact, your questions could be construed as a smoke screen. Whether we wanted Alexander Todorov here or not is of no consequence. He was murdered in *your* city, *your* country. Edinburgh is not without its problems with race and creed—Polish workers have found themselves attacked. Wearing the wrong football shirt can be provocation enough."

Rebus looked towards Clarke. "Talk about a smoke screen . . ."

"I am speaking the truth." Stahov's voice was beginning to tremble, and he made an effort to calm himself. "What my consulate requires, Inspector, is to be kept informed of developments. That way, we can reassure Moscow that your investigation has been rigorous and fair, and they in turn can advise your government of our satisfaction."

Rebus and Clarke seemed to consider this. Rebus unfolded his arms and slipped his hands into his pockets.

"There's always the possibility," he said quietly, "that Mr. Todorov was attacked by someone with a grudge. That person *could* be a member of the Russian community here in Edinburgh. I'm assuming the consulate keeps a list of nationals living and working here?"

"My understanding, Inspector, was that Alexander Todorov was just another victim of this city's street crime."

"Foolish to rule anything out at this stage, sir."

"And that list *would* come in handy," Clarke stressed.

Stahov looked from one detective to the other. Rebus

hoped he'd make up his mind soon. One error they'd made in opting for IR3—it was bloody freezing. The Russian's overcoat looked toasty, but Rebus reckoned Siobhan was going to start shivering soon. He was surprised their breath wasn't visible in the air.

"I will see what I can do," Stahov said at last. "But quid pro quo—you will keep me informed of developments?"

"Give us your number," Clarke told him. The young Russian seemed to take this as agreement.

Rebus knew it was anything but.

There was a package waiting for Siobhan Clarke at the front desk. Rebus had gone outside for a cigarette and to see whether Stahov had a chauffeur. Clarke opened the padded envelope and found a CD inside, with the single word "Riordan" written on it in thick black pen. It told her a lot about Charles Riordan that he used his own name, in place of Todorov's. She took the CD upstairs, but there was no machine to play it on. So instead she headed for the car park, passing Rebus as he came in.

"Big black Merc waiting for him," Rebus confirmed. "Guy wearing shades and gloves at the helm. Where are you off to?"

She told him, and he said he wouldn't mind joining her, though warning that he "might not last the pace." In the end, though, the pair of them sat in Clarke's car for a solid hour and a quarter, engine running so the heater stayed on. Riordan had recorded everything: some chat between audience members, then the introduction by Abigail Thomas, Todorov's half hour and the Q and A session after, most of the questions steering clear of politics. As the applause died and the audience dispersed, Riordan's mic was still picking up chatter.

"He's an obsessive," Clarke commented.

"I hear you," Rebus agreed. Almost the last thing they heard was a muttered snatch of Russian. "Probably," Rebus speculated, "saying 'Thank Khrushchev that's over.'"

"Who's Khrushchev?" Clarke asked. "Some friend of Jack Palance?"

The recital itself had been riveting, the poet's voice by turns sonorous, gruff, elegiac, and booming. He performed some of his work in English, some in Russian, but the majority in both—usually Russian first, English after.

"Sounds like Scots, doesn't it?" Clarke had asked at one point.

"Maybe to someone from England," Rebus had retorted. Okay, so she'd walked into that one, as so often before—her "southern" accent had been easy prey for Rebus since the moment they'd met. This time, she'd refused to rise to him.

"This one," she'd said at another point, "is called 'Raskolnikov'—I remember it from the book. Raskolnikov's a character in *Crime and Punishment*."

"A book I'd probably read before you were even born."

"You've read Dostoevsky?"

"You think I'd lie about something like that?"

"What's it about, then?"

"It's about guilt. One of the great Russian novels, in my opinion."

"How many others have you read?"

"That's neither here nor there."

Now, as she turned the CD off, he swiveled towards her. "You've listened to the show, you've been through Todorov's book—have you found *anything* resembling a motive for his killing?"

"No," she conceded. "And I know what you're thinking—Macrae's going to treat it as a mugging gone wrong."

"Which is pretty well how the consulate wants to see it handled, too."

She gave a slow, thoughtful nod. "So who did he have sex with?" she eventually asked.

"Is it relevant?"

"We won't know till we know. Most likely candidate is Scarlett Colwell."

"Because she's a stunner?" Rebus sounded dubious.

"Can't bear to think of her with anyone else?" Clarke teased.

"What about Miss Thomas at the Poetry Library?" But this time Clarke gave a snort.

"I don't see her as a contender," she explained.

"Dr. Colwell didn't seem so sure."

"Which probably says more about Dr. Colwell than Ms. Thomas."

"Maybe young Colin had a point," Rebus plowed on. "Or it's just as likely our red-blooded poet picked up a tart in Glasgow." He saw Clarke's look. "Sorry, I should have said 'sex worker'—or has the terminology changed again since I last got my knuckles rapped?"

"Keep going and I'll rap them again." She paused for a moment, eyes still fixed on him. "Funny to think of you reading *Crime and Punishment*." She took a deep breath. "I did a search on Harry Goodyear."

"Thought you might." He turned his attention to the

windscreen and the bleak car park beyond. Clarke could see that he wanted to wind down the window so he could smoke. But the smell was out there, lying in wait just above the level of the tarmac.

"He was a pub landlord in Rose Street, mid-eighties," she said. "You were a detective sergeant. You helped put him away."

"He was dealing drugs from the premises."

"He died in jail, didn't he? Just a year or two after . . . bad heart or something. Todd Goodyear wouldn't long have been out of nappies." She paused in case he had anything to add, then went on. "Todd's got a brother, did you know that? Name's Sol, been on our radar a few times. I say that, but actually he lives in Dalkeith, making him E Division's problem. Guess what he's been in trouble for."

"Drugs?"

"So you know about him?"

Rebus shook his head. "Educated guess."

"And you didn't know Todd Goodyear was in the police?"

"Believe it or not, Shiv, I don't keep tabs on the grandkids of villains I locked up two decades back."

"Thing is, we didn't just get Sol for possession — we tried to have him for dealing, too. Court gave him the benefit of the doubt."

Rebus turned towards her. "How do you know all this?"

"I was in the office before you this morning. Few minutes on the computer and one phone call to Dalkeith CID. Rumor at the time was Sol Goodyear was dealing on behalf of Big Ger Cafferty."

She could see straightaway that she'd struck a nerve:

Cafferty was unfinished business — *big* unfinished business — his name top of Rebus's to-do list. Cafferty had made a decent fist of looking like a retired villain, but Rebus and Clarke knew better.

Cafferty still ran Edinburgh.

And had found himself a place at the top of *her* list, too.

"Is any of this leading somewhere?" Rebus asked, turning his attention back to the windscreen.

"Not really." She ejected the CD from its slot. The radio blasted into life — Forth One, the DJ talking twenty to the dozen. She switched it off. Rebus had noticed something.

"Didn't know there was a camera there," he said. He meant at the corner of the building, between the first and second stories. The camera was pointing into the car park.

"They reckon it stops vandalism. Reminds me actually — think there's any point looking at city-center footage from the night Todorov was killed? Bound to be cameras at the west end of Princes Street, maybe on Lothian Road, too. If someone was shadowing him . . ." She let the sentence drift.

"It's an idea," he admitted.

"Needle in a haystack," she added. His silence seemed to confirm it, and she rested her head against the back of the seat, neither of them in any hurry to go back inside. "I remember reading in a paper that we've got the most surveillance of any country in the world; more CCTV in London than the whole of the USA . . . can that be right?"

"Can't say I've noticed it reducing the crime stats." Rebus's eyes narrowed. "What's that noise?"

Clarke saw that Tibbet was gesturing from an upstairs window. "I think we're wanted."

"Maybe guilt got the better of our killer and he's come to hand himself in."

"Maybe," Clarke said, not believing it for one moment.

8

"Been here before?" Rebus asked, once they'd passed through the metal detector. He was scooping loose change back into his pocket.

"Got the guided tour soon after it opened," Clarke admitted.

There were indented shapes in the ceiling; Rebus couldn't tell if they were supposed to be Crusader-style crosses. Plenty of activity in the main entrance hall. Tables had been set up for the tour parties, ID badges lying on them and placards to say which groups were expected. Staff were everywhere, ready to direct visitors to the reception desk. At the far end of the hall, some school kids in uniform were settling down for an early lunch.

"First time for me," Rebus told Clarke. "Always wondered what four hundred million pounds looks like . . ."

The Scottish Parliament had divided public opinion from the moment its plans were revealed in the media. Some thought it bold and revolutionary, others wondered at its quirks and its price tag. The architect had died before completing the project, as had the man who'd commissioned it. But it was built now and working, and Rebus had to admit that the debating chamber, whenever he'd seen it on the TV news, looked a bit special.

When they told the woman at the reception desk that they were here to see Megan Macfarlane, she printed out a couple of visitor passes. A call to the MSP's office confirmed that they were expected, and another member of staff stepped forward and asked them to follow him. He was a tall, brisk-stepping figure and, like the receptionist, probably not a day under sixty-five. They followed him down corridors and up in a lift and down more corridors.

"Plenty of concrete and wood," Rebus commented.

"And glass," Clarke added.

"The special, expensive kind, of course," Rebus speculated.

Their guide said nothing until they turned yet another corner and found a young man waiting for them.

"Thanks, Sandy," the man said, "I'll take it from here."

As the guide headed back the way they'd just come, Clarke thanked him, and received a little grunt of acknowledgment. Maybe he was just out of breath.

"My name's Roddy Liddle," the young man was telling them. "I work for Megan."

"And who exactly *is* Megan?" Rebus asked. Liddle stared at him as if he were maybe making a joke. "All our boss told us," Rebus explained, "was to come down here and talk to someone with that name. Apparently she phoned him."

"It was me who did the phoning," Liddle said, making it sound like yet another arduous task that he'd taken in his stride.

"Good for you, son," Rebus told him. The "son" obviously rankled. Liddle was in his early twenties and reckoned he was already well on his way in politics. He looked Rebus up and down before deciding to dismiss him as irrelevant.

"I'm sure Megan will explain." Having said which, Liddle turned and led them to the end of the corridor.

The MSPs' private offices were well proportioned, with desks for staff as well as the politicians themselves. It was Rebus's first sighting of one of the infamous "think pods"—little alcoves with curved windows and a cushioned seat. This was where the MSPs were supposed to come up with blue-sky ideas. It was also where they found Megan Macfarlane. She rose to greet them.

"Glad you could come at such short notice," she said. "I know you're busy on the inquiry, so I won't keep you long." She was short and slim and impeccably groomed, not a hair out of place and with just the right amount of makeup. She wore half-moon glasses that rested most of the way down her nose, so that she peered over them at the two detectives. "I'm Megan Macfarlane," she said, inviting them to make introductions of their own. Liddle was back behind his desk, staring at messages on his computer. Rebus and Clarke gave their names, and the MSP looked around for places to sit, before having a better idea.

"We'll go downstairs and get a coffee. Roddy, can I bring you one back?"

"No thanks, Megan. One cup a day's plenty for me."

"Good point—I don't need to be in the chamber later on?" She waited till he'd shaken his head, then focused her gaze on Clarke. "Diuretic effects, you know, doesn't do to be caught short when you're halfway through a point of order . . ."

They went back the way they'd come and found themselves descending an impressive staircase, Macfarlane announcing that the "Scot Nats" had high hopes for May's elections.

"Latest polls put us five points clear of Labour. Blair's unpopular, and so is Gordon Brown. The Iraq war, cash for peerages — it was one of my colleagues who started that investigation. Labour's panicking because Scotland Yard say they've uncovered 'significant and valuable material.'" She gave a satisfied smile. "Scandal seems to be our opponents' middle name."

"So it's the protest vote you're after?" Rebus asked.

Macfarlane didn't seem to feel this merited any sort of reply.

"If you win in May," Rebus went on, "do we get a referendum on independence?"

"Absolutely."

"And we suddenly become a Celtic tiger?"

"The Labour Party has been failing the people of Scotland for fifty years, Inspector. It's time for a change."

Queuing at the counter, she announced that this would be her "treat." Rebus ordered an espresso, Clarke a small cappuccino. Macfarlane herself opted for a black coffee into which she poured three sachets of sugar. There were tables nearby, and they chose an empty one, pushing aside the leftover crockery.

"We're still in the dark," Rebus said, lifting his cup. "I hope you don't mind me getting straight to the point, but as you said yourself, we've got a murder inquiry waiting for us back at base."

"Absolutely," Macfarlane agreed. Then she paused for a moment, as if to marshal her thoughts. "How much do you know about me?" she began by asking.

Rebus and Clarke shared a look. "Until we were told to come see you," Rebus obliged, "neither of us had ever heard of you."

The MSP, trying not to show any pain, blew across the surface of her coffee before taking a sip.

"I'm a Scottish Nationalist," she said.

"That much we'd guessed."

"And that means I'm passionate about my country. If Scotland is to flourish in this new century—and flourish outside the confines of the UK—we need enterprise, initiative, and investment." She counted these three off on her fingers. "That's why I'm an active member of the URC—the Urban Regeneration Committee. Not that our remit is purely urban, you understand; in fact, I've already proposed a name change in order to make that clear."

"Forgive me for interrupting," Clarke said, having noted Rebus's agitation, "but can I ask what any of this has to do with us?"

Macfarlane lowered her eyes and gave a little smile of apology. "I'm afraid when I'm passionate about something, I do tend to rabbit on."

Rebus's glance towards Clarke said it all.

"This unfortunate incident," Macfarlane was saying, "involving the Russian poet . . ."

"What about it?" Rebus prompted.

"Right now, a group of businessmen is in Scotland—a very *prosperous* group, and all of them Russian. They represent oil, gas, and steel, and other industries besides. They are looking to the future, Inspector—Scotland's future. We need to ensure nothing jeopardizes the links and relationships that we've painstakingly fostered over the past several years. What we certainly *don't* want is anyone thinking we're not a welcoming country, a country that embraces cultures and nationalities. Look at what happened to that young Sikh lad . . ."

"You're asking us," Clarke summarized, "if this was a racial attack?"

"One of the group has voiced that concern," Macfarlane admitted. She looked towards Rebus, but he was staring at the ceiling again, still not sure about it. He'd heard that its concave sections were supposed to look like boats. When he turned his attention back to the MSP, her worried face demanded some reassurance.

"We can't rule anything out," he decided to tell her instead. "Could have been racially motivated. The Russian consulate told us as much this morning—there've been attacks on some of the migrant workers from Eastern Europe. So it's certainly a line we'll be following."

She looked shocked by these words, just as he'd intended. Clarke was hiding her smile behind a raised cup. Rebus decided there was more fun to be had. "Would any of these businessmen have met with Mr. Todorov recently? If so, it would be helpful to talk to them."

Macfarlane was saved from answering by the appearance of a new arrival. Like Rebus and Clarke, he wore a badge that proclaimed him a visitor.

"Megan," he drawled, "I saw you from the reception desk. Hope I'm not interrupting?"

"Not at all." The MSP could hardly disguise her relief. "Let me get you a coffee, Stuart." Then, to Rebus and Clarke: "This is Stuart Janney, from First Albannach Bank. Stuart, these are the officers in charge of the Todorov case." Janney shook hands before pulling over a chair.

"I hope you're both clients," he said with a smile.

"State of my finances," Rebus informed him, "you should be happy I'm with the competition."

Janney made a show of wincing. He'd been carrying

his trench coat over one arm, and now folded it across his lap. "Grim news about that murder," he said, while Macfarlane rejoined the queue at the counter.

"Grim," Rebus echoed.

"From what Ms. Macfarlane just said," Clarke added, "I'm guessing she's already spoken with you about it."

"Happened to come up in conversation this morning," Janney acknowledged, running a hand through his blond hair. His face was freckled, the skin pink, reminding Rebus of a younger Colin Montgomerie, and his eyes were the same dark blue as his tie. Janney seemed to have decided that further explanation was needed. "We were on the phone to one another."

"Are you something to do with these Russian visitors?" Rebus asked. Janney nodded.

"FAB never turns away prospective customers, Inspector."

FAB: it was how most people referred to the First Albannach Bank. It was a term of affection, but behind it lay one of the biggest employers — and probably the most profitable company — in Scotland. The TV adverts showed FAB as an extended family, and were filmed almost as mini-soaps, while the bank's brand-new corporate HQ — built on greenbelt land, despite the protests — was a city in miniature, complete with shopping arcade and cafés. Staff could get their hair done there, or buy food for the evening meal. They could use the gym or play a round of golf on the company's own nine-hole course.

"So if you're looking for someone to manage that overdraft . . ." Janney handed out business cards. Macfarlane laughed when she saw it, before passing him his black coffee. Interesting, Rebus thought: he takes it the same way she does. But he'd bet that if Janney was out with an important customer, whatever the customer ordered would be Janney's drink of choice, too. The Police College at Tulliallan had run a course on it a year or two back: Empathic Interviewing Techniques. When questioning a witness or a suspect, you tried to find things you had in common, even if that meant lying. Rebus had never really got round to trying it, but he could tell that someone like Janney would be a natural.

"Stuart's incorrigible," the MSP was saying. "What have I told you about touting for business? It's unethical." But she was smiling as she spoke, and Janney gave a quiet chuckle, while sliding his business cards closer to Rebus and Clarke.

"Mr. Janney," Clarke began, "tells us the pair of you were discussing Alexander Todorov."

Megan Macfarlane nodded slowly. "Stuart has an advisory role in the URC."

"I didn't think FAB would be pro-Nationalist, Mr. Janney," Rebus said.

"Completely neutral," Janney stressed. "There are twelve members of the Urban Regeneration Committee, Inspector, representing five political parties."

"And how many of them did you speak to on the phone today?"

"So far, only Megan," the banker admitted, "but then it's not *quite* lunchtime." He made show of checking his watch.

"Stuart is our three-I consultant," Macfarlane was saying. "Inward Investment Initiatives."

Rebus ignored this. "Did Ms. Macfarlane ask you to drop by, Mr. Janney?" he asked. When the banker looked to the MSP, Rebus had his answer. He turned his attention to Macfarlane herself. "Which businessman was it?"

She blinked. "Sorry?"

"Which one was it who seemed so concerned about Alexander Todorov?"

"Why do you want to know?"

"Is there any reason I *shouldn't* know?" Rebus raised an eyebrow for effect.

"The Inspector's got you cornered, Megan," Janney was saying with a lopsided smile. He got a baleful look in return, which had gone by the time Macfarlane turned towards Rebus.

"It was Sergei Andropov," she stated.

"There was a Russian president called Andropov," Clarke commented.

"No relation," Janney told her, taking a sip of coffee. "At HQ, they've taken to calling him Svengali."

"Why's that, sir?" Clarke sounded genuinely curious.

"The number of takeovers he's finessed, the way he built up his own company into a global player, the boards he's won round, the strategies and gamesmanship . . ." Janney sounded as if he could go on all day. "I'm pretty sure," he said, "it's meant as a term of endearment."

"Sounds like he's endeared himself to you, at any rate," Rebus commented. "I'm guessing First Albannach would love to do business with these big shots."

"We already do."

Rebus decided to wipe the smile off the banker's face. "Well, Alexander Todorov happened to bank with you, too, sir, and look what happened to him."

"DI Rebus has a point, sir," Clarke interrupted. "Any chance you could get us details of Mr. Todorov's accounts and most recent transactions?"

"There are protocols . . ."

"I understand, sir, but they might help us find his killer, which in turn would put your clients' minds at rest."

Janney gave a thoughtful pout. "Is there an executor?"

"Not that we know of."

"Which branch was his account with?"

Clarke stretched out her arms and gave a shrug and a hopeful smile.

"I'll see what I can do."

"We appreciate it, sir," Rebus told him. "We're based at Gayfield Square." He made show of studying his surroundings. "Not quite as grand as this, but then it didn't bankrupt the taxpayer either . . ."

9

It was a quick run from the Parliament to the City Chambers. Rebus told the staff at reception that they had a 2:00 p.m. appointment with the Lord Provost and were hellish early, but could they leave their car parked outside anyway? Everyone seemed to think that was fine, which caused Rebus to beam a smile and ask if they could fill in the time by saying hello to Graeme MacLeod. More passes, another security check, and they were in. As they waited for the lift, Clarke turned to Rebus.

"I meant to say, you handled Macfarlane and Janney pretty well."

"I guessed as much from the way you let me do most of the work."

"Is it too late for me to withdraw the compliment?" But they were both smiling. "How long till they find out we've nicked a parking space under false pretenses?"

"Depends whether they bother to ask the Lord Prov's secretary." The lift arrived and they got in, descending two stories below ground level to where a man was waiting. Rebus introduced him to Clarke as Graeme MacLeod, and MacLeod led them into the CMF Room, explaining that CMF stood for Central Monitoring Facility. Rebus had been there before, but Clarke hadn't, and her eyes widened a little as she saw the array of closed-circuit monitors, dozens of them, three deep and with staff manning desks of computers in front of them.

MacLeod liked it when visitors were impressed and needed no prompting to give his little speech.

"Ten years the city's had CCTV," he began. "Started with a dozen cameras in the center, now we've got over a hundred and thirty, with more due to be introduced shortly. We maintain a direct link to the Police Control Center at Bilston, and about twelve hundred arrests a year are down to things we spot in this stuffy wee room."

The room was certainly warm — heat from all the monitors — and Clarke was shrugging off her coat.

"We're open 24/7," MacLeod went on, "and can track a suspect while telling the police where to find them." The monitors had numbers above them, and MacLeod pointed to one. "That's the Grassmarket. And if Jenny here" — meaning the woman seated at the desk — "uses the little keypad in front of her we can swivel the camera and zoom in on anyone parking their car or coming out of a shop or pub."

Jenny showed how it was done, and Clarke nodded slowly.

"The picture's very clear," she commented. "And in color — I was expecting black and white. Don't suppose you've any cameras on King's Stables Road?"

MacLeod gave a dry chuckle. "I knew that's what you'd be after." He reached for a logbook and flicked back a couple of pages. "Martin was manning the decks that night. He tracked the police cars and ambulance." MacLeod ran a finger along the relevant entry. "Even had a look back at what footage there was but didn't spot anything conclusive."

"Doesn't mean there's nothing there."

"Absolutely."

"Siobhan here," Rebus said, "was telling me there's more CCTV in the UK than any other country."

"Twenty percent of all the closed-circuit cameras in the world, one for each and every dozen of us."

"So quite a lot then?" Rebus muttered.

"You save all the footage?" Clarke asked.

We do what we can. It goes onto hard disk and video, but there are guidelines we have to follow . . ."

"What Graeme means," Rebus explained for Clarke's benefit, "is that he can't just go handing material to us — Data Protection Act, 1997."

MacLeod was nodding. "Ninety-eight actually, John. We can give you what we've got, but there are hoops to be gone through first."

"Which is why I've learned to trust Graeme's judgment." Rebus turned to MacLeod. "And I'm guessing you've been through the recordings with whatever the digital equivalent is of a fine-toothed comb?"

MacLeod smiled and nodded. "Jenny gave me a hand. We had the photos of the victim from the various news agencies. I think we've picked him up on Shandwick Place. He was on foot and unaccompanied. That's at just gone ten. Next time we see him is half an hour later on Lothian Road. But as you've guessed, we've no cameras on King's Stables Road itself."

"Did you get the sense anyone was following him?" Rebus asked.

MacLeod shook his head. "And neither did Jenny."

Clarke was studying the screens again. "A few more years of this and I'll be out of a job."

MacLeod laughed. "I doubt that. Surveillance is a

tricky balancing act. Invasion of privacy is always an issue, and the civil rights people oppose us every step of the way."

"Now there's a surprise," Rebus muttered.

"Don't tell me you'd want one of our cameras peering in through your own window?" MacLeod teased.

Clarke had been thinking. "Charles Riordan picked up the tab at the curry house at nine forty-eight. Todorov left there and headed into town along Shandwick Place. How come it took him half an hour to travel quarter of a mile to Lothian Road?"

"He stopped for a drink?" Rebus guessed.

"Riordan mentioned Mather's or the Caledonian Hotel. Wherever he went, Todorov was back on the street at ten forty, meaning he'd have been outside the car park five minutes later." She waited for Rebus to nod his agreement.

"Shutters go down on the car park at eleven," he added. "The attack must've been quick." Then, to MacLeod: "What about afterwards, Graeme?"

MacLeod was ready for this. "The passerby who found the body called it in at twelve minutes past eleven. We took a look at the footage from the Grassmarket and Lothian Road ten minutes either side of that time." He gave a shrug. "Just the usual pub-goers, office parties, late-night shoppers . . . no crazed muggers legging it with a hammer swinging from their hand."

"Be handy if we could take a look at that," Rebus stated. "We might know faces you don't."

"Fair enough."

"But you'd want us to jump through the hoops?"

MacLeod had folded his arms, the gesture providing an answer in itself.

* * *

They were heading back through the reception area, Rebus breaking open a fresh packet of cigarettes, when an attendant in some sort of official garb stopped them. It took a moment for Rebus to register that the Lord Provost herself was there, too, her gold chain of office hanging around her neck. She didn't look particularly happy.

"I believe we have an appointment?" she was asking. "Though nobody seems to know about it except you two."

"Bit of a cock-up there," Rebus apologized.

"So not just a ploy to grab yourselves a precious parking bay?"

"Perish the thought."

She glared at him. "Just as well you're going — we need that space for more important visitors."

Rebus could feel his grip tightening on the cigarettes. "What could be more urgent than a murder inquiry?" he asked.

She caught his meaning. "The Russian poet? We need that one cleared fast."

"To appease the moneymen of the Volga?" Rebus guessed. Then, after a moment's thought: "How much does the council have to do with them? Megan Macfarlane tells us her Urban Regeneration Committee is involved."

The Lord Provost was nodding. "But there's council input, too."

"So you're glad-handing the fat cats? Good to see my council tax being put to such good use."

The Lord Provost had taken a step forwards, glare intensifying. She was readying a fresh salvo when her attendant cleared his throat. Through the window, a long black car could be seen trying to maneuver itself through the arch in front of the building. The Lord Provost said nothing, just turned from Rebus and was gone. He gave her five seconds, then made his own exit, Clarke at his shoulder.

"Nice to make friends," she said.

"I'm a week from retirement, Shiv, what the hell do I care?"

They walked a few yards down the pavement, then stopped while Rebus got his cigarette lit.

"Did you see the paper this morning?" Clarke asked. "Andy Kerr won Politician of the Year last night."

"And who's he when he's at home?"

"Man who brought in the smoking ban."

Rebus just snorted. Pedestrians were watching the official-looking car draw to a halt in front of the waiting Lord Provost. Her liveried attendant stepped forward to open the back door. Tinted windows had shielded the passenger from view, but as he stepped out Rebus immediately guessed he was one of the Russians. Big coat, black gloves, and a chiseled, unsmiling face. Maybe forty years old, hair short and well groomed with some graying at the temples. Steely gray eyes that took in everything, Rebus and Clarke included, even as he was shaking the Lord Provost's hand and answering some remark she'd made. Rebus sucked smoke deep into his lungs and watched as the party disappeared back inside.

"Looks like the Russian consulate's going into the taxi business," Rebus stated, studying the black Mercedes.

"Same car Stahov had?" Clarke guessed.

"Could be."

"What about the driver?"

"Hard to tell."

Another official had appeared and was gesturing for them to move their car so the chauffeur could park. Rebus held up a single digit, meaning one minute. Then he noticed that Clarke was still wearing her visitor's badge.

"Better hand them back," he said. "You take this." He held out the half-smoked cigarette towards her, but she was reluctant, so instead he balanced it on a windowsill nearby. "Watch it doesn't blow away," he warned, taking her badge and unclipping his own.

"I'm sure they don't need them," she commented. Rebus just smiled and headed for reception.

"Thought we better give you these," he told the woman behind the desk. "You can always recycle them, eh? We've all got to do our bit." He was still smiling, so the receptionist smiled back.

"By the way," he added, leaning over the desk, "that bloke with the Lord Provost—was it who I think it was?"

"Some sort of business tycoon," the woman said. Yes, because the visitors' log was sitting there in front of them, and the last name to be entered—entered with what looked like thick blue ink from a fountain pen—was the same one she uttered now.

"Sergei Andropov."

"Where to?" Clarke asked.

"The pub."

"Do you have one in mind?"

"Mather's, of course."

But as Clarke drove them down Johnston Terrace,

Rebus told her to take a detour, a series of left turns bringing them into King's Stables Road from the Grass-market end. They drew to a halt outside the multistory, and saw that Hawes and Tibbet were busy. Clarke sounded the horn as she turned off the ignition. Tibbet turned and waved. He'd been sticking flyers on wind-screens — POLICE INCIDENT: INFORMATION RE-QUIRED. Hawes was setting up a sandwich board on the pavement next to the exit barriers — a larger version of the flyer, exact same wording. There was a grainy photograph of Todorov: "Around 11 p.m. on Wednesday 15 November a man was attacked within the confines of this car park, dying from his injuries. Did you see anything? Was anyone you know parked here on that evening? Please call the incident room . . ." The number given was a police switchboard.

"Just as well," Rebus pointed out, "seeing as there's no one currently home at CID."

"Macrae was saying much the same thing," Hawes agreed, studying her handiwork. "Wanted to know how many more officers we'd be needing."

"I like my teams small and perfectly formed," Rebus replied.

"Obviously not a Hearts fan," Tibbet added in an un-dertone.

"You a Hibs fan then, Colin, same as Siobhan here?"

"Livingston," Tibbet corrected him.

"Hearts have got a Russian owner, haven't they?"

It was Clarke who answered. "He's Lithuanian actu-ally."

Hawes interrupted to ask where Rebus and Clarke were headed.

"The pub," Clarke announced.

"Lucky you."

"Business rather than pleasure."

"So what do Colin and me do after this?" Hawes's eyes were on Rebus.

"Back to base," he told her, "to await the torrent of phone calls."

"And," Clarke suddenly remembered, "I need someone to call the BBC for me. See if they'll send us a copy of Todorov on *Question Time*. I want to see just how much of a stirrer he really was."

"They ran a bit of it on the news last night," Colin Tibbet announced. "There was a package about the case, and that was all the footage of him they seemed to have."

"Thanks for sharing," Clarke told him. "Maybe *you* could get on to the Beeb for me?"

He gave a shrug, indicating willingness. Clarke's attention was drawn to the stack of flyers he still held. Though they were printed on various colors of paper, most seemed to be a particularly lurid pink.

"We wanted them in a hurry," Tibbet explained. "This was what was on offer."

"Let's go," Rebus told Clarke, making for the car, but Hawes had other ideas.

"We should be doing the follow-up interviews with the witnesses," she called. "Me and Colin could do it."

Rebus pretended to think for all of five seconds before turning down the offer.

Back in the car, he stared at the No Entry sign that was denying them direct access to Lothian Road.

"Think I should chance it?" Clarke asked.

"Up to you, Shiv."

She gnawed at her bottom lip, then executed a three-point turn. Ten minutes later, they were on Lothian Road, passing the other end of King's Stables Road. "Should've chanced it," Rebus commented. Two further minutes and they were parking on the yellow lines outside Mather's, having disregarded a road sign warning them they could turn into Queensferry Street only if they were a bus or a taxi. The white van in front had done the selfsame thing and the estate car behind them was following suit.

"A regular little law-breaking convoy" was Rebus's comment.

"I despair of this town," Clarke said, teeth bared. "Who thinks up the traffic management?"

"You need a drink," Rebus informed her. He didn't get into Mather's much, but he liked the place. It was old-fashioned, with few chairs, most of them occupied by serious-looking men. Early afternoon, and Sky Sports was on the television. Clarke had brought a few of the flyers with her — yellow in preference to pink — and went around the tables with them, while Rebus held one up in front of the barman's face.

"Two nights ago," he said, "around ten o'clock, maybe a little after."

"Wasn't my shift," the barman answered.

"Then whose was it?"

"Terry's."

"And where's Terry?"

"In his kip, most likely."

"Is he on again tonight?" When the barman nodded, Rebus pressed the flyer on him. "I want a phone call from him, whether he served this guy or not. No phone call, it's you I'll blame."

The barman just gave a twitch of the mouth. Clarke was standing next to Rebus. "Guy over in the corner seems to know you," she said. Rebus looked and nodded, then walked over to the table, Clarke following.

"All right, Big?" Rebus said by way of greeting.

The man drinking alone — half of heavy and an inch of whisky — seemed to be enjoying his berth, one foot up on the chair next to him, a hand scratching his chest. He was wearing a faded denim shirt, undone to below the breastbone. Rebus hadn't seen him in maybe seven or eight years. He called himself Podeen — Big Podeen. Ex-navy, ex-bouncer, looking his age now, his huge, weather-beaten face caving in on itself, most of the teeth having disappeared from the fleshy-lipped mouth.

"Not bad, Mr. Rebus." There were no handshakes, just slight tilts of the head and occasional eye contact.

"This your local, then?" Rebus asked.

"Depends how you mean."

"Thought you were living down the coast."

"That was years back. People change, move on." There was a pouch of tobacco on the table, next to a lighter and cigarette papers. Podeen picked it up and began to play with it.

"Got something for us?"

Podeen puffed out his cheeks and exhaled. "I was here two nights back, and your man there wasn't." He nodded towards the flyer. "Know who he is, though, used to see him in here round about closing time. Bit of a nighthawk, if you ask me."

"Like yourself, Big?"

"And your good self, too, I seem to remember."

"Pipe and slippers these days, Big," Rebus told him. "Cocoa and in bed by ten."

"Can't see it somehow. Guess who I bumped into

the other day—our old friend Cafferty. How come you never managed to put him away?"

"We got him a couple of times, Big."

Podeen wrinkled his nose. "A few years here and there. He always seemed to get back off the canvas, though, didn't he?" Podeen's eyes met Rebus again. "Word is, you're for the gold watch. Not a bad heavy-weight career, Mr. Rebus, but that's what they'll always say about you . . ."

"What?"

"That you lacked the knockout punch." Podeen lifted his whisky glass. "Anyway, here's to the twilight years. Maybe we'll start seeing you in here more often. Then again, most of the pubs in this city, you'd have to keep your back to the wall—plenty of grudges, Mr. Rebus, and once you're not the law anymore . . ." Podeen gave a theatrical shrug.

"Thanks for cheering me up, Big." Rebus glanced towards the flyer. "Did you ever talk to him?" Podeen made a face and shook his head. "Anyone else in here we should be asking?"

"He used to stand at the bar, as near the door as possible. It was the drink he liked, not the company." He paused for a moment. "You've not asked me about Cafferty."

"Okay, what about him?"

"He said to say hello."

Rebus stared him out. "Is that it?"

"That's it."

"And where did this earth-shattering exchange take place?"

"Funnily enough, just across the road. I bumped into him as he was coming out of the Caledonian Hotel."

*   *   *

Which was their next destination. The vast pink-hued edifice had two doors. One led into the hotel's reception area and boasted a doorman. The other took you directly into the bar, which was open to residents and waifs alike. Rebus decided he was thirsty and ordered a pint. Clarke said she'd stick to tomato juice.

"Been cheaper across the road," she commented.

"Which is why you're paying." But when the bill came, he slapped a five-pound note on it, hoping for change.

"Your chum in Mather's was right, wasn't he?" Clarke ventured. "When I go out for the night, I always keep watch on who's coming and going, just in case I see a face I know."

Rebus nodded. "Number of villains we've put away, stands to reason some of them are back on the street. Just make sure you frequent a better class of watering hole."

"Like this place, for instance?" Clarke looked around her. "What do you think Todorov would see in it?"

Rebus thought for a moment. "Not sure," he conceded. "Maybe just a different sort of vibe."

"Vibe?" Clarke echoed with a smile.

"Must've picked that up from you."

"I don't think so."

"Tibbet then. Anyway, what's wrong with it? It's a perfectly decent word."

"It just doesn't sound right, coming from you."

"Should have heard me in the sixties."

"I wasn't born in the sixties."

"Don't keep reminding me." He'd downed half his drink and signaled for the barman, flyer at the ready. The barman was short and stick-thin with a shaved head.

He wore a tartan waistcoat and tie, and looked at Todorov's photo for only a few seconds before starting to nod, bald pate gleaming.

"He's been in a few times recently."

"Was he in two nights ago?" Clarke asked.

"I think so." The barman was concentrating, brow furrowed. Rebus knew that sometimes the reason people concentrated was to think up a convincing lie. The badge on the barman's waistcoat identified him only as Freddie.

"Just after ten," Rebus prompted. "He'd already had a few drinks."

Freddie was nodding again. "Wanted a large cognac."

"He just stayed for one?"

"I think so."

"Did you speak to him?"

Freddie shook his head. "But I know who he is now — I saw about it on the news. What a hellish thing to happen."

"Hellish," Rebus agreed.

"Did he sit at the bar?" Clarke asked. "Or was he at a table?"

"The bar — always the bar. I knew he was foreign, but he didn't act like a poet."

"And how do poets act, in your experience?"

"What I mean is, he just sat there with a scowl on his face. Mind you, I did see him writing stuff down."

"The last time he was in?"

"No, before that. Had a wee notebook he kept taking from his pocket. One of the waitresses thought maybe he was an undercover inspector or doing a review for a magazine. I told her I didn't think so."

"The last time he was here, you didn't see the note-book?"

"He was talking to somebody."

"Who?" Rebus asked.

Freddie just shrugged. "Another drinker. They sat pretty much where you two are." Rebus and Clarke shared a look.

"What were they talking about?"

"Pays not to eavesdrop."

"It's a rare bartender who doesn't like to listen in on other people's conversations."

"They might not have been talking in English."

"What then — Russian?" Rebus's eyes narrowed.

"Could be," Freddie seemed to concede.

"Got any cameras in here?" Rebus was looking around him. Freddie shook his head.

"Was this other drinker male or female?" Clarke asked.

Freddie paused before answering. "Male."

"Description."

Another pause. "Bit older than him . . . stockier. We dim the lights at night, and it was a busy session . . ." He shrugged an apology.

"You're being a great help," Clarke assured him. "Did they talk for long?" Freddie just shrugged again. "They didn't leave together?"

"The poet left on his own." Freddie sounded confident about this at least.

"Don't suppose cognac comes cheap in here," Rebus commented, taking in his surroundings.

"Sky's the limit," the barman admitted. "But when you've a tab running, you tend not to notice."

"Not until your bill's handed to you at checkout,"

Rebus agreed. "Thing is, though, Freddie, our Russian friend wasn't a resident here." He paused for effect. "So whose tab are we talking about?"

The barman seemed to realize his mistake. "Look," he said, "I don't want to get into trouble . . ."

"You certainly don't want to get into trouble with *me,*" Rebus confirmed. "The other man was a guest?"

Freddie looked from one detective to the other. "I suppose so," he said, seeming to deflate. Rebus and Clarke locked eyes.

"If you were here from Moscow on a business trip," she said quietly, "maybe some kind of delegation . . . which hotel would you stay at?"

There was only one way to answer that, but in reception the staff said they couldn't help. Instead, they called for the duty manager, and Rebus repeated his question.

"Any Russian businessmen bunking here?"

The duty manager was studying Rebus's warrant card. When he handed it back, he asked if there was a problem.

"Only if your hotel continues to obstruct me in a murder inquiry," Rebus drawled.

"Murder?" The duty manager had introduced himself as Richard Browning. He wore a crisp charcoal suit with a checked shirt and lavender tie. Color flooded his cheeks as he repeated Rebus's word.

"A man left the bar here a couple of nights back, got as far as King's Stables Road, and was beaten to death. Means the last people who saw him were the ones knocking back cocktails in your hotel." Rebus had taken a step closer to Richard Browning. "Now, I can get my hands on your registration list and make sure I interview every single guest — maybe set up a big table next to the concierge desk so that it's nice and public . . ." Rebus paused. "I *can* do that, but it'll take time and it'll be messy. Or . . ." Another pause. "You can tell me what Russians you have staying here."

"You could also," Clarke added, "go through the bar receipts and find the names of anyone who paid for a large cognac some time after ten on the night before last."

"Our guests have the right to their privacy," Browning argued.

"We only want names," Rebus told him, "not a list of whatever porn they've been watching on the film channel."

Browning stiffened his spine.

"Okay," Rebus apologized, "this isn't that sort of hotel. But you *do* have some Russians staying here?"

Browning admitted as much with a nod. "You know there's a delegation in town?" Rebus assured him he did. "To be honest, we only have three or four of them. The rest are spread around the city — the Balmoral, George, Sheraton, Prestonfield . . ."

"Don't they get along?" Clarke asked.

"Just not enough presidential suites to go round," Browning sniffed.

"How much longer are they here?"

"A few days — there's a trip to Gleneagles planned, but they're keeping their rooms, saves checking out and checking in again."

"Nice to have the option," Rebus commented. "How soon can we have the names?"

"I'm going to have to talk to the general manager first."

"How soon?" Rebus repeated.

"I really can't say," Browning spluttered. Clarke handed him a card with her mobile number.

"Sooner the better," she nudged him.

"Else it'll be a table by the concierge," Rebus added.

They left Browning nodding to himself and staring at the floor.

The doorman saw them coming and held open the door. Rebus handed him one of the lurid flyers by way of a tip. As they crossed to Clarke's car—which she'd parked in an empty cab rank—Rebus saw a limo drawing to a halt, the black Merc from the City Chambers and the same figure emerging from the back: Sergei Andropov. Again, he seemed to sense eyes on him and returned Rebus's stare for a moment before entering the hotel. The car cruised around the corner and entered the hotel's car park.

"Same driver Stahov had?" Clarke asked.

"Still didn't get a good enough look," Rebus told her. "But that reminds me of something *I* meant to ask when we were inside—namely, what the hell is a respectable hotel like the Caledonian doing letting Big Ger Cafferty over its threshold?"

10

They waited until 6:00 p.m. to do the witness interviews, reckoning there'd be a better chance of finding people at home. Roger and Elizabeth Anderson lived in a detached 1930s house on the southern edge of the city with views to the Pentland Hills. The path leading through the garden to the front door was lit, allowing them to take in the impressive rockeries and an expanse of lawn that could well have been trimmed with nail scissors.

"A little hobby for Mrs. Anderson?" Clarke guessed.

"Who knows—maybe she's the highflyer and he stays at home."

But when Roger Anderson opened the door he was dressed in his work suit, the tie loosened and top shirt-button undone. He held the evening paper in one hand and had pushed his reading glasses to the top of his head.

"Oh, it's you," he said. "Wondered when you'd get round to us." He headed back indoors, expecting them to follow. "It's the police," he called to his wife. Rebus gave her a smile when she arrived from the kitchen.

"See you've not put the wreath up yet," he said, gesturing towards the front door.

"She had me throw it in the bin," Roger Anderson said, using the remote to turn off the TV.

"We're about to sit down to dinner," his wife pointed out.

"This won't take long," Clarke assured her. She'd brought a folder with her. PCs Todd Goodyear and Bill Dyson had typed up their initial notes. Goodyear's were immaculate, Dyson's riddled with spelling mistakes. "It wasn't you who actually found the body, was it?" Clarke asked.

Elizabeth Anderson had taken a few more steps into the room, standing just behind her husband's chair, the chair Roger Anderson was sinking back into without bothering to ask if either detective would like to sit. Rebus, however, was happier standing—it meant he could cruise the room, taking it all in. Mr. Anderson had laid his newspaper down on the coffee table next to a crystal tumbler of what smelled like three parts gin to one of tonic.

"We heard the girl screaming," the man was saying, "went over to see what was happening. Thought she'd been attacked or something."

"You were parked . . ." Clarke pretended to be scouring the notes.

"In the Grassmarket," Mr. Anderson stated.

"Why there, sir?" Rebus broke in.

"Why not there?"

"Just seems a fair walk from the church. You were at a carol service, yes?"

"That's right."

"Bit early in the year for it?"

"The Christmas lights go on next week."

"It finished pretty late, didn't it?"

"We had a spot of supper afterwards." Anderson

sounded indignant that any questions at all needed to be asked of him.

"You didn't think to use the multistory?"

"Closes at eleven — wasn't sure we'd be back at the car by then."

Rebus nodded. "You know the place then? Know its opening hours?"

"I've used it in the past. Thing is, the Grassmarket doesn't cost anything after six thirty."

"Got to be careful with the pennies, sir," Rebus agreed, looking around the large, well-furnished room. "It says in the notes you work in . . . ?"

"I'm on the staff at First Albannach."

Rebus nodded again, pretending not to be surprised. Dyson hadn't actually bothered to make a note of Anderson's profession.

"You're bloody lucky to find me home so early," Anderson went on. "Been hellish busy recently."

"Do you happen to know someone called Stuart Janney?"

"Met him many times. . . . Look, what's any of this got to do with the poor sod who died?"

"Probably nothing at all, sir," Rebus admitted. "We just like to build up as full a picture as possible."

"Another reason we park in the Grassmarket," Elizabeth Anderson said, voice not much above a whisper, "is that it's well lit, and there are always people about. We're very careful that way."

"Didn't stop you taking a scary route to get there," Clarke pointed out. "That time of night, King's Stables Road's pretty well deserted."

Rebus was peering at a selection of framed photographs in a cabinet. "You on your wedding day," he mused.

"Twenty-seven years ago," Mrs. Anderson confirmed.

"And is this your daughter?" He knew the answer already: half a dozen photos time-lined the girl's life.

"Deborah. She'll be home from college next week."

Rebus nodded slowly. Seemed to him that the most recent pictures were half hidden behind framed memories of a gap-toothed infant and schoolgirl. "I see she's been going through a Goth stage." Meaning the hair suddenly turning jet black, the heavily kohled eyes.

"Again, Inspector," Roger Anderson interceded, "I don't see what possible bearing any of this—"

Rebus waved the objection aside. Clarke looked up from the notes she'd been pretending to read.

"I know it's a stupid question," she said with a smile, "but you've had time to think back over everything, so is there anything you can add? You didn't see anyone else, or hear anything?"

"Nothing," Mr. Anderson stated.

"Nothing," his wife echoed. Then, after a moment: "He's quite a famous poet, isn't he? We've had reporters on the phone."

"Best not to say anything to them," Rebus advised.

"I'd love to know how the hell they got to hear about us in the first place," her husband growled. "Is this the end of it, do you think?"

"I'm not sure I understand."

"Will you lot keep coming back, even though we've nothing to tell you?"

"Actually, you need to come to Gayfield Square to make a formal statement," Clarke told them. She pulled another of her business cards out of the folder. "You can call this number first and ask for DC Hawes or DC Tibbet."

"What's the bloody point?" Roger Anderson asked.

"It's a murder inquiry, sir," Rebus responded crisply. "A man was beaten to a pulp, and the killer's still out there. Our job is to find him . . . sorry if that inconveniences you in any way."

"You don't sound too sorry, I must say," Anderson grumbled.

"Actually, Mr. Anderson, my heart bleeds — apologies if that doesn't always come across." Rebus turned as if readying to leave, but then paused. "What sort of car is it, by the way, the one you need to keep parked where there's plenty of light?"

"A Bentley — the Continental GT."

"From which I take it you don't work in the mailroom at FAB?"

"Doesn't mean I didn't start there, Inspector. Now if you'll excuse us, I think I can hear our dinner shriveling on the hob."

Mrs. Anderson put a hand to her mouth in horror and darted back into the kitchen.

"If it's burnt," Rebus said, "you can always console yourself with a couple more gins."

Anderson decided not to grace this with an answer, and rose to his feet instead, the better to usher the two detectives off the property.

"Did you have a good supper?" Clarke asked casually, slipping the notes back into her folder. "After the carols, I mean."

"Pretty good, yes."

"I'm always on the lookout for a new restaurant."

"I'm sure you can afford it," Anderson said, with a smile that suggested the opposite. "It's called the Pompadour."

"I'll make sure he's paying." Clarke nodded towards Rebus.

"You do that," Anderson told her with a laugh. He was still chuckling when he closed the door on them.

"No wonder his wife likes the garden," Rebus muttered. "Chance for some time away from that pompous prick." He started down the path, reaching into his pocket for a cigarette.

"If I tell you something interesting," Clarke teased, "will you buy me dinner at the Pompadour?"

Rebus busied himself with his lighter, nodding a reply.

"There was a copy of its menu sitting on the concierge's desk."

Rebus exhaled a plume of smoke into the night sky. "Why's that then?"

"Because," Clarke told him, "the Pompadour is the restaurant at the Caledonian Hotel."

He stared at her for a moment, then turned back to the door and gave it a couple of thumps with his fist. Roger Anderson looked less than delighted, but Rebus wasn't about to give him the chance to complain.

"Before he was attacked," he stated, "Alexander Todorov was drinking in the bar at the Caledonian."

"So?"

"So you were in the restaurant — you didn't happen to see him?"

"Elizabeth and I didn't go near the bar. It's a big hotel, Inspector . . ." Anderson was closing the door again. Rebus thought about wedging a foot in to stop him; probably been years since he'd done anything like that. But he couldn't think of any other questions, so he just kept his gaze on Roger Anderson until the solid wooden door was between them. Even then, he focused on it for a few seconds more, willing the man to open up again. But Anderson was gone. Rebus headed back down the path.

"What do you think?" Clarke asked.

"Let's go talk to the other witness. After that, I'll give you my best guess."

Nancy Sievewright's flat was on the third story of a Blair Street tenement. There was an illuminated sign across the street, advertising a basement sauna. Farther up the steep incline, smokers were huddled outside a bar and there were a few yips and yells from Hunter Square, where the city's homeless often held court until moved on by the police.

There wasn't much light in the tenement's doorway, so Rebus held his cigarette lighter under the intercom, while Clarke made out the various names. Rented flats and a shifting population, meaning some of the buzzers boasted half a dozen names alongside, with scrawled amendments on peeling bits of gummed paper. Sievewright's name was just about legible, and when Clarke pressed the button the door clicked open without anyone bothering to check who wanted in. The stairwell was well enough lit, with some bags of rubbish at the bottom and a stack of several years' worth of unwanted telephone directories.

"Someone's got a cat," Rebus said, sniffing the air.

"Or an incontinence problem," Clarke agreed. They climbed the stone steps, Rebus pausing at each level as though studying the various names on the doors, but really just catching his breath. By the time he reached the third floor, Clarke had already rung the bell. The door was opened by a young man with tousled hair and a week's growth of dark beard. He wore eyeliner and a red bandanna.

"You're not Kelly," he said.

"Sorry to disappoint you." Clarke was holding up her warrant card. "We're here to see Nancy."

"She's not in." He sounded instantly defensive.

"Did she tell you about finding the body?"

"What?" The young man's mouth fell open and stayed that way.

"You a friend of hers?"

"Flatmate."

"She didn't tell you?" Clarke waited for a response that didn't come. "Well, anyway, this is just a backup call. She's not done anything wrong—"

"So if you'll kindly let us in," Rebus interrupted, "we'll try to ignore the smell of Bob Hope wafting into our faces." He gave what he hoped was an encouraging smile.

"Sure." The young man held the door open a little wider. Nancy Sievewright's head appeared around her bedroom door.

"Hello, Nancy," Clarke said, stepping into the hall. There were boxes everywhere—stuff for recycling, stuff to be thrown out, stuff that hadn't made it into the flat's limited cupboard space. "Just need to check a few things with you."

Nancy was in the hallway, closing her bedroom door after her.

She wore a short tight skirt with black leggings and

a crop top, which showed off her midriff and a studded belly button.

"I'm just on my way out," she said.

"I'd put another layer on," Rebus suggested. "It's perishing."

"Won't take a moment," Clarke was reassuring the teenager. "Where's the best place to talk?"

"Kitchen," Nancy stated. Yes, because the sweet smell of dope was coming from behind another closed door, probably the living room. There was music, too, something rambling and electronic. Rebus couldn't place it, but it reminded him a bit of Tangerine Dream.

The kitchen was narrow and cluttered, seemed the flatmates existed on takeaways. The window had been left open a couple of inches, which did little to lessen the smell from the sink.

"Someone's missed their turn to do the washing-up," Rebus commented.

Nancy ignored him. She had folded her arms and was waiting for a question. Clarke went back into her folder again, bringing out Todd Goodyear's impeccable report and another business card.

"We'd like you to come down to Gayfield Square some time soon," Clarke began, "and give a proper signed statement. Ask for either of these officers." She handed over the card. "Meantime, we just want to check a couple of things. You were on your way back here when you found the victim?"

"That's right."

"You'd been to a friend's in . . ." Clarke pretended to look at the report. She was expecting Nancy to finish the sentence, but the teenager seemed to be having trouble remembering. "Great Stuart Street," Clarke reminded her. Nancy nodded in agreement. "What's your friend's name, Nancy?"

"What do you need that for?"

"It's just the way we are, we like as much detail as we can get."

"Her name's Gill."

Clarke wrote the name down. "Surname?" she asked.

"Morgan."

"And what number does she live at?"

"Sixteen."

"Great." Clarke wrote this down, too. "Thanks for that."

The living room door opened, and a female face peered out, disappearing again after meeting Rebus's glare.

"Who's your landlord?" Rebus decided to ask Nancy. She gave a shrug.

"I give the rent to Eddie."

"Is Eddie the one who answered the door?"

She nodded, and Rebus took a couple of steps back into the hall. On top of one of the cardboard boxes sat a pile of mail. As Clarke asked another question, he sifted through it, stopping at one envelope in particular. In place of a stamp, there was a business frank, and alongside it the name of the company: MGC Lettings. Rebus dropped the letter and listened to Nancy's answer.

"I don't know if the car park was locked up—what difference does it make?"

"Not much," Clarke seemed to concede.

"We think the victim was attacked there," Rebus added. "He either staggered along to the lane where you found him, or else he was carried there."

"I didn't *see* anything!" the teenager wailed. Tears were welling in her eyes, and she had wrapped her arms more tightly around her. The living room door opened again, and Eddie emerged into the hall.

"Stop hassling her," he said.

"We're not hassling her, Eddie," Rebus told him. The young man blanched when he realized Rebus now had his name. He held his ground a further moment or two for pride's sake, then retreated. "Why didn't you tell him what had happened?" Rebus asked Nancy.

She was shaking her head slowly, having blinked back the tears. "Just want to forget all about it."

"Can't blame you for that," Clarke sympathized. "But if you *do* remember anything . . ." She was pointing towards the business card.

"I'll call you," Nancy agreed.

"And you'll come to the station, too," Clarke reminded her, "any time Monday." Nancy Sievewright nodded, looking utterly dejected. Clarke threw a glance towards Rebus, wondering if he had any other questions. He decided to oblige.

"Nancy," he asked quietly, "have you ever been to the Caledonian Hotel?"

The teenager gave a snort. "Oh yeah, I'm in there all the time."

"Seriously, though."

"What do you think?"

"I'll take that as a no." Rebus gave a little jerk of his head, signaling to Clarke that it was time to go. But before they did, he shoved open the living room door. The place was a haze of smoke. There was no ceiling light, just a couple of lamps fitted with purple bulbs and a row of thick white candles on the mantelpiece. The coffee table was covered with cigarette papers, torn bits of card, and shreds of tobacco. Apart from Eddie, there were three figures sprawled on the sofas and the floor. Rebus just nodded at them, then retreated. "Do you do anything yourself?" he asked Nancy. "A bit of blaw maybe?" She was opening the front door.

"Sometimes," she admitted.

"Thanks for not lying," Rebus said. There was a girl on the doorstep: Kelly, presumably. She was probably the same age as Nancy, but the makeup would get her into most over-twenty-one nightspots.

"Bye then," Nancy told the two detectives. As the door closed, they could hear Kelly asking Nancy who they were, along with Nancy's muffled reply that they worked for the landlord. Rebus gave a snort.

"And guess who that landlord would be?" He watched Clarke give a shrug. "Morris Gerald Cafferty — as in MGC Lettings."

"I knew he had a few flats," Clarke commented.

"Hard to turn a corner in this city and not find Cafferty's paw prints nearby." Rebus was thoughtful for a moment.

"She was lying," Clarke stated.

"About the friend she was visiting?" Rebus nodded his agreement.

"Why would she lie?"

"Probably a hundred good reasons."

"Her stoner buddies, for example." Clarke was starting back down the stairs. "Is it worth trying to talk to someone called Gill Morgan at 16 Great Stuart Street?"

"Up to you," Rebus said. He was looking over his shoulder towards the door of Nancy Sievewright's flat. "She's an anomaly, though."

"How so?"

"Every other bugger in this case seems to use the Caledonian like a home from home."

Clarke was smiling a little smile as the door opened behind them. It stayed open as Nancy Sievewright padded down the stairs towards them.

"There's something you can do for me," she said, voice lowered.

"What's that, Nancy?"

"Keep that creep away from me."

The two detectives shared a look. "Which creep is that?" Clarke asked.

"The one with the wife, the one who phoned 999 . . ."

"Roger Anderson?" Rebus's eyes had narrowed.

Nancy gave a nervous nod. "He was round here yesterday. I wasn't in, but he must have waited. He was parked outside when I got back."

"What did he want?"

"Said he was worried about me, wanted to make sure I was all right." She was heading back up the steps again. "I'm done with that."

"Done with what?" Rebus called, but she didn't answer, just closed the door softly after her.

"Bloody hell," Clarke whispered. "What was all that about?"

"Something to ask Mr. Anderson. Funny, I was just thinking to myself that Nancy looks a bit like his daughter."

"How did he get her address?"

Rebus just shrugged. "It'll keep," he stated, after a moment's thought. "I've another little mission for you tonight . . ."

*   *   *

Another little mission: meaning she was on her own when she met with Macrae in his office. He'd been out to some function or other and was dressed in a dinner jacket and black bow tie. There was a driver waiting outside to take him home. As he sat behind his desk, he removed the tie and undid his top button. He'd fetched himself a glass of water from the cooler and was waiting for Clarke to say something. She cleared her throat, cursing Rebus. His reasoning: Macrae would listen to her. That was the whole of it.

"Well, sir," she began, "it's about Alexander Todorov."

"You've got someone in the frame?" Macrae had brightened, but only until she shook her head.

"It's just that we think there may be more to it than a mugging gone wrong."

"Oh yes?"

"We've not got much in the way of evidence as yet, but there are a lot of . . ." A lot of what? She couldn't think of a convincing way of putting it. "There are a lot of leads we need to follow, and mostly they point away from a random attack."

Macrae leaned back in his chair. "This sounds like Rebus," he stated. "He's got you in here arguing *his* corner."

"Doesn't mean I don't agree with him, sir."

"Sooner you're free of him the better." Clarke prickled visibly, and Macrae gave a little wave of apology. "You know what I mean, Siobhan. How long till he goes? A week . . . and what happens then? Will the case be closed by the time he packs his bags?"

"Doubtful," Clarke conceded.

"Meaning *you'll* be left with it, Siobhan."

"I don't mind that, sir."

Macrae stared at her. "Reckon it's worth a few more days, this hunch of his?"

"It's more than a hunch," Clarke stressed. "Todorov connects to a number of people, and it's a matter of ruling them out rather than ruling anything in."

"And what if there's less to this than meets the eye? We've been here before with John after all."

"He's solved a lot of cases in his time," Clarke stated.

"You make a good character witness, Siobhan." Macrae was smiling tiredly. "I know John outranks you," he said eventually, "but I want you in charge of the Todorov murder. Makes things easier, as he himself would admit."

Clarke nodded slowly but said nothing.

"Two or three days — see what you can come up with. You've got Hawes and Tibbet — who else are you going to bring aboard?"

"I'll let you know."

Macrae grew thoughtful again. "Someone from the Russian embassy spoke to Scotland Yard . . . and *they* spoke to our dear Chief Constable." He sighed. "If he knew I was letting John Rebus anywhere near this, he'd have kittens."

"They make nice pets, sir," Clarke offered, but Macrae just glowered.

"It's why *you're* in charge, Siobhan, not John. Is that clear?"

"Yes, sir."

"I'm guessing he's skulking nearby, waiting for you to report back to him?"

"You know him too well, sir."

Macrae made a little gesture with his hand, telling her she was dismissed. She wandered back through the CID suite and down to the lobby, where she saw a face she recognized. Todd Goodyear had either finished a shift or was working undercover, dressed as he was in black straight-leg denims and a black padded bomber jacket. Clarke made show of trying to place him.

"The Todorov crime scene? PC Goodyear?"

He nodded, and glanced towards the folder she was still carrying. "You got my notes?"

"As you can see . . ." She was playing for time, wondering why he was there.

"Were they all right?"

"They were fine." He looked keen for a bit more than that, but she just repeated the word "fine," then asked what he was doing.

"Waiting for you," he owned up. "I'd heard tell you worked late."

"Actually, I just got here twenty minutes ago."

He was nodding. "I was outside in the car." He glanced over her shoulder. "DI Rebus isn't with you?"

"Look, Todd, what the hell is it you want?"

Goodyear licked his lips. "I thought PC Dyson told you — I'm after a stint with CID."

"Good for you."

"And I wondered if you maybe needed someone . . ." He let the sentence drift off.

"With Todorov, you mean?"

"It'd be a chance for me to learn. That was my first murder scene . . . I'd love to know what happens next."

"What happens next is a lot of slogging, most of it with nothing to show at the end."

"Sounds great." He offered her a grin. "I write a good

report, DS Clarke . . . I don't miss too many tricks. I just feel I could be doing *more*."

"Persistent little sod, aren't you?"

"Let me try to convince you over a drink."

"I'm meeting someone."

"Tomorrow, then? I could buy you a coffee."

"Tomorrow's Saturday, and DCI Macrae hasn't put together a budget."

"Meaning no overtime?" Goodyear nodded his understanding.

Clarke thought for a moment. "Why me rather than Rebus? He's the ranking officer."

"Maybe I thought you'd be a better listener."

"Meaning more gullible?"

"Meaning just what I said."

Clarke took another moment to make up her mind. "Actually, it's me in charge of this case, so let's meet for that coffee first thing Monday morning. There's a place on Broughton Street I sometimes use." She named it, and a time.

"Thanks, DS Clarke," Goodyear said. "You won't regret it." He held out his hand and they shook on it.

DAY FOUR

Monday 20 November 2006

11

S iobhan Clarke was ten minutes early, but Goodyear was already there. He was in his uniform, but with the same bomber jacket as Friday night covering it and zipped to the neck.

"Embarrassed to be seen in it?" Clarke asked.

"Well, you know what it's like . . ."

She did indeed. Long time since she'd worn a constabulary uniform, but the job was still something you didn't always readily own up to. Parties she'd been to, people always seemed a bit less comfortable once they knew what she did for a living. It was the same on a night out, guys either losing interest or else making too many jokes: *Going to cuff me to your bedposts? Wait till you see my truncheon. Don't worry about the neighbors, I'll come quietly, officer . . .*

Goodyear was back on his feet, asking what she'd like. "They're on the case," she assured him. Her regular cappuccino was being prepared, so all Goodyear had to do was pay for it and fetch it over. They were seated on stools at a table by the window. It was a basement, so all they could see was a passing parade of legs at street level. Gusts of rain were blowing in from the North Sea; everyone was hurrying to be somewhere else. Clarke turned down his offer of sugar and told him to relax.

"You're not at a job interview," she said.

"I thought I was," he replied with a nervy little laugh, showing a line of slightly crooked teeth. His ears stuck out a little bit, too, and his eyelashes were very fair. He was drinking a mug of filter coffee, and the crumbs on his plate were evidence of an earlier croissant. "Good weekend?" he asked.

"*Great* weekend," she corrected him. "Hibs won six–one, and Hearts lost to Rangers."

"You're a Hibs fan." He nodded slowly to himself, filing the information away. "Were you at the game?"

She shook her head. "It was at Motherwell. I had to content myself with a film."

"*Casino Royale*?"

She shook her head. "*The Departed*." They lapsed into silence, until a thought struck Clarke. "How long were you waiting before I got here?"

"Not too long. Woke up early and thought I might as well . . ." He took a deep breath. "To be honest, I wasn't sure I'd find this place, so I left plenty of time. I always err on the side of caution."

"Duly noted, PC Goodyear. So tell me a bit about yourself."

"Like what?"

"Anything."

"Well, I'm guessing you know who my granddad was . . ." He looked up at her and she nodded. "Most people seem to, whether they say as much to my face."

"You were young when he died," Clarke said.

"I was four. But I hadn't seen him for the best part of a year. Mum and Dad wouldn't take me with them."

"To the prison, you mean?" It was Goodyear's turn to nod.

"Mum fell apart a bit. . . . She was always highly

strung, and her parents thought her a class above my dad. So when *his* dad ended up in jail, that seemed all the proof they needed. Added to which, my dad always liked drowning his own sorrows." He offered a rueful smile. "Maybe some people would be better off never marrying."

"But then there'd be no Todd Goodyear."

"God must have had his reasons."

"Does any of it explain why you joined the police?"

"Maybe—but thanks for not making a straight assumption. So many people have tried spelling it out to me like that. 'You're atoning, Todd' or 'You're showing not all Goodyears are cut from the same cloth.'"

"Lazy thinking?" Clarke guessed.

"How about you, DS Clarke? What made you become a cop?"

She considered a moment before deciding to tell him the truth. "I think I was reacting against my parents. They were typical liberal lefties, growing up in the sixties."

"The only way to rebel was to become the Establishment?" Goodyear smiled and nodded his understanding.

"Not a bad way of putting it," Clarke agreed, lifting her cup to her lips. "What does your brother think of it all?"

"You know he's been in trouble a few times?"

"I know his name's on our books," Clarke admitted.

"You've been checking up on me?" But Clarke wasn't about to answer that. "I never see him." Goodyear paused. "Actually, that's not strictly true—he's been in hospital, and I went to visit him."

"Nothing serious?"

"He got himself into some stupid argument in a pub. That's just the way Sol is."

"Is he older than you or younger?"

"Two years older. Not that you'd ever have known it — when we were kids, neighbors used to say how much more mature than him I seemed. They just meant I was better behaved — plus I used to do the shopping and stuff . . ." He seemed lost in the past for a moment, then shook his head clear. "DI Rebus," he said, "has a bit of history with Big Ger Cafferty, doesn't he?"

Clarke was surprised by the change of subject. "Depends what you mean," she said warily.

"It's just gossip among the uniforms. The pair of them are supposed to be close."

"They detest one another," Clarke heard herself say.

"Really?"

She nodded. "I sometimes wonder how it'll pan out . . ." She was almost talking to herself, because it had crossed her mind often these past few weeks. "Any particular reason why you're asking?"

"When Sol started dealing, I think he was talked into it by Cafferty."

"You think or you know?"

"He's never admitted it."

"Then what makes you so sure?"

"Are cops still allowed to have hunches?"

Clarke smiled, thinking of Rebus again. "It's frowned upon."

"But that doesn't stop it happening." He studied what little was left in his mug. "I'm glad you've put my mind at rest about DI Rebus. You didn't sound surprised when I mentioned Cafferty."

"Like you said, I did some checking."

He gave a smile and a nod, then asked if she wanted a refill.

"One's enough for now." Clarke drained her cup, taking only a few seconds to make up her mind. "You're based at Torphichen, right?"

"Right."

"And can they spare you for a morning?" Goodyear's face brightened like a kid at Christmas. "I'll give them a call," Clarke went on, "and tell them I've snaffled you for a few hours." She wagged a finger in his face. "Just a few hours, mind. Let's see how we get on."

"You won't regret it," Todd Goodyear said.

"That's what you said on Friday — better make sure I don't." My case, Clarke was thinking, and my team . . . and here was her first little bit of recruiting. Maybe it was his naked enthusiasm, reminding her of the cop she'd been, too, once upon a time. Or the notion of rescuing him from his time-serving partner. Then again, with Rebus on the cusp of retirement, a buffer between herself and her remaining colleagues might prove handy . . .

Being selfish or being kind? she asked herself.

Was it possible for an action to be both?

Roger Anderson had reversed halfway down his drive when he spotted the car blocking the gates. The gates themselves were electric and had swung open at the push of a button, but there was a Saab on the roadway, stopping him getting out.

"Of all the inconsiderate bloody . . ." He was wondering which neighbor was responsible. The Archibalds two doors down always seemed to have workmen in or visitors staying. The Graysons across the road had a couple of sons home for the winter from their gap years. Then there were the cold callers and the people dropping leaflets and cards through the door. . . . He sounded the Bentley's horn, which brought his wife to the dining room window. Was there someone in the Saab's passenger seat? No . . . they were in the bloody driving seat! Anderson thumped on the horn a couple more times, then undid his seat belt and got out, stomping towards the offending vehicle. The window on the driver's side was sliding down, a face peering out at him.

"Oh, it's you." One of the detectives from last night . . . Inspector something.

"DI Rebus," Rebus reminded the banker. "And how are you this morning, Mr. Anderson?"

"Look, Inspector, I *do* intend coming to your station sometime today . . ."

"Whenever suits you, sir, but that's not the reason I'm here."

"Oh?"

"After we left you on Friday, we paid a call to the other witness — Miss Sievewright."

"Oh yes?"

"She told us you'd been to see her."

"That's right." Anderson glanced over his shoulder, as if checking his wife was out of earshot.

"Any particular reason, sir?"

"Just wanted to make sure she hadn't suffered any . . . well, she'd had a nasty shock, hadn't she?"

"Seems you gave her another one, sir."

Anderson's cheeks had flushed. "I only went round there to—"

"So you've said," Rebus interrupted. "But what I'm wondering is, how did you know her name and address? She's not in the phone book."

"The officer told me."

"DS Clarke?" Rebus was frowning. But Anderson shook his head.

"When our statements were being taken. Or rather, just after. I'd offered to run her home, you see. He happened to mention her name and Blair Street both."

"And you wandered up and down Blair Street looking for a buzzer with her name on?"

"I don't see that I've done anything wrong."

"In which case, I'm sure you'll have told Mrs. Anderson all about it."

"Now look here . . ."

But Rebus was starting his ignition. "We'll see you at the station later . . . and your good lady wife, too, of course."

He pulled away with the window still open and left it that way for the first few minutes. This time of the morning, he knew the traffic would be sluggish heading back into town. He'd had only the three pints last night, but his head felt gummy. Saturday he'd watched a bit of TV, ruing another obituary — the footballer Ferenc Puskás. Rebus had been in his teens when the European Cup Final had come to Hampden. Real Madrid against Eintracht Frankfurt, Real winning 7–3. One of the great games, and Puskás one of the greatest players. The young Rebus had found Hungary, the footballer's home country, in an atlas, and had wanted to go there.

Jack Palance, and now Puskás, both gone forever. That was what happened with heroes.

So: Saturday night at the Oxford Bar, sorrows drowned, any and all conversations forgotten by the next morning. Sunday: laundry and the supermarket, and news that a Russian journalist called Litvinenko had been poisoned in London. That had made Rebus sit up in his chair, increasing the volume on the TV. Gates and Curt had joked about poisoned umbrella tips, but here was the real-life equivalent. One theory was that a meal in a sushi restaurant had contained the poison, the Russian mafia to blame. Litvinenko was in hospital under armed guard. Rebus had decided against calling Siobhan; it was just a coincidence after all. He'd been agitated, waking each morning to dread. His last weekend as a serving officer; his last week now beginning. Siobhan had done all right on Friday night, and had even looked a little bit sheepish when explaining that Macrae wanted her spearheading the case.

"Makes sense to me" was all Rebus had said, getting in the drinks. He thought he knew the way Macrae would be thinking. *Less to this than meets the eye. . . .* That was the way Siobhan said he had put it. But it would keep Rebus occupied until retirement day, after which Siobhan would be persuaded to return to route one: a mugging gone wrong.

"Makes sense to me," he repeated now, heading down a rat run. Ten minutes later, he was parking at Gayfield Square. No sign of Siobhan's car. He went upstairs and found Hawes and Tibbet seated together at the same desk, staring at the mute telephone.

"No joy?" Rebus guessed.

"Eleven calls so far," Hawes said, tapping the notepad in front of her. "One driver who exited the car park at nine fifteen on the night in question and therefore had nothing at all to tell us but wanted to chat anyway." She glanced up at Rebus. "He enjoys hill walking and jogging, if you're interested." Without bothering to look, she could sense Tibbet grinning beside her, and gave him an elbow in the ribs.

"He was on the phone to Phyl for half an hour," Tibbet added after stifling a grunt.

"Who else have we got?" Rebus asked.

"Anonymous cranks and practical jokers," Hawes replied. "And one guy we're hoping will call back. He started talking about a woman hanging around on the street, but the line went dead before I could get any details."

"Probably just saw Nancy Sievewright," Rebus cautioned. But he was thinking: why would Nancy be "hanging around"? "I've got a job for the pair of you," he said, reaching for Hawes's notepad and finding a clean sheet. He jotted down the details of Nancy's "friend" Gill Morgan. "Go see if this checks out. Sievewright reckons she was on her way home from Great Stuart Street. Even if there's someone by that name living at the address, give them a bit of a grilling."

Hawes stared at the page. "You think she's lying?"

"Seemed to have trouble remembering. But she'll probably have primed this pal of hers."

"I can usually tell when someone's spinning me a line," Tibbet stated.

"That's because you're a good cop, Colin," Rebus told him. Tibbet puffed out his chest a little, which Hawes noticed with a laugh.

"You've just been spun a line," she pointed out to her partner. Then, rising to her feet: "Let's go." Tibbet followed her sheepishly, pausing in the doorway.

"You okay manning the phones?" he asked Rebus.

"It rings, and I pick it up . . . does that about cover it?"

Tibbet was trying not to scowl as Hawes returned to fetch him. "By the way," she said to Rebus, "if you get bored you can watch the telly — we got hold of that video Siobhan wanted."

Rebus noticed it lying on the desk. It was marked with the words *Question Time*.

"You might learn something" was the parting shot from the doorway, made by Tibbet rather than Hawes. Rebus was quietly impressed.

"We'll make a man of you yet, Colin," he muttered under his breath, reaching out to pick up the tape.

12

Charles Riordan wasn't at the studio. The receptionist told them he was spending the morning at home and, when asked, provided them with an address in Joppa. It was a fifteen-minute drive away and took them past the flat gray waters of the Firth of Forth. At one point, Goodyear tapped the side window.

"Cat and dog home back there," he said. "I went once, thinking I'd get a pet. In the end, I couldn't choose . . . told myself I'd go back some day."

"I've never had a pet," Clarke said. "Find it hard enough taking care of myself."

He laughed at that. "Any boyfriends?"

"One or two down the years."

He laughed again. "I meant just now."

She took her eyes off the road long enough to give him a look. "You're trying too hard, Todd."

"Just nervous."

"That why you're asking so many questions?"

"No, not at all. I'm just . . . well, I suppose I'm interested."

"In me?"

"In everybody." He paused. "I think we're put here for a purpose. Never find out what it is if you don't ask questions."

"And your 'purpose' is to pry into my love life?"

He gave a little cough, face reddening. "I didn't mean it like that."

"Back in the café, you talked about God's purpose — is this where you tell me you're religious?"

"Well, as a matter of fact, I am. Is there anything wrong with that?"

"Nothing at all. DI Rebus used to be, too, and I've managed to cope with him all these years."

"Used to be?"

"In that he went to church . . ." She thought for a moment. "Actually, he went to dozens of them, a different one every week."

"Looking for something he couldn't find," Goodyear guessed.

"He'd probably kill me for telling you," Clarke warned.

"But you're not religious yourself, DS Clarke?"

"Lord, no," she said with a smile. "Hard to be, in this line of work."

"You reckon?"

"All the stuff we deal with . . . people gone bad, hurting themselves and others." She gave him another glance. "Isn't God supposed to have made us in his or her image?"

"An argument that might take us the rest of the day."

"Instead of which, I'll ask if you've got a girlfriend."

He nodded. "Her name's Sonia, works as a SOCO."

"And what did the two of you get up to at the weekend — apart from church, obviously?"

"She had a hen party Saturday. I didn't see much of her. Sonia's not a churchgoer . . ."

"And how's your brother doing?"

"Okay, I think."

"You mean you don't know?"

"He's out of hospital."

"I thought you said it was a punch-up?"

"There was a knife . . ."

"His or the other guy's?"

"The other guy's, hence Sol's stitches."

Clarke was thoughtful for a moment. "You said your mum and dad fell apart when your granddad went to jail . . ."

Goodyear leaned back into his seat. "Mum started on medication. Dad walked out soon after and hit the bottle harder than ever. There were days I'd bump into him outside the shops and he wouldn't even recognize me."

"Tough on a young kid."

"Sol and me mostly stayed with our aunt Susan, Mum's sister. House wasn't really big enough, but she never complained. I started going with her to church on Sundays. Sometimes she was so tired, she nodded off in the pew. Used to have a bag of sweets with her, and this one time they slid from her lap and started rolling across the floor." He smiled at the memory. "Anyway, that's about all there is to it."

"Just as well—we're nearly there." They were heading down Portobello High Street and—a first for Clarke—without being held up by roadworks. Two more minutes, and they were turning off Joppa Road and cruising a street of terraced Victorian houses.

"Number eighteen," Goodyear said, spotting it first. Plenty of curbside parking—Clarke reckoned most people had taken their cars to work. She pulled on the hand brake and turned off the ignition. Goodyear was already striding down the path.

"All I need," she muttered to herself, undoing her seat

belt, "is a bloody holy-roller . . ." Not that she meant it: as soon as the words were out of her mouth, she knew where she'd got them — or at least their sentiment.

John Rebus.

She'd only just reached Goodyear as the door opened, Charles Riordan looking surprised to be face-to-face with a police uniform. He recognized Clarke, however, and ushered the two officers inside.

The hallway was lined with bookshelves but no books. Instead, all the available space was taken up with old-fashioned reels of tape and boxes of cassettes.

"Come in if you can get in" was Riordan's comment. He led them into what should have been the living room but had been fitted out as a studio, complete with acoustic baffling stapled to the walls and a mixing desk surrounded by more cartons of cassettes, minidiscs, and reel-to-reels. Cables snaked underfoot, microphones lay in the dust, and the curtains covering the only window looked half an inch thick.

"Riordan Mansions," Charles Riordan announced.

"Can I take it you're not married?" Clarke asked.

"Was once, but she couldn't hack it."

"The equipment, you mean?"

But Riordan shook his head. "I like to make recordings." He paused meaningfully. "Of everything. After a while, it started to get to Audrey." He slipped his hands into his pockets. "So what can I do for you today, officers?"

Clarke was looking around the room. "Are we being taped, Mr. Riordan?"

Riordan gave a chuckle and, by way of answer, pointed to a slender black microphone.

"And the other day at your studio?"

He nodded. "I used DAT. Though these days I'm more into digital."

"I thought DAT *was* digital?" Goodyear asked.

"But it's tape — I'm talking about straight to the hard drive."

"Would you mind turning it off?" Clarke asked, making it sound like the demand it really was. Riordan shrugged and hit a switch on the mixing desk.

"More questions about Alexander?" he asked.

"One or two, yes."

"You got the CD?"

Clarke nodded. "Thanks for that."

"He was a great performer, wasn't he?"

"He was," Clarke acknowledged. "But what I really wanted to ask you about was the night he died."

"Yes?"

"After the curry, you said you parted company. You were heading home, and Mr. Todorov was going to find a drink?"

"That's right."

"And you added that it was a toss-up whether he went to Mather's or the Caledonian Hotel — why those two in particular, Mr. Riordan?"

Riordan gave a shrug. "He was going to have to walk past both of them."

"And a dozen more besides," Clarke countered.

"Maybe he'd mentioned them to me."

"You don't remember?"

"Is it important?"

"It could be." Clarke glanced towards Goodyear. He was playing the game: shoulders back, legs slightly parted, hands clasped in front of him . . . and saying nothing. He looked *official*. Clarke doubted Riordan would pay any attention to the prominent ears or the crooked teeth or the eyelashes . . . all he'd be seeing was a uniform, focusing his mind on the gravity of the situation.

Riordan had been rubbing his chin thoughtfully. "Well, I suppose he *must* have mentioned them," he said.

"But not on the night you met?" Clarke watched Riordan shake his head. "So he didn't have a rendezvous planned?"

"How do you mean?"

"After you split up, Mr. Todorov headed straight for the bar at the Caledonian. He got talking to someone there. Just wondered if it was a regular thing."

"Alexander liked people: people who'd buy him drinks and listen to his stories and then tell him a few of their own."

"Never thought of the Caledonian as a place for story-telling."

"You're wrong—hotel bars are perfect. You meet strangers there, and you spill your life out for the twenty or thirty minutes that you're with them. It's quite incredible what people will tell complete strangers."

"Maybe because they *are* strangers," Goodyear interrupted.

"The constable has a good point," Riordan said.

"But how do *you* know this, Mr. Riordan?" Clarke asked. "Can I assume you've done some covert taping in places like the Caledonian?"

"Plenty of times," Riordan admitted. "And on trains and buses—people snoring or talking to themselves or plotting the overthrow of the government. Tramps on park benches and MPs at the hustings; ice-skaters and picnickers and love rats on the phone to their mistresses." He turned to Goodyear. "My little hobby," he explained.

"And when did it turn to an obsession, sir?" Goodyear asked politely. "Some time before your wife left you, I'd imagine."

The smile fell from Riordan's face. Realizing he'd slipped up, Goodyear risked a glance towards Clarke. She was shaking her head slowly.

"Are there any other questions?" Riordan asked coldly.

"You can't think of anyone Alexander Todorov could have been drinking with at the hotel?" Clarke persisted.

"No." Riordan was moving towards the door. Goodyear mouthed the word "sorry" at Clarke as the pair of them followed their host into the hallway.

Back in the car, Clarke told Goodyear not to worry. "I think we'd had about all we were going to get."

"All the same, I should have left the talking to you."

"A lesson learned," Clarke said, turning the ignition.

13

W hat's Sonny Jim doing here?" Rebus asked. He was leaning back in his chair, feet up on the desk, the remote for the video recorder in his hand, having just frozen the TV picture.

"He's on secondment from Torphichen," Clarke stated. Rebus stared at her, but she refused to make eye contact. Todd Goodyear had his hand stretched out for shaking. Rebus turned his attention to it, but ignored the offer. Goodyear let his arm fall back to his side, and Clarke gave a vexed sigh.

"Anything good on the box?" she eventually asked.

"That video you wanted." Rebus seemed already to have dismissed the new arrival from his mind. "Come and take a look." He let the program run again but turned the sound most of the way down. A panel of politicians and pundits was being asked questions by a savvy-looking audience. Large letters on the floor between the two groups spelled out the word EDINBURGH.

"Filmed at The Hub," Rebus explained. "I went to a jazz concert there, recognized it straight off."

"You like jazz?" Goodyear asked, only to be ignored.

"Do you see who I see?" Rebus was asking Clarke.

"Megan Macfarlane."

"Funny she didn't mention it," Rebus mused. "When

the presenter was doing the introductions, he said she's number two in the SNP and likely to take over when her leader jacks it in. Making her, in the presenter's words, 'candidate for president of an independent Scottish state.'"

"And the rest of the panel?"

"Labour, Tories, and Lib Dems."

"Plus Todorov." The poet was seated next to the presenter at the semicircular desk. He seemed relaxed, doodling with his pen on some paper. "How's he doing?"

"Knows more about politics than I do," Rebus admitted, "and seems to have an opinion on everything."

Goodyear had folded his arms and was concentrating on the screen. Rebus gave Clarke another look, this time achieving eye contact. She shrugged, then narrowed her eyes slightly, warning him off. Rebus turned towards Goodyear.

"You know I helped put your granddad away?"

"Ancient history," the young man said.

"Maybe so, but if it's going to be an issue, best tell me now."

"It's not an issue." Goodyear was still staring at the screen. "What's the deal with this woman Macfarlane?"

"She's a Scot Nat MSP," Clarke explained. "Has a vested interest in us not shaking things up."

"Because of all the Russian tycoons in town?" Goodyear saw that Clarke was impressed. "I read the papers," he explained. "So Macfarlane had a little chat, but neglected to say that she knew the victim?"

"That's the size of it." Rebus was showing more interest in the new recruit.

"Well, she's a politician. Last thing she wants is bad

PR—and being linked to a murder inquiry probably counts as a negative." Goodyear offered a shrug, analysis complete.

The TV show was coming to an end, the dapper presenter announcing that the following week's episode would be coming from Hull. Rebus turned off the tape and stretched his spine.

"Anyway," he asked, "where've you two been?"

"Riordan," Clarke stated, starting to fill him in on the meeting. Halfway through, Hawes and Tibbet returned and had to be introduced to Todd Goodyear. Hawes had brought cakes for the office, and apologized to Goodyear that there wasn't one left over.

"I don't have a sweet tooth," he replied with a shake of the head. Tibbet had spent a few months in uniform at Torphichen, just before his promotion to CID, and asked about old colleagues. Rebus got stuck into his slice of caramel shortbread while Clarke boiled the kettle. She checked, but there was no sign of Macrae.

"Meeting at HQ," Rebus explained as she placed a mug on his desk. Then, in an undertone: "Have you cleared the Sundance Kid with him?"

"Not yet." She glanced over to where Goodyear was chatting easily with Tibbet and Hawes, and even managing to make them both laugh.

"Bringing a uniform in on a murder case?" He kept his voice low. "Sure you know what you're doing?"

"DCI Macrae put me in charge."

"Meaning you're responsible for any and all fuckups."

"Thanks for reminding me."

"How much do you know about him?"

"I know he's young and he's keen, and he's spent too long hanging around with a dead weight."

"I hope you're not drawing parallels, DS Clarke." Rebus slurped from the mug.

"Perish the thought, DI Rebus." She looked towards Goodyear again. "I'm just giving him a taster, that's all — couple of days and he'll be back to West End. Besides, Macrae wanted a few more recruits to the cause . . ."

Rebus nodded slowly, slid from his chair, and wandered over, his hand landing on Goodyear's shoulder.

"It was you who took the statement from Nancy Sievewright?" he checked. Goodyear nodded. "When she said she'd just been passing by, did you get any sort of an inkling?"

The young man thought for a moment, holding his bottom lip between his teeth. "Not really," he said at last.

"You either did or you didn't."

"In which case, I didn't."

Rebus nodded, turning to Hawes and Tibbet. "What did you get in Great Stuart Street?"

"Gill Morgan does live there, and she knows Nancy Sievewright."

Rebus stared at Hawes. "But?"

Tibbet didn't want to be left out. "But," he said, "we got the feeling she was parroting something she'd been told to say."

Rebus turned back to Goodyear. "And DC Tibbet can tell when someone's spinning him a line. . . . What does that tell you?"

Goodyear gave his lip another gnaw. "She's asked a

friend to cover for her, because she was lying to us that night."

"Lying to *you*," Rebus corrected him, "and you didn't even know it." Having made his point, he seemed to dismiss the constable again, turning to Hawes and Tibbet. "What's Morgan like?"

Hawes: "Lives in a nice flat . . . doesn't seem to be sharing with anyone."

"Just her name on the door," Tibbet added.

"Works as a model, so she says. But no jobs today. If you're asking me, though, she's got credit at the Bank of Mum and Dad."

"Different league from Sievewright," Rebus commented, waiting for Clarke to nod agreement. "So how do they know one another?"

Hawes and Tibbet seemed at a loss. Rebus made a tutting sound, a teacher whose star pupils had eventually slipped up.

"I think they just know each other socially," Tibbet blurted out.

Rebus glared at him. "Attend the same regattas, you mean?"

Hawes felt compelled to come to her partner's defense. "She wasn't *that* posh."

"Just making a point, Phyl," Rebus told her.

"Maybe we should bring her in," Clarke suggested.

"Your call, Shiv," Rebus reminded her. "You're the one Macrae's put in charge."

This was news to Hawes and Tibbet. Goodyear meantime was studying Rebus as though wondering how a sergeant could suddenly outrank an inspector. The ringing phone broke the silence. Rebus, being closest, picked it up.

"Todorov inquiry, DI Rebus speaking."

"Oh . . . hello." The voice was male and tremulous. "I called earlier . . ."

Rebus caught Hawes's eye. "About a woman, sir? We appreciate you taking the trouble to phone back."

"Yes, well . . ."

"So what is it I can do for you, Mr. . . . ?"

"Do I have to give my name?"

"This can be as confidential as you like, sir, but a name would be nice."

"By 'confidential' you mean . . . ?"

I mean spit it out! Rebus wanted to yell into the receiver. But instead he kept his voice level and pleasant, thinking of something he'd once been told: sincerity is everything—when you can fake that, the sky's the limit.

"Well, all right, then," the caller was saying, "my name's—" He broke off again. "I mean, you can call me George."

"Thank you, George."

"George Gaverill."

"George Gaverill," Rebus repeated, watching Hawes add the name to her notepad. "Now what is it you'd like to say, George? My colleague mentioned something about a woman . . ."

"Yes."

"And you're calling because you saw our flyers at the car park?"

"On the sandwich board outside the car park," the man corrected Rebus. "I'm sure it's nothing. I mean, I saw it on the news . . . the poor guy was mugged, wasn't he? I don't think she could have done it."

"You're probably right, sir. All the same, we try to

gather up as much information as we can, helps us build a picture." Rebus was rolling his eyes. Clarke made a circular motion with her finger: *keep him talking.*

"I wouldn't want my wife to think it was anything other than what it actually was," Gaverill was saying.

"Absolutely. So this woman, sir . . . ?"

"The night that man was murdered—" The voice broke off abruptly, and Rebus thought he'd lost him. But then he heard breathing on the line. "I was walking along King's Stables Road . . ."

"What time was this?"

"Ten . . . maybe ten fifteen."

"And there was a woman?"

"Yes."

"I'm with you so far, sir." Rebus rolled his eyes again.

"She propositioned me."

It was Rebus's turn to pause. "By which you mean . . . ?"

"Just what I say: she wanted to have sex, though she put it rather more crudely."

"And this was on King's Stables Road?"

"Yes."

"Near the car park?"

"Outside the car park, yes."

"A prostitute?"

"I suppose so. I mean, it's not every day something like that happens—not to me, at any rate."

"And what did you say to her, sir?"

"I turned her down, naturally."

"And this was around ten or quarter past?"

"Something like that, yes."

Rebus shrugged, letting the others know he wasn't

sure what he was getting. He really wanted a description, but it would be easier face to face. Moreover, Gaverill's eyes would tell Rebus whether he was dealing with just another crank.

"Is there any way," he began quietly, "I could persuade you to come to the station? I can't stress how vital your information might be."

"Really?" Gaverill perked up for a moment, but only a moment. "My wife, though . . . I couldn't possibly . . ."

"You could make some excuse, I'm sure."

"Why do you say that?" the man barked suddenly.

"I just thought . . ." But the line had gone dead. Rebus cursed under his breath and dropped the phone back onto the desk. "In the movies, someone would have traced the call."

"I've never heard of a sex worker operating from that street or anywhere near," Clarke commented skeptically.

"Sounded genuine enough," Rebus felt bound to counter.

"Reckon Gaverill's his real name?"

"I'd put money on it."

"Then we look him up in the phone book." Clarke turned to Hawes and Tibbet. "Get on to it."

They got on to it, while Rebus tapped the phone, willing it to ring again. When it did, he snatched the receiver up.

"I shouldn't have done that," Gaverill was saying. "It was rude of me."

"Don't blame you for being a little cautious, sir," Rebus assured him. "We were just hoping you'd phone again. This is one of those cases where we're desperate for a break of some kind."

"But she wasn't a mugger or anything."

"Doesn't mean she didn't see something. We reckon the victim was attacked just before eleven. If she was in the area . . ."

"Yes, I see what you mean."

Hawes and Tibbet had done the deed. A piece of paper was waved under Rebus's nose: phone number and address for George Gaverill.

"Tell you what," Rebus said into the phone, "this call must be costing you money. Let me ring you back — are you on the 229 number?"

"Yes, but I don't want . . ." The rest of the sentence died with a gurgle in Gaverill's throat.

"Now then," Rebus said, a little more steel in his voice, "we either come round to question you at your home, Mr. Gaverill, or you come and see us here at Gayfield Square — which is it to be?"

Sounding like a chastened child, Gaverill told Rebus to give him half an hour.

But before Gaverill arrived, there were three other visitors. Roger and Elizabeth Anderson were first. And after Hawes and Tibbet had taken them to an interview room, Nancy Sievewright turned up. Rebus asked the front desk to put her in one of the spare rooms — "but not IR3" — and give her a cup of tea.

"Don't want her seeing Anderson," he explained to Clarke.

She nodded. "We need to talk to Anderson anyway, see what he says to Nancy's story."

"Already done," Rebus admitted. Her gaze hardened, but all he did was shrug. "Happened to be out that way this morning, thought I might as well ask him about it."

"What did he say?"

"He was worried about her. Got her name and address from . . ." Rebus turned towards Todd Goodyear. "Wasn't you, was it?"

"Must've been Dyson," Goodyear said.

"That's what I thought. Anyway, I've warned him off." He seemed to think for a moment, then asked Clarke if she wanted to take Goodyear with her and get Sievewright's formal statement. "Part of Todd's learning curve," he argued.

"You're forgetting one thing, John—*I'm* in charge."

"Only trying to be helpful." Rebus had stretched his arms, all innocence.

"Thanks, but I'd rather hear what Gaverill's got to say."

"I get the feeling he'll be easily intimidated. He trusts me now, but when he comes up against three of us . . ." He started to shake his head. "Don't want him clamming up again."

"Let's wait and see" was all Clarke said. Rebus gave another shrug and wandered over to the window.

"Meantime," he said, "want to hear my theory?"

"Your theory of what?"

"Why he's so sweaty about his wife finding out."

"Because," Goodyear piped up, "she'll think he accepted the offer."

But Rebus was shaking his head. "Quite the reverse, young Todd. Would DS Clarke like to hazard a guess?"

"Slay us with an insight," she said instead, folding her arms.

"What else is there on King's Stables Road?" Rebus asked.

"Castle Rock," Goodyear offered.

"And?"

"A churchyard," Clarke added.

"Exactly," Rebus said. "And on the corner of that churchyard you'll find an old lookout tower. It was used a couple of centuries back to keep watch for body snatchers — and to my mind they should put it back into use. Dodgy place at night, that churchyard . . ." He let his words hang in the air.

"Gaverill's gay," Clarke speculated, "and his wife doesn't know it?"

Rebus shrugged but seemed pleased that she'd reached the same conclusion as him.

"So he was hardly going to take up the woman's offer," Goodyear continued, nodding to himself.

At which point the phone buzzed. It was the front desk, letting them know George Gaverill was waiting for them.

They'd already decided that he should be brought to the CID suite — just that little bit more welcoming than an interview room. But first Rebus shook him warmly by the hand and led him along the corridor to IR2, where he asked him to put his eye to the peephole.

"See the young woman?" Rebus asked quietly.

"Yes," Gaverill whispered back.

"She the one?"

Gaverill turned towards him. "No," he stated. Rebus stared at the man. Gaverill was about five and a half feet tall, thin-boned and pale-faced with mousy brown hair and some sort of rash on his face. He was probably in his early forties, and Rebus got the feeling the rash could have been with him since his teens.

"Sure?" Rebus asked.

"Fairly sure. This woman was a bit taller, I'd say. Not as young and not as skinny."

Rebus nodded and led him back the way they'd come, before climbing the stairs to CID. He shook his head when Clarke made eye contact — no identification. She gave a twitch of the mouth and held up the latest *Evening News*. There was a photo of the man called Litvinenko; he was attached to wires in his hospital bed and the poison had made him lose his hair.

"Coincidence" was all Rebus said as Clarke introduced herself to Gaverill.

"Can't thank you enough for coming, sir."

Goodyear meantime was busy on the phone, taking notes from someone who'd called the hotline and looking less than thrilled. Clarke had gestured for Gaverill to sit down.

"Can we get you anything?" she asked.

"I just want this over and done with."

"Well then," Rebus intervened, "we'll get straight to business. Maybe you can tell us in your own words exactly what happened?"

"Like I told you, Inspector, I was on King's Stables Road, around quarter past ten, and there was this woman loitering there, close to the car park exit. I reckoned she was waiting for someone, but when I was making to pass her, she spoke to me."

"And what did she say?"

"She asked if I wanted . . ." Gaverill swallowed hard, his Adam's apple bouncing.

"A fuck?" Rebus offered.

"Exact words," Gaverill agreed.

"Was any sort of a price mentioned?"

"She told me it was . . . I think she said 'no strings,'

something like that. No strings, no comebacks. Said she just wanted a . . ." But he still couldn't bring himself to say it.

"And this was going to happen right where you stood?" Rebus sounded disbelieving.

"Maybe in the car park . . ."

"Did she say as much?"

"I don't really remember. I'd started walking away. To be honest with you, I was a bit shocked."

"I can imagine," Clarke sympathized. "What a hellish thing to happen. So can you tell us what she looked like?"

"Well, she was . . . I'm not sure exactly. About the same height as me . . . a bit older than the lass downstairs, though I'm not very good at ages — women's ages, I mean."

"Lots of makeup?"

"Some makeup . . . and perfume, but I couldn't tell you what kind."

"Would you say she looked like a prostitute, Mr. Gaverill?" Rebus asked.

"Not the kind you see on TV, no. She wasn't dressed provocatively. She had a coat on with a hood. It was cold that night, don't forget."

"A coat with a hood?"

"Like a duffel coat maybe . . . or a bit longer than a duffel . . . I'm not terribly sure." He gave a nervous little laugh. "I wish I could be more help."

"You're doing fine," Rebus assured him.

"Better than fine," Clarke added.

"To be honest with you," Gaverill went on, "when I played it back in my mind, I decided she was probably a wee bit bonkers. I remember one time, there was a woman on the steps of a church by Bruntsfield Links, and she was lying there with her legs in the air, skirt hiked up, and it turned out she'd escaped from the Royal Ed . . ." He seemed to think some explanation was needed. "That's where they keep the—"

"Psychiatric patients," Clarke interrupted him with a nod.

"Well, I was only a bairn when that happened, but I still remember it."

"Not the sort of thing you'd forget," Rebus agreed. "Surprised it didn't put you off women for life." He gave a laugh so Gaverill would take it as a joke, but Clarke's eyes warned him to go easy.

"Irene's a special woman, Inspector," Gaverill stated.

"I'm sure she is, sir. Been married a while?"

"Nineteen years—she was the first real girlfriend I ever had."

"First and last, eh?" Rebus offered.

"Mr. Gaverill," Clarke interrupted, "would you be willing to do us one further favor? I'd like an identification officer to work with you on a composite of the woman's face. Do you think that might be possible?"

"Right now?" Gaverill checked his watch.

"Soon as possible, while the memory's still fresh. We could have someone here in ten or fifteen minutes . . ." Meaning half an hour.

"Meant to ask, Mr. Gaverill," Rebus butted in, "what's your line of work?"

"Auctions," Gaverill told him. "I pick stuff up and sell it on."

"Flexible hours," Rebus argued. "You can always explain to Irene that you were with a punter."

Clarke gave a little cough, but Gaverill hadn't read anything into Rebus's words. "Ten minutes?" he asked.

"Ten or fifteen," Clarke assured him.

Lunchtime sandwiches: they'd given their orders to Goodyear, Rebus stressing that it was all part and parcel of the training. Roger and Elizabeth Anderson had gone home; so had Nancy Sievewright. Hawes and Tibbet had gleaned nothing new from either interview. Rebus was studying the computer image of a woman's face. Gaverill had insisted that most of it be left in shadow, the hood pulled low over the forehead.

"Nobody we know," Clarke said, not for the first time. Gaverill had just left, and not in the best of moods — it had taken almost an hour for the ID expert, with the help of his laptop, printer, and software, to put together the e-fit.

"Could be anybody," Rebus said in response to Clarke's statement. "Still . . . let's say she was there, whoever she is."

"You buy Gaverill's story?"

"You mean you don't?"

"He seemed genuine to me," Goodyear piped up, before quickly adding, "for what it's worth."

Rebus gave a snort and dumped the remains of his filled roll into the bin, brushing his shirt free of crumbs.

"So now," Hawes added, "we've got a woman trying to lure men into the car park to have quick, meaningless sex with her?" She paused. "I can see where Siobhan has a problem."

"Tends not to happen too often," Clarke agreed, "unless the boys know different?"

Rebus looked to Tibbet and Tibbet looked to Goodyear; none of them said anything.

"A hooker, then," Tibbet decided to offer.

"Sex worker," Rebus corrected him.

"But the Andersons and Nancy Sievewright walked right past the car park and didn't see a woman in a hood."

"Doesn't mean she wasn't there, Colin," Rebus pointed out.

"There's a term for it, isn't there?" Goodyear asked. "When a woman sets a man up . . ."

"Honey trap," Rebus told him. "So are we back to the mugging theory again? It's not an MO I've come across—not in Edinburgh. And here's another thing—Forensics say Todorov had had sex that day."

The room was quiet for a moment as they tried to untangle the various threads. Clarke sat with her elbows on the desk, face in her hands. Eventually she looked up.

"Is there anything at all stopping me from coming to the obvious conclusion, and taking that conclusion to DCI Macrae? Victim was robbed, beaten, left for dead." She nodded towards the e-fit. "And here's the only suspect we have."

"So far," Rebus cautioned. "But Macrae said we've got a few days to keep digging, so why not use them?"

"And dig where exactly?"

Rebus tried to think of an answer but gave up. He gestured for Clarke to follow him into the corridor, Hawes and Tibbet looking hurt by the snub. Rebus paused at the top of the stairs. Clarke was approaching, arms folded.

"Are you sure," Rebus asked her, "that Phyl and Col are okay with Goodyear suddenly appearing on the team?"

"How do you mean?"

"I mean he's not one of us."

She stared at him. "I don't think they're the ones with the problem." She paused before continuing. "Do you remember your first day in CID?"

"Vaguely."

"I remember mine like it was yesterday. The way everybody kept saying I was 'fresh meat,' I thought they were vampires." She unfolded her arms, rested her hands on her hips. "Todd wants that taste of CID, John."

"Sounds like he's got his teeth into you, at any rate."

Her smile became a scowl, but the thought of vampires had given Rebus a notion. "Might be a long shot," he said, "but the guard at the car park said something about one of the bosses, the only one that ever went near the place. He called her the Reaper. Want to know why?"

"Okay then, why?" Clarke was determined not to be placated.

"On account," Rebus told her, "of the hood she always wears."

14

Gary Walsh was in the car park's security shack, having relieved Joe Wills about an hour before. With the jacket of his uniform undone and his shirt tieless, he looked fairly relaxed.

"Money for old rope, this," Rebus teased him as he knocked on the half-open door. Walsh slid his feet from the tabletop and pulled out his earphones, turning off the CD player. "What're you listening to?"

"Primal Scream."

"And what would you have done if I'd been one of the bosses?"

"Reaper's the only one we ever see."

"So you said. . . . Anyone told her about the murder?"

"She got it from a reporter."

"And?" Rebus was studying a newspaper next to the radio: that afternoon's *Evening News* with the crossword already done.

Walsh just shrugged. "Wanted to see the blood."

"She sounds lovely."

"She's all right."

"Got a name for her?"

Walsh was studying him. "You nicked anybody yet?"

"Not yet."

"What do you want to talk to Cath for?"

"That's her name — Cath?"

"Cath Mills."

"Does she look anything like this?"

Walsh took the picture of the hooded woman from Rebus and stared at it unblinkingly, then shook his head.

"Sure?" Rebus said.

"Nothing like her." Walsh handed the picture back. "Who's it supposed to be?"

"Witness saw a woman hanging around outside on the night Todorov was murdered. It's a question of ruling people out."

"Well, you can rule the Reaper out straightaway — Cath wasn't here that night."

"All the same, I'll take her phone number."

Walsh pointed to a corkboard behind the door. "It's up there."

Rebus started jotting down the mobile number. "How often does she drop by?"

"Maybe a couple of times a week — once on Joe's shift, once on mine."

"Ever had trouble with the local prossies?"

"Didn't know there *were* any."

Rebus was closing his notebook when the buzzer sounded. Walsh was looking at one of the monitors: a driver was out of his car and standing at the exit barrier.

"Is there a problem?" Walsh asked into the microphone.

"Bloody thing's just chewed up my ticket."

Walsh rolled his eyes for Rebus's benefit. "Been doing that a lot," he told him. He pushed a button and the barrier started to rise, the driver getting back behind his steering wheel without so much as a "thanks" or "good-bye."

"Going to have to close that exit," Walsh muttered, "till they come and fix it."

"Never a dull moment, eh?"

Walsh gave a snort. "This woman," he said, rising to his feet, "reckon she had anything to do with it?"

"Why do you ask?"

Walsh was buttoning his uniform. "You don't get many women muggers, do you?"

"Not many," Rebus conceded.

"And it *was* a mugging? I mean, papers say the guy's pockets were emptied."

"Looks that way." Rebus paused for a moment. "You lock up at eleven, right?"

"Right."

"That's pretty much when the body was found."

"Oh aye?"

"But you didn't see anything?"

"Nothing."

"You'd have driven right past Raeburn Wynd."

Walsh just shrugged. "I didn't see anything and I didn't hear anything. I certainly didn't see a woman in a cloak. Probably have scared the life out of me, with that graveyard across the road . . ." He broke off, brow furrowing.

"What is it?" Rebus asked.

"Probably nothing — just thinking about those ghost tours they do . . . dressing up in costumes, putting a fright on the tourists . . ."

"I don't think our mystery woman was in that sort of game." But Rebus knew what he meant. You saw them at night, wandering up and down the Royal Mile: guides dressed as vampires or God-knew-what. "Besides, I've never heard of them doing walking tours down here."

"Cemetery's not safe enough," Walsh agreed, ready to leave the kiosk. He'd picked up a glossy plastic sign with the words Out of Order on it. Rebus preceded him out.

"Ever get any hassle from that quarter?" Rebus asked.

"Couple of junkies wanting a handout. . . . If you ask me, they beat that poor bugger up in the stairwell last year."

"Your colleague told me about that — never solved?"

Walsh gave a snort, which was all the answer Rebus needed. "Any idea which station did the investigating?"

"It was before I started here." Walsh's eyes narrowed. "Is it because this guy's foreign, or because he's a bigwig?"

"Not sure I get you." They were heading down the ramp towards the exit level.

"Is that why you're spending so much time on it?"

"It's because he was murdered, Mr. Walsh," Rebus stated, getting out his mobile.

Megan Macfarlane had been to some meeting in Leith. Roddy Liddle said she could probably manage ten minutes at the Starbucks just uphill from the Parliament, so that was where Clarke and Todd Goodyear were waiting. Goodyear was drinking tea, while Clarke's own Americano had come with the requested extra shot of espresso. She'd also splashed out on two slices of carrot cake, though Goodyear had tried paying.

"My treat," she'd insisted. Then had asked at the till for a receipt, just in case she could finesse it as an expense. They sat at a table near the window, with a view of the darkening Canongate. "Daft place to put a parliament," she commented.

"Out of sight, out of mind," Goodyear offered.

She smiled at that, and asked him what he thought of CID so far. He considered for a moment before answering.

"I like that you've kept me on."

"So far," she warned.

"And you seem to click as a team — I like that, too. The case itself . . ." His voice drifted off.

"Spit it out."

"I think maybe all of you — and this isn't a criticism — are a little bit in thrall to DI Rebus."

"Can you be a 'little bit' in thrall?"

"You know what I mean, though . . . he's old, experienced, seen a lot of action down the years. So when he has hunches, you tend to follow them."

"It's just the way some cases go, Todd — you drop a pebble in water, and the ripples start to spread."

"But it's not like that at all, is it?" He pulled his chair closer to the table, warming to his argument. "It's actually linear. The crime is committed by a person, and the job of CID is to find them. Most of the time, that's pretty straightforward — they feel guilty and hand themselves in, or someone witnesses the crime, or they're already known to us and their prints or DNA give them away." He paused. "I get the feeling DI Rebus hates those sorts of cases, the ones where the motive's too easy to spot."

"You barely *know* DI Rebus." Clarke prickled.

Goodyear seemed to sense he'd gone too far. "All I mean is, he likes things to be complex, gives him more of a challenge."

"Less to this than meets the eye — that's what you're saying?"

"I'm saying we should keep an open mind."

"Thanks for the advice." Clarke's voice was as chilled as the carrot cake. Goodyear stared into his mug and looked relieved when the door opened and Megan Macfarlane approached the table. She was toting about three kilos of ring binder, which she let clatter to the floor. Roddy Liddle had gone to the counter to order their drinks.

"The hoops we have to go through," Macfarlane complained. She gave Todd Goodyear a questioning smile and Clarke made the introductions.

"I'm a great fan," Goodyear told the MSP. "I admired the stand you took on the tram system."

"You wouldn't happen to have a few thousand friends who think the same way?" Macfarlane had collapsed into her chair, eyes staring ceilingwards.

"And I've always supported independence," Goodyear went on. She angled her head towards him before turning to Clarke.

"I like this one better," she commented.

"Speaking of DI Rebus," Clarke said, "he's sorry he can't make it along this afternoon. But he was the one who happened to spot your *Question Time* appearance—we're wondering why you didn't mention it."

"Is that all?" Macfarlane sounded irritated. "I thought maybe you'd arrested someone."

"Did you just meet Mr. Todorov that one time?" Clarke persisted.

"Yes."

"So you met at the studio?"

"The Hub," Macfarlane corrected. "Yes, we were all due to rendezvous there an hour before recording."

"I thought it went out live," Goodyear interrupted.

"Not quite," the MSP insisted. "Of course, Jim

Bakewell, being a Labour *minister*, had to turn up fashionably late—floor staff didn't like that, which might explain why he got so little screen time." She perked up again at the memory, and gave Liddle a blessing as he arrived with her black coffee and a single espresso for himself. He dragged a chair over so he could be part of the company, and shook hands with Goodyear.

"Think we'll start to hear rumors, Roddy?" Macfarlane asked, pouring a first sachet of sugar into her drink. "Me being seen with a uniformed police officer?"

"Very likely," Liddle drawled, lifting the tiny cup to his mouth.

"You were saying about Mr. Todorov," Clarke prompted.

"She wants to know about *Question Time*," Macfarlane explained to her assistant. "Thinks I must be hiding something."

"Just wondering," Clarke interrupted, "why you didn't think to mention it."

"Tell me, Sergeant, have any of the other politicos who shared the stage with the victim come forward with their reminiscences?" The question didn't seem to require an answer. "No, because they'd have said much the same as me—our Russian friend necked some wine, crammed a few sandwiches into his face, and said nary a word to us. I rather got the impression he wasn't a great fan of politicians as an overall species."

"What about after the show?"

"Taxis were waiting . . . he grunted his good-byes and left, tucking a spare bottle of wine under his jacket." She paused. "How any of this aids your inquiry is a mystery to me."

"That was the only time you met him?"

"Didn't I just say so?" She looked to her assistant for confirmation. Clarke decided to look at him, too.

"What about you, Mr. Liddle?" she asked. "Did you talk to him at The Hub?"

"I introduced myself— 'surly,' I'd have called him. There's usually a nonpolitician on the show, and there's always a rigorous pre-interview. The researcher who'd talked with Todorov didn't sound too thrilled— you could tell by her notes that he hadn't been forthcoming. To this day, I don't know why they had him on."

Clarke thought for a moment. Charles Riordan had said that Todorov liked to chat to people, yet the drinker in Mather's had said he hardly uttered a word. And now Macfarlane and Liddle were saying much the same. Did Todorov have two sides to his personality? "Whose idea would it have been to book him on the show?" she asked Liddle.

"Producer, presenter, one of the crew . . . I dare say anyone can propose a guest."

"Could it have been," Goodyear interrupted, "a case of sending a message to Moscow?"

"I suppose so," Macfarlane conceded, sounding impressed.

"How do you mean?" Clarke asked Goodyear.

"There was a journalist killed there awhile back. Maybe the BBC wanted people to know you can't stifle free speech so easily."

"Someone stifled it eventually, though, didn't they?" Liddle added. "Or we wouldn't be having this conversation. And look at what happened to that poor bloody Russian in London . . ."

Macfarlane was scowling at him. "That's *exactly* the kind of rumor we want to clamp down on!"

"Of course, of course," he mumbled, busying himself with his already empty cup.

"So, just to recap," Clarke announced into the silence, "the two of you saw Mr. Todorov at the *Question Time* recording, but didn't get much of a conversation going. You hadn't met him before, and you didn't see him again afterwards—is that the way you'd like me to phrase it in my report?"

"Report?" Macfarlane fairly barked the word.

"Not for public consumption," Clarke reassured her. Then, after a moment's beat, she delivered her coup de grâce: "Until the trial, of course."

"I've already stressed, Sergeant, that we have some influential investors in town, and it might not take much to spook them."

"But you'd agree, wouldn't you," Clarke countered, "that we need to show them how scrupulous and thorough our police force is?"

Macfarlane seemed about to say something to that, but her phone was trilling. She turned away from the table as she answered.

"Stuart, how are things?"

Clarke guessed "Stuart" might be the banker, Stuart Janney.

"I hope you got them all a booking at Andrew Fairlie?" Macfarlane had got to her feet and was on the move. She headed outside, glancing through the window as she continued her conversation.

"It's the restaurant at Gleneagles," Liddle was explaining.

"I know," Clarke told him. Then, for Goodyear's benefit: "Our economic saviors are staying the night there—nice big dinner and a round of golf after breakfast." She asked Liddle who would be picking up the tab. "The hard-pressed taxpayer?" she guessed. He gave a shrug and she turned back to Goodyear. "Still reckon the meek will inherit the earth, Todd?"

"Psalm 37, verse 11," Goodyear intoned. But now Clarke's own phone was ringing. She picked it up and held it to her ear. John Rebus wanted a progress report.

"Just getting a bit of Scripture from PC Goodyear," she told him. "The meek inheriting the earth and all of that."

15

Rebus had only called because he was bored. But within a minute of Clarke answering his call, a black VW Golf was roaring to a curbside stop outside the car park. The woman who emerged had to be Cath Mills, so Rebus cut the call short.

"Miss Mills?" he said, taking a step towards her. With late-afternoon darkness had come biting gusts of wind, scudding in from the North Sea. He didn't know what he'd been expecting "the Reaper" to be wearing—a full-length cape maybe. But in fact her coat was more like a parka with fur-trimmed hood. She was in her late thirties, tall, with red hair in a pageboy cut and black-rimmed spectacles. Her face was pale and rounded, lips reddened with lipstick. She looked nothing like the picture in his pocket.

"Inspector Rebus?" she assumed, giving a short-lived shake of the hand. She wore black leather driving gloves, which she plunged into her pockets afterwards. "I hate this time of year," she muttered, checking the sky. "Dark when you get up, dark when you go home."

"You keep regular hours?" Rebus asked.

"Job like this, there's always something needs dealing with." She glowered at the Out of Order sign next to the nearest exit barrier.

"So were you out and about on Wednesday night?"

She was still looking at the barrier. "Home by nine, I seem to think. Problem at our facility in Canning Street — shift hadn't turned up. I got the attendant to pull a double, so that was that." Slowly, she turned her attention to Rebus. "You're asking about the night the man was killed."

"That's right. Pity your CCTV's worse than useless . . . might've given us something to work with."

"We didn't install it with slaughter in mind."

Rebus ignored this. "So you didn't happen to pass here around ten o'clock on the night it happened?"

"Who says I did?"

"No one, but we've a woman matching your description . . ." Okay, so he was stretching it, but he wanted to see how she would react. All she did was raise an eyebrow and fold her arms.

"And how," she asked, "did you happen to get my description in the first place?" She glanced towards the car park. "Boys been telling tales out of school? I'll have to see to it they're disciplined."

"Actually, all they said was that you sometimes wear a hood. A pedestrian happened to spot a woman hanging around, and she was wearing a hood, too . . ."

"A woman with her hood up? At ten o'clock on a winter's night? And this is your idea of narrowing the field?"

All of a sudden, Rebus wanted the day to be over. He wanted to be seated on a bar stool with a drink before him and everything else left far behind. "If you weren't here," he said with a sigh, "just say so."

She thought this over for a moment. "I'm not sure," she said at last, drawing the words out.

"What do you mean?"

"Might liven things up, being a suspect in a police case . . ."

"Thanks, but we get quite enough time wasters as it is. The worst offenders," he added, "we might even prosecute."

Her face opened into a smile. "Sorry," she apologized. "Been a long, grueling day; I probably picked the wrong person to tease." Her attention was back on the barrier. "I suppose I should talk to Gary, make sure he's reported that." She peeled back a glove to look at her wristwatch. "Just about see me through to the end of play . . ." She brought her eyes back to Rebus's. "After which I dare say I can be located in Montpelier's."

"Wine bar in Bruntsfield?" It had taken Rebus only a couple of seconds to place it.

Her smile widened. "Thought you looked the kind who'd know," she said.

In the end, he stayed for three drinks — blame the "Third Glass Free" promotion. Not that he was drinking glasses of anything: three small bottles of imported lager, keeping his wits about him. Cath Mills was a pro, her own three drinks adding up to a whole bottle of Rioja. She'd parked her car around the corner, since she lived in a flat nearby and could leave it there overnight.

"So don't think you can have me for drunk driving," she'd said with a wag of the finger.

"I'm walking, too," he'd answered, explaining that his own flat was in Marchmont.

When he'd entered the bar, assailed by loudspeaker music and office chatter, she'd been waiting in a booth at the back.

"Hoping I wouldn't find you?" he'd speculated.

"Don't want to seem too easy, do I?"

The conversation had mostly been about his job, plus the usual Edinburgh rants: the traffic, the roadworks, the council, the cold. She'd warned him that there wasn't much of a story to her own life.

"Married at eighteen, divorced by twenty; tried again at thirty-four, and it lasted all of six months. Should have known better by then, shouldn't I?"

"You can't always have been a parking supervisor, though?"

Indeed not: office job after office job, then her own little consulting business, which had plummeted to earth after two and a half years, not helped by Husband Two hoofing it with the savings.

"I was a PA after that but couldn't hack it . . . bit of time on the dole and trying to retrain, then this came along."

"My line of work," Rebus had said, "I hear people's stories all the time — they always hold back the interesting stuff."

"Then take me in for questioning," she'd replied, stretching her arms wide.

Eventually, he'd got her to say a little about Gary Walsh and Joe Wills. She, too, suspected Wills of drinking on the job, but had yet to catch him.

"Being a detective, you could find out for me."

"It's a private eye you need. Or set up a few more CCTV cameras without him knowing about it."

She'd laughed at that, before telling the waitress she was ready for her free drink.

After an hour, they were checking their watches and giving little smiles across the table to each other. "What about you?" she'd asked. "Found anyone who'll put up with you?"

"Not for a while. I was married, one daughter — in her thirties now."

"No office romances? High-pressure job, working in a team . . . I know how it is."

"Hasn't happened to me," he'd confirmed.

"Bully for you." She sniffed and gave a twitch of the mouth. "I've given up on one-night stands . . . more or less." The twitch becoming another smile.

"This has been nice," he'd said, aware of how awkward it sounded.

"You won't get into trouble for consorting with a suspect?"

"Who's going to tell?"

"Nobody needs to." And she'd pointed towards the bar's own CCTV camera, trained on them from a corner of the ceiling. They'd both laughed at that, and as she shrugged back into her parka he'd asked again: "*Were* you there that night? Be honest now . . ." And she'd shaken her head, as much of an answer as he was going to get.

Outside, he'd handed her a business card with the number of his mobile on it. No peck on the cheek or squeeze of the hand: they were two scarred veterans, each respectful of the other. On his way home, Rebus had stopped for fish and chips, eating them out of the little cardboard box. They didn't come wrapped in newspaper anymore, something to do with public health. Didn't taste the same either, and the portions of haddock had been whittled away. Blame overfishing in the North Sea. Haddock would soon be a delicacy; either that or extinct. He'd finished by the time he arrived at his tenement, pulling himself up the two flights of stairs. There was no mail waiting, not even a utility bill. He switched on the lights in the living room and selected some music, then called Siobhan.

"What's up?" she asked.

"Just wondered where we go from here."

"I was thinking of going to the fridge for a can of something."

"Time was, that would have been *my* line."

"The times are a-changing."

"And *that's* one of mine, too!"

He could hear her laughing. Then she asked how his interview with Cath Mills had gone.

"Another dead end."

"Took long enough to drive down it."

"Didn't see the point of coming back to base." He paused. "Thinking of reporting me for bad time-keeping?"

"I'll give you the benefit of the doubt. What's the music you're playing?"

"It's called *Little Criminals*. There's a track on it called 'Jolly Coppers on Parade.' "

"Not someone au fait with the police then . . ."

"It's Randy Newman. There's another title of his I like: 'You Can't Fool the Fat Man.' "

"And would the fat man be yourself, by any chance?"

"Maybe I'll keep you guessing." He let the silence linger for a moment. "You're starting to side with Macrae, aren't you? You think we should be concentrating on the mugger file?"

"I've put Phyl and Colin on it," Clarke conceded.

"You're losing your bottle?"

"I'm not losing *anything*."

"Okay, I put that badly . . . It's good to be cautious, Shiv. I'm not about to blame you for it."

"Think about it for a second, John. Was Todorov followed from the Caledonian Hotel? Not according to your CCTV wizard. Did a prostitute proposition him? Maybe, and maybe her pimp jumped in with a length of lead pipe. Whatever happened, the poet was in the wrong place at the wrong time."

"That much we agree on."

"And getting up the noses of MSPs, Russian tycoons, and First Albannach Bank isn't going to get us anywhere."

"But it's fun, isn't it? What's the point of a job if you're not having fun?"

"It's fun for *you*, John . . . it's always been fun for you."

"So humor me, my last week at work."

"I thought that's what I *was* doing."

"No, Shiv, what you're doing is writing me off. That's what Todd Goodyear is about—he's your number two, same way you used to be mine. You're already starting to train him up, and probably enjoying it, too."

"Now hang on a sec . . ."

"And I'm guessing he's also a means to an end—as long as you've got him with you, you don't have to choose between Phyl and Col."

"With insights like that, it's a wonder you never got farther up the ladder."

"Thing about that ladder, Shiv, each rung you climb there's another arse waiting to be licked."

"What a lovely image."

"We all need some poetry in our lives." He told her he'd see her tomorrow—"always supposing I'm needed"— and ended the call. Sat there another five minutes wondering if she'd call back, but she didn't. There was something too cheery about Randy Newman's delivery, so Rebus turned off the album. Plenty of darker stuff he could play— early King Crimson or Peter Hammill, for example— but instead he walked around the silent flat, going from room to room, and ended up in the hallway with the keys to the Saab in his hand.

"Why the hell not?" he told himself. It wasn't as if it would be the first time, and he doubted it would be the last. Wasn't drunk enough for it to be a problem. He locked the flat and headed down the stairwell, out into the night. Unlocked the Saab and got in. It was only a five-minute drive, and took him past Montpelier's again. A right-hand turn off Bruntsfield Place, then one more right and he was parking in a quiet street of detached Victorian-era houses. He'd been here so often, he'd started to notice changes: new lampposts or new pavements. Signs had gone up warning that come March the parking would be zoned. It had already happened in Marchmont; hadn't made it any easier to find a space. A few rubbish dumpsters had come and gone. He'd heard the Polish accents of the workmen. Extensions had been added to some homes, and the garages dismantled in two separate gardens. Plenty of comings and goings during the day, but much quieter in the evening. Practically every house had its own driveway, but cars from neighboring streets would park up overnight. No one had ever paid attention to Rebus. In fact, one dog walker had started to mistake him for a local, and would nod and smile or offer a hello. The dog itself was small and wiry and looked less trusting, turning away from him the one time he'd tried crouching down to pat it.

That had been a rare occurrence: mostly he stayed in the car, hands on the steering wheel, window rolled down, and a cigarette between his lips. The radio could be playing. He wouldn't even be watching the house necessarily, but he knew who lived there. Knew, too, that there was a coach house in the back garden, which was where the bodyguard lived. One time, a car had stopped when it was halfway through the driveway gates. The bodyguard was in the front, but it was the back window that had slid soundlessly down, the better for the passenger to make eye contact with the watching Rebus. The look was a mixture of contempt, frustration, and maybe even pity — though this last would have been imitation.

Rebus doubted Big Ger Cafferty had ever in his adult life felt an emotion like pity for another human being.

DAY FIVE
Tuesday 21 November 2006

16

The air still smoldered, the charred smell almost overpowering. Siobhan Clarke held a handkerchief to her mouth and nose. Rebus stubbed out his breakfast underfoot.

"Bloody hell" was all he could think to say.

Todd Goodyear had heard the news first and had phoned Clarke, who was halfway to the scene before she decided to call Rebus. They now stood on a roadway in Joppa while the fire crew gathered up the spent coils of hose. Charles Riordan's house was a shell, the windowpanes gone, roof collapsed.

"Can we go in yet?" Clarke asked one of the firemen.

"What's the rush?"

"I'm just asking."

"Talk to the boss . . ."

Some of the firemen were sweating, rubbing smudges of soot across their foreheads. They'd taken off their oxygen tanks and masks. They were talking among themselves, like a gang after a rumble, debating their roles in the action. A neighbor had brought them water and juice. More neighbors were standing in their doorways or gardens, while onlookers from farther afield shuffled and whispered. It was a D Division call and two suits from Leith CID had already asked Clarke what Gayfield Square's interest was.

"Witness in a case" was all she'd told them: no point giving away anything more. The suits hadn't been happy about it and were now keeping their distance, phones held to their ears.

"Reckon he was at home?" Rebus asked Clarke.

She shrugged. "Remember what we were talking about last night?"

"You mean the argument we were having? Me reading way too much into Todorov's death?"

"Don't rub it in."

Rebus decided to play devil's advocate. "Could be an accident, of course. And hey, maybe we'll find him alive and well at his studio."

"I've tried calling—no answer as yet." She nodded towards a curbside TVR. "Woman two doors down says that's his car. He parked it last night—she knows it was him because of the noise it makes." The TVR's windscreen was shrouded in ash. Rebus watched two more firemen step gingerly over some timbers on their way into what was left of the house. Some of the shelves were still visible in the hallway, though most had been destroyed.

"Fire investigator on his way?" Rebus asked.

"On *her* way," Clarke corrected him.

"The march of progress . . ." An ambulance crew had turned up, too, but were now checking their watches, unwilling to waste much more time. Todd Goodyear came bounding forward, dressed in a suit rather than a uniform. He nodded a greeting at Rebus and started leafing back through his notebook.

"How many of those do you get through a month?" Rebus couldn't help asking. Clarke gave him a warning look.

"I've talked to the neighbors either side of him," Goodyear reported to Clarke. "They're in a state of shock, of course—terrified their own houses might be about to explode. They want to get back in and save a few bits and pieces, but the brigade's not having it. Seems Riordan came home at eleven thirty. After that, not a peep from him."

"The way he'd soundproofed the house . . ."

Goodyear nodded enthusiastically. "Unlikely they'd have heard anything. One of the fire officers says the acoustic baffling was probably part of the problem—it can be incredibly flammable."

"Riordan didn't have any visitors in the night?" Clarke asked.

Goodyear shook his head. He couldn't help glancing towards Rebus, as if expecting some sort of praise or appraisal.

"You're in mufti" was all Rebus said.

The constable's eyes swiveled between the two detectives. Clarke cleared her throat before speaking.

"If he's working with us, I thought he'd look less conspicuous . . ."

Rebus tried staring her out, then nodded slowly, though he knew she was lying. The suit had been Goodyear's idea, and now she was covering for him. Before he could say anything, a red car with flashing light roared into view, stuttering to a halt.

"The fire inspector," Clarke announced. The woman who emerged from the car was elegant and businesslike and seemed straight off to have the brigade's attention and respect. Officers started pointing at parts of the smoke-streaked building, obviously giving their side of the story, while the two detectives from Leith hovered nearby.

"Think we should introduce ourselves?" Clarke asked Rebus.

"Sooner or later," he told her. But she'd already decided and was striding towards the cluster of bodies. Rebus followed, indicating for Goodyear to hang back. The constable seemed reluctant, hopping from pavement to roadway and back again. Rebus had attended plenty of house fires, including one he'd ended up being accused of starting. There'd been a fatality that time, too. . . . Not much fun for the pathologists, when there were victims to be identified. He'd almost burned his own flat down once, as well, falling into a stupor on the sofa with the cigarette hanging from his mouth. He'd woken to smouldering fabric and a plume of sulfurous smoke.

Easily done . . .

Clarke was shaking hands with the FI. Not everyone looked happy: the firefighters reckoned CID should leave them to get on with it. Natural reaction, and one Rebus could sympathize with. All the same, he started lighting another cigarette, reckoning it might get him noticed.

"Bloody menace," one of the brigade dutifully muttered. Mission accomplished. The FI's name was Katie Glass, and she was telling Clarke what happened next: locating any victims, securing breached gas sources, checking the obvious.

"Meaning anything from a chip pan left on the heat to an electrical fault."

Clarke nodded along until Glass had finished, then explained about the homeowner's role in an ongoing investigation, aware of Leith CID listening in.

"And that makes you suspect something?" Glass guessed. "So be it, but I always like to enter a scene with an open mind— preconceptions mean you can miss things." She moved towards the garden gate, flanked by firefighters and watched by Rebus and Clarke.

"There's a café back in Portobello," Rebus said, giving a final glance towards the gutted house. "Fancy a fry-up?"

Afterwards, they headed to Gayfield Square, where Hawes and Tibbet, feeling abandoned, welcomed them with frowns. They soon perked up at news of the fire and asked if it meant they could put the HMF away. Goodyear asked what that was.

"Habitual Mugger File," Hawes explained.

"Not an official term," Tibbet added, slapping a hand against the pile of box files.

"Thought they'd all be on computer," Goodyear commented.

"If you're applying for the job . . . ?"

But Goodyear waved the offer aside. Clarke was seated at her desk, tapping it with a pen.

"What now, boss?" Rebus asked, receiving a glare for his efforts.

"I need to talk to Macrae again," she said at last, though she could see his office was empty. "Has he been in?"

Hawes shrugged. "Not since we got here."

"Travel in together?" Rebus asked, all innocence. It was Colin Tibbet's turn to glower at him.

"This changes everything," Clarke was saying quietly.

"Unless it was an accident," Rebus reminded her.

"First Todorov, now the man he spent his final evening with . . ." It was Goodyear who had spoken, but Clarke was nodding her agreement.

"Could all be a horrible coincidence," Rebus argued. Clarke stared at him.

"Christ, John, *you* were the one seeing conspiracies! Now it looks like we've got a connection, you're pouring cold water on it!"

"Isn't that what you do with a fire?" When he saw the blood shooting up Clarke's neck, he knew he'd gone too far. "Okay, say you're right—you still need to run it past Macrae. And meantime, we wait to hear if they find a body. And supposing they do, we then wait to see what Gates and Curt make of it." He paused. "That's what's called 'procedure'—you know it as well as I do." Clarke knew he was right, and he watched as her shoulders relaxed a little and she dropped the pen onto the desk, where it rolled and settled.

"For once John's not wrong," she told the room, "much as it galls me to say it." She smiled, and he smiled back with a little bow from the waist.

"Had to happen once in my career," he said. "Better late than never, I suppose." There were more smiles, and Rebus felt it at that moment. The inquiry had been on the go for days, but only now had everything changed.

Despite the scowls and the sniping, they really were a team.

Which was how Macrae found them when he walked into the CID suite. Even he seemed to sense a change of atmosphere. Clarke gave him her report, keeping everything simple. The phone rang on Hawes's desk, and Rebus wondered if it was another response to their public appeal. He thought again of the prostitute, trying to do business on a no-through-road, and of Cath Mills, stoking up on Rioja. Todorov was attractive to women—and attracted by them, no doubt. Could a stranger have lured him to his doom with an offer of sex? It was straight out of le Carré . . .

Hawes was off the phone and advancing towards Rebus's desk. "They found the body" was all she needed to say.

Rebus knocked on Macrae's door, relaying the message with a look and a nod. Clarke asked the boss if she could be excused. Back in the main body of the kirk, she asked Hawes for details.

"Male, they think. Under a collapsed section of ceiling in the living room."

"Meaning the studio room," Goodyear interrupted, reminding them all that he, too, had been to the producer's home.

"They've got their own team taking photographs and the like," Hawes went on. "Body is on its way to the mortuary."

To be placed in the Decomposing Room, Rebus didn't doubt. He wondered how Todd Goodyear would react to seeing a crispy one.

"We should go there," Clarke told him. But Rebus was shaking his head.

"Take Todd," he offered. "Part of that CID learning curve . . ."

Hawes was on the phone to CR Studios, giving them the news while confirming that Riordan himself hadn't actually turned up so far that day. Colin Tibbet's task was to chase up Richard Browning at the Caledonian Hotel. How long did it take to go through an evening's worth of bar tabs? If Rebus didn't know better, he'd have said Browning was chancing his arm, hoping CID would forget all about it. When a face appeared around the door, Rebus was the only one not doing anything.

"There's someone downstairs," the desk sergeant said. "Looking to hand in a list of Russians. . . . Could it be the Hearts first team for Saturday?"

But Rebus knew who and what it was: Nikolai Stahov from the consulate; Russian nationals based in Edinburgh. Again, Stahov had taken his time, and Rebus doubted they'd have much use for the list — the landscape had changed since they'd first asked for it. All the same, and for want of anything better to do, he nodded and said he'd be down straightaway.

But when he opened the door to the reception area, the man studying the posters on the walls was not Stahov.

It was Stuart Janney.

"Mr. Janney," Rebus said, holding out a hand and trying not to show his surprise.

"It's Detective Inspector . . . ?"

"Rebus," he reminded the banker.

Janney nodded, as if in apology for not having remembered. "I'm just handing in a message." He'd lifted an envelope from his pocket. "Didn't expect someone of your caliber to be on the receiving end."

"Likewise, I didn't know you ran errands for the Russian consulate."

Janney managed a smile. "I ran into Nikolai at Gleneagles. He happened to find the envelope in his pocket . . . mentioned he was supposed to bring it in."

"You told him you'd save him the trouble?"

Janney gave a shrug. "No big deal."

"How was the golf?"

"I didn't play. FAB was giving a presentation, which

happened to coincide with the visit by our Russian friends."

"That *is* a coincidence. Anyone would think you were stalking them."

Now Janney laughed, head back. "Business is business, Inspector, and, lest we forget, good for Scotland."

"True enough—that why you're keeping in with the SNP, too? Reckon they'll be running the show next May?"

"As I said at our first encounter, the bank has to stay neutral. On the other hand, the Nats are making a strong showing. Independence may be a ways off, but it's probably inevitable."

"And good for business?"

Janney gave a shrug. "They're pledging to drop the rate of corporation tax."

Rebus was examining the sealed envelope. "Did Comrade Stahov happen to mention what's in here?"

"Russian nationals living locally. He said it's to do with the Todorov case. I can't really see the connection myself . . ." Janney let the sentence hang, as if ready for Rebus's explanation, but all Rebus did was tuck the envelope inside his jacket.

"How about Mr. Todorov's bank statements?" he asked instead. "Any further forward with them?"

"As I said, Inspector, there are procedures. Sometimes, without the benefit of an executor, the wheels grind slow . . ."

"So have you done any deals yet?"

"Deals?" Janney seemed not to understand.

"With these Russians I'm supposed to be tiptoeing around."

"It's nothing to do with tiptoeing — we just don't want them getting the wrong idea."

"About Scotland, you mean? A man's dead, Mr. Janney — not much we can do to change that."

The door next to the reception desk opened, and DCI Macrae appeared. He was dressed in coat and scarf, ready to leave.

"Any news on the fire?" he asked Rebus.

"No, sir," Rebus told him.

"Nothing from the postmortem?"

"Not yet."

"But you still think it ties to the poet fellow?"

"Sir, this is Mr. Janney. He works for First Albannach Bank."

The two men shook hands. Rebus hoped his boss would take the hint, but just in case, he added the information that Janney was going to provide details of Todorov's bank account.

"Am I to understand," Janney said, "that someone else has died?"

"House fire," Macrae barked. "Friend of Todorov's."

"Gracious me."

Rebus had extended his own hand towards the banker. "Well," he interrupted, "thanks again for dropping by."

"Yes," Janney conceded, "you must have a lot on your plate."

"The whole help-yourself buffet," Rebus acknowledged with a smile.

The two men shook hands. For a moment, it looked as if Macrae and the banker might leave the station together. Rebus didn't like the idea of Macrae spilling any more of the buffet, so told him he needed a word. Janney exited alone, and Rebus waited until the door had closed. But it was Macrae who spoke.

"What do you think of Goodyear?" he asked.

"Seems proficient." Macrae seemed to be expecting some caveat, but Rebus shrugged his shoulders instead and left it at that.

"Siobhan appears to agree with you." Macrae paused. "There'll be a few changes to the team when you retire."

"Yes, sir."

"I reckon Siobhan's about ready for a step up to inspector."

"She's been ready for years."

Macrae nodded to himself. "What was it you wanted to speak to me about?" he eventually asked.

"It'll keep, sir," Rebus assured him. He watched the boss head for the exit and considered stepping into the car park for a smoke. But instead, he headed back upstairs, tearing open the envelope and studying the names. There were a couple of dozen, but no other details—nothing like addresses or a list of occupations. Stahov had been scrupulous to the point of adding his own name at the very bottom—maybe he'd done it for a laugh, knowing the sheet itself was of no possible use to the inquiry. But as Rebus pushed open the door to the CID suite, he saw that Hawes and Tibbet were on their feet, keen to tell him something.

"Spit it out," he said.

Tibbet was holding out another sheet of paper. "Fax from the Caledonian. Several of the hotel residents bought brandies at the bar that night."

"Any of them Russian?" Rebus asked.

"Have a look."

So Rebus took the fax from him and saw three names

staring back at him. Two were complete strangers, but didn't sound foreign. The third wasn't foreign either, but it sent the blood thrumming in his ears.

Mr. M. Cafferty.

M for Morris. Morris Gerald Cafferty.

"Big Ger," Hawes explained, with no necessity whatsoever.

17

Rebus had only the one question: bring him in, or question him at his house?

"My decision, not yours," Siobhan Clarke reminded him. She'd been back from the mortuary half an hour and seemed to be nursing a headache. Tibbet had made her a coffee, and Rebus had watched her press two tablets from their foil enclosure into the palm of her hand. Todd Goodyear had thrown up only the once, in the mortuary car park, though there had been another crisis point on the way back to Gayfield Square when they passed some men laying tarmac.

"Something about the smell," he'd explained.

He now looked pale and shaken, but kept telling everyone he was all right — whether they wanted to hear it or not. Clarke had gathered them round so she could tell them what Gates and Curt had told her: male, five ten, rings on two fingers of the right hand, gold watch on one wrist, and with a broken jaw.

"Maybe a roof beam fell on him," she speculated. The victim hadn't been tied to any piece of furniture, and neither his hands nor his feet had been bound. "Just lying in a heap on the living room floor. Probable cause of death: smoke inhalation. Gates did stress that these were preliminary findings . . ."

Rebus: "Still makes it a suspicious death."

Hawes: "Which means it's ours."

"And ID?" Tibbet asked.

"Dental records, if we're lucky."

"Or the rings?" Goodyear guessed.

"Even if they belonged to Riordan," Rebus told him, "doesn't mean Riordan was the last man wearing them. I had a case ten or twelve years back, guy being done for fraud tried faking his own death . . ."

Goodyear nodded slowly, beginning to see.

After which, Rebus divulged his own news, before asking his question.

Clarke sat with the fax in one hand, head resting in the other.

"This," she said, "just keeps getting better and better. Then, raising her eyes to meet Rebus's: "Interview Room 3?"

"IR3 it is," he said, "and remember to wrap up warm."

Cafferty, however, sat with his chair slid back from the table, one leg crossed over the other and hands behind his head, for all the world as if he were in the parlor back home.

"Siobhan," he said as she walked into the room, "always a great delight. Doesn't she look businesslike, Rebus? You've trained her to perfection."

Rebus closed the door and took up position by the wall, Clarke easing herself onto the chair opposite Cafferty. He gave her a little bow, inclining the great dome of his head but keeping the hands where they were.

"I was wondering when you would pull me in," he said.

"So you knew it was coming?" Clarke had placed a

blank pad of paper on the table and was taking the top off her pen.

"With DI Rebus only days away from the scrap heap?" The gangster glanced in Rebus's direction. "I knew you'd dream up some pretext for giving me grief."

"Well, as it happens, we've got slightly *more* than a pretext—"

"Did you know, Siobhan," Cafferty broke in, "that John here sits outside my house of an evening, making sure I'm tucked up in bed? I'd say that level of protection goes somewhat beyond the call of duty."

Clarke was trying not to be deflected. She placed her pen on the table, but then had to stop it rolling towards the edge. "Tell us about Alexander Todorov," she began.

"Say again?"

"The man you bought a tenner's worth of cognac for last Wednesday night."

"In the bar of the Caledonian Hotel," Rebus added.

"What? The Polish guy?"

"Russian, actually," Clarke corrected him.

"You live a mile and a half away," Rebus pressed on. "Makes me wonder why you'd need a room."

"To get away from you, maybe?" Cafferty made show of guessing. "Or just because I can afford one."

"And then you sit in the bar, buying drinks for strangers," Clarke added.

Cafferty unlinked his hands so he could raise a finger, as if to stress a point. "Difference between Rebus and me—*he'd* sit in the bar all night and buy drinks for no bugger." He gave a cold chuckle. "This is the sum total of why you've dragged me here—because I bought some poor immigrant a drink?"

"How many poor immigrants do you reckon would wander into that bar?" Rebus asked.

Cafferty made show of thinking, closing his sunken eyes and then opening them again. They were like dark little pebbles in his huge pale face. "You have a fair point," he admitted. "But the man was still a stranger to me. What's he gone and done?"

"He's gone and been murdered," Rebus said, with as much restraint as he could muster. "And as of right now, you're the last person who saw him alive."

"Whoa there." Cafferty looked from one detective to the other. "The poet guy, the one I saw in the papers?"

"Attacked on King's Stables Road, maybe fifteen or twenty minutes after drinking with you. What was it the pair of you fell out about?"

Cafferty ignored Rebus and concentrated on Clarke. "Do I need my solicitor here?"

"Not as yet," she said levelly. Cafferty smiled again.

"Are you not wondering, Siobhan, why I'm asking you and not Rebus? He outranks you, after all." Now he turned back to Rebus. "But you're days from the scrap heap, just like I say, while Siobhan here's still on the way up. If the pair of you have got a case on the go, my guess is that Old Man Macrae will have seen sense and put Shiv in charge."

"Only my friends get to call me Shiv."

"My apologies, Siobhan."

"Far as you're concerned, I'm Detective Sergeant Clarke."

Cafferty whistled through his teeth and slapped one meaty thigh. "Trained her to perfection," he repeated. "And rare entertainment with it."

"What were you doing at the Caledonian Hotel?" Clarke asked, as if he'd never spoken.

"Having a drink."

"And staying in a room?"

"It can be murder, finding a taxi home."

"So how did you meet Alexander Todorov?"

"I was in the bar . . ."

"Alone?"

"But only because I wanted to be — unlike DI Rebus there, I have plenty of friends I can drink and have a laugh with. I'm betting *you'd* be fun to drink with, too, DS Clarke, so long as misery-guts was elsewhere."

"And Todorov just happened to sit next to you?" Clarke was guessing.

"I was on a stool at the bar. He was standing, waiting to get served. Barman was crafting a cocktail, so we had a minute or two to talk. I liked him well enough to put his drink on my tab." Cafferty offered an exaggerated shrug. "He slugged it, said thanks, and buggered off."

"He didn't offer to buy one back?" Rebus asked. He took the poet to be a drinker of the old school; etiquette would have demanded no less.

"Actually he did," Cafferty admitted. "I told him I was fine."

"Here's hoping the CCTV backs you up," Rebus commented.

For the first time, Cafferty's mask slipped a little, though the unease was momentary at best. "It will," he stated.

Rebus just nodded slowly while Clarke suppressed a smile. Good to know they could still rattle Cafferty.

"Victim was beaten without mercy," Rebus went on.

"If I'd thought about it, I'd've had you in the frame from the word go."

"You always did like framing people." Cafferty turned his gaze on Clarke. So far all she'd added to the top sheet of paper was a sequence of doodles. "Three, four times a week, he's in that old banger of his, parked on the street outside my house. Some people would cry 'harassment' — what do you think, DS Clarke? Should I apply for one of those restraining orders?"

"What did the two of you talk about?"

"Back to the Russian guy again?" Cafferty sounded disappointed. "Far as I can recollect, he said something about Edinburgh being a cold city. I probably said he was dead right."

"Maybe he meant the people rather than the climate."

"And he'd *still* have been right. I don't mean you, of course, DS Clarke — you're a little ray of sunshine. But those of us who've lived here all our lives, well, we can be on the morose side, wouldn't you agree, DI Rebus? A pal of mine told me once it's because we've never stopped being invaded — a silent invasion, to be sure, quite a pleasant invasion, and sometimes more a trickle than an onslaught, but it's made us . . . prickly — some more than most." Giving a sly glance towards Rebus.

"You've still not explained why you were paying for a room at the hotel," Rebus stated.

"I thought I had," Cafferty countered.

"Only if you mistake us for half-wits."

"I agree, 'half-wits' would be stretching it." Cafferty gave another chuckle. Rebus had slipped his hands into his trouser pockets, the better to curl them into unseen fists. "Look," Cafferty went on, seeming suddenly to tire of the game, "I bought a drink for a stranger, somebody mugged him, end of story."

"Not until we know the who and the why," Rebus corrected him.

"What else did you talk about?" Clarke added.

Cafferty rolled his eyes. "He said Edinburgh was cold, I said yes. He said Glasgow was warmer, I said maybe. His drink arrived, and we both said 'cheers.' . . . Come to think of it, he had something with him. What was it? A compact disc, I think."

Yes, the one Charles Riordan had given him. Two dead men sharing a curry. Rebus clenching and unclenching his hands. Clenching and unclenching. Cafferty, he realized, stood for everything that had ever gone sour — every bungled chance and botched case, suspects missed and crimes unsolved. The man wasn't just the grit in the oyster, he was the pollutant poisoning everything within reach.

And there's no way I can take him down, is there?

Unless God really was up there, handing Rebus this last slim chance.

"The disc wasn't on the body," Clarke was saying.

"He took it with him," Cafferty stated. "Slipped it into one of his pockets." He patted his right-hand side.

"Meet any other Russians in the bar that night?" Rebus asked.

"Now you mention it, there were some rum accents — I thought they must be Gaels or something. Soon as they started with the ceilidh songs, I swore I'd be heading for bed."

"Did Todorov speak to any of them?"

"How should I know?"

"Because you were with him."

Cafferty slapped both hands against the greasy table-top. "*One* drink I had with him!"

"So you say." *Got you rattled again, you bastard!*

"Meaning you were the last person he spoke with before he died," Clarke reinforced.

"You're saying I followed him? Put the boot in him? Fine, let's take a look at this CCTV of yours . . . let's get the barman in here to say how late I stayed at the bar. You've obviously seen my tab — what time was it signed for? I didn't move from that place until gone midnight. Room full of witnesses . . . signed bar tab . . . CCTV." He held up three fingers triumphantly. There was silence in IR3. Rebus eased himself from the wall and took the couple of steps that left him standing beside Cafferty's chair.

"Something happened in that bar, didn't it?" he said, his voice not much above a whisper.

"Sometimes I wish I had your fantasy life, Rebus, I really do."

There was a sudden knock at the door. Clarke released the breath she'd been holding and called out for whoever it was to come in. Todd Goodyear edged nervously around the door.

"What do you want?" Rebus snapped. Goodyear's eyes were on the gangster, but the message was for Clarke.

"Fire investigator's got some news."

"Is she here?" Clarke asked.

"In the suite," he confirmed.

"Fresh blood," Cafferty drawled, measuring Goodyear from head to toe. "What's your name, son?"

"PC Goodyear."

"A police constable out of uniform?" Cafferty

smiled. "CID must be desperate. Is he your replacement, Rebus?"

"Thanks, Goodyear" was all Rebus said, nodding to let the young man know he was dismissed. Cafferty, however, had other ideas. "Used to know a heid-the-ba' called Goodyear . . ."

"Which one?" Todd Goodyear decided to ask. Cafferty's smile turned into a laugh.

"You're right—there was old Harry, used to run a pub on Rose Street. But I was thinking of more recent times."

"Solomon Goodyear," Todd stated.

"That's the one." Cafferty's eyes gleamed. "Sol, everyone calls him."

"My brother."

Cafferty nodded slowly. Rebus was gesturing for Goodyear to hoof it, but Cafferty's stare held the young man captive. "Now I think of it, Sol *did* have a brother . . . never seemed to want to talk about him, though. Does that make you the black sheep, PC Goodyear?" He was laughing again.

"Tell the FI we'll be there in a minute," Clarke interrupted, but still Goodyear didn't move.

"Todd?" Rebus's use of his first name seemed to break the spell. Goodyear nodded and disappeared around the door again.

"Nice kid," Cafferty mused. "He'll be your pet project then, DS Clarke, for when Rebus slopes off into the sunset, just like you used to be Rebus's." When neither detective spoke, Cafferty decided to quit while he was ahead. He stretched his spine, arms extended to either side, and started getting to his feet. "We done here?"

"For the moment," Clarke conceded.

"You don't want me to make a statement or anything?"

"Wouldn't be worth the paper it was written on," Rebus growled.

"Get all the digs in while you can," Cafferty advised. He was at eye level with his old adversary. "See you tonight maybe — same time, same place. I'll be thinking of you, freezing in your car. Speaking of which, it was a nice touch turning off the heating in here — it'll make my room at the hotel feel all the cozier."

"Speaking of the Caledonian," Clarke decided to add, "you bought a lot of drinks that night — eleven, according to your tab."

"Maybe I was thirsty — or just generous." His gaze settled on her. "I can be the generous sort, Siobhan, when the circumstances are right. But then you know that already, don't you?"

"I know a lot of things, Cafferty."

"Oh, I'm sure of that. Maybe we can talk about them while you give me a lift back into town."

"Bus stop's across the road," Rebus said.

18

Something happened in that bar," Rebus repeated as
he walked with Clarke back to the CID suite.

"So you said."

"Cafferty was there for a reason. He's never squan-
dered so much as a quid in his life, so what's he doing
booked into one of the dearest hotels in town?"

"I doubt he'll tell us."

"But his stay happens to coincide with the oligarchs."
She looked at him, and he gave a shrug. "Looked it up in
the dictionary. Thought maybe it had to do with oil."

"It means a small group of powerful people, right?"
Clarke checked.

"Right," Rebus confirmed.

"Thing is, John, we've also got this woman at the car
park . . ."

"Cafferty could have put her there. He's owned a fair
few brothels in his time."

"Or she could be nothing to do with it. I'm going to
have Hawes and Tibbet talk to the witnesses, see if the
e-fit jogs any memories. But meantime, there's a more
pressing question — namely, what the hell are you doing
running a one-man stakeout on Big Ger Cafferty?"

"I prefer 'vendetta' to 'stakeout.' " She seemed ready
to say something, but he held up his hand. "I was outside
his place last night, as it happens, and he was at home."

"So?"

"So he's keeping a room at the Caledonian, but not spending much time there." They had arrived at the door to CID. "And that means he's up to something." Rebus opened the door and went in.

Katie Glass had been given a mug of strong-looking tea and was studying it warily.

"DC Tibbet always does that," Rebus warned her. "If you want tannin poisoning, feel free to drink up."

"I might pass," she said, placing the mug on the corner of a desk. Rebus introduced himself and shook her hand. Clarke thanked her for coming in and asked if she'd found something.

"Early days," Glass hedged.

"But . . . ?" Rebus nudged, knowing there was more.

"We may have a source for the fire: small glass bottles filled with a chemical of some kind."

"What kind of chemical?" Clarke asked, folding her arms. All three were standing, while Hawes and Tibbet listened in from behind their desks. Todd Goodyear was standing by one of the windows, staring out. Rebus wondered if he'd been tracking Cafferty's departure.

"Gone for analysis," the fire inspector was saying. "If I had to guess, I'd say maybe it was cleaning fluid of some kind."

"Household cleaner?"

Glass shook her head. "Bottles were too small. But this was a man who had a lot of tapes in his house . . ."

"Cassette cleaner," Rebus stated. "For wiping oxidation off the heads of the cassette decks."

"Impressive," Glass said.

"I used to have a thing about hi-fi."

"Well, at least one of the bottles looks like someone

had wadded some tissue into its neck. It was sitting in the midst of a pile of melted tape casings."

"In the living room?"

Glass nodded.

"So you think it was deliberate?"

Now she shrugged. "Thing is, if you wanted to kill someone in a fire, usually you'd go to town — slosh petrol around the place, that sort of thing. This was a couple of sheets of loo roll and a small bottle of something flammable."

"I think I see what you're getting at," Rebus told her. "Maybe Riordan wasn't the target." He paused to see if anyone would beat him to it. "The tapes were," he eventually explained.

"The tapes?" Hawes asked, forehead creasing.

"Piled around the little homemade pyre."

"Meaning what exactly?"

"That Riordan had something somebody wanted."

"Or something they didn't want anyone else to have," Clarke added, running a finger beneath her chin. "Is there anything at all left of those tapes, Katie?"

Glass gave another shrug. "Most of the tape itself is done to a crisp. Some of the casings fared a little better."

"So there could still be writing on them?"

"It's possible," Glass conceded. "We've got a slew of stuff that the fire didn't quite get to — dunno how playable any of it will be. Heat, smoke, and water may have done their bit. We've also got some of the deceased's recording equipment — again, the stuff on the hard disks might be salvageable." She didn't sound optimistic.

Rebus caught Siobhan Clarke's eye. "Right up Ray Duff's street," he said.

Goodyear had turned away from the window and was trying to catch up. "Who's Ray Duff?"

"Forensics," Clarke explained. But she was focusing on Rebus. "How about the engineer at Riordan's studio? He might be able to help."

"Could have kept backups," Tibbet piped up.

"So," Glass said, folding her arms, "do I send the stuff here, or to Forensics, or the dead man's studio? Whatever the answer, I'll have to keep your D Division colleagues in the loop."

Rebus thought for a moment, then puffed out his cheeks, exhaled noisily, and said: "DS Clarke's in charge."

Freddie the barman was on duty again. Rebus had spent a few minutes outside the Caledonian Hotel, smoking a cigarette and watching the choreography of passing traffic. Two taxis were parked in the cab rank, the drivers chatting to each other. The Caledonian's liveried doorman was giving directions to a couple of tourists. The elaborate clock at the corner of Fraser's department store was being photographed, presumably by another tourist. There never seemed to be enough rooms in Edinburgh for these visitors; new hotels were always being proposed, considered, and constructed. He could think of five or six off the top of his head, all opening within the past ten years, and with more to come. It gave the impression of Edinburgh as a boomtown. More people than ever seemed to want to work there, or visit, or do business. The Parliament had brought plenty of opportunities. Some argued that independence would spoil things, others that it would build on the success while dealing with devolution's failings. It interested him that a hard-nosed executive like Stuart Janney would cozy up to a nationalist like Megan Macfarlane. But not as much as these Russian visitors interested him. Big place, Russia, and rich in all manner of resources. You could drop Scotland into it dozens of times over. So why were these men here? Rebus was more than curious.

He finished the cigarette and headed indoors, sliding onto one of the bar stools and offering Freddie a reasonably hearty "good afternoon." For a couple of seconds, Freddie mistook him for a guest—he knew the face, after all. He placed a coaster in front of Rebus and asked what he was having.

"The usual," Rebus teased, enjoying the barman's confusion. Then he shook his head. "I'm the cop from Friday. But I'll take a dram with a spot of water in it, so long as it's on the house."

The young man hesitated, but eventually turned to the array of spirits bottles.

"A malt, mind," Rebus warned him. There was no one else in the bar, no one at all. "Bit of a graveyard, this time of day."

"I'm on a double shift—the quiet suits me fine."

"Me, too. Means we can talk that bit more freely."

"Talk?"

"We've got the bar tabs from the night that Russian came in. Remember? He sat right here, and one of your guests bought him a cognac. Guest's name is Morris Gerald Cafferty."

Freddie placed the whisky in front of Rebus, and filled a small glass jug with tap water. Rebus dribbled some into the malt and thanked the barman.

"You'll know Mr. Cafferty?" he persisted. "Last time we spoke, you pretended you didn't. Might explain why you tried pulling a flanker, telling me Todorov could've been talking Russian to the man who bought him the drink. Can't say I blame you, Freddie — Cafferty's not a man you'd want to get on the wrong side of." He paused. "Problem is, same goes for me."

"I was confused, that's all — it was a busy night. Joseph Bonner was in with a party of five . . . Lady Helen Wood at another table with half a dozen friends . . ."

"No problem remembering names now, eh, Freddie?" Rebus gave a smile. "But it's Cafferty I'm interested in."

"I know the gentleman," the barman eventually conceded.

Rebus's smile widened. "Maybe it's because he gets called 'gentleman' that he stays here. Wouldn't happen everywhere in the city, believe me."

"I know he's been in trouble down the years."

"No secret," Rebus agreed. "Maybe he mentioned it himself and told you to get a copy of that book about him, the one that came out last year?"

Freddie couldn't help smiling back. "Gave me a copy, actually — signed and everything."

"He's generous that way. Comes in here most days, would you say?"

"He checked in a week ago; due to leave us in a couple of days."

"Funny," Rebus said, pretending to concentrate on the contents of his glass, "that just about coincides with all these Russians."

"Does it?" The way Freddie said it, he knew damned well what Rebus was up to.

"Can I remind you," Rebus said, voice hardening, "I'm looking into a murder . . . two murders actually. The night the poet came in here, he'd just had a meal and a drink with a man who's now turned up dead. It's getting serious, Freddie — something you need to bear in mind. You don't want to say anything, fine by me, I'll just arrange to have a patrol car come and pick you up. We'll put you in cuffs and make you comfortable in one of our excellent cells while we get the interrogation room ready . . ." He paused, letting it sink in. "I'm trying to be nice here, Freddie, doing my best to be things like 'understated' and 'people-centered.' That can all change." He tipped the last of the whisky down his throat.

"Get you another?" the barman asked, his way of saying he was going to cooperate. Rebus shook his head.

"Tell me about Cafferty," he said instead.

"Comes in most evenings. You're right about the Russians — if it looks like none of them are coming in, he doesn't linger. I know he tries the restaurant, too — has a look around and if they're not there, he won't stay."

"What about if they *are* there?"

"Takes a table nearby. Same thing in here. I get the feeling he didn't know them before, but he knows some of them now."

"So they're all friendly and chatty?"

"Not exactly — they've not got much English. But each of them has a translator — usually some good-looking blonde . . ."

Rebus thought back to the day he'd seen Andropov outside the hotel and the City Chambers: no glamorous assistant. "They don't all need a translator," he said.

Freddie was nodding. "Mr. Andropov speaks English fairly fluently."

"Which means he probably speaks it better than Cafferty."

"I do sometimes get that impression. Other thing I

felt was that maybe *they* weren't strangers when they met . . ."

"What do you mean?"

"First time they ran into one another in here, it was like they didn't need introductions. Mr. Andropov, when he shook hands with Mr. Cafferty, he sort of gripped his arm at the same time . . . I dunno." Freddie shrugged. "Just seemed like they knew one another."

"How much do you know about Andropov?" Rebus asked.

Freddie shrugged again. "He tips well, never seems to drink very much — usually bottles of water, he insists on Scottish."

"I meant what do you know of his background?"

"Nothing at all."

"Me neither," Rebus admitted. "So how many times have Cafferty and Andropov met?"

"I've seen them in here a couple of times . . . the other barman, Jimmy, says he saw them having a chin-wag one time, too."

"What do they talk about?"

"Not a clue."

"You better not be holding back on me, Freddie."

"I'm not."

"You said Andropov's English was better than Cafferty's."

"But not from hearing them in conversation."

Rebus was gnawing away at his bottom lip. "So what does Cafferty talk to *you* about?"

"Edinburgh, mostly — the way it used to be . . . how things have changed . . ."

"Sounds riveting. Nothing about the Russians?"

Freddie shook his head. "Said the best moment of his life was the day he went 'legit.'"

"He's about as legit as a twenty-quid Rolex."

"I've been offered a few of those in my time," the barman mused.

"Something I noticed about all the Russian gentlemen — nice watches. Tailored suits, too. But their shoes look cheap; I can never understand that. People should take better care of their feet." He decided Rebus merited an explanation. "My girlfriend's a chiropodist."

"The pillow talk must be scintillating," Rebus muttered, staring at the empty room and imagining it full of Russian tycoons and their translators.

And Big Ger Cafferty.

"Night the poet was in here," he said, "he just had the one drink with Cafferty and then left . . ."

"That's right."

"But what did Cafferty do?" Rebus was remembering that bar tab: eleven drinks in total.

Freddie thought for a moment. "I think he stayed for a bit . . . yes, he was here till I closed up, more or less."

"More or less?"

"Well, he may have nipped to the toilet. Actually, he went over to Mr. Andropov's booth. There was another gentleman there, a politician, I think."

"You think?"

"Whenever they come on the telly, I turn the sound down."

"But you recognized this man?"

"Like I say, I think he's something to do with the Parliament."

"Which booth was this?" The barman pointed, and

Rebus slid from his stool and headed over to it. "And Andropov was where?" he called.

"Move in a bit further . . . yes, there."

From where Rebus was now sitting, he could see only the nearest end of the bar. The stool he'd just risen from, the one Todorov had taken, was hidden from view. Rebus got to his feet again and walked back to Freddie.

"You sure you've not got cameras in here?"

"We don't need them."

Rebus thought for a moment. "Do me a favor, will you?" he said. "Next time you get a break, find a computer."

"There's one in the Business Center."

"Log on to the Scottish Parliament Web site. There'll be about a hundred and twenty-nine faces there . . . see if you can match one of them."

"My breaks tend to be twenty minutes."

Rebus ignored this. He gave Freddie his card. "Call me as soon as you've got a name." Perfect timing: the door was swinging open, a couple of suits coming in. They looked as though some deal had done them a few favors.

"Bottle of Krug!" one of them barked, ignoring the fact that Freddie was busy with another customer. The barman's eyes met Rebus's, and the detective nodded to let him know he could go back to his job.

"Bet they're not even tippers," Rebus said under his breath.

"Maybe not," Freddie acknowledged, "but at least they'll pay for their drinks . . ."

19

Clarke decided to take the call outside, so Goodyear wouldn't hear her asking Rebus if he was going senile.

"We've already been warned off," she said into the phone, her voice just above a whisper. "What grounds have we got for pulling him in?"

"Anyone willing to drink with Cafferty has got to be dodgy," she heard Rebus explain.

She gave a sigh she hoped he'd hear. "I don't want you going within a hundred yards of the Russian delegation until we have something a bit more concrete."

"You always spoil my fun."

"When you grow up, you'll understand." She ended the call and went back into the CID suite, where Todd Goodyear had plugged in a tape deck borrowed from one of the interview rooms. Turned out Katie Glass had been toting a couple of evidence sacks' worth of stuff from Riordan's house. Goodyear had carried them up from the boot of her car.

"Drives a Prius," he'd commented.

When the bags were opened, the smell of burnt plastic filled the room. But some of the tapes were intact, as were a couple of digital recorders. Goodyear had slotted a cassette tape home, and as Clarke walked in through the door he pressed the play button. The machine didn't have much of a loudspeaker, and they leaned down either side of it, the better to listen. Clarke could hear chinks and clinks and distant, indistinguishable voices.

"A pub or a café or something," Goodyear commented. The hubbub continued for a few more minutes, interrupted only by a cough much closer to the microphone.

"Riordan, presumably," Clarke offered.

Getting bored, she told Goodyear to fast-forward. Same location, same clutter of the overheard everyday.

"You couldn't dance to it," Goodyear admitted. Clarke got him to eject the tape and turn it over. They appeared to be in a railway station. There was the platform master's loud whistle, followed by the sound of a train moving off. The microphone then headed back to the station concourse, where people mingled and waited, probably watching the arrivals or departures board. Someone sneezed, and Riordan himself said, "Bless you." A couple of women were caught in the middle of a conversation about their partners, and the mic seemed to follow them as they headed for a food kiosk, discussing which filled baguettes took their fancy. Purchases made, it was back to gossiping about their partners again as they queued for coffee at a separate kiosk. Clarke heard the espresso machine at work, a sudden announcement over the station tannoy masking the dialogue. She heard the towns Inverkeithing and Dunfermline being mentioned.

"Must be Waverley," she said.

"Could be Haymarket," Goodyear hedged.

"Haymarket doesn't have a sandwich bar as such."

"I bow to your superior knowledge."

"Even when I'm wrong, you should bow anyway."

He did so, giving a courtier-style flourish of the hand, and she smiled.

"He was obsessive," Clarke stated, Goodyear nodding his agreement.

"You really think his death is linked to Todorov?" he asked.

"As of this moment, it's a coincidence . . . but there are precious few murders in Edinburgh—now we get two in a matter of days, and the victims just happen to know one another."

"Meaning you don't really think it's coincidence at all."

"Thing is, Joppa is a D Division call, and we're B Division. If we don't argue our corner, Leith CID will take it."

"Then we should claim it."

"Which means persuading DCI Macrae that there's a connection." She stopped the tape and ejected it. "Reckon they're all going to be like that?"

"Only one way to find out."

"There'll be hundreds of hours of the stuff."

"We don't know that; fire could have made a lot of it unlistenable. Best for one of us to check it first, then pass anything difficult on to Forensics or the engineer at Riordan's studio."

"True." Clarke still didn't share Goodyear's enthusiasm. She was thinking back to her own days in uniform . . . not that long ago, really, in the span of things. She'd been every bit as keen as Goodyear, confident that she would make a difference to each and every case—and maybe, just now and then, a *telling* difference. It had happened sometimes, but the glory had been grabbed by someone more senior—not Rebus, she was thinking back to before their pairing. Her at St. Leonard's, being told that it was all about teamwork, no room for egos and prima donnas. Then Rebus had arrived, his old station having burned to the ground— wiring gone bad. She had to have a little smile to herself at that.

Wiring gone bad: a fair description of Rebus himself at times. Bringing with him to St. Leonard's his mistrust of "teamwork," his two-decades-plus of bets hedged, lines crossed, and rules broken.

And at least one very personal vendetta.

Goodyear was suggesting they give one of the little digital recorders a listen. There was no external speaker, but the headphones from Goodyear's iPod fitted one of the sockets. Clarke didn't really fancy pushing the little buds into her own ears, so told him he could do the listening. But after about half a minute and the pressing of buttons in various configurations, he gave up.

"That's one for our friendly specialist," he said, moving to the next machine.

"I meant to ask," Clarke said, "how you felt meeting Cafferty."

Goodyear considered his answer. "Just looking at him," he said eventually, "you can see he's full of sin. It's in his eyes, the way he looks at you, the way he carries himself . . ."

"You judge people by the way they look?"

"Not all the time." He did a bit more button pushing, earphones still in place, and then held up a finger to let her know he was getting something. After a moment's listening he made eye contact. "You're not going to believe this." He unplugged himself and offered her the earphones. Reluctantly, she held them either side of her head, close to her ears but not touching. He'd rewound a little, and now she heard voices. Tinny little voices, but words she recognized:

"After you split up, Mr. Todorov headed straight for the bar at the Caledonian. He got talking to someone there . . ."

"That's me," she said. "He told us he wasn't recording!"

"He lied. People do sometimes."

Clarke gave him a scowl and listened to a bit more, then told Goodyear to fast-forward. He did, but there was silence.

"Go back again," she ordered.

What was she hoping for? Riordan's last moments, captured for posterity? His attacker's voice? Riordan gaining some measure of justice from beyond the grave?

Only silence.

"Further back."

Clarke and Goodyear himself, winding up their questioning of Riordan in his living room.

"We're the last thing on it," she stated.

"Does that make us suspects?"

"Any more wisecracks, you're back in the woolly suit," she warned him.

Goodyear looked contrite. "Woolly suit," he repeated. "I've not heard that one before."

"Picked it up from Rebus," Clarke admitted.

So many things he'd given her . . . not all of them useful.

"I don't think he likes me," Goodyear was telling her.

"He doesn't *like* anyone."

"He likes you," Goodyear argued.

"He tolerates me," Clarke corrected him. "Different thing entirely." She was staring at the machine. "I can't believe he recorded us."

"If you ask me, *not* being recorded by Mr. Riordan would have put us in the minority."

"True enough."

Goodyear picked up another of the clear plastic sacks and gave it a shake. "Plenty more for us to listen to."

She nodded, then leaned across and patted his shoulder. "Plenty for *you* to listen to, Todd," she corrected him.

"Learning curve?" he guessed.

"Learning curve," she agreed.

"Want to do something tonight?" Phyllida Hawes asked. She was driving, Colin Tibbet her passenger. It annoyed her that he would sit with one hand gripping the door handle, as if ready to eject should her skills suddenly desert her. Sometimes she would put the wind up him on purpose, accelerating towards the vehicle in front or taking a turn at the last possible and unsignaled second. Serve him right for doubting her. One time, he'd told her she drove as though they'd just nicked the car from a forecourt.

"Could go for a drink," he offered.

"Now *there's* a novelty."

"Or we could *not* go for a drink." He thought for a moment. "Chinese? Indian?"

"With ideas as radical as these, Col, you should be running a brains trust."

"You're in a mood," he stated.

"Am I?" she replied icily.

"Sorry," he said.

Another thing that was starting to annoy her: rather than argue his corner, he'd concede on just about any and every point.

Until eight weeks back, Hawes had had a lover — a live-in lover at that. Colin had managed a few single-nighters and one girl who'd actually stuck with him for the best part of a month. Somehow, three weeks ago, they'd fallen into bed together after a night on the piss. Neither had really recovered from it since waking up, faces an inch apart, horror dawning.

It was an accident.

Best put behind us.

And never mentioned.

Forget it ever happened . . .

But how could they? It *had* happened, and despite herself she'd quite like for it to happen again. She had transferred her annoyance with herself on to Colin, in the hope he might do something about it, but he was like some sort of sponge, just soaking it all up.

"Wouldn't surprise me," he said now, "if Shiv takes us all for a drink tonight. Keep the team together — it's what good managers do."

"What you mean is, better that than having John Rebus to herself."

"You may have a point."

"On the other hand," Hawes added, "could be she'll want young Todd all to herself . . ."

He turned towards her. "You don't really think so?"

"Women work in mysterious ways, Colin."

"So I've noticed. Why do you think she brought him on to the team?"

"Maybe she just fell for his charms."

"Seriously, though."

"The DCI's put her in charge. Means she can recruit who she likes, and young Todd wasn't backwards at coming forwards."

"She was easy to persuade?" Tibbet's forehead was creased in thought.

"Doesn't mean you can persuade her to put your name forward for promotion."

"That's not what I was thinking," Tibbet assured her. He looked through the windscreen. "It's next right, isn't it?"

Hawes refused to signal, and crossed the traffic only when there was a bus bearing down on them.

"I wish you wouldn't do that," Tibbet said.

"I know," Phyllida replied with a thin-lipped smile. "But when you're driving a car you've just nicked from a forecourt . . ."

They were headed — Shiv's orders — to Nancy Sieve-wright's flat. Had to ask her about the woman in the cowl. Very word Shiv had used — "cowl" — Hawes checking afterwards that she hadn't meant "hood."

"Hood or cowl, Phyl, what's the difference exactly?" Shiv having grown prickly these past couple of weeks.

"Just here on the left," Colin Tibbet was saying. "There's a space further down."

"Which I couldn't possibly have spotted without you, DC Tibbet." To which he gave no reaction whatsoever.

The door to the communal stairwell had been wedged open, so they decided not to bother with the intercom. Once you crossed the threshold you were in a cold, shadowy place. The white wall-tiles had been damaged and now sported graffiti tags. Voices echoed from somewhere above. A woman, by far the louder of the two. The deeper male bass was softer, entreating.

"Just get the fuck away from me! Why can't you take a telling?"

"I think you know why."

"I don't fucking well care!"

The couple seemed unaware of the two new arrivals who were climbing towards them.

The man: "Look, if you'll only talk to me for a moment."

Interrupted by Colin Tibbet: "Is there a problem here?" His ID open, letting them know who — and more importantly *what* — he was.

"Christ, what now?" the man uttered in exasperation.

"Pretty much what I was asking myself thirty seconds ago, sir," Hawes told him. "It's Mr. Anderson, isn't it? My partner and I took the statements from you and your wife."

"Oh, yes." Anderson had the good grace to look embarrassed. Hawes saw that one of the doors on the next landing up was wide open. That would be Nancy Sievewright's flat. Hawes met the eyes of the underfed, underdressed girl.

"We interviewed you, too, Nancy," she said.

Sievewright nodded her agreement. "Two birds with one stone," Colin Tibbet stated.

"I didn't realize," Hawes said, "you two knew one another."

"We *don't!*" Nancy Sievewright exploded. "He just keeps coming here!"

"Grossly unfair," Anderson snarled. Hawes shared a look with Tibbet. They knew what they had to do.

"Let's get you inside," Hawes told Sievewright.

"And if you'll come downstairs with me, sir," Tibbet

said to Anderson. "There's a question we were hoping to ask you . . ."

Sievewright stomped back into her flat and made straight for the narrow kitchen, where she picked up the kettle and filled it. "The other two, I thought they were going to deal with it."

Meaning, Hawes guessed, Rebus and Clarke. "Why does he keep coming round?" she asked.

Sievewright tugged at a straggle of hair above one ear. "No idea. Says he wants to check I'm all right. But when I tell him I am, he comes back again! I think he hangs around until he knows I'm in the flat on my own . . ." She twisted the hair into a tighter skein. "Fuck him," she said defiantly, hunting among the mugs on the drainer for the one least likely to poison her.

"You could make a formal complaint," Hawes told her, "explain he's harassing you . . ."

"Reckon that would stop him?"

"It might," Hawes said, believing it about as much as the girl herself did. Sievewright had rinsed her chosen mug and now dumped a tea bag into it. She patted the kettle, willing it to boil.

"Social call, was it?" she asked at last.

Hawes rewarded her with a friendly smile. "Not exactly. Some new information's come to light."

"Meaning you've not arrested anybody."

"No," Hawes admitted.

"So what's this information?"

"A woman in a hood, seen hanging around the exit to the multistory." Hawes showed her the e-fit. "If she was still there, you'd have walked right past her."

"I didn't see anyone . . . I've already *told* you this!"

"Easy, Nancy," Hawes said quietly. "Calm yourself down."

"I'm calm."

"The tea's a good idea."

"I think the kettle's knackered." Sievewright was resting the palm of her hand against it.

"No, it's fine," Hawes reassured her. "I can hear it."

Sievewright was staring at the kettle's reflective surface. "Sometimes we try to see how long we can stay touching it while it boils."

"We?"

"Me and Eddie." She gave a sad little smile. "I always win."

"Eddie being . . . ?"

"My flatmate." She looked at the detective. "We're not a couple."

The front door creaked, and they turned to look down the passageway. It was Colin Tibbet.

"He's gone," Tibbet told them.

"Good riddance," Sievewright muttered.

"Did he tell you anything?" Hawes asked her partner.

"Seemed adamant neither he nor his wife saw any woman in a hood. He asked if maybe it was a ghost of some kind."

"I meant," Hawes said, voice toneless, "did he say why he was giving Nancy here such a hard time?"

Tibbet shrugged. "Told me she'd had this great shock, and he wanted to be sure she wasn't bottling it up. 'Storing up trouble for later,' I think his exact words were."

Sievewright, one hand still pressed to the kettle, gave a hoot of derision.

"Very noble of him," Hawes said. "And the fact that his act of charity isn't at all what Nancy wants . . . ?"

"He promised to stay away."

"Fat chance," Sievewright sneered.

"That kettle's nearly boiled," Tibbet felt it necessary to warn her, having just noticed what she was doing with her hand. He was rewarded with something that was between a grimace and a smile.

"Anyone care to join me?" Nancy Sievewright offered.

20

The headline on page five of the *Evening News* was "Das Kapitalists." The story below it recounted a dinner at one of Edinburgh's Michelin-rated restaurants. The party of Russians had booked the whole place. Fourteen sat down to a dinner of foie gras, scallops, lobster, veal, sirloin, cheese, and dessert, washed down with several thousand pounds' worth of champagne, white Burgundy, and venerable red Bordeaux, finishing with port from before the Cold War. Six grand in total. The reporter liked the fact that the champagne—Roederer Cristal—had been a favorite with the tsars of prerevolutionary Russia. None of the diners was identified by name. Rebus couldn't help wondering if Cafferty had slimed his way onto the guest list. Another story on the page opposite stated that the murder rate was down—there had been ten in the past year, twelve the year before that.

They were seated around a large corner table in a Rose Street pub. The place was about to get noisy: Celtic were readying to kick off against Manchester United in the Champions' League and the big-screen TV was the focus of most drinkers' attentions. Rebus closed the paper and tossed it back towards Goodyear, who was seated across from him. He realized he'd missed the last bit of Phyllida Hawes's story, so got her to repeat Anderson's words: *storing up trouble for later.*

"I'll give him 'trouble,'" he muttered. "And he can't say I didn't give him fair warning . . ."

"So far," Colin Tibbet said, "we've only got one sighting of the mystery woman." Having noticed that Todd Goodyear had taken off his tie, he was now in the process of removing his own.

"Doesn't mean she wasn't there," Clarke told him. "Even if she played no part, she might have seen something. There's a line in one of Todorov's poems about averting your eyes so you'll never have to testify."

"And what's that supposed to mean?" Rebus asked her.

"She could be lying low for a reason—people don't always want to get involved."

"Sometimes," Hawes agreed, "they have good reason *not* to get involved."

"Do we still think Nancy Sievewright's holding something back?" Clarke asked.

"That friend of hers was definitely spinning us a yarn," Tibbet said.

"So maybe we need to go over her story again."

"Anything so far from those tapes?" Hawes was asking. Clarke shook her head and gestured towards Goodyear.

"Just that the deceased liked to listen in to people's conversations," he obliged, "even if it meant following them around."

"Bit of a weirdo, then?"

"One way of looking at it," Clarke conceded.

"Christ's sake," Rebus butted in, "there's a bigger picture you're not looking at—Todorov's last stop before ending up dead . . . a drink with Big Ger Cafferty, and some of the Russians not ten yards away!" He rubbed a hand across his forehead.

"Can I just ask one thing?"

Rebus stared at Goodyear. "And what's that, young Todd?"

"Don't take the Lord's name in vain."

"You taking the piss?"

But Goodyear was shaking his head. "I'd look on it as a great favor . . ."

"Which church do you go to, Todd?" Tibbet asked.

"St. Fothad's in Saughtonhall."

"That where you live?"

"Where I grew up," Goodyear corrected Tibbet.

"I used to go to the kirk," Tibbet went on. "Stopped when I was fourteen. My mum died from cancer, couldn't see the point after that."

" 'God is the place that always heals over,' " Goodyear recited, " 'however often we tear it.' " He smiled. "That's from a poem, though not one of Todorov's. Seems to make sense of it all — to me, at any rate."

"Hell's teeth," Rebus said. "Poems and quotations and the Church of Scotland. I don't come to pubs for a sermon."

"You're not alone," Goodyear told him. "Plenty of Scots try to hide their cleverness. We don't *trust* clever people."

Tibbet was nodding. "We're supposed to be 'all Jock Tamson's bairns' — meaning we're all the same."

"And not allowed to be different." Goodyear was nodding back at him.

"See what you're going to miss when you retire?" Clarke said, her eyes on Rebus. "Intellectual debate."

"I'm getting out just in time, then." He started to rise

to his feet. "Now if you eggheads will excuse me, I've got a tutorial with Professor Nicotine . . ."

Rose Street was busy: a hen-night pub crawl, the women dressed in identical T-shirts marked with the words Four Weddings and a Piss-Up. They blew kisses at Rebus as they passed him, but were then stopped by a crowd of young men heading in the opposite direction. A stag do by the look of it, the groom-to-be spattered with shaving foam, eggs, and flour. Office workers eased past, on their way home after a couple of bevvies. There were tourist families, too, not sure what to make of the hens and stags, and men hurrying to catch the match.

The door opened behind Rebus, and Todd Goodyear stepped out. "Wouldn't have taken you for a smoker," Rebus told him.

"I'm headed home." Goodyear was shrugging himself back into his suit jacket. "I left cash on the table for the next round."

"Prior engagement, is it?"

"Girlfriend."

"What's her name?"

Goodyear hesitated, but couldn't seem to think of a valid excuse not to tell Rebus. "Sonia," he said. "She's one of the SOCOs."

"Was she there last Wednesday?"

Goodyear nodded. "Short blond hair, mid-twenties . . ."

"Can't place her," Rebus admitted. Goodyear looked tempted to take this as an insult, but changed his mind.

"You used to be a churchgoer, didn't you?" he asked instead.

"Who told you that?"

"Just something I heard."

"Best not to believe rumors."

"Even so, I get the feeling I'm right."

"Maybe you are," Rebus conceded, blowing smoke into the air. "Years back, I tried a few different churches. Didn't find any answers."

Goodyear nodded slowly. "What Colin said sums up a lot of people's experience, doesn't it? A loved one dies, and we blame God. Is that what happened with you?"

"Nothing happened with me," Rebus stated stonily, watching the hen party move off in search of its next watering hole. The stags were watching, too, one or two debating whether to follow.

"Sorry," Goodyear was apologizing, "just nosy . . ."

"Well, don't be."

"Are you going to miss the job?"

Rebus rolled his eyes. "Here he goes again," he complained to the sky above. "All I want is a peaceful smoke, and now it's *Question Time*."

Goodyear smiled a further apology. "I better get going while I still can."

"Before you do . . ."

"Yes?"

Rebus studied the tip of his cigarette. "Cafferty in the interview room . . . was that the first time you'd met him?" Goodyear nodded. "He knew your brother, and your granddad, too, if it comes to that." Rebus looked up and down the street. "Your granddad's pub was the next block, wasn't it? Forget what it was called . . ."

"Breezer's."

Rebus nodded slowly. "When he went to court, I was the one in the witness box."

"I didn't know that."

"Three of us made the bust, but I was the one who gave evidence."

"Have you ever been in that position with Cafferty?"

"He got put away both times." Rebus spat onto the pavement. "Shiv tells me your brother was in a fight. Is he all right?"

"I think so." Goodyear was looking uncomfortable. "Look, I'd better get going."

"You do that. I'll see you tomorrow."

"Night, then."

"Night," Rebus said, watching him leave. Didn't seem a bad kid. Decent enough cop. Maybe Shiv could do something with him. . . . Rebus remembered Harry Goodyear pretty well. Guy's pub had been notorious — speed, coke, and a bit of pot, all being shifted from the place, Harry himself a small-timer, in and out of trouble. Rebus had wondered at the time, how did he get a pub license? Reckoned money had changed hands, someone on the council pitching for him. Friends could always be bought. Time was, Cafferty himself had owned a number of councillors. That way, he stayed one step ahead; cheap at whatever the price. He'd tried buying Rebus, too, but that was never going to run — Rebus had learned his lesson by then.

"Not my fault Grandpa Goodyear died in the clink . . ."

He stubbed out the cigarette and turned towards the door, but then paused. What was waiting for him inside? Another drink, plus a table of youngsters — Shiv, Phyl, and Col would be discussing the case, bouncing ideas around. And what exactly could Rebus add to the mix? He took out another cigarette and lit it, then started walking.

He took a left onto Frederick Street and a right into Princes Street. The castle was being illuminated from below, its shape picked out against the night sky. The fun fair was under construction in Princes Street Gardens, along with the market stalls and booths parked at the foot of the Mound. It would be a magnet for shoppers in the run-up to Christmas. He thought he could hear music: maybe the open-air ice rink was being tested out. Groups of kids were weaving their way past the shop fronts, paying him not the slightest heed. When did I become the invisible man? Rebus asked himself. Catching his reflection in a window he saw heft and bulk. Yet these kids teemed past as if he had no place in their version of the world.

Is this how ghosts feel? he wondered.

He crossed at the traffic lights and pushed open the door to the bar of the Caledonian Hotel. The place was busy. Jazz was playing on the hi-fi, and Freddie was busy with a cocktail shaker. A waitress was waiting to take her tray of drinks over to a table filled with laughter. Everyone looked prosperous and confident. Some of them held mobile phones to their ears, even as they spoke to the person next to them. Rebus felt a moment's irritation that someone had taken his stool. In fact, all the stools were taken. He bided his time until the barman had finished pouring. The waitress moved off, balancing the tray on her hand, and Freddie saw Rebus. The frown he gave told Rebus that the situation had changed. The bar was no longer empty, and Freddie would be unwilling to talk.

"Usual, please," Rebus said anyway. And then: "You weren't exaggerating about the double shift . . ."

This time, when the whisky arrived, the bill came with it. Rebus smiled to let Freddie know this was fine with him. He trickled a few drops of water into the glass and swirled it in his hand, sniffing the contents as he scanned the room.

"They've gone, in case you're wondering," Freddie told him.

"Who?"

"The Russians. Checked out this afternoon, apparently. Winging their way back to Moscow."

Rebus tried not to look too deflated by this news. "What I was wondering," he said, "is whether you've got that name for me."

The barman nodded slowly. "I was going to phone you tomorrow." The waitress had arrived with another order, and he went to fill it. Two large helpings of red wine and a glass of the house champagne. Rebus started listening in on the conversation next to him. Two businessmen with Irish accents, eyes glued to the football on the soundless TV. Some property deal had failed to come off, and they were drowning their sorrows.

"And God grant them a lingering death" seemed to be the toast of choice. One of the things Rebus liked best about bars was the chance to eavesdrop on other people's lives. Did that make him a voyeur, not so very different from Charles Riordan?

"Any chance we get to screw them over . . ." one of the Irishmen was saying. Freddie had returned the champagne bottle to the ice bucket and was coming back to Rebus's end of the bar.

"He's Minister for Economic Development," the barman explained. "Ministers are listed first on the Parliament's Web site. Might've taken a while otherwise . . ."

"What's he called?"

"James Bakewell."

Rebus wondered why he knew the name.

"Saw him on the TV a few weeks back," Freddie was saying.

"On *Question Time*?" Rebus guessed. The barman was nodding. Yes, because Rebus had seen Bakewell there, too, arguing the toss with Megan Macfarlane while Alexander Todorov sat between them. Jim, everyone seemed to call him . . . "And he was in here with Sergei Andropov, same night as the poet?" Freddie kept nodding.

And the same night, too, as Morris Gerald Cafferty. Rebus rested his hands against the bar, letting them take his weight. His head was swirling. Freddie had moved to take another order. Rebus thought back to the tape of *Question Time*. Jim Bakewell had been New Labour with some of the rough edges left untreated. Either he wouldn't let the image consultants near him, or that *was* his image. Late forties with a mop of dark brown hair and wire-framed spectacles. Square-jawed and blue-eyed and self-deprecating. He'd got a lot of respect north of the border for the way he'd resigned a safe seat at Westminster to stand for the Scottish Parliament. This made him a rare beast indeed. Seemed to Rebus that a lot of the political talent was still drawn to London. Freddie hadn't mentioned any minders, which Rebus also found interesting. If Bakewell had been meeting the Russians in an official capacity, surely there'd have been assistants and advisers on hand. The Minister for Economic Development . . . late-night drinks with a foreign businessman . . . Big Ger Cafferty crashing the party. . . . Too many questions were hammering away at the inside of Rebus's skull. It was as if his brain had developed a pulse. Finishing the drink, he left some money on the bar and decided it was time to head home. His phone alerted him to a text message. Siobhan was wondering where he'd got to.

"Took you long enough," he muttered to himself. As he passed the Irishmen, one of them was leaning in towards the other.

"If he dies on Christmas morning," he was confiding in a booming voice, "that'll be tinsel enough for me . . ."

Two ways to leave the hotel: the bar's own door, or through reception. Rebus wasn't sure why he chose the latter. As he crossed the lobby, two men had just emerged through the revolving door. The one in front he recognized: the man who'd been driving Andropov.

The other was Andropov himself. He had seen Rebus, and his eyes were narrowing, wondering where he knew him from. Rebus gave a little bow of the head as they approached each other.

"Thought you'd all gone home," he said, trying to sound casual.

"I'm staying a few more days." There wasn't much of an accent at all. Rebus could tell Andropov was still trying to place him.

"Friend of Cafferty's," he pretended to explain.

"Ah yes." The chauffeur was standing just the other side of Rebus, hands clasped in front of him, feet splayed. Chauffeur *and* bodyguard.

"The few extra days," Rebus inquired of Andropov, "business or pleasure?"

"Usually I find business a distinct pleasure." It sounded like a line he'd used dozens of times before, always expecting a laugh or a smile. Rebus obliged as best he could.

"Seen Mr. Cafferty today?" he asked eventually.

"I'm sorry, I seem to have forgotten your name . . ."

"I'm John," Rebus told him.

"And your connection to Cafferty . . . ?"

"I was wondering the same about you, Mr. Andropov." Rebus decided he'd already been rumbled. "It's fine to hobnob with the great and the good, being fawned over by politicians of all creeds and colors . . . but when you start cozying up to a career criminal like Cafferty, alarm bells are bound to start ringing."

"You were at the City Chambers," Andropov announced with a wag of one gloved finger. "And then you were outside the hotel here."

"I'm a detective, Mr. Andropov." Rebus held up his warrant card, and Andropov examined it.

"Have I done something wrong, Inspector?"

"A week back, you were having a little chat with Jim Bakewell and Morris Gerald Cafferty."

"What if I was?"

"There was another man in the bar — a poet called Todorov. Less than twenty minutes after walking out of here, he was murdered."

Andropov was nodding. "A great tragedy. The world has an apparent need of poets, Inspector. They are, so they tell us, its 'unacknowledged legislators.' "

"I'd say they've got a bit of competition in that department."

Andropov decided to ignore this. "Several people," he said instead, "inform me that your police force may not be investigating Alexander's death as a simple street attack. Tell me, Inspector, what do *you* think happened?"

"A story best told at my police station. Would you be willing to drop in for an interview, Mr. Andropov?"

"I can't see that anything would be gained from that, Inspector."

"I'll assume that's a no."

"Let me offer my own theory." Andropov took a step closer, mimicked by his driver. "*Cherchez la femme,* Inspector."

"Meaning what exactly?"

"You don't speak French?"

"I know what it means; I'm just not sure what you're getting at."

"In Moscow, Alexander Todorov had something of a reputation. He was forced to leave his teaching post after accusations of improper conduct. Female students, you know, and apparently the younger the better. Now, if you'll excuse me . . ." Andropov was obviously heading for the bar.

"Hooking up with your gangster friend again?" Rebus guessed. Andropov ignored him and kept walking. The driver, however, decided that Rebus merited a final baleful look, the kind that said, *You, me, and a dark alley . . .*

The look Rebus gave him back carried another message, no less threatening. *You're on my list, pal, you and your boss both.*

Outside once again in the crisp night air, he decided he might try walking home. His heart was pounding, mouth dry, blood coursing through him. He gave it a few hundred yards, then hailed the first taxi he saw.

DAY SIX

Wednesday 22 November 2006

21

The sound engineer was called Terry Grimm, and the secretary was Hazel Harmison. They seemed shell-shocked, and with good reason.

"We've no idea what to do," Grimm explained. "I mean . . . do we get paid at month's end? What do we do about all the jobs we've got on our books?"

Siobhan Clarke nodded slowly. Grimm was seated at the mixing desk, swiveling nervously on his chair. Harmison was standing by her desk, arms folded. "I'm sure Mr. Riordan will have made some kind of provision . . ." But Clarke wasn't sure of that at all. Todd Goodyear was staring at all the machinery, the banks of knobs and dials, switches and slider controls. In the pub last night, Hawes had hinted that really it should be either her or Tibbet who accompanied Clarke today. It made Siobhan wonder again if she'd brought Goodyear into the team precisely because she didn't want to have to make that choice.

"Can neither of you sign company checks?" Clarke asked now.

"Charlie wasn't that trusting," Hazel Harmison piped up.

"The company accountant's the one to speak to."

"Except he's on holiday."

"Someone else at his firm, then?"

"One-man band," Grimm stated.

"I'm sure it'll all work out," Clarke remarked crisply. She'd had enough of their bellyaching. "Reason we're here is, some of Mr. Riordan's recordings have been salvaged from the house. Most, however, went up in smoke. I'm wondering if he kept copies."

"Might be some in the storeroom," Grimm conceded. "I was always warning that he didn't back up enough . . ." He met her eyes. "The hard disks didn't make it?"

"Mostly not. We've brought some stuff with us, wondered if maybe you'd have better luck than us."

Grimm gave a shrug. "I can take a look." Clarke handed her car keys to Goodyear.

"Fetch up the bags," she said. The phone had started ringing, and Harmison picked it up.

"CR Studios, how can I help you?" She listened for a moment. "No, I'm sorry," she began to apologize. "We can't take on any new work at the moment, due to unforeseen circumstances."

Clarke still had the engineer's attention. "You could go it alone," she told him quietly. "I mean the two of you . . ." Glancing towards Harmison. He nodded and got up, walked over to the desk, and gestured for the telephone. "One moment, please," Harmison said into the mouthpiece. "I'm just going to hand you over to Mr. Grimm."

"How can I help?" Terry Grimm asked the caller. Harmison wandered over towards Clarke, her arms folded again, as if to form a shield against further blows.

"First time I was here," Clarke said, "Terry hinted that Mr. Riordan recorded *everything*."

The secretary nodded. "One time, the three of us went out for dinner. They brought something we hadn't ordered. Charlie pulled this little recorder from his pocket and played it back to the staff, proving it was them to blame." She was smiling at the memory.

"There've been times I'd have done the same," Clarke acknowledged.

"Me, too. Plumbers who promise to be there at eleven . . . people on the phone who say the check's in the post . . ."

Clarke was smiling now, too. But Harmison's face fell again.

"I feel so sorry for Terry. He's worked every bit as hard as Charlie, probably put in more hours, truth be told."

"What sort of work have you got on just now?"

"Radio ads . . . couple of audiobooks . . . plus editing the Parliament project."

"What Parliament project?"

"You know they have a Festival of Politics every year?"

"I didn't, actually."

"Had to happen—we've got festivals for everything else. This coming year, there's an artist they've commissioned to put something together. He works in video and so on, and he wanted a sound collage to go with whatever it is he's doing."

"So you've been taping stuff at the Parliament?"

"Hundreds of hours of it." Harmison nodded towards the battery of machines. But Grimm was clicking his fingers, gaining her attention.

"I'll just put my assistant back on," he was telling the caller. "And she'll fix up a meeting."

Harmison fairly trotted towards the desk and the appointments diary. Clarke reckoned it was his use of "assistant" that had done it. No longer a mere secretary or receptionist . . .

Grimm was nodding in gratitude as he approached Clarke. "Thanks for the tip," he said.

"Hazel was just telling me about the Festival of Politics."

Grimm turned his eyes heavenwards. "What a nightmare. Artist hadn't a clue what he wanted. Bounces around between Geneva and New York and Madrid. . . . We'd get the occasional e-mail or fax. Get me some sounds of a debate, but make sure it's heated. All the meetings of one of the committees . . . some of the guided tours . . . interviews with visitors. . . . He'd be vague as hell, then tell us we hadn't done what he wanted. Luckily we kept all his e-mails."

"And of course Charlie would have taped any meetings or phone calls?"

"How did you guess?"

"Hazel told me."

"Well, our artist friend *loved* that. I mean, not everyone likes it when they find out they've been secretly taped . . ."

"I can imagine," Clarke drawled.

"But he thought it was hysterical."

"Sounds like a big project, though."

"Nearly done. I put together two hours of collage, and so far he seems to like it. Plans to use it with some video installation at the Parliament building." Grimm gave a shrug, which seemed to sum up his attitude to "artists."

"What's his name?"

"Roddy Denholm."

"And he's not based in Scotland?"

"Has a flat in the New Town but never seems to be there."

The intercom buzzed, letting them know Goodyear

was back with the spools of tape and the digital recorders.

"What is it you think we might get from them?"
Grimm asked, staring at the polythene sacks as Goodyear placed them on the floor.

"To be honest, I'm not sure," Clarke admitted. Hazel
Harmison had finished making the appointment and was
now staring in morbid fascination at the sacks. She'd
folded her arms once more, but it wasn't proving at all
effective.

"Did you make the appointment for today or tomorrow?" Grimm asked her, hoping to divert her attention.

"Midday tomorrow."

"This recording you've been doing at the Parliament . . ." Clarke addressed Grimm. "You said you'd
been taping one of the committees — mind if I ask
which one?"

"Urban Regeneration," he stated. "Not exactly a caul-
dron of human drama, believe me."

"I believe you," Clarke told him. Interesting all the
same. "So was it you doing the actual recording rather
than Mr. Riordan?"

"Both of us."

"That committee's chaired by Megan Macfarlane,
isn't it?"

"How do you know that?"

"You might say I've got an interest in politics. Mind if
I take a listen?"

"To the Urban Regeneration Committee?" He sounded
nonplussed. "You've gone beyond an 'interest in politics,'
Sergeant . . ."

She took the bait: "And into what?"

"Masochism," he stated, turning towards the mixing desk.

"Gill Morgan?" Rebus asked into the intercom. He was standing outside a door on Great Stuart Street. Cars rumbled across the setts, taking drivers and passengers to Queen Street and George Street. The morning rush hour wasn't quite over, and Rebus had to lean down, ear pressed to the intercom's loudspeaker, to make out the eventual reply.

"What is it?" The voice sounded bleary.

"Sorry if I woke you," Rebus pretended to apologize. "I'm a police officer. A few follow-up questions regarding Miss Sievewright."

"You've got to be joking." Bleary *and* irritated.

"Wait till you hear the punch line."

But she'd missed that: the setts sending tremors through a lorry. Rather than repeat himself, Rebus just asked to be let in.

"I need to get dressed."

He repeated the request, and the buzzer sounded. He pushed open the door into the communal stairwell and climbed the two flights. She'd left her door ajar for him, but he gave a knock anyway.

"Wait in the living room!" she called, presumably from her bedroom. Rebus could see the living room. It was at the end of a wide hall, the sort that often got called a "dining hallway," meaning you were supposed to have a table there and entertain your friends to supper rather than have them traipse all over your actual living room. It seemed to him a very Edinburgh thing. Welcoming, but not very. The living room itself boasted stark white walls to complement stark white furniture. It was like walking into an igloo. The floor-

boards had been stripped and varnished, and he concentrated
on them for a moment, trying to avoid becoming snow-blind.
It was a big room with a high ceiling and two huge windows.
He couldn't imagine that Gill Morgan shared with anyone,
the place was too tidy. There was a flat-screen TV on the
wall above the fireplace and no ornaments anywhere. It was
like the rooms in the Sunday newspaper supplements, the
ones designed to be photographed rather than lived in.

"Sorry about that," a young woman said, walking into
the room. "I realized after I'd let you in that you could be
anybody. The officers the other day carried ID—can I see
yours?"

Rebus got out his warrant card, and as she studied it, so he
studied her. She was tiny—almost elfin. Probably not even
five feet tall, and with a pointy little face and almond-shaped
eyes. Brown hair tied into a ponytail, and arms the thickness
of pipe cleaners. Hawes and Tibbet had said she was a model
of some kind . . . Rebus found that hard to believe. Weren't
models supposed to be tall? Satisfied with his credentials,
Morgan had sunk into a white leather armchair, tucking her
legs beneath her.

"So how can I help you, Detective Inspector?" she asked,
hands clasped to her knees.

"My colleagues said you have a modeling career, Miss
Morgan—must be going well for you?" He made show of
admiring the living room's proportions.

"I'm moving into acting, actually."

"Really?" Rebus tried to sound interested. Most people
would have responded to his original question by asking
what business it was of his, but not Gill Morgan. In her universe, talking about herself came naturally.

"I've been taking classes."

"Would I have seen you in anything?"

"Probably not yet," she preened, "but there's some screen work on the horizon."

"Screen work? That's impressive . . ." Rebus lowered himself onto the chair opposite her.

"Just a small part in a television drama . . ." Morgan seemed to feel the need to play down the significance, no doubt in the hope that he'd think she was being modest.

"Exciting, all the same," he told her, playing along. "And it probably helps explain something we've been wondering about."

Now she looked puzzled. "Oh?"

"When my colleagues spoke to you, they could see you were trying to feed them a line. Fact that you say you're an actor explains why you thought you'd get away with it." He leaned forward, as if to take her into his confidence. "But here's the thing, Miss Morgan, we're now investigating *two* murders, and that means we can't afford to get sidetracked. So before you get into serious trouble, maybe you should own up."

Morgan's lips were the same pale color as her cheeks. Her eyelids fluttered, and for a moment he thought she might faint.

"I don't know what you mean," she said.

"I wouldn't give up those lessons just yet—looks to me like you've got a few things to learn about delivering a line. The blood's left your face, your voice is shaking, and you're blinking like you've been caught in someone's headlights." Rebus sat back again. He'd been here five minutes, but he thought he could read the whole of Gill Morgan's life in what he'd seen of her so far: cushy upbringing, parents who poured money and love over her, schooled in the art of confidence, and never having faced a challenge she couldn't sweet-talk her way out of.

Until now.

"Let's take it slowly," he said in a softening voice, "ease you into it. How did you meet Nancy?"

"At a party, I think."

"You think?"

"I'd been to a few bars with some friends . . . we ended up at this party and I can't remember if Nancy was already there or if she'd somehow attached herself to the group along the way."

Rebus nodded his understanding. "How long ago was this?"

"Three or four months. Around Festival time."

"I'm guessing the two of you come from different backgrounds."

"Absolutely."

"So what did you find in common?" She didn't seem to have a ready answer. "I mean, something must have helped you bond?"

"She's just good fun."

"Why do I get the feeling you're lying again? Is it the shaky voice or the fluttering eyelids?"

Morgan leapt to her feet. "I don't have to answer any of your questions! Do you know who my mother is?"

"Wondered how long it would take," Rebus said with a satisfied smile. "Go on then, impress me." He clasped his hands behind his head.

"She's the wife of Sir Michael Addison."

"Meaning he's not your actual father?"

"My father died when I was twelve."

"And you kept his surname?" Color had flooded back into the young woman's cheeks. She'd decided to sit down again, but keeping her feet on the floor this time. Rebus unclasped his hands and rested them on the chair arms. "So who's Sir Michael Addison?" he asked.

"Chief executive of First Albannach Bank."

"A useful sort to know, I'm guessing."

"He rescued my mother from alcoholism," Morgan stated, eyes boring into Rebus's. "And he loves both of us very much."

"Nice for you, but it doesn't help the poor sod who ended up dead on King's Stables Road. Your friend Nancy found the body, then lied to us about where she'd been heading home from. She gave *your* name, Gill, and *your* address. Meaning she must think you're one hell of a friend, the kind who'd go to jail on her behalf rather than tell the truth . . ."

He didn't realize his voice had risen, but when he stopped, there was a moment's reverberation from the walls.

"You think your stepdad would want you doing that, Gill?" he went on, voice softening again. "You think your poor mum would want that?"

Gill Morgan had bowed her head and seemed to be analyzing the backs of her hands. "No," she said quietly.

"No," Rebus agreed. "Now tell me, if I were to ask you right now where Nancy lives, could you give me an answer?"

A single tear dropped into the young woman's lap. She squeezed her eyes with thumb and forefinger, then blinked any further tears back. "Somewhere off the Cowgate."

"Doesn't sound to me," Rebus said, "as if you really know her all that well. So if the two of you aren't what you might call bosom buddies, why are you covering for her?"

Morgan said something he didn't catch. He asked her to repeat it. She glared at him, and this time the words were unmistakable.

"She was buying me drugs." She let the words sink in. "Buying *us* drugs, I should say—some for her, and some for me. Just a bit of pot, nothing to send civilization crashing to its knees."

"Is that how you became friends?"

"I dare say it's part of the reason." But Morgan couldn't really see the point of lying. "Maybe quite a *lot* of the reason."

"The party you met her at, she brought dope with her?"

"Yes."

"Was she sharing or selling?"

"We're not talking about some Medellín cartel here, Inspector . . ."

"Cocaine, too?" Rebus deduced. Morgan realized she'd said too much. "And you had to protect her because otherwise she was going to—pardon the pun—grass you up?"

"Is that the punch line you were talking about?"

"I didn't think you'd heard that."

"I heard."

"So Nancy Sievewright wasn't here that night?"

"She was supposed to turn up at midnight with my share. It annoyed me at the time, because I'd had to rush home."

"Where from?"

"I've been helping out one of my drama teachers. He has a sideline running one of those nighttime walking tours of the city."

"Ghost tours, you mean?"

"I know they're preposterous, but the tourists like them and it's a bit of a giggle."

"So you're one of the actors? Jumping out from the shadows and going 'Boo!'?"

"I have to play several roles, actually." She sounded hurt by his glibness. "And between setups, I have to run like blazes to the next location, changing costume as I go."

Rebus remembered Gary Walsh saying something about the ghost tours. "Where does it happen?" he asked now.

"St. Giles to the Canongate, same route each night."

"Do you know of any tours that take in King's Stables Road?"

"No."

Rebus nodded thoughtfully. "So who exactly do you play?"

She gave a puzzled laugh. "Why the interest?"

"Indulge me."

She puckered her lips. "Well," she said at last, "I'm the plague doctor . . . I have to wear a mask like a hawk's beak—the doctor would fill it with potpourri to ward off the stench from his patients."

"Nice."

"And then I'm a ghost . . . and sometimes even the Mad Monk."

"Mad Monk? Bit of a challenge for a woman, isn't it?"

"I only have to do a bit of moaning and groaning."

"Yes, but they can see you're not a bloke."

"The hood covers most of my face," she explained, smiling again.

"Hood?" Rebus echoed. "I wouldn't mind having a look at that."

"The costumes stay with the company, Inspector. That way, when one actor's off sick, they can use another as cover."

Rebus nodded as if satisfied by the explanation. "Tell me," he asked, "did Nancy ever come to see you perform?"

"A couple of weeks back."

"Enjoy herself, did she?"

"Seemed to." She gave another nervy little laugh. "Am I walking into some trap here? I can't see what any of this has to do with your case."

"Probably nothing," Rebus assured her.

Morgan grew thoughtful. "You're going to talk to Nancy now, aren't you? She'll know I've told you."

"Afraid you may be in the market for another supplier, Miss Morgan. Shouldn't worry, though—there are plenty of them about." Rebus got to his feet. She followed suit, standing on tiptoe and still below the height of his chin.

"Is there . . ." She swallowed back the rest of the question but decided she had to know. "Is there any reason why my mother might get to hear of this?"

"Depends, really," Rebus said, after a moment's pretend thought. "We catch the killer . . . it comes to trial . . . the timeline is gone through minute by minute. Defense is going to want some doubt in the jury's minds, and that means showing any witnesses to be less than trustworthy. They show Nancy's original statement to be a pile of dung, and it all starts to smell from then on in . . ." He gazed down at her. "That's the worst-case scenario," he offered. "Might never happen."

"Which is another way of saying it might."

"You should have told the truth from the start, Gill. Lying is all very well for an actor, but out here in the real world we tend to call it perjury."

22

I'm not sure I can take all this in," Siobhan Clarke admitted. They were gathered in the CID suite. Clarke was pacing up and down in front of the Murder Wall. She passed by photos of Alexander Todorov in life and in death, a photocopied pathology report, names and phone numbers. Rebus was polishing off a ham salad sandwich, washed down with polystyrene tea. Hawes and Tibbet sat at their desks, swaying gently in their chairs, as if in time to a piece of music only they could hear. Todd Goodyear was sipping milk from a half-liter carton.

"Want me to recap for you?" Rebus offered. "Gill Morgan's stepdad runs First Albannach, she buys drugs from Nancy Sievewright, and she has ready access to a hooded cape." He shrugged as if it was no big deal. "Oh, and Sievewright knew about the cape, too."

"We need to bring her in," Clarke decided. "Phyl, Col — go fetch."

They managed a synchronized nod as they rose from their chairs. "What if she's not there?" Tibbet asked.

"Find her," Clarke demanded.

"Yes, boss," he said, sliding his jacket back on. Clarke was glaring at him, but Rebus knew Tibbet hadn't been trying for sarcasm. He'd called her "boss" because that was what she was. She seemed to sense this, and glanced towards Rebus. He balled up the wrapper from his sandwich, and missed the waste bin by about three feet.

"She doesn't seem like a dealer to me," Clarke said.

"Maybe she's not," Rebus responded. "Maybe she's just a friend who likes to share."

"But if she charges for that share," Goodyear argued, "doesn't that make her a dealer?" He had walked over to the waste bin and picked up Rebus's wrapper, making sure it found its target. Rebus wondered if the young man was even aware that he'd done it.

"So if she wasn't at Gill Morgan's flat that night, where was she?" Clarke asked.

"While we're adding ingredients to the broth," Rebus interrupted, "here's another for you. Barman at the hotel saw Andropov and Cafferty with another man the night Todorov was murdered. The man in question is a Labour minister called Jim Bakewell."

"He was on *Question Time*," Clarke stated. Rebus nodded slowly. He'd decided not to mention his own run-in with Andropov at the Caledonian.

"Did he talk to the poet?" Clarke asked.

"I don't think so. Cafferty bought Todorov a drink at the bar, then, when the poet hoofed it, he went and joined Andropov and Bakewell at their table. I sat where they'd been sitting — there's a blind spot, doubtful Andropov saw Todorov."

"Coincidence?" Goodyear offered.

"We've not much room for that in CID," Rebus told him.

"Doesn't that mean you often see connections where none exist?"

"Everything's connected, Todd. Six degrees of

separation, they call it. I'd've thought a Bible-thumper would concur."

"I've never thumped a Bible in my life."

"You should try it — good way of letting off steam."

"When you two boys have quite finished," Clarke chided them. "You want us to talk to this Bakewell character?" she asked Rebus.

"At this rate, we'd be as well precognosing the whole Parliament," Goodyear stated.

"How do you mean?" Rebus asked.

So then it was their turn to tell him about their morning: Roddy Denholm's project and the Urban Regeneration Committee recordings. As if to prove the point, Goodyear held up a box of DAT tapes.

"Now if only we had a player," he said.

"One's on its way from Howdenhall," Clarke reminded him.

"Hours and hours of fun," he muttered, laying the small cassettes out in a row across the desk in front of him. He stood them on their sides, as if attempting to build a run of dominoes.

"I think the allure of CID is beginning to wane," Rebus suggested to Clarke.

"You could be right," she agreed, giving the desk a nudge so that the tape cases fell over.

"Think we need to talk to Megan Macfarlane again?" was Rebus's next question.

"On what grounds?"

"That she probably knew Riordan. Funny she has links to both the victims . . ."

Clarke was nodding, without looking entirely convinced. "This case is a bloody minefield," she eventually groaned, turning back to the Murder Wall. Rebus noticed for the first time that a photo of Charles Riordan had been added to the collection.

"A single killer?" he suggested.

"Let me just go ask the Ouija board," she shot back.

"Not in front of the children," Rebus teased her. Goodyear had found a biscuit wrapper on the floor and was tidying it into the bin.

"We've got cleaners to do that, Todd," Rebus reminded him. Then, to Siobhan Clarke: "One killer or two?"

"I really don't know."

"Close enough — the correct answer should be 'doesn't matter.' All that's important at this stage is that we're treating the two deaths as connected."

She nodded her agreement. "Macrae's going to want the team enlarged."

"The more the merrier."

But when her eyes drilled into his, he could see she wasn't confident. She'd never led a full-scale inquiry before. The death at the G8 last year had been kept low-key, so as not to grab headlines. But once the media got to hear that they were dealing with a double murder, they'd be resetting their front pages and demanding plenty of action and a quick result.

"Macrae's going to want a DI heading it up," Clarke stated. Rebus wished Goodyear wasn't there — the pair of them could talk properly. He shook his head.

"Make your case," he said. "If you've anyone in mind for the team, tell him. That way you get the people you want."

"I've already got the people I want."

"Aww, isn't that sweet? But what the public needs to hear is that there's a twenty-strong force of detectives prowling the badlands, hot on the villain's scent. Five of

us in a room in Gayfield Square doesn't have the same
ring to it."

"Five was enough for Enid Blyton," Clarke said with
a thin smile.

"Worked for Scooby-Doo, too," Goodyear added.

"Only if you include the dog," Clarke corrected him.
Then, to Rebus: "So who do I start annoying first—
Macrae, Macfarlane, or Jim Bakewell?"

"Go for the hat trick," he told her. The phone on his
desk started ringing, and he picked it up.

"DI Rebus," he announced to the caller. He pursed
his lips, gave a couple of grunts in response to whatever
was being said, and let the receiver clatter back into its
cradle.

"The chiefs are demanding a sacrifice," he explained,
hauling himself to his feet.

James Corbyn, Chief Constable of Lothian and Borders
Police, was waiting for Rebus in his office on the second
floor of the Fettes Avenue HQ. Corbyn was in his early
forties, a parting in his black hair and a face that shone
as though freshly shaved and cologned. People usually
paid too much attention to the Chief Constable's groom-
ing, as a way of not staring at the oversized mole on his
right cheek. Officers had noticed that, when interviewed
on TV, he always stayed right of screen, so that the other
side of his face would be in profile. There had even been
discussion as to whether the blemish most resembled the
coastline of Fife or a terrier's head. His initial nickname
of Trouser Press had soon been supplanted by the more
telling Mole Man, which Rebus seemed to think was
also the name of a cartoon villain. He'd met Corbyn only
three or four times, never (so far) for a pat on the back or

a congratulatory handshake. Nothing he'd heard over the phone had suggested a change of script this time round.

"In you come, then," Corbyn himself snapped, having opened his door just wide enough to stick his head around. By the time Rebus rose from the corridor's only chair and pushed the door all the way open, Corbyn was back behind his large and unfeasibly tidy desk. There was a man seated across from the Chief Constable. He was bulky and balding, with an overfed face tinged pink by hypertension. He rose up just long enough to shake Rebus's hand, introducing himself as Sir Michael Addison.

"She works fast, your stepdaughter," Rebus told the banker. And Addison was no slouch himself; no more than ninety minutes since Rebus had left Gill Morgan's flat, and here they all were. "Nice to have friends, isn't it?"

"Gill's explained everything," Addison was saying. "Seems she's fallen in with a bad lot, but her mother and I will deal with that."

"Her mother knows, does she?" Rebus decided to probe.

"We're hoping that may not be necessary . . ."

"Wouldn't want her falling off the wagon," Rebus agreed.

The banker seemed stunned by this; Corbyn took the silence as his cue. "Look, John, I can't see what you've got to gain from pressing the point." His use of Rebus's first name was a message that they were all on the same side here.

"What point might that be, sir?" Rebus asked, refusing to play along.

"You know what I mean. Young girls are susceptible . . . maybe Gill was scared to tell the truth."

"Because she'd be losing her supplier?" Rebus pretended to guess. He turned towards Addison. "The friend's called Nancy Sievewright, by the way — mean anything to you?"

"I've never met her."

"One of your colleagues has, though — name of Roger Anderson. Seems he can't keep away from her."

"I know Roger," Addison admitted. "He was there when that poet's body was found."

"Found by Nancy Sievewright," Rebus stressed.

"And does any of this," Corbyn broke in, "really concern Gill?"

"She lied to a murder inquiry."

"And now she's told you the truth," Corbyn pressed. "Surely that's good enough?"

"Not really, sir." He turned to Addison. "Here's another name for you — Stuart Janney."

"Yes?"

"He works for you, too."

"He works for the bank rather than for me personally."

"And spends his days hanging out with MSPs and trying to protect dodgy Russians."

"Now wait a minute." Addison's fleshy face had gone from pink to red, highlighting razor rash at the neck.

"I've just been talking with my colleagues," Rebus plowed on, "about how everything's connected. Country the size of Scotland, city as small as Edinburgh, you start to see the truth of it. Your bank's hoping to do some big deals with the Russians, isn't it? Maybe you took some time out of your busy schedule for a round of golf with them at Gleneagles? Stuart Janney making sure everything went smoothly . . . ?"

"I really don't see what any of this has to do with my stepdaughter."

"Might be a bit embarrassing if it turns out she's linked to the Todorov murder . . . doesn't matter how many degrees of separation you try to make out there are. She leads straight to you, straight to the top of FAB. Don't suppose Andropov and his pals will be too thrilled with that."

Corbyn banged his fists against the table, eyes like burning coals. Addison was shaking, levering himself to his feet. "This was a mistake," he was saying. "I blame myself for not wanting to see her hurt."

"Michael," Corbyn started to say, but then broke off, having nothing with which to finish the sentence.

"I notice your stepdaughter hasn't taken your surname, sir," Rebus said. "Doesn't stop her asking for favors, though, does it? And that lovely apartment of hers—owned by the bank, is it?"

Addison's overcoat and scarf were hanging on a peg behind the door, and that was his destination.

"An appeal to common decency, that's all," the banker was saying, more to himself than anyone else. He'd managed to get one arm into a sleeve but was struggling with the other. Nevertheless, his need to get out was too great, and the coat was hanging off him as he left. The door stayed open. Corbyn and Rebus were on their feet, facing each other.

"That seemed to go well," Rebus commented.

"You're a bloody fool, Rebus."

"What happened to 'John'? Reckon he'll hike your mortgage, just out of spite?"

"He's a good man — and a personal friend," Corbyn spat.

"And his stepdaughter is a lying drug user." Rebus offered a shrug. "Like they say, you can't choose your family. You *can,* however, choose your friends . . . but FAB's friends seem to be a fairly rum bunch, too."

"First Albannach is one of the few bloody success stories this country has!" Corbyn erupted again.

"Doesn't make them the good guys."

"I suppose you opt to see yourself as the 'good guy'?" Corbyn let out a jagged laugh. "Christ, you've got a nerve."

"Was there anything else, sir? Maybe a neighbor who wants CID to focus its scant resources on the theft of a garden gnome?"

"Just one last thing." Corbyn had seated himself again. His next three words were spaced evenly. "You . . . are . . . history."

"Thanks for the reminder."

"I mean it. I know you've got three days left till retirement, but you're going to spend them on suspension."

Rebus stared hard at the man. "Isn't that just a tiny bit petty and pathetic, sir?"

"In which case, you're going to love the rest of it." Corbyn took a deep breath. "If I hear you've so much as crossed the threshold at Gayfield Square, I'll demote each and every officer within your compass. What I want you to do, Rebus, is crawl away from here and tick off the days on the calendar. You're no longer a serving detective and never will be." He held out the palm of one hand. "Warrant card, please."

"Want to fight me for it?"

"Only if you're ready to spend time in the cells. I *think*

we could hold you for three days without too much trouble." The hand twitched, inviting Rebus's cooperation. "I can think of at least three chief constables before me who would love to be here right now," Corbyn cooed.

"Me, too," Rebus agreed. "We'd get a barbershop quartet going and sing about the fuckwit sitting in front of us."

"And *that*," Corbyn added triumphantly, "is the reason you're being suspended."

Rebus couldn't believe the hand was still there. "You want my warrant card," he said quietly, "send the boys round for it." He turned and headed for the door. There was a secretary standing there, clutching a file to her chest, eyes and mouth gawping. Rebus confirmed with a nod that her ears had not deceived her, and mouthed the word "fuckwit," just to be on the safe side.

Outside in the car park he unlocked his Saab, but then stood there, hand on the door handle, staring into space. For a while now, he'd known the truth — that it wasn't so much the underworld you had to fear as the *overworld*. Maybe that explained why Cafferty had, to all purposes and appearances, gone legit. A few friends in the right places and deals got done, fates decided. Never in his life had Rebus felt like an insider. From time to time he'd tried — during his years in the army and his first few months as a cop. But the less he felt he belonged, the more he came to mistrust the others around him with their games of golf and their "quiet words," their stitchups and handshakes, palm greasing and scratching of backs. Stood to reason someone like Addison would go straight to the top; he'd done it because he could, because in his world it felt entirely justified and correct. Rebus had to admit, though, he'd underestimated Corbyn, hadn't expected him to pull that particular trick. Kicked into touch until gold-watch day.

"Fuckwit," he said out loud, this time aiming the word at no one but himself.

That was that, then. End of the line, end of the job. These past weeks, he'd been trying so hard not to think about it—throwing himself into other work, *any* work. Dusting off all those old unsolveds, trying to get Siobhan interested, as if she didn't have more than enough on her plate in the here and now—a situation unlikely to change in the future. The alternative was to take the whole lot home with him . . . call it his retirement gift; something to keep his brain active when the idea of the pub didn't appeal. For three decades now, this job of his had sustained him, and all it had cost him was his marriage and a slew of friendships and shattered relationships. No way he was ever going to feel like a civilian again; too late for that; too late for him to change. He would become invisible to the world, not just to reveling teenagers.

"Fuck," he said, drawing the word out way past its natural length.

It was the casual arrogance that had flipped his switch, Addison sitting there in the full confidence of his power—and the stepdaughter's arrogance, too, in thinking one weepy phone call would make everything better. It was, Rebus realized, how things worked in the overworld. Addison had never woken from a beating in a piss-stained tenement stairwell. His stepdaughter had never worked the streets for money for her next fix and the kids' dinner. They lived in another place entirely—no doubt part of the buzz Gill Morgan got from mixing with the likes of Nancy Sievewright.

The same buzz Corbyn got from having one of the most powerful men in Europe come to him with a favor.

The same buzz Cafferty got, buying drinks for businessmen and politicians . . . Cafferty: unfinished business, and likely to remain that way if Rebus heeded Corbyn's orders. Cafferty unfettered, free to commute between underworld and overworld. Unless Rebus went back indoors right now and apologized to the Chief Constable, promising to toe the line.

The scrap heap's hurtling towards me as it is . . . give me this one last chance . . . please, sir . . . please . . .

"Aye, right," Rebus said, yanking open the car door and stabbing the key into the ignition.

23

Nancy, we're going to record this, okay?"

Sievewright's mouth twitched. "Do I need a lawyer?"

"Do you want a lawyer?"

"Dunno."

Clarke nodded for Goodyear to switch on the deck. She'd slotted home both tapes herself — one for them and one for Sievewright. But Goodyear was hesitating, and Clarke had to remind herself that he'd not done this sort of thing before. Interview Room 1 felt stuffy and sweltering, as if it was sucking all the heat from the rooms around it. The central heating pipes hissed and gurgled and couldn't be turned down. Even Goodyear had taken off his jacket, and there were damp patches beneath his arms. Yet IR3, two doors along, was freezing, maybe because IR1 was keeping all the heat to itself.

"That one and that one," she explained, pointing to the relevant buttons. He pressed them, the red light came on, and both tapes started running. Clarke identified herself and Goodyear, her final few words drowned by the scrape of his chair as he drew it in towards the desk. He gave a little grimace of apology, and she repeated herself, then asked Sievewright to state her name, before adding date and time to the recording. Formalities done with, she sat back a little in her chair. The Todorov file was in

front of her, autopsy photo uppermost. She had padded
the file itself with blank sheets of copy paper, to make
it seem more impressive and, perhaps, more threatening. Goodyear had nodded admiringly. Same went for
the postmortem photo, plucked from the Murder Wall to
remind Sievewright of the grim seriousness of the case.
The young woman certainly looked unnerved. Hawes
and Tibbet had explained nothing of their appearance at
her door, and had kept tight-lipped during the drive to
Gayfield Square. Sievewright had then been left in IR1
for the best part of forty minutes, without any offer of tea
or water. And when Clarke and Goodyear had come in,
they'd both been carrying a fresh brew—even though
Goodyear himself had insisted he wasn't thirsty.

"For effect," Clarke had told him.

Next to the file on the table sat Clarke's mobile phone,
and next to that a pad of paper and a pen. Goodyear, too,
was bringing out a notebook.

"Now then, Nancy," Clarke began. "Want to tell
us what you were really up to the night you found the
victim?"

"What?" Sievewright's mouth stayed open long after
the question had left it.

"The night you were out at your friend's flat . . ."
Clarke made show of consulting the file. "Gill Morgan."
Her eyes met Sievewright's. "Your good friend Gill."

"Yes?"

"Your story was that you'd been round to her flat and
were on your way home. But that was a lie, wasn't it?"

"No."

"Well, somebody's lying to us, Nancy."

"What's she been saying?" The voice taking on a
harder edge.

"We're led to believe, Nancy, that you were on your way *to* her flat, not from it. Did you have the drugs on you when you tripped over the body?"

"What drugs?"

"The ones you were going to share with Gill."

"She's a lying cow!"

"I thought she was your friend? Enough of a friend to stick to the story you gave her."

"She's lying," Sievewright repeated, eyes reduced to slits.

"Why would she do that, Nancy? Why would a *friend* do that?"

"You'd have to ask her."

"We already have. Thing is, her story fits with other facts in the case. A woman was seen hanging around outside the car park . . ."

"I already told you, I never saw her."

"Maybe because you *were* her?"

"I look nothing like that picture you showed me!"

"See, she was offering herself for sex, and we know why some women will do that, don't we?"

"Do we?"

"Money for drugs, Nancy."

"What?"

"You needed the money to buy drugs you could sell on to Gill."

"She'd already given me the money, you dozy cow!"

Clarke didn't bother replying, just waited for Nancy's outburst to sink in. The teenager's face crumpled, and she knew she'd said more than she should.

"What I mean is . . . ," she stumbled, but the lie wouldn't come.

"Gill Morgan gave you money to buy her some dope,"

Clarke stated. "To be honest with you—and this is for the record—I couldn't give a monkey's. Doesn't sound to me like you're some big-shot dealer. If you had been, you'd have scarpered that night rather than sticking around to wait for us. But that makes me think you didn't have anything on you at the time, which means you were either waiting to score or on your way to score."

"Yes?"

"I wouldn't mind knowing which it was."

"The second one."

"On your way to meet your dealer?"

Sievewright just nodded. "Nancy Sievewright nods," Clarke said for the benefit of the slowly spooling tapes. "So you weren't hanging around outside the car park?"

"I already said, didn't I?"

"Just want to make sure." Clarke made show of turning to another page in the file. "Ms. Morgan has ambitions to be an actress," she stated.

"Yeah."

"Ever seen her in anything?"

"Don't think she's *been* in anything."

"You sound skeptical."

"First she was going to write for the papers, then it was TV presenting, then modeling . . ."

"What we might call a gadfly," Clarke agreed.

"You call it what you want."

"Must be fun, though, hanging out with her?"

"She gets good invites," Sievewright admitted.

"But she doesn't always take you with her?" Clarke guessed.

"Not often." Sievewright shifted in her chair.

"I forget, how did you two meet?"

"At a party in the New Town . . . got talking to one

of her pals in a pub, and he said I could tag along with them."

"You know who Gill's father is?"

"I know he must have a few quid."

"He runs a bank."

"Figures."

Clarke turned to another sheet of paper. Really, she wanted Rebus there, so she could bounce ideas off him and let him do some of the running while she collected her thoughts between rounds. Todd Goodyear looked stiff and uncertain and was gnawing away at his pen like a beaver with a particularly juicy length of timber.

"She works on one of the city's ghost tours, did you know that?" Clarke asked eventually.

"Can I get a drink or something?"

"We're nearly done."

Sievewright scowled, like a kid on the verge of a major sulk. Clarke repeated her question.

"She took me along with her one time," the teenager admitted.

"How was it?"

Sievewright shrugged. "Okay, I suppose. Bit boring, really."

"You weren't scared?" The question received a snorted response. Clarke closed the file slowly, as if winding up. But she had a few more questions. She waited until Sievewright was readying to get up before asking the first of them. "Remember the cloak Gill wears?"

"What cloak?"

"When she's being the Mad Monk."

"What about it?"

"Ever seen it at her flat?"

"No."

"Has she ever been to your flat?"

"Came to a party once."

Clarke pretended to spend a few moments considering this. "You know I'm not going to be chasing you for drugs offenses, Nancy, but I wouldn't mind knowing your dealer's address."

"No chance." The teenager sounded adamant. She was still poised to get up; in her mind, she was already leaving, meaning she'd want to give quick answers to any further questions. Clarke rapped her fingernails against the closed file.

"But you know him pretty well?"

"Says who?"

"I'm guessing you had some dope on you at that first party; explains how you made friends so quickly."

"So?"

"So you're not going to give me a name?"

"Bloody right I'm not."

"How did you meet him?"

"Through a friend."

"Your flatmate? The one with the eyeliner?"

"None of your business."

"The day I was there, quite an aroma was wafting from the living room . . ." Sievewright stayed tight-lipped. "You in touch with your parents, Nancy?"

The question seemed to throw the young woman. "Dad did a runner when I was ten."

"And your mum?"

"Lives in Wardieburn."

Not the city's most salubrious neighborhood. "See her much?"

"Is this turning into a social work interview?"

Clarke smiled indulgently. "Had any more trouble from Mr. Anderson?"

"Not yet."

"You think he'll be back?"

"He better think twice."

"Funny thing is, he works for Gill's dad's bank."

"So what?"

"Gill's never taken you to any of their parties? No possibility Mr. Anderson could have met you there?"

"No," Sievewright stated. Clarke let the silence linger, then leaned back in her chair and placed her palms on the tabletop.

"Again, just to be clear, you're not a prostitute and he's not one of your clients?" Sievewright glared at her, forming some sort of comeback. Clarke didn't give her the chance. "I think that's us, then," she said. "I want to thank you for coming in."

"Didn't have much choice," Sievewright complained.

"Interview ends at . . ." Clarke checked the time, announced it for the benefit of the recorder, then switched the machine off and ejected both tapes, sealing them in separate polythene bags. She handed one to Sievewright. "Thanks again." The young woman snatched the bag. "PC Goodyear will see you out."

"Do I get a lift home?"

"What are we, a taxi service?"

Sievewright gave a curl of the lip, letting Clarke know what she thought of that. Goodyear led her outside, while Clarke gave a twitch of her head to let him know she'd see him upstairs. Once the door was closed, Clarke lifted her phone to her ear.

"You caught all of that?"

"Pretty much," Rebus's voice said. She could hear him lighting up.

"This is going to cost us both a fortune in phone bills."

"That depends on where you do the interviews," he told her. "Anywhere outside the station, I can sit in. It's only Gayfield itself Corbyn told me to avoid."

Clarke slipped the cassette tape into the file and tucked it under her arm. "Do you think I got everything I could out of her?" she asked.

"You did fine. It was good to leave some of the big questions till the end . . . had me wondering if you were going to remember to ask them."

"Did I leave anything out?"

"Not that I can think of."

She was out in the corridor now, glad to find it about eight degrees cooler.

"One thing, though," Rebus was adding. "Why did you ask about her parents?"

"Not sure really. Maybe it's because we see so many like her — single-parent household, mum probably holding down a job, giving the daughter time to be led astray . . ."

"Are you going to go all liberal on me?"

"Growing up in Wardieburn . . . and then suddenly you're going to parties in the New Town."

"And pushing drugs," Rebus reminded her. Clarke shouldered open the door to the car park. He was there in his Saab, phone to his ear and a cigarette in his other hand. She folded her phone shut as she opened the passenger-side door and slid in, closing it after her. Rebus had put his own phone back in his pocket.

"That everything?" he asked, holding out a hand for the file.

"As much as I could photocopy without the troops suspecting."

He removed the inch-deep block of unsullied copy paper. "You learned all the right tricks, Kwai Chang Caine."

"Does that make you Master Po?"

"Didn't think you were old enough for *Kung Fu*."

"Old enough for the reruns." She watched him place the file on the back seat. "All through the interview, I was praying you wouldn't cough or sneeze."

"Couldn't risk lighting a ciggie either," Rebus replied. She stared at him, but he was avoiding eye contact.

"How come," she asked eventually, "you couldn't play nice, just this once?"

"People like Corbyn seem to push my buttons," he explained.

"Making them part of the majority," she chided him.

"Maybe so," he admitted. "Are you going to interview Bakewell at the Parliament?" She nodded slowly. "Am I invited?"

"Remind me, what does it mean to be 'on suspension'?"

"Last time I looked, Shiv, the public were allowed into the Parliament building. Buy the man a coffee, and I could be seated at the next table over."

"Or you could go home and let me talk to Corbyn, see if I can change his mind."

"Won't happen," he stated.

"Which — you going home or him changing his mind?"

"Both."

"God give me strength," she sighed.

"Amen to that . . . and speaking of the Almighty, I didn't hear much from young Todd during the interview."

"He was there to observe."

"It's all right, you know . . . you can admit that you missed me."

"Weren't you just saying that I covered all the bases?"

She watched Rebus shrug. "Maybe there were bases she kept hidden from us."

"You're telling me you'd have teased the dealer's name out of her?"

"Twenty quid says I'll have it by day's end."

"If Corbyn gets wind that you're still on the case . . ."

"But I won't be, DS Clarke. I'll be a civilian. Not much he can do about that, is there?"

"John . . . ," she began to caution, but broke off, knowing she'd be wasting her breath. "Keep me posted," she muttered at last, opening the car door and easing herself out.

"Notice something?" he asked. She leaned back down into the car.

"What?"

He waved his arm, taking in the car park. "The smell's gone. . . . Wonder if that's an omen." He was smiling as he turned the key in the ignition, leaving Clarke with an unasked question:

Good omen or bad?

24

"Nancy at home?" Rebus asked Sievewright's flatmate when the young man answered the door.

"No."

No, because she'd been walking up Leith Street when Rebus had passed her in his Saab. Meaning he had maybe a twenty-minute start on her, always supposing she'd head straight for her flat.

"It's Eddie, right?" Rebus said. "I was here a few days ago."

"I remember."

"Didn't catch your surname, though."

"Gentry."

"As in Bobbie Gentry."

"Not many people know her these days."

"I'm older than most people—got a couple of her albums at home. Mind if I come in?" Rebus noted that Gentry had lost his bandanna but still wore the smudgy eyeliner. "She told me to be here at three," he lied blithely.

"Someone was at the door for her a while back . . ." Gentry was reluctant, but Rebus's stare told him resistance was futile. He opened the door a little wider, and Rebus gave a little bow of the head as he walked in. The living room smelled of stale tobacco and something that could have been patchouli oil—been awhile since Rebus had come across that particular scent. He wandered over to the window and peered down onto Blair Street.

"Tell you a funny story," he said, back still to Eddie Gentry. "There's a warren of basements across the way where bands used to practice. Owner was thinking of re-developing, so he got some builders in. They were work-ing in these tunnels — miles and miles of them — and they started to hear unearthly groans . . ."

"The massage parlor next door," Gentry said, cutting to the punch line.

"You've heard it." Rebus turned from the window and studied some of the album sleeves — actual LPs rather than CDs. "Caravan," he commented. "Canterbury's fin-est . . . didn't know people still listened to them." There were other sleeves he recognized: the Fairports and Davey Graham and Pentangle.

"Somebody studying archaeology?" he guessed.

"I like a lot of the old stuff," Gentry explained. He nodded towards the corner of the room. "I play guitar."

"So you do," Rebus agreed, seeing a six-string acous-tic nestling on its stand, a twelve-string lying on the floor behind it. "Any good?"

In answer, Gentry picked up the six-string and settled on the sofa, legs crossed beneath him. He started to play, and Rebus realized that he'd grown the fingernails long on his right hand, each one a ready-made plectrum. Rebus knew the tune, even if he couldn't place it.

"Bert Jansch?" he guessed over the closing chord.

"From that album he did with John Renbourn."

"Haven't listened to it in years." Rebus nodded his appreciation. "You're pretty good, son. Shame you can't make a living from it, eh? Might have stopped you from dealing drugs."

"What?"

"Nancy's told us all about it."

"Whoa, wait a minute." Gentry put his guitar aside and rose to his feet. "What's that you're saying?"

"A deaf musician?" Rebus sounded impressed.

"I heard the words, I just don't know why she would say that."

"Night the poet was killed, she was picking up a delivery from the guy you introduced her to."

"She didn't say that." Gentry was trying to sound confident, but his eyes told Rebus a different story. "I didn't introduce her to *anybody!*"

Rebus shrugged with his hands in his pockets. "No skin off my nose," he commented. "She says you're dealing, you say you're not. . . . We all know there's stuff being smoked here."

"Stuff she gets from her boyfriend," Gentry burst out. But then he corrected himself. "He's not even her boyfriend . . . she just thinks he is."

"Who's this?"

"I don't know. I mean, he's been here a couple of times, but he just calls himself Sol—says it's Latin for 'the sun.' Not that he strikes me as *that* bright."

Rebus laughed as if this were the best joke he'd heard in a while, but Gentry wasn't smiling.

"I can't *believe* she'd try dropping me in it," he muttered to himself.

"She dropped a pal of hers in it, too," Rebus revealed. "Got her to provide an alibi." Rebus let his final word hang in the air.

"Alibi?" Gentry echoed. "Christ, you think *she* killed that guy?"

Rebus offered another shrug. "Tell me," he said, "does

Nancy own anything like a cape or a cloak? Sort of thing a monk might wear?"

"No." Gentry sounded bewildered by the question.

"Have you ever met her friend Gill?"

"Hooray Henrietta from the New Town?" Gentry screwed up his face.

"You know her, then?"

"She came to a party awhile back."

"I hear that she throws a good party, too. You could offer to play a set."

"I'd rather stick pins in my eyes."

"You're probably right, same as I'd rather listen to Dick Gaughan than James Blunt." Rebus sniffed loudly, drawing a handkerchief from his pocket. "This Sol character . . . got an address for him?"

"Afraid not."

"Not to worry." Rebus was over at the window again, putting the handkerchief back as he gazed down on the street. Not long now till Nancy Sievewright returned. Top of Leith Street, then North Bridge and Hunter Square. . . . "Do you sing as well as play?"

"A little bit."

"But not in a band?"

"No."

"You should get yourself up to Fife. Friend of mine says there's some sort of acoustic scene up there."

Gentry was nodding. "I've played Anstruther."

"Funny to think of the East Neuk as the center of anything . . . used to be it was shut winter and weekends."

Gentry smiled. "Wait there, will you?" He was gone from the living room less than a minute. When he came back, he was holding something out towards Rebus — a CD in a clear plastic pocket. There was a folded square of white paper with the titles of three tracks listed. "My demo," Gentry announced proudly.

"That's great," Rebus said. "After I've played it, do you want it back?"

"I can burn another one," Gentry said with a shake of the head.

Rebus patted the disc against the palm of his left hand. "I really appreciate that, Eddie. As long as *you* appreciate that it's not a bung of some kind."

Gentry looked horrified. "No, I just thought . . ."

But Rebus touched him on the shoulder and assured him he was only joking. "I'd best be off," he said. "Thanks again." He gave a little wave with the CD and made for the hallway and the front door. With the door closed behind him, he started down the stairs, just as Nancy Sievewright was making her way up, still holding the sealed polythene bag with the interview tape inside. Rebus offered her a nod and a smile but said nothing. All the same, he could feel her watching his descent. At the bottom, he looked up— sure enough, she hadn't moved.

"Just told him," Rebus called to her.

"Told who what?" she called back.

"Your flatmate, Eddie," he answered. "The one you tried fobbing us off with . . ."

He exited the tenement and unlocked his car. It was parked illegally but had managed to avoid a ticket.

"My lucky day," he told himself. He'd finally got round to installing a CD player in the Saab. He drew Gentry's offering from its sleeve and slotted it home, then studied the titles of the songs.

"Meg's Mons."

"Minstrel in Pain."

"Reverend Walker Blues."

He liked them already. With the volume low, he took out his phone and called Siobhan Clarke.

"Tell me you're in the pub" was her opening line.

"Blair Street, actually — and you owe me twenty notes."

"I don't believe you."

"You won't when I tell you." He paused for dramatic effect. "Sievewright gets her stuff from someone called Sol. Her flatmate thinks he's named himself after the sun, but we know differently, don't we?"

"Sol Goodyear?"

"I take it Todd's not within earshot?"

"Making me a coffee."

"Isn't that sweet of him?"

"Sol Goodyear?" she repeated, as if she still couldn't take it in. Eventually, she asked him what he was listening to.

"Nancy's flatmate plays guitar."

"I'm assuming he's not in the car with you."

"Probably shouting the odds at Sievewright as we speak. But he did give me a demo he made."

"That was good of him. Bet you can't remember the last time you listened to anything made after 1975."

"You gave me that Elbow album . . ."

"True." The tangent had run its course. "So now we need to add Todd's brother to the list?"

"Nice to stay busy," Rebus consoled her. "Do you have a time for Jim Bakewell yet?"

"Haven't been able to track him down."

"And Macrae?"

"Wants to add another twenty or so bodies to the team."

"As long as they're warm ones . . ."

"He's even thinking of bringing Derek Starr back from Fettes."

"Which would mean relegating you to vice-captain?"

"If only I had some vices . . ."

"Should have listened to me, Shiv. I could've given you a few tips. Will I see you later at the pub?"

"Might have an early night actually . . . no offense."

"None taken, but don't think I'll forget about that twenty." Rebus ended the call and turned the music up a little. Gentry was humming along to the melody, and Rebus wasn't sure if it was meant to be picked up by the mic. It was still the first track, "Meg's Mons." He wondered if Meg was a real woman. Peering at the slip of paper in the clear plastic sleeve, he thought he could make out writing on the other side. He pulled out the track listing and unfolded it. Sure enough, on the back was written the name of the studio where Gentry had recorded his demo.

CR Studios.

25

Rebus sat in front of his own personal video monitor. Graeme MacLeod had placed him in a corner of the room and had piled the videotapes next to him. Edinburgh city center's west end, the night of the Todorov killing.

"You're going to get me shot," MacLeod had complained, fetching the tapes from their locked cupboard.

Rebus had been sitting for an hour in the Central Monitoring Facility, sometimes hitting Search and sometimes Pause. There were cameras on Shandwick Place, Princes Street, and Lothian Road. Rebus was looking for evidence of Sergei Andropov or his driver, or maybe Cafferty. Or anyone else attached to the case, come to that. So far he had nothing at all to show for his efforts. The hotel would have its own surveillance, of course, but he doubted the manager would hand it over without a fight, and he couldn't see himself persuading Siobhan to put in the request.

There was something soothing about the unhurried voyeurism going on around him. One act of vandalism reported, and one known shoplifter tracked along George Street. The camera operators seemed as passive as any daytime TV viewers, and Rebus wondered if there might be some reality show to be made from it. He liked the way the staff could control the remote cameras using a joystick, zooming in on anything suspicious. It didn't feel like the police state the media were always predicting. All the same, if he worked here every day, he'd be careful of himself on the street, for fear of being caught picking his nose or scratching his backside. Careful in shops and restaurants, too.

And probably with no interest in the TV at home.

MacLeod was back at Rebus's shoulder. "Anything?" he asked.

"I know you've been over this footage more than once, Graeme, but there are a few faces I may know that you don't."

"I'm not having a moan."

"If I were in your shoes, I'd be thinking the same."

"Just a pity we didn't have a camera in King's Stables Road."

"Hardly anyone uses it at night, I've noticed that. Plenty of people turning into Castle Terrace, but almost no one into King's Stables."

"And no woman in a hood?"

"Not yet."

MacLeod consoled Rebus with a pat on the shoulder, then went back to work. It didn't make sense to Rebus: why would some woman be hanging around there, doling out offers of sex? They had only the one witness's word for it. Could it have been some fantasy he'd been harboring? Rebus felt his vertebrae snap back into place as he stretched his spine. He wanted a break, but knew if he took one he might not be tempted back. He could always go home — it was what everybody wanted. But then his phone rang, and he scooped it from his pocket. Caller ID: Siobhan.

"What's up?" he asked, cupping the phone to his mouth so he wouldn't be overheard.

"Megan Macfarlane's just called DCI Macrae. She's not happy you've been harassing Sergei Andropov." She paused. "Want to tell me about it?"

"Happened to run into him last night."

"Whereabouts?"

"Caledonian Hotel."

"Your regular watering hole?"

"No need for sarcasm, young lady."

"And you didn't think to let me in on it?"

"I really did just bump into him, Shiv. No big deal."

"To you maybe, but Andropov seems to think it is, and now Megan Macfarlane thinks so, too."

"Andropov's Russian, probably used to politicians controlling the police . . ." Rebus was thinking out loud.

"Macrae wants to see you."

"Tell him I'm banned from Gayfield."

"I've told him. He was furious about that, too."

"Corbyn's fault for not alerting him."

"That's what I said."

"Any word from Jim Bakewell's office?"

"No."

"So what are you up to?"

"Trying to make space for the new recruits. Four have arrived from Torphichen and two from Leith."

"Anyone we know?"

"Ray Reynolds."

"He's not even a good imitation of a detective," Rebus stated. Then he asked her if she was going to do anything about Sol Goodyear.

"Soon as I've worked out what to say to Todd," she decided.

"Good luck with that."

One of the CCTV operators suddenly called to her colleague that she had the shoplifter on Camera 10, entering the bus station. Clarke's groan was almost audible.

"You're at the City Chambers," she stated.

"We'll make a detective of you yet."

"You're on suspension, John."

"It keeps slipping my mind."

"Studying the tapes from that night?"

"Correct."

"Trying to place who at the scene exactly?"

"Who do you think?"

"Why in God's name would Cafferty want a Russian poet killed?"

"Maybe he gets annoyed when verses don't rhyme. By the by, here's a strange one for you—that CD Sievewright's flatmate gave me was recorded at Riordan's studio."

"Yet another coincidence." But she was silent for a moment. "Think it's worth talking to the engineer about?"

"You're mob-handed, Shiv—it's worth chasing every single lead, no matter how brittle."

"I'm not great at delegating."

"Me neither. Still headed straight home from work?"

"That's the plan."

"I'll be thinking of you, then."

"John, just promise me one thing—no more drinks at the Caledonian Hotel."

"Yes, boss. Talk to you later." He ended the call but sat there staring at the phone. Macrae, Macfarlane, and Andropov—all annoyed as hell with him.

"Good," he said quietly, reaching for the next videotape.

*   *   *

"Can I ask you about your brother?"

Clarke had led Todd Goodyear into the corridor for a bit of privacy. She'd already set the new recruits to work. Some were studying the "bible" — the collating of everything pertaining to the case — while others had been assigned the Riordan tapes. It wasn't exactly a collection of the brightest and the best — no CID unit wanted to give up its star players to a rival team. A detective from Goodyear's own station had recognized him and asked what he thought he was up to, "masquerading as a proper cop."

"Sol?" Goodyear was asking now, looking puzzled. "What about him?"

"He was in a fight — what night was that?"

"Last Wednesday."

Clarke nodded. Same night Todorov was attacked. "Can you give me an address for him?"

"What's going on?"

"Turns out he might know Nancy Sievewright."

"You're kidding me." He'd started laughing.

"No joke," she assured him. "We think he was her dealer. Did you know he was still in the game?"

"No." The blood was rising up Goodyear's neck.

"So I need his address."

"I don't know it. I mean, it's somewhere around the Grassmarket . . ."

"I thought he lived in Dalkeith."

"Sol's always on the move."

"How did you know he'd been in a fight?"

"He called me."

"So you're still in touch?"

"He has my mobile number."

"Meaning you've got his?"

Goodyear shook his head. "He keeps changing it."

"This fight he had . . . any idea where it happened?"

"A pub in Haymarket."

Clarke nodded to herself. The SOCO, Tam Banks, had got a message about the incident, hadn't he? Mentioned it at the Todorov scene. A stabbing. . . . "So you don't keep in touch, but he phones you when he's been stabbed?"

Goodyear ignored this. "What does it matter if he knows Nancy Sievewright?"

"Just another loose end that needs tying."

"We've got more of those than a frayed rug." Clarke offered up a tired smile, and Goodyear sighed, shoulders slumping. "When you find Sol's address, do you want me along?"

"Can't happen," she said. "You're his brother."

He nodded his understanding.

"I'm assuming West End took an interest in the stabbing?" she asked. Meaning the police station on Torphichen Place. Goodyear nodded again.

"They asked him a few questions at A&E. By the time I saw him, he'd been transferred to a ward. Just the one night, for observation."

"Do you think he told the officers anything?"

Goodyear shrugged. "All he said was, he was having a drink and this guy took against him. It moved outside, and Sol came off worst."

"And the other guy?"

"Didn't say anything about him." Goodyear bit his bottom lip. "If Sol's connected . . . does that mean a conflict of interest? Back to my old station and uniform?"

"I'll have to ask DCI Macrae."

He nodded again, but dolefully this time. "I didn't

know he was still dealing," he stressed. "Maybe Sieve-wright's lying . . ."

Clarke imagined herself placing a hand on his arm, offering comfort. But in the real world, she just moved past him and back into the already overcrowded CID suite. Chairs had been borrowed from the interview rooms, and she had to weave between them as she made for her desk. There was another officer stationed there. He apologized but didn't move. Three more detectives were huddled around Rebus's desk. Clarke picked up her phone and called Torphichen. She was patched through to CID and found herself talking to Detective Inspector Shug Davidson.

"Want to thank you," he chuckled, "for taking Ray Reynolds off our hands." She looked across the room towards Reynolds, a detective constable these past nine years, promotion never on the cards. He was standing in front of the Murder Wall and rubbing his stomach as if preparing for another of his infamous belches.

"That's good," she told Davidson, "because I'm after a favor in return."

"What's this I hear about John getting booted into touch?"

"News travels . . ."

"Age has not softened him—that's a quote from somewhere."

"Listen, Shug, do you remember last Wednesday night, a fight outside a pub at Haymarket?"

"Sol Goodyear, you mean?"

"That's right."

"You've got his brother on secondment, I'm told. Seems like a decent bloke. I think he's embarrassed about Sol—and rightly so. Sol's got a fair bit of form."

"So this fight he got into . . . ?"

"If you ask me, there was money owed by one of his punters. Guy didn't fancy paying up, so decided to have a go at Sol. We're considering making it attempted murder."

"Todd says he was only in hospital the one night."

"With eight stitches in his side. More of a slice than a proper stabbing, meaning he got lucky."

"You caught the attacker?"

"He's pleading self-defense, naturally. Name's Larry Fintry—Crazy Larry, he gets called. Should be in the nuthouse, if you ask me."

"Care in the community, Shug."

"Aye, with the pharmaceuticals dispensed by Sol Goodyear."

"I need to speak to Sol," Clarke said.

"Why's that?"

"The Todorov murder. We think the girl who found the body was on her way to Sol's."

"More than likely," Davidson agreed. "Last address I have for him is Raeburn Wynd."

Clarke's whole body froze for a moment. "That's where we found the body."

"I know." Davidson was laughing. "And if Sol hadn't been getting himself stabbed at Haymarket around the exact same time, I might have thought to mention it earlier."

In the end, she took Phyllida Hawes with her. Tibbet had looked distraught, as if fearing Siobhan had already made up her mind who should replace her at sergeant level when she was promoted. She hadn't bothered reminding him that she would have little or no say over anyone's fate. Instead, she had simply told him that he was in charge until her return, which perked him up a little.

They'd taken Clarke's car, sticking to shoptalk interrupted only occasionally by awkward silences — Hawes wanting to know about life post-Rebus (but not daring to ask), while Clarke didn't quite get round to bringing up Hawes's relationship with Tibbet. It was a mercy when the car finally stopped at the foot of Raeburn Wynd. The lane was L-shaped. From the main road, all you could see were garages and lockups, but around the corner, buildings which at one time would have housed horses and their coaches had been turned into mews flats.

"None of the neighbors heard anything?" Hawes asked.

"Might send the team out to ask them again and flash that e-fit," Clarke considered.

"Can Ray Reynolds be one of them, please?"

Clarke managed a smile. "Didn't take long."

"I'd heard the stories," Hawes said, "but nothing quite prepares you . . ."

They'd turned the corner into the mews proper. Clarke stopped at one of the doors, checked the address she'd copied into her notebook, and pressed the bell. After twenty seconds, she tried again.

"I'm coming!" someone yelled from within. There was the sound of feet thumping down a flight of stairs, and the door was opened by Sol Goodyear. Had to be him: same eyelashes and ears as his brother.

"Solomon Goodyear?" Clarke checked.

"Christ, what do you lot want?"

"Well spotted. I'm DS Clarke, this is DC Hawes."

"Got a warrant?"

"Want to ask you a couple of questions about the murder."

"What murder?"

"The one at the bottom of your street."

"I was in hospital at the time."

"How's the wound?"

He lifted his shirt to show a large white compress, just above the waistband of his underpants. "Itches like buggery," he admitted. Then, catching on: "How did you know about it?"

"DI Davidson at Torphichen filled me in. Mentioned Crazy Larry, too. Bit of a tip for you, actually — before you square up to someone, always check their nick-name."

Sol Goodyear snorted at that, but still didn't show any great desire to let them in. "My brother's a cop," he said instead.

"Oh, yes?" Clarke tried to sound surprised. She reckoned Sol would try this line on any police officer he met.

"He's still in uniform, but not for much longer. Todd's always been a fast-track kind of guy. He was the white sheep of the family." He gave a little laugh at what Clarke assumed was another of his well-rehearsed lines.

"That's a good one," Hawes obliged, managing to sound as though she meant the opposite. The laugh died in Sol Goodyear's throat.

"Well, anyway," he sniffed, "I wasn't here that night. They didn't discharge me till the evening after."

"Did Nancy come to see you at the hospital?"

"Nancy who?"

"Your girlfriend Nancy. She was on her way here

when she tripped over the body. You were going to sell her some stuff for a friend of hers."

"She's not my girlfriend," he stated, having decided in the blinking of an eye that there was no point lying about things they already knew.

"She seems to think she is."

"She's mistaken."

"You're just her dealer, then?"

He scowled as though pained by this turn in the conversation. "What I am, officer, is the victim of a stabbing. The painkillers I'm on make it highly unlikely that anything I say could be used in a court of law."

"Clever boy," Clarke said, sounding admiring, "you know your loopholes."

"Learned the hard way."

She nodded slowly. "I've heard it was Big Ger Cafferty got you started on the selling — do you still see him?"

"Don't know who you're talking about."

"Funny, I've never heard of a stabbing affecting someone's memory before . . ." Clarke looked to Hawes for confirmation of this.

"Think you've got the patter, don't you?" Sol Goodyear was saying. "Well try this for a payoff."

And with that, he slammed the door in their faces. From behind it, as he started climbing the stairs again, could be heard a stream of invective. Hawes raised an eyebrow.

"Bitches *and* lesbians," she repeated. "Always nice to learn something new about yourself."

"Isn't it?"

"So now we've got one brother involved, I suppose that means the other has to be taken off the case?"

"That's a decision for DCI Macrae."

"How come you didn't tell Sol we've got Todd working with us?"

"Need-to-know basis, Phyl." Clarke stared at Hawes. "You in a hurry to see the back of PC Goodyear?"

"Just so long as he remembers he *is* a PC. Now that the suite's filling up, he's looking too comfortable in that suit of his."

"Meaning what exactly?"

"Some of us have worked our way out of uniform, Siobhan."

"CID's a closed shop, is it?" Clarke turned away from Hawes and started moving, but stopped abruptly at the corner. From where she stood, it was about sixty feet to the spot where Alexander Todorov was murdered.

"What are you thinking?" Hawes asked.

"I'm wondering about Nancy. We're assuming she was on her way to Sol's when she found the body. But she could've walked up here, rung his bell a few times, maybe thumped on his door . . ."

"Not knowing he's been injured in a brawl?"

"Exactly."

"And meantime Todorov's managed to stagger from the car park . . ."

Clarke was nodding.

"You think she saw something?" Hawes added.

"Saw or heard. Maybe hid around this corner, while Todorov's attacker followed him and delivered the final blow."

"And her reason for not telling us any of this . . . ?"

"Fear, I suppose."

"Fear'll do it every time," Hawes concurred. "What was that line from Todorov's poem . . . ?"

" 'He averted his eyes/Ensuring he would not have to testify.' "

"The sort of lesson Nancy might have learned from Sol Goodyear."

"Yes," Clarke agreed. "Yes, she might."

26

Rebus was eating a bag of crisps and listening again to Eddie Gentry's CD on his car stereo. Except that it wasn't stereo exactly, one of the speakers having packed in. Didn't really matter when it was just one man and his guitar. He'd already finished the first packet of crisps, plus a curried vegetable samosa bought from a corner shop in Polwarth and washed down with a bottle of still water, which he tried to persuade himself made it a balanced meal. He was parked at the bottom end of Cafferty's street and as far as possible from any of the streetlamps. For once, he didn't want the gangster spotting him. Then again, he couldn't even be sure Cafferty was at home: the man's car was in the driveway, but that didn't mean much in itself. Some of the house lights were on, but maybe just to deter intruders. Rebus couldn't see any sign of the bodyguard who lived in the coach house to the rear of the property. Cafferty never seemed to use him much, leading Rebus to believe he was on the payroll for reasons of vanity rather than necessity. Siobhan had texted a couple of times, ostensibly to ask if he fancied supper one night. He knew she'd be wondering what he was up to.

Two hours he'd been parked there, for no good reason. The fifteen-minute break spent at the corner shop had given Cafferty ample time to head out without Rebus being any the wiser. Maybe for once the gangster would be using his room at the Caledonian. As a surveillance, it was laughable, but then he wasn't even sure it *was* a surveillance. Might be it was just a pretext for not going home, where the only thing waiting was a reissue of Johnny Cash's *Live at San Quentin* that he hadn't got round to playing. Kept forgetting to put it in the car, and wondered how it would sound on a single speaker. First stereo he'd ever owned, one of the speakers had packed in after only a month. There was a track on a Velvet Underground album, all the instruments on one channel, vocals on the other, so that he couldn't listen to both together. It had taken him ages to buy his first CD player, and even now he preferred vinyl. Siobhan said it was because he was "willful."

"Either that or I've just not got the herd mentality," he'd argued back. These days, she had an MP3 player and bought stuff online. He would tease her by asking if he could take a look at the album cover or lyric sheet.

"You're missing the big picture," he'd told her. "A good album should be more than the sum of its parts."

"Like police work?" she'd guessed, smiling. He hadn't bothered admitting that he was just coming to that . . .

He'd finished the crisps and folded the bag into a narrow strip so he could tie it into a knot. Didn't know why he did that, just seemed neater somehow. A mate back in army days had done it, and Rebus had followed suit. It made a change from putting a match under the empty packet and watching it shrivel to a miniature version of itself, like something from a doll's house. Simple pleasures, same as sitting in a car on a quiet nighttime street, music playing and belly full. He would give it another hour. He had the Who's *Endless Wire* for when he got fed up of Gentry. Hadn't yet worked out what the title meant, but because he'd bought the CD at least he had the lyrics.

A car was reversing out of some gates up the road. Looked to Rebus very much like Cafferty's gates, Cafferty's car. Being driven by the bodyguard, because there was a reading light on in the back seat, illuminating Cafferty's dome of a head. He seemed to be peering at some papers. Rebus waited. The car was turning downhill, meaning it would drive straight past him. He ducked down, waiting until its lights had passed. It signaled right, and Rebus turned the ignition, doing a three-point turn and following. At the Granville Terrace junction, Cafferty's car jumped out in front of a double-decker bus. Rebus had to wait for traffic to clear, but knew there was nothing Cafferty could do now until Leven Street. He stayed behind the bus until it signaled to pick up passengers, then moved out and past it. There was a gap of a hundred yards between him and the car in front. Eventually its brake lights glowed as it reached the traffic lights at the King's Theatre. As Rebus crawled nearer, he saw that something was wrong.

It wasn't Cafferty's car.

He drew up behind it. The car in front of it, stopped on red, wasn't Cafferty either. No way the bodyguard could have passed both cars and got through the lights while they were still on green. Rebus had been behind the bus for maybe a couple of minutes. There had been the Viewforth crossroads, but he'd looked both ways and seen no sign of Cafferty. Had to have turned sharpish down one of the narrow side streets, but which one? He did another three-point turn, a taxi sounding a complaint as it waited to follow him back along Gilmore Place. There were a

few boardinghouses whose front gardens had been paved
and turned into car parking, but none of the vehicles
matched Cafferty's Bentley.

"You wait two solid hours and then you lose him
at the first hurdle," Rebus muttered to himself. There
was a convent, its gates open, but Rebus doubted he'd
find the gangster there. Roads off to left and right, but
none looked promising. At the Viewforth traffic lights
he turned the car again. This time he signaled left and
headed down a narrow one-way street towards the canal.
It wasn't well lit and wouldn't be used much this time of
night, meaning he'd stick out like a sore thumb, so when
a curbside parking space appeared, he reversed into it.
There was a bridge across the canal, but it was blocked
to everything except bikes and pedestrians. As Rebus
headed that way on foot, he finally saw the Bentley. It
was parked up next to some wasteland. A couple of canal
boats were moored for the night, smoke billowing from
the chimney of one of them. Rebus hadn't been down
this way in ages. New blocks of flats had appeared from
somewhere, but it didn't look as though many of them
were occupied. Then he saw a sign stating that they were
"serviced apartments." The Leamington Lift Bridge was
a construction of wrought iron with a wooden roadway. It
could be raised to let barges and pleasure boats through,
but otherwise lay level with either bank of the canal. Two
men were standing in the middle of it, their shadows
thrown onto the water by a near-as-dammit full moon.
Cafferty was doing the talking, throwing out his arms to
illustrate each point. The focus of his interest seemed to
be the canal's far bank. There was a walkway stretching
from Fountainbridge to the city limits and beyond. At one
time it had been a treacherous spot, but a new footpath

had been built and the canal seemed a lot cleaner than
Rebus remembered it. Beyond the footpath stood a high
wall, behind which, Rebus knew, was one of Edinburgh's
redundant industrial sites. Until about a year back, it had
been a brewery, but now most of the buildings were in
the process of being dismantled, the steel mash tuns removed. Time was, the city had boasted thirty or forty
breweries. Now, Rebus seemed to think there was just the
one, not too far away on Slateford Road.

When the other man half turned to concentrate on
what Cafferty was saying, Rebus recognized the silhou-
ette of Sergei Andropov's distinctive face. The door to
Cafferty's car opened, but only so his driver could get
out to light a cigarette. Rebus heard another door, almost
like an echo of the first. He decided to pretend he was on
his way home, tucked his hands into his jacket, hunched
his shoulders, and started walking. Risking just the one
glance back over his shoulder, he saw that there was another car parked alongside Cafferty's. Andropov's driver
had decided on a cigarette break, too. Cafferty and the
Russian, meantime, had crossed the bridge and were still
deep in conversation. Rebus wished he'd thought to bring
a microphone of some kind — the engineer at Riordan's
studio would have obliged. As it was, he couldn't make
out anything. What was more, he was headed away from
the scene, and it would raise suspicions were he suddenly
to turn and retrace his steps. He passed a car workshop,
locked up tight for the night. Past it were some tenement
flats. He thought about going inside, climbing a flight, and
peering from the stairwell window. Instead, he stopped
and lit a cigarette, then pretended to take a phone call,
holding the mobile close to his face. He started walking
again, but slowly, aware of the two men on the opposite

bank. Andropov gave a whistle, and gestured to the drivers to stay put. Rebus saw that the canal was coming to an end at a recently built basin, complete with a couple of more permanent-looking barges, one of which had a For Sale sign taped to its only window. New buildings had been thrown up here, too: office blocks, restaurants, and a bar with plenty of glass frontage and outside tables, which were being used tonight only by hardened smokers. One of the units was still to let, and Rebus couldn't see much action in the restaurants. The bar had a cash machine to one side of it, and he paused to use it, risking another glance towards the approaching figures.

But they weren't there anymore.

He looked in through the windows of the bar and saw that they were removing their coats. Even from here, Rebus could hear pounding music. Several TV sets were also on the go, and the clientele was predominantly young and studenty. The only person who paid attention to the new arrivals was their waitress, who bounded over with a smile and took their order. No way Rebus could go in — the place wasn't so busy that he'd be able to hide in the throng. And even supposing he did go in, he'd never get close enough to hear anything. Cafferty had chosen wisely: not even Riordan would have stood a chance. The two men could have a chat without fear of eavesdroppers. What to do next . . . ? Plenty of dark corners out here, meaning he could bide his time and freeze his backside. Or he could retreat to his car. The two men would have to return to their own cars eventually. With a hundred quid extracted from the machine, Rebus made his choice. He walked back along the other side of the canal, crossed at the Leamington Bridge, and hummed to himself as he passed the piece of wasteground. Not that the two drivers paid any attention, they were too busy talking to each other. Rebus doubted Cafferty's man spoke any Russian, meaning Andropov's driver must have a decent grasp of English.

Once installed in the Saab, Rebus considered switching the engine on, so he could have some heat. But an idling motor might make the guards curious, so he rubbed his hands together and drew his coat more tightly around him. It was a further twenty minutes before anything happened. He hadn't caught sight of Andropov and Cafferty, but both cars were on the move. He followed them back to Gilmore Place. They signaled to turn right at the Viewforth junction, and then right again at Dundee Street. Two minutes later they were pulling to a halt outside the bar. While one of its sides faced the canal, the other fronted Fountainbridge. Traffic here was busier, with plenty of parked cars. Rebus found a space near the old Co-op Funeral Home. Major works were in progress, and one building had lost everything but its façade, while a new construction rose up to fill the space behind. It was all insurance companies and banks around here, Rebus seemed to think, which made him think also of Sir Michael Addison, Stuart Janney, and Roger Anderson—First Albannach men all. In his wing mirror, he could see that the two cars were idling but hadn't bothered to switch off their lights or engines. Give it a couple of years, he'd probably be empowered to arrest them under some CO_2 injunction. Except that he wouldn't be here in a couple of years . . .

"Bingo," he said to himself as Andropov and Cafferty emerged. They got into their separate cars and headed off, passing Rebus and making towards Lothian Road. Again, Rebus followed: harder to lose them this time. As they passed the end of King's Stables Road, Rebus felt his stomach tighten at the prospect that they might end up at the car park, but they stayed on the main drag and turned into Princes Street, Charlotte Square, and Queen Street. When passing Young Street, Rebus glanced down it towards the Oxford Bar.

"Not tonight, my love," he cooed, blowing it a kiss.

At the end of Queen Street, they forked left onto Leith Walk, passing Gayfield Square. Great Junction Street, North Junction Street, and they were on the waterfront to the west of Leith itself. More redevelopment was happening here, blocks of apartments rising from what had been dockland and industrial estates.

"Hardly the tourist trail, Sergei," Rebus muttered as the cars pulled over again. There was another car already sitting there, hazard lights on. Rebus drove past—no way he could park, the streets were deserted. Instead, he took the first turning he came to, did another of the three-pointers he was becoming so expert in, and crawled back to the junction. He signaled right and passed the three cars. Same deal: Cafferty and Andropov standing on the pavement, Cafferty with his arms stretched wide as if to encompass *everything*. But this time with two new attendants: Stuart Janney and Nikolai Stahov. The consular official stood with his gloved hands behind his back, a Cossack hat on his head. Janney looked thoughtful, arms folded, nodding to himself.

"Gang's all here," Rebus commented.

There was a petrol station with its lights still on, so he pulled into the forecourt and dribbled some unleaded into the tank. Bought chewing gum from the cashier when he paid, and stood beside the pump, unwrapping a piece slowly and making as if to check messages on his phone. The cashier kept staring out at him, and he knew this wasn't an act he could keep up for long. He looked back along the street, but couldn't make out much. Cafferty still seemed to be holding the floor. A car had pulled up at the pump behind him. Two men got out. One busied himself with the nozzle while the other gave a few stretches and started walking towards the kiosk, but then seemed to change his mind and headed towards Rebus instead.

"Evening," he said. He was big, bigger than Rebus. His belt was on its last notch and looked ready to snap. His head was shaved, some gray showing through. Pudgy face like an overfed baby who still objected every time the breast was taken away. Rebus just nodded a reply, flicking the gum wrapper into a bin.

The new arrival was studying Rebus's car. "Bit of a clunker," he offered, "even as Saabs go."

Rebus looked back at the man's own car. Vauxhall Vectra with a black paint job.

"Least I own mine," he said.

The man gave a smile and a nod, as if to admit that, yes indeed, his belonged to the company. "He wants a word," he said, giving a flick of the head in the Vectra's direction.

"Oh aye?" Rebus seemed more interested in the packet of gum.

"Maybe you should talk to him, DI Rebus," the man continued, a gleam in his eye as he clocked the effect: an emergency stop on the gum chewing.

"Who are you?" Rebus asked.

"He'll tell you. I've got to pay for the petrol." The man moved off. Rebus stood his ground a moment. The cashier was looking interested. The man at the Vectra was concentrating on the pump's meter. Rebus decided to go see him.

"You wanted me," he said.

"Believe me, Rebus, you're the *last* thing I want." The man was neither tall nor short, fat nor thin. His hair was brown, eyes somewhere between brown and green and set in the blandest of faces. Always blending in, and instantly forgettable — perfect for surveillance work.

"I'm assuming you're CID," Rebus went on. "Don't know you, though, which means you're from out of town."

The man released his grip on the pump as the meter hit thirty pounds dead. He seemed satisfied with this outcome and replaced the nozzle in its holster. Only then, as he replaced the cap and wiped his hands on his handkerchief, did he deign to focus his attention on the man standing before him.

"You're Detective Inspector John Rebus," he stated. "Based at Gayfield Square police station, B Division, Edinburgh."

"Let me write this down in case I forget." Rebus made show of reaching into a pocket for his notebook.

"You have a problem with authority," the man went on, "which is why everyone's so relieved you're about to retire. They've only just stopped short of putting up bunting at Fettes HQ."

"Seems you know all there is to know about me," Rebus conceded. "And so far all I know about you is that you drive the sort of overpowered cockmobile favored by a certain type of cop . . . usually the kind who's happiest investigating other cops."

"You think we're the Complaints?"

"Maybe not, but you seem to know who they are."

"I've been on their receiving end a couple of times myself," the man confided. "You're not a proper cop otherwise."

"Makes me a proper cop, then," Rebus added.

"I know," the man said quietly. "Now get in and let's do some proper talking."

"My car's . . ." But as Rebus looked over his shoulder, he saw that the baby-faced giant had somehow squeezed in behind the Saab's steering wheel and was turning the ignition.

"Don't worry," Rebus's new friend assured him, "Andy knows a thing or two about cars." He was getting back into the Vectra's driving seat. Rebus walked around to the passenger side and climbed in. The big man—Andy—had left a dent in the seat. Rebus looked around for clues as to the men's identity.

"I like your thinking," the driver admitted. "But when you're undercover, you try not to give the game away."

"I can't be much good, then, seeing how you had no trouble spotting me."

"Not much good, no."

"While your pal Andy couldn't look more like a copper if he had the word tattooed on his forehead."

"Some people think he looks like a bouncer."

"Bouncers tend to have that bit more refinement."

The man had lifted a mobile phone for Rebus to see. "Want me to relay that to him while he's in charge of your vehicle?"

"Maybe later," Rebus said. "So who are you, then?"

"We're SCD," the stranger said. Short for SCDEA, the Scottish Crime and Drugs Enforcement Agency. "I'm DI Stone."

"And Andy?"

"DS Prosser."

"What can I do to help you, DI Stone?"

"You can start by calling me Calum, and I hope it's all right to call you John?"

"Nice and friendly, eh, Calum?"

"Let's just aim for civil and see how it goes."

The Saab was already signaling to turn off the main road. They entered the car park of a casino, not far from Ocean Terminal, where the Saab pulled to a stop, Stone drawing up alongside.

"Andy seems to know his way around," Rebus commented.

"Football routes only. Andy's a Dunfermline fan, comes through here to watch his team play Hibs and Hearts."

"Not for much longer, the way the Pars are struggling."

"A sore point."

"I'll bear that in mind . . ."

Stone had turned in his seat, the better to meet Rebus face-to-face. "I'm being straight with you, because I think any other approach might see your hackles rise. I hope you'll offer me the same courtesy." He paused for a moment. "Why are you so interested in Cafferty and the Russian?"

"A case I'm working."

"The Todorov killing?"

Rebus nodded. "Last drink he had before he died happened to be with Cafferty. Andropov was in the bar at the same time."

"You think the pair of them are in cahoots?"

"I just wasn't sure how."

"And now . . . ?"

"Andropov's looking to buy a huge swathe of Edinburgh," Rebus guessed. "With Cafferty as his middleman."

"Could be," Stone conceded. Rebus was looking out of the passenger-side window towards his own car. Prosser seemed to be thumping the dodgy speaker with his foot.

"Not sure Andy shares my taste in music," Rebus commented.

"Depends on whether you listen to nothing but Strathspey reels . . ."

"We may have a problem."

Stone pretended to laugh. "Bit unusual, isn't it?" he asked. "A one-man stakeout? Is CID around these parts really that short of bodies?"

"Not everyone wants to work nights."

"Tell me about it—wife's sometimes so surprised to see me, I keep thinking she must have the milkman hidden in the wardrobe."

"You don't wear a wedding ring."

"No, I don't. While you, John, are divorced with a grown-up daughter."

"Anyone would think it was me you were interested in rather than Andropov."

"I couldn't care less about Andropov. Authorities in Moscow are a gnat's bollock away from charging him with God-knows-what—fraud and deception and bribery . . ."

"He seems pretty relaxed about it. Is that because he's thinking of relocating?"

"Wait and see. But for what it's worth, whatever the reason for him being here, it seems legit."

"Even with Cafferty in tow?"

"Thing about crooks, John, ninety percent of everything they do is completely kosher."

Rebus considered for a moment, the word *overworld* reverberating in his head. "So if it's not Andropov you're after . . ."

"We've got your friend Cafferty in our sights, John, and this time he's going down. Reason your name flashed on the radar—all those run-ins down the years. But he's *ours,* John. Six of us have been slaving over him these past seven months. We've got phone taps and forensic accountants and a lot more besides, and we aim to have him in jail shortly with his ill-got gains reverting to the Exchequer." Stone looked pleased with himself, but his eyes were cold, bright marbles. "Only thing that could mess it up is someone blundering in, hell-bent on their own half-baked theories and stoked by long-held prejudice." Stone was shaking his head slowly. "Can't let that happen, John."

"Or in other words—butt out."

"If I told you to do that," Stone continued quietly, "I have the suspicion you'd do exactly the opposite, just for the hell of it." In the Saab, Prosser's head had disappeared from view as he wrestled with the door panel.

"What are you going to charge Cafferty with?"

"Maybe drugs, maybe money laundering . . . tax evasion's always a good one. He doesn't think we know about his various offshore accounts . . ."

"Those forensic accountants you were mentioning?"

"They're so good, they have to stay anonymous—there'd be a price on their heads otherwise."

"I can imagine." Rebus was thoughtful for a moment. "Anything tying Cafferty and Andropov to Alexander Todorov?"

"Only that Andropov knew him in Moscow."

"Knew Todorov?"

"From years back . . . same school or college or something."

"So you know a bit about Andropov . . . tell me, what's his connection to Cafferty? I mean, he's a different league, isn't he?"

"Listen to yourself, John . . . pushing sixty and frisky as a pup." Stone laughed again, but this time it sounded genuine. "You want Cafferty put away—that much is clear. But the best chance we have of giving you that little retirement gift is if you leave *us* to get on with it. Cafferty's not going to go to jail because you've been busy tailing him. He's going to be brought down by a paper trail: shell companies, VAT dodges, banks in Bermuda and Lithuania, sweeteners and payoffs and doctored balance sheets."

"That why you're busy tailing him?"

"We heard Cafferty on the phone to his lawyer, saying you'd pulled him in. Lawyer wanted to make an official complaint—called it 'harassment'; Cafferty wouldn't have it, said it was actually 'a bit flattering.' That's what got us worried, John—don't want a loose cannon out there, not when we're readying to attack. We know you've been watching Cafferty's house—we've seen you do it. But I'm betting *you've* never seen *us*."

"That's because you're so much better at it than I am," Rebus said.

"You better believe it." Stone leaned back in his seat, a gesture which seemed to have some significance for Prosser. The Saab's door opened, and the fat man got out, tugging at the handle on the Vectra's passenger side.

"How's my hi-fi?" Rebus asked him.

"Good as new."

Rebus turned his attention back to Stone. The detective handed him his business card.

"Be good," Stone said. "Leave the stakeouts to the professionals."

"I'll sleep on it" was all Rebus said. He got into his Saab and tried the stereo. The wonky speaker was working again, no sign of damage to the grille or door panel. Had to admit, he was impressed with that, but he managed not to let it show. Reversed out of the car park and made his way back to the main road. His options: a left turn into the city, or a right towards where he'd last seen Cafferty and Andropov. He signaled left and waited for the traffic to clear.

Then took the right turn.

But all three cars had gone. Rebus cursed under his breath. He could keep cruising, or maybe try the Caledonian Hotel. He could head to Cafferty's house and check if he was back.

"Just go home, John," he told himself.

So that was what he did, working his way through Canonmills and the New Town and the Old Town, along the Meadows and then left into Marchmont itself and Arden Street. Where a parking space—the universe's small reward for his labors—awaited him. As did two flights of stairs. He wasn't breathing too hard at the top. Got a glass of water from the kitchen and gulped it, then poured in a fresh inch to carry through to the living room. Added the same amount of whisky and stuck Johnny Cash on the hi-fi before collapsing into his chair. But the Man in Black wasn't right. Rebus felt a bit guilty, ejecting the CD. Cash had Fife roots, he seemed to recall. Photos of him in some old newspaper visiting his hereditary home in Falkland. Rebus stuck John Martyn on instead, *Grace and Danger,* one of the great breakup albums. Dark and brooding and feeling just about perfect.

"Fuck," Rebus announced, the single word summing up the day's adventures. He didn't know how to feel about the SCD men. Yes, he wanted Cafferty taken out of the game. But suddenly it was important that it be *him* making the bone-crunching tackle. So it couldn't *just* be about Cafferty; it was about the means and method, too. Years he'd been fighting the bastard, and now technology and some bespectacled pen pusher might end up finishing the job. No mess, no fuss, no blood.

There should be mess.

There should be fuss.

John Martyn was singing about some people being crazy. A little later, he would move on to "Grace and Danger" itself, followed by "Johnny Too Bad."

"Singing my whole life story," John Rebus told his whisky glass. What the hell was he going to do with himself if Cafferty was out of bounds? If Stone and his men did actually manage to put the gangster away, cleanly and coldly?

There should be mess.

There should be fuss.

There should be blood . . .

DAY SEVEN

Thursday 23 November 2006

27

Rebus was parked on the other side of Gayfield Square from the police station. He had a pretty good view of the news crews. TV cameras were being erected or dismantled, depending on how early the teams had arrived. Journalists paced the pavement, mobile phones pressed to their ears, keeping a respectful distance from one another so as not to be tempted into a bit of eavesdropping. Photographers were wondering how to get anything usable from the dismal cop-shop frontage. Rebus had watched a trickle of suits climb the steps and enter the building. He recognized some — Ray Reynolds, for example. Others were new to him, but they all looked like CID, meaning they'd been seconded to the team. Rebus bit into the remains of his breakfast roll and chewed slowly. When buying the roll, he'd added a coffee, newspaper, and orange juice to the order. Skimming through the paper, he'd found more news of the ailing Litvinenko — the poisoning still a mystery — but no mention of Todorov and only a paragraph on Charles Riordan, at the foot of which he was directed to the obituary columns farther back. He learned that Riordan had worked on various rock tours in the 1980s, including Big Country and Deacon Blue. One of the musicians was quoted as saying that "Charlie could mix a sweet sound in an aircraft hangar." Further back in time, he'd been a session musician, appearing on albums by Nazareth, Frankie Miller, and the Sutherland Brothers, which meant Rebus probably owned stuff he'd played on.

"Wish I'd known," he'd said to himself.

Staring out at the media scrum, he wondered who had leaked the information that the Todorov and Riordan deaths were being linked. Didn't really matter; bound to come out sooner or later. But it did mean he'd lost an opportunity for leverage. There was a favor he was after, and it would have been nice to offer the tidbit in return . . .

Still no sign of his quarry, however. But an official-looking car had drawn up, Corbyn stepping out, pausing for photos in his smart uniform, shiny cap, and black leather gloves. A morale booster for the troops would be the excuse, but Rebus knew Corbyn would have been alerted to the media. Nothing warmed a chief constable more than a hungry news gathering. He'd have them eating out of his hand. Rebus punched Siobhan's number into his phone.

"High Hiedyin alert," he warned her.

"Who and where?"

"Corbyn himself, posing for the press. Give him two minutes, and he'll be in your face."

"Meaning you're nearby . . ."

"Don't worry, he can't see me. How's it all going?"

"We're going to have to speak to Nancy Sievewright yet again."

"Has she had any more grief from the banker?"

"Not that I know of." Clarke paused. "So what else are you up to, apart from this morning's stakeout?"

"To tell you the truth, I'm just relieved I don't have to come in . . . not with officers of the caliber of Rat-Arse Reynolds to contend with."

"Don't."

"Thought I saw young Todd heading inside, too, clean suit and everything . . ."

"Yes."

"I was thinking you might've dropped him, now his brother's part of the deal."

"Phyl shares your interest, but Todd's busy reviewing about two hundred hours of committee tapes made by Charles Riordan. Should keep him out of harm's way."

"And you've kept the Chief informed?"

"That's my call, not yours."

Rebus tutted, and watched as Corbyn gave a final wave to the reporters before entering the reception area. "He's inside," he said into the mouthpiece.

"Suppose I'd better get ready to look surprised."

"*Pleasantly* surprised, Shiv. Might get you an extra brownie point."

"I'm going to talk to him about your suspension."

"You'll be on a hiding to nothing."

"Even so . . ." She drew in some breath. "And talk of the devil . . ." The phone went dead in Rebus's hand. He flipped it shut and drummed his fingers against the steering wheel.

"Where are you, Mairie?" he muttered. But just as he uttered these words, Mairie Henderson appeared around the corner from East London Street, moving briskly uphill towards the police station. She had a notebook in one hand, pen and Dictaphone in the other, and a large black satchel slung over one shoulder. Rebus sounded his horn, but she paid no heed. He tried again with the same lack of effect, and didn't want to attract any attention other than hers. So he gave up and got out of the car, taking up position next to it with hands in pockets.

Henderson was in conversation with one of her colleagues. Then she collared a photographer and asked him what shots he'd been taking. Rebus recognized him, thought his name was Mungo or something, knew he'd worked with Mairie in the past. A text arrived on her phone and she checked it while still talking to the snapper, before punching some buttons and making a call. Phone to her ear, she moved away from the mêlée towards the patch of grass that sat in the middle of Gayfield Square. There was some litter there — empty wine bottles and fast-food wrappers — which she frowned at as she spoke. Then she lifted her eyes and saw Rebus. He was smiling. She kept her gaze on him as she spoke. Conversation over, she skirted the patch of grass. Rebus was back in the car; no point letting anyone else see him. Mairie Henderson climbed into the passenger seat, holding her satchel on her lap.

"What's up?" she said.

"And hello to you, Mairie. How's the newspaper business?"

"Crumbling at the seams," she admitted. "Between the freesheets and the Internet, readers willing to pay for their news are rapidly disappearing."

"And ad revenue with them?" Rebus guessed.

"Meaning cutbacks." She sighed.

"Not so much work for a freelancer like yourself?"

"There are still plenty of stories, John, it's just that the editors are loath to pay for them. Haven't you noticed the tabloids — they advertise for *readers* to send in news and pics . . ." She rested her head against the back of the seat, closing her eyes for a moment. Rebus felt an unexpected jab of sympathy. He'd known Mairie for years, during which time they'd traded tips and information. He'd never before known her to sound so beaten.

"Maybe I can help," he offered.

"Todorov and Riordan?" she guessed, opening her eyes and turning to face him.

"The very same."

"How come you're out here rather than in there?" She gestured towards the police station.

"Because I'm after a favor."

"Meaning you want me to do some digging?"

"You know me too well, Mairie."

"I know I've done you plenty of favors in the past, John, and the scales never seem to balance."

"Might be different this time."

She laughed tiredly. "Another line you always use."

"All right then, call it your retirement gift to me."

She studied him more closely. "I'd forgotten you were on your way out."

"I'm *already* out. Corbyn's suspended me."

"Why did he do that?"

"I badmouthed a pal of his called Sir Michael Addison."

"The banker?" Her intonation lifted along with her spirits.

"There's a tie—a loose tie—between him and Todorov."

"How loose?"

"The whole six degrees."

"Intriguing nevertheless."

"Knew you'd think so."

"And you'll tell me the story?"

"I'll tell you what I can," Rebus corrected her.

"In return for what exactly?"

"A man called Andropov."

"He's the Russian industrialist."

"That's right."

"Recently in town as part of a trade delegation."

"They all went home; Andropov stayed."

"I didn't know that." She pursed her lips. "So what is it you want to know?"

"Who he is and how he got his money. Again, there's a hookup to Todorov."

"In that they're both Russian?"

"I've heard they knew one another, back in the mists of time."

"And?"

"And the night Todorov died, he was drinking in the same bar as his old classmate."

Mairie Henderson let out a low, sustained whistle. "No one else has this?"

Rebus shook his head. "And there's plenty more."

"If I run a story, your bosses are bound to guess the source."

"The source is back to being a civilian in a couple of days."

"Meaning no comebacks?"

"No comebacks," he agreed.

Her eyes narrowed. "I'm betting there's plenty more dirt you could be dishing."

"Saving it for my memoirs, Mairie."

She studied him again. "You'll be needing a ghost-writer," she informed him. Didn't sound like she was joking.

The *Scotsman* newspaper was based in an up-to-date facility at the bottom of Holyrood Road, opposite the BBC and the Parliament building. Although Mairie Henderson had left her full-time job there several years back, she was still a known face and carried her own security pass.

"How did you wangle that?" Rebus asked as he signed himself in at reception. Henderson tapped the side of her nose as Rebus pinned on his visitor badge. The office behind the reception desk was large and open-plan and seemed to be staffed by a skeleton crew of only nine or ten bodies. Rebus said as much, and Henderson told him that he was living in the past.

"Doesn't take many hands to produce a paper these days."

"You don't sound too enthusiastic."

"The old building had a bit of character to it. And so did the old newsroom, everyone scuttling around like mad trying to put a story together. Editor with his sleeves rolled up, effing and blinding. Subs smoking like chimneys and trying to sneak puns into the copy . . . cutting and pasting by hand. Everything's just gotten so . . ." She sought the right word. "Efficient," she eventually said.

"Being a cop was more fun in the old days, too," Rebus assured her, "but we also made more mistakes."

"At your age, you're allowed to be nostalgic."

"But you're not?"

She just shrugged and sat herself at a vacant computer, gesturing for him to pull up a chair. A middle-aged man with a scraggy beard and wearing half-moon glasses walked past and said hello.

"Hiya, Gordon," Henderson replied. "Remind me of the password, will you?"

"Connery," he said.

She thanked him and then, watching him leave, gave a

little smile. "Half the people in here," she told Rebus, her voice lowered, "think I'm still on the payroll."

"Handy to be able to waltz in." He watched her tap in the password and start to search the computer for the name Andropov.

"First name?" she asked.

"Sergei."

She searched again, halving the initial results.

"We could have logged onto the Internet anywhere," Rebus told her.

"This isn't the Internet as such; it's a database of news stories."

"From the *Scotsman*?"

"And every other paper you can think of." She tapped the screen. "Just over five hundred hits," she stated.

"Seems a lot."

She gave him a look. "It's minuscule. Want me to print the pages, or are you happy to scroll?"

"Let's see how I get on."

She rose from her chair and slid it aside so Rebus could roll his own chair closer to the screen. "I'm going to do the rounds, see what the gossip is."

"What do I say if anyone asks me what I'm up to?"

She thought for a moment. "Tell them you're the economics editor."

"Fair enough."

She left him to it, climbing the stairs to the next level. Rebus started clicking and reading. The first few stories concerned Andropov's business dealings. With perestroika had come a loosening of state controls on industry, allowing men like Andropov to buy into base metals, mining and the rest. Andropov had specialized in zinc, copper, and aluminum, before branching out into coal and steel. Ventures into gas and oil had stalled, but in other areas he'd made a killing. Too big a killing, perhaps, leading the authorities to investigate him for corruption. Depending on which investigative journalist you turned to, Andropov was either a martyr or a crook. After twenty minutes, Rebus tried refining the search by adding "background" to the keywords. He was rewarded with a potted biography of Andropov. Born 1960, the same year as Alexander Todorov, in the Zhdanov suburb of Moscow, also the same as Todorov.

"Well, well," Rebus muttered to himself. There was no information as to which schools or colleges Andropov had attended. His early life, it seemed, hadn't been investigated at all. Rebus tried cross-referencing Andropov's name with Todorov but drew a blank. But while he was looking at the entries for Todorov — seventeen thousand of them worldwide; Mairie had been right about Andropov's five hundred being small beer — he tried finding information on the poet's university career. Some of his lectures could be downloaded, but there was no mention of improprieties with students. Maybe Andropov had been spinning him a line.

"Hello." The bearded man was back.

"Morning," Rebus said. He seemed to remember that the man's name was Gordon, and Gordon was now peering over his shoulder at the screen.

"I thought Sandy was covering the Todorov story," he commented.

"Yes," Rebus said. "I'm just adding background."

"Ah." Gordon nodded slowly, as though this made sense. "So Sandy's still stuck outside Gayfield Square?"

"Last I heard," Rebus agreed.

"What's the betting the cops screw it up, as per?"

"I wouldn't risk my shirt on it," Rebus said, voice hardening.

"Well, shoulder to the grindstone, nose to the mill . . ." Gordon was laughing as he moved away.

"Prick," Rebus said, just loud enough to be overheard. Gordon stopped in his tracks, but didn't turn round, and started walking again after a moment. Either thought he'd misheard or didn't want to start something. Rebus got back to his reading, switching from Todorov to Andropov again, and almost immediately came across a name he recognized: Roddy Denholm. Seemed that Russia's New Rich liked to buy art. The prices paid at auction were hitting record highs. A plutocrat wasn't a plutocrat without the obligatory Picasso or Matisse. Rebus put some of the news stories onto the screen. They were accompanied by photos taken at sales in Moscow, New York, and London. Five million there, ten million here . . . Andropov was mentioned only tangentially, as someone with a taste for up-to-the-minute art, predominantly British. As such, he bought judiciously from galleries and shows rather than the likes of Sotheby's or Christie's. Recent purchases included two Alison Watts and work by Callum Innes, David Mach, Douglas Gordon, and Roddy Denholm. Siobhan had mentioned Denholm to Rebus—the guy doing the art show at the Parliament, Riordan working for him. The journalist writing the piece had added that "as all these artists are Scottish, Mr. Andropov may be starting to specialize." Rebus jotted down the names and started some new searches. A further fifteen minutes passed before Mairie Henderson returned with two coffees.

"Milk, no sugar."

"It'll do, I suppose," Rebus said by way of thanks.

"What did you say to Gordon?" She had pulled her chair in next to his.

"Why?"

"Seemed to think you'd taken against him."

"Some people are touchy."

"Whatever you said, he's come to the conclusion you must be management."

"I always thought I had it in me . . ." Rebus glanced away from the screen long enough to give her a wink. "If I hit the print button, where do the pages appear?"

"That machine over there." She pointed towards a corner of the room.

"So I'd have to walk all the way over there to collect them?"

"You're management, John. Get someone to do it for you . . ."

28

The reporters had drifted away from Gayfield Square. Maybe because it was approaching lunchtime, or some other story had broken. Siobhan Clarke had been in a meeting with DCI Macrae and the Chief Constable. Corbyn wasn't enthusiastic about leaving her in charge, despite Macrae's spirited defense.

"Let's get DI Starr back from Fettes," Corbyn had insisted.

"Yes, sir," Macrae had said, capitulating at the last.

Afterwards, he'd sighed and told Clarke the Chief Constable was right. Clarke had just shrugged and watched him pick up the phone, asking to be connected to Derek Starr. Within half an hour, Starr himself, coiffeured and cuff-linked, was in the CID suite and gathering the team together for what he termed "a pep talk."

"Isn't a PEP a pension scheme?" Hawes asked beneath her breath, her way of telling Clarke she was on her side. Clarke smiled back to let her know she appreciated it.

Having had only the briefest of briefings in Macrae's office, Starr focused on the "tenuous links" between the two deaths and insisted that they not read too much into them "at this early stage." He wanted the team divided in two, with one group concentrating on Todorov and the other on Riordan. Then, turning his attention to Siobhan Clarke: "You'll be the nexus, DS Clarke. Meaning if there *are* points of connection between the two cases, you'll collate them." Looking around the room, he asked if everyone understood how he wanted things to work. The murmurs of assent were drowned out by a sustained belch from Ray Reynolds.

"Chili con carne," he stated, by way of apology, as officers nearby wafted notebooks and sheets of paper. The phone on Clarke's desk rang and she picked it up, pressing a finger in her other ear to muffle the rest of Starr's oration.

"DS Clarke," she announced.

"Is DI Rebus there?"

"Not at the moment. Can I help at all?"

"It's Stuart Janney."

"Ah yes, Mr. Janney. This is DS Clarke, we met at the Parliament."

"Well, DS Clarke, your man Rebus asked for details of Alexander Todorov's bank account . . ."

"You've got them?"

"I know it's taken awhile, but there were protocols . . ."

Clarke caught Hawes's eye. "Where are you just now, Mr. Janney?"

"Bank HQ."

"Could a couple of my colleagues come and collect them?"

"Don't see why not; save me a trip." Janney sniffed as he spoke.

"Thank you, sir. Will you be there for the next hour?"

"If I'm not, I'll leave the envelope with my assistant."

"Very kind of you."

"How's the investigation going?"

"We're making progress."

"Glad to hear it. Papers this morning seem to think you're connecting Todorov's death to that house fire."

"Don't believe everything you read."

"Extraordinary, nevertheless."

"If you say so, Mr. Janney. Thanks again." Clarke put the phone down and turned back to Phyllida Hawes. "I'm getting you and Col out of here. Go to First Albannach's HQ and pick up Todorov's bank details from a man called Stuart Janney."

"Thank you," Hawes mouthed.

"And while you're gone, I might make myself scarce, too. Nancy Sievewright's going to be sick of the sight of me . . ."

Starr was clapping his hands, signaling that the meeting was at an end, "unless anyone's got a really stupid question." His eyes raked the room, daring any hand to be raised. "Right, then," he barked, "let's go to work!"

Hawes rolled her eyes and squeezed through the throng to where Colin Tibbet was standing, seemingly in thrall to Derek Starr. Siobhan Clarke found Todd Goodyear sidling up next to her.

"You think DI Starr's going to want me kept on?" he asked quietly.

"Just keep your head down and hope he doesn't notice you."

"And how do I do that?"

"You're going through all those committee tapes, right?" She watched Goodyear nod. "Just keep doing that, and if he asks who you are, explain that you're the only sod willing to take on such a thankless task."

"I'm still not sure what it is you think I might find."

"Search me," Clarke confessed. "But you never know your luck."

"Okay then." Goodyear sounded far from convinced. "And you're going to be liaison between the two halves of the inquiry?"

"Always supposing that's what a 'nexus' is."

"Does that mean you'll be giving the press conferences?"

Clarke responded with a snort. "Derek Starr's not going to let anyone hog the cameras except him."

"He looks more like a salesman than a detective," Goodyear commented.

"That's because he is," Clarke agreed. "And the thing he's selling is himself. Problem is, he's bloody good at it."

"You're not jealous?" They were being jostled by other detectives, as everyone tried to find a patch of office they could claim as their own.

"DI Starr will go far," she said, leaving it at that. Goodyear watched as she slung her bag over one shoulder.

"You're going somewhere," he stated.

"Well spotted."

"Anything I can help with?"

"You've got all those tapes to listen to, Todd."

"What's happened to DI Rebus?"

"He's in the field," Clarke explained, reckoning the fewer people who knew about the suspension, the better.

Especially when Rebus, despite — or more accurately *because of* — the suspension, was most definitely still on the case.

Nancy Sievewright hadn't been at all happy when Clarke had announced herself at the intercom. But at last she'd come downstairs and told the detective that she wanted hot chocolate.

"There's a place near the top of the street."

Inside the café, they ordered their drinks and settled on opposing leather couches. Sievewright looked like she'd not had enough sleep. She was still wearing a short skirt, threads trailing from it, and a thin denim jacket, but her legs were wrapped in thick black tights and there were knitted fingerless gloves on her hands. She'd asked for whipped cream and marshmallows in her drink, and she cupped the mug between her palms as she sipped and chewed.

"Any more grief from Mr. Anderson?" Clarke asked. Sievewright just shook her head. "We spoke to Sol Goodyear," Clarke continued. "You didn't tell us he lived in the same street the body was found."

"Why should I?"

Clarke just shrugged. "He doesn't seem to see himself as your boyfriend."

"He's protecting me," Sievewright snapped back.

"From what?" Clarke asked, but the young woman wasn't about to answer that. There was music playing quite loudly, and a speaker in the ceiling directly overhead. It was some sort of dance track with a pulsing rhythm and it was giving Clarke a headache. She went to the counter and asked for it to be turned down. The assistant obliged, albeit grudgingly and with minimal effect.

"Why I like this place," Sievewright said.

"The surly staff?"

"The music." Sievewright peered at Clarke over the rim of her mug. "So what *did* Sol say about me?"

"Just that you're not his girlfriend. Speaking to him got me wondering, though . . ."

"What about?"

"About the night of the attack."

"It was some nutter in a pub . . ."

"I don't mean the attack on Sol; I'm talking about the poet. You were on your way to buy stuff from Sol. So you either stumbled across the body on your way *up* the lane, or on your way back down . . ."

"What's the difference?" Sievewright was shuffling her feet, looking down at them as if they were no longer under her control.

"Quite a big difference, actually. Remember when I came to your flat that first time?"

Sievewright nodded.

"There was something you said . . . the *way* you said something. And I was thinking about it yesterday after I'd been talking to Sol."

The young woman took the bait. "What?" she asked, trying not to sound too interested.

"You told us: 'I didn't *see* anything.' But you put the stress on 'see' when I'm guessing most people would have emphasized the 'anything.' Made me wonder if you were doing that thing of not quite telling the truth but at the same time managing not to tell an outright lie."

"You've lost me." Sievewright's knees were bouncing like pistons.

"I think maybe you'd gone to Sol's door, rung the bell, and waited. You knew he was expecting you. Maybe you stood there for a while, thinking he'd be back soon. Maybe you tried his mobile, but he wasn't answering."

"Because he was getting himself stabbed."

Clarke nodded slowly. "So you're outside his flat, and suddenly you hear something at the bottom of the lane. You go to the corner and take a look."

But Sievewright was shaking her head emphatically.

"Okay then," Clarke conceded, "you don't *see* anything, but you do hear something, don't you, Nancy?"

The young woman looked at her for a long time, then broke off eye contact and took another slurp of hot chocolate. When she spoke, the music covered whatever it was she said.

"I didn't catch that," Clarke apologized.

"I said yes."

"You heard something?"

"A car. It pulled up and . . ." She paused, lifting her eyes to the ceiling in thought. Eventually, she looked at Clarke again. "First off, there was this groaning. I thought maybe a drunk was about to be sick. His words seemed all slurred. Could have been saying something in Russian, though. That would make sense, wouldn't it?" She seemed keen for Clarke to agree, so Clarke nodded again.

"And then a car?" she prompted.

"It pulled up. Door opened, and I heard this noise, just a dull sort of thump and no more groans."

"How can you be sure it was a car?"

"Didn't sound like a van or a lorry."

"You didn't look?"

"By the time I turned the corner, it was gone. There was just a body slumped next to the wall."

"I think I know why you screamed," Clarke stated. "You thought it was Sol?"

"At first, yes. But when I got close, I saw it wasn't."

"Why didn't you run?"

"That couple arrived. I did try to leave, but the man told me I should stay. If I'd scarpered, it'd have looked bad for me, wouldn't it? And he could've given you my description."

"True enough," Clarke admitted. "What made you think it might be Sol?"

"When you deal drugs, you make enemies."

"Such as?"

"The bastard who knifed him outside the pub."

Clarke was nodding thoughtfully. "Any others?"

Sievewright saw what she was getting at. "You think maybe they killed the poet by mistake?"

"I'm not sure." How much sense did it make? The trail of blood led back to the multistory, meaning whoever had attacked Todorov must've known he wasn't Sol Goodyear. But as for the coup de grâce . . . well, it could have been the same person, but not necessarily. And Sievewright was spot on — dealers made enemies. Maybe she would put that point to Sol himself, see if he had any names for her. Likelihood was, of course, that he'd keep them to himself, maybe intent on exacting his own revenge. She imagined Sol rubbing at the ragged line of stitches, as if trying to erase them. Imagined the two boys growing up, Sol and his wee brother, Todd, granddad dead in jail and parents going to pieces. At what point had Todd decided to cut his brother adrift? And had Sol suffered as a result?

"Can I get another?" Sievewright was asking, lifting her empty mug.

"Your turn to pay," Clarke reminded her.

"I've got no money."

Clarke sighed and handed her a fiver. "And get me another cappuccino," she said.

29

H e's a hard man to pin down," Terence Blackman said, fluttering his hands.

Blackman ran a gallery of contemporary art on William Street in the city's west end. The gallery consisted of two rooms with white walls and sanded wooden flooring. Blackman himself was barely five feet tall, skinny with a slight paunch, and was probably thirty or forty years older than he dressed. The thatch of brown hair looked dyed, and might even have been an expensive weave job. An assortment of nips and tucks had stretched the skin tight over the face, so that Blackman's range of expressions was limited. According to the Web, he acted as Roddy Denholm's agent.

"So where is he now?" Rebus asked, stepping around a sculpture that looked like a mass brawl of wire coat hangers.

"Melbourne, I think. Could be Hong Kong."

"Any of his stuff here today?"

"There's actually a waiting list. Half a dozen buyers, money no object."

"Russians?" Rebus guessed.

Blackman stared at him. "I'm sorry, Inspector, why was it you wanted to see Roddy?"

"He's been working on a project at the Parliament."

"An albatross around all our necks." Blackman sighed.

"Mr. Denholm needed bits and pieces of recording done, and the man responsible has turned up dead."

"What?"

"His name's Charles Riordan."

"Dead?"

"I'm afraid so. There was a fire . . ."

Blackman slapped his palms to his cheeks. "Are the tapes all right?"

Rebus stared at him. "Nice of you to show concern, sir."

"Oh, well, yes, of course it's a terrible tragedy for the family and . . . um . . ."

"I think the recordings are fine."

Blackman gave silent thanks and then asked what this had to do with the artist.

"Mr. Riordan was murdered, sir. We're wondering if he'd recorded something he shouldn't have."

"At the Parliament, you mean?"

"Any reason why Mr. Denholm chose the Urban Regeneration Committee for his project?"

"I've not the faintest idea."

"Then you see why I need to talk to him. Maybe you've got a number for his mobile?"

"He doesn't always answer."

"Nevertheless, a message could be left."

"I suppose so." Blackman didn't sound keen.

"So if you could give me the number," Rebus pressed. The dealer sighed again and gestured for Rebus to follow him, unlocking a door at the back of the room. It was a cramped office, the size of a box room and with unframed canvases and uncanvased frames everywhere.

Blackman's own phone was charging, but he unplugged it and pressed the keys until the artist's number showed on the screen. Rebus punched it into his own phone, while asking how much Denholm's work tended to fetch.

"Depends on size, materials, man-hours . . ."

"A ballpark figure."

"Between thirty and fifty . . ."

"Thousand pounds?" Rebus awaited the dealer's nodded confirmation.

"And how many does he knock out each year?"

Blackman scowled. "As I told you, there's a waiting list."

"So which one did Andropov buy?"

"Sergei Andropov has a good eye. I'd happened to acquire an early example of Roddy's work in oils, probably painted the year he left Glasgow School of Art." Blackman lifted a postcard from the desk. It was a reproduction of the painting. "It's called *Hopeless*."

To Rebus, it looked as if a child had taken a line for a walk. Hopeless just about summed it up.

"Fetched a record price for one of Roddy's pre-video works," the dealer added.

"And how much did you pocket, Mr. Blackman?"

"A percentage, Inspector. Now if you'll excuse me . . ."

But Rebus wasn't about to let go. "Nice to see my taxes going into your pocket."

"If you mean the Parliament commission, you've no need to worry — First Albannach Bank is underwriting the whole thing."

"As in paying for it?"

Blackman nodded abruptly. "Now you really must excuse me . . ."

"Generous of them," Rebus commented.

"FAB is a tremendous patron of the arts."

It was Rebus's turn to nod. "Just a couple more questions, sir—any idea why Andropov is moving into Scottish art?"

"Because he likes it."

"Is the same true of all these other Russian millionaires and billionaires?"

"I've no doubt some are buying for investment, others for pleasure."

"And some as a way of letting everyone else know how rich they are?"

Blackman offered the thinnest of smiles. "There may be an element of that."

"Same as with their Caribbean yachts—mine's bigger than yours. And the mansions in London, the jewelry for the trophy wife . . ."

"I'm sure you're right."

"Still doesn't explain the interest in Scotland." They'd moved back out of the office into the gallery space.

"There are old ties, Inspector. Russians revere Robert Burns, for example, perhaps seeing him as an ideal of Communism. I forget which leader it was—Lenin, maybe—who said that if there was to be a revolt in Europe, it would most likely start in Scotland."

"But that's all changed, hasn't it? We're talking capitalists, not Communists."

"Old ties," Blackman repeated. "Maybe they still think there's a revolution on the cards." And he smiled wistfully, making Rebus think the man had at one time been a card carrier. Hell, why not? Rebus had grown up in Fife, solidly working class and full of coal mines. Fife had elected Britain's first—maybe even the *only*—

Communist MP. In the 1950s and '60s there'd been plenty of Communist councillors. Rebus wasn't old enough for the General Strike, but he remembered an aunt telling him about it—barricades erected, towns and villages cut off—UDI, basically. The People's Kingdom of Fife. He had a little smile to himself, nodding at Terence Blackman.

"By revolution, you mean independence?"

"Could hardly make a worse fist of it than the current lot . . ." Blackman's mobile was ringing, and he pulled it from his pocket, walking away from Rebus and giving a little flick of the hand, hinting at dismissal.

"Thanks for your time," Rebus muttered, heading for the door.

On the pavement outside he tried the artist's number. It rang and rang until an automated voice told him to leave a message. He did so, then tried another number. Siobhan Clarke picked up.

"Enjoying your leisure time?" she asked.

"You're one to talk—is that an espresso machine I hear?"

"Had to get out of the station. Corbyn's brought Derek Starr back."

"We knew it would happen."

"We did," she conceded. "So I'm having a bit of a blather with Nancy Sievewright. She tells me that the night of the Todorov killing, she was at Sol's house trying to get some stuff. Only Sol was otherwise occupied, as we now know. But Nancy heard a car draw up and someone jump out and whack our poet across the back of the head."

"So he was attacked twice?"

"It would seem so."

"Same person each time?"

"Don't know. I was beginning to wonder if Sol himself might have been the intended target second time around."

"It's a possibility."

"You sound skeptical."

"Is Nancy in earshot?"

"Popped to the loo."

"Well, for what it's worth, how about this: Todorov's jumped in the car park, that much we know. He staggers into the night, but the attacker calmly gets into his or her car and follows, decides to finish the job."

"Meaning the car was in the multistory?"

"Not necessarily . . . could've been parked on the street. Is it worth another trip to the City Chambers? Go back through the video. Up till now, we were looking at pedestrians . . ."

"Ask your friend at Central Monitoring to bring us number plates for any cars going in or out of King's Stables Road?" She seemed to be considering it. "Thing is, Starr's busily rewinding to the mugging scenario."

"You've not told him about the car?"

"Not yet."

"Are you going to?" he asked teasingly.

"The alternative being, keep it to myself, just like you would? Then if I'm right and he's wrong, I get the applause?"

"You're learning."

"I'll have to mull it over." But he could tell she was already half-convinced. "So what are you up to? I hear traffic."

"Bit of window-shopping."

"Pull the other one." She paused again. "Nancy's coming back. I better hang up . . ."

"Tell me, did Starr make one of his 'into the breach' speeches?"

"What do you think?"

"I'll bet Goodyear lapped it up."

"I'm not so sure. Col liked it, though . . . I've sent him and Phyl to First Albannach. Janney's got Todorov's account details."

"Took him long enough."

"Well, he's had a lot on his plate—wining and dining the Russians at Gleneagles . . ."

Not to mention, Rebus could have added, hanging around the Granton seafront with Cafferty and Andropov. . . . Instead, he said his good-byes and hung up. Looked around him at the small shops: women's boutiques mostly. Realized he was a two-minute walk from the Caledonian Hotel.

"Why the hell not?" he asked himself. Answer: no reason at all.

At reception, he asked for "Mr. Andropov's room." But no one was answering. The clerk asked if he wanted to leave a message, but he shook his head and sauntered into the bar. It wasn't Freddie serving. This bartender was young and blond and had an East European accent. To her opening question, Rebus replied that he'd have a Highland Park. She offered him ice, and he sensed she was new either to the job or to Scotland. He shook his head and asked where she was from.

"Cracow," she said. "In Poland."

Rebus just nodded. His ancestors had come from Poland, but that was as much as he knew about the place.

He slid onto a stool and scooped up some nuts from a bowl.

"Here we are," she said, placing the drink in front of him.

"And some water, please."

"Of course." She sounded flustered, annoyed to have made the mistake. About a pint of tap water arrived in a jug. Rebus added the merest dribble to the glass and swirled it in his hand.

"Meeting someone?" she asked.

"He's here to see me, I think." Rebus turned towards the speaker. Andropov must have been sitting in the same booth, the one with the blind spot. He managed a smile, but his eyes were cold.

"Henchman not with you?" Rebus asked.

Andropov ignored this. "Another bottle of water," he told the barkeeper. "And no ice this time."

She nodded and took the bottle from a fridge, unscrewing it and pouring.

"So, Inspector," Andropov was saying, "is it really me you're looking for?"

"Just happened to be in the area. I was visiting Terence Blackman's gallery."

"You like art?" Andropov's eyebrows had gone up.

"I'm very keen on Roddy Denholm. Especially those early ones where he got the preschool kids to do some doodles."

"I think you are being mocking." Andropov had picked up his drink. "On my room," he instructed the bartender. Then, to Rebus: "Join me, please."

"This *is* the same booth?" Rebus asked as they got settled.

"I'm not sure I understand."

"The booth you were in the night Alexander Todorov was here."

"I didn't even know he was in the bar."

"Cafferty paid for his drink. After the poet had gone, Cafferty then came over here and joined you." Rebus paused. "You and the Minister for Economic Development."

"I'm impressed," Andropov seemed to admit. "Really I am. I can see you are not a man to cut corners."

"Can't be bought off, either."

"I'm sure of that, too." The Russian gave another smile; again, it didn't reach his eyes.

"So what were you chatting about with Jim Bakewell?"

"Strange as it may seem, we were discussing economic development."

"You're thinking of investing in Scotland?"

"I find it such a welcoming country."

"But we've none of the stuff you're interested in — no gas or coal or steel . . ."

"You do have gas and coal, actually. And oil, of course."

"About twenty years' worth."

"In the North Sea, yes — but you're forgetting the waters to the west. Plenty of oil in the Atlantic, Inspector, and eventually we will master the technology, allowing us to extract it. Then there are the alternative energies — wind and wave."

"Don't forget all that hot air in the Parliament." Rebus took a sip of his drink, savoring it. "Doesn't explain why you're eyeing up derelict land in Edinburgh."

"You *do* keep a watchful eye, don't you?"

"Comes with the territory."

"Is it because of Mr. Cafferty?"

"Could be. How did you two get to know one another?"

"Through business, Inspector. All of it aboveboard, I assure you."

"That why the authorities back in Moscow are preparing to take you down?"

"Politics," Andropov explained with a pained expression. "And a refusal to grease the necessary palms."

"So you're being made an example of?"

"Events will run their course . . ." He lifted his glass to his lips.

"A lot of rich men are in jail in Russia. You're not scared of joining them?" Andropov just shrugged. "Lucky you've made plenty of friends here — not just Labour, but the SNP, too. Must be nice to feel so wanted." Still the Russian said nothing, so Rebus decided on a change of topic. "Tell me about Alexander Todorov."

"What would you like to know?"

"You mentioned that he got kicked out of his teaching post for being too friendly with the students."

"Yes?"

"I'm not finding anything about it in the records."

"It was hushed up, but plenty of people in Moscow knew."

"Funny, though, that you'd tell me that and forget to mention that the two of you grew up together — same age, same neighborhood . . ."

Andropov looked at him. "Once again, I admit I'm impressed."

"How well did you know him?"

"Hardly at all. I'm afraid I came to represent everything Alexander detested. He would probably use words like 'greed' and 'ruthlessness,' while I prefer 'self-reliance' and 'dynamism.' "

"He was an old-fashioned Communist?"

"You know the English word 'bolshie'? It has its roots in 'bolshevism,' a Russian word. The Bolsheviks were fairly ruthless themselves, but these days 'bolshie' just means awkward or stubborn . . . that's what Alexander was."

"You knew he was living in Edinburgh?"

"I think I saw it mentioned in a newspaper."

"Did the two of you meet?"

"No."

"Funny he started drinking here . . ."

"Is it?" Andropov shrugged again and took another sip of water.

"So here you both are in Edinburgh, two men who grew up together, famous in your separate ways, and you didn't think to get in touch?"

"We would have had nothing to say to one another," Andropov declared. Then: "Would you like another drink, Inspector?"

Rebus noticed that he'd finished the whisky. He shook his head and started to rise from the booth.

"I'll be sure to mention to Mr. Bakewell that you dropped by," Andropov was saying.

"Mention it to Cafferty, too, if you like," Rebus retorted. "He'll tell you, once I get my teeth into something, I don't let go."

"And yet the pair of you seem very similar. . . . A pleasure talking to you, Inspector."

Outside, Rebus tried to get a cigarette lit in the swirling breeze. He had his head tucked into his jacket when the taxi pulled up, which meant he escaped the attention of Megan Macfarlane and Roddy Liddle, the MSP and her assistant marching into the hotel lobby, eyes fixed ahead of them. Rebus, blowing smoke skywards, wondered if Sergei Andropov would hesitate to tell them, too, about his recent visitor . . .

30

As Siobhan Clarke walked into the narrow CID room at West End police station, there was applause. Only two of the six desks were occupied, but both men wanted to show their appreciation.

"Feel free to keep Ray Reynolds as long as you like," DI Shug Davidson added with a grin, before introducing her to a detective constable called Adam Bruce. Davidson had his feet up on the desk, chair tilted back.

"Nice to see you hard at it," Clarke commented. "Where's everyone else?"

"Probably getting some Christmas shopping done. Can I expect a little something from you this year, Shiv?"

"I was thinking of sticking some gift wrap on Ray and posting him back."

"Don't you dare. Any joy with Sol Goodyear?"

"I'm not sure 'joy' is quite the right word."

"He's a sod, isn't he? Couldn't be more different from his brother. You know Todd goes to church on a Sunday?"

"So he said."

"Talk about chalk and cheese . . ." Davidson was shaking his head slowly.

"Can we talk about Larry Fintry instead?"

"What about him?"

"Is he on remand?"

Davidson gave a snort. "Cells are bursting at the seams, Shiv — you know that as well as I do."

"So he's out on bail?"

"Anything short of genocide and cannibalism these days, bail's a nap."

"So where can I find him?"

"He's in a hostel up in Bruntsfield."

"What sort of hostel?"

"Addiction problems. Doubt he'd be there this time of day, though." Davidson checked his watch. "Hunter Square or the Meadows, maybe."

"I was just in a café off Hunter Square."

"See any nutters hanging around?"

"I saw a few street people," Clarke corrected him. She'd noticed that although Bruce was glued to a computer screen, he was actually playing Minesweeper.

"The benches behind the old hospital," Davidson was saying, "he likes to hang out there sometimes. Might be a bit chilly, though. Drop-in centers on the Grassmarket and Cowgate are another possibility. . . . What is it you want him for?"

"I'm starting to wonder if there might be a price on Sol Goodyear's head."

Davidson gave a hoot. "Little turd's not worth it."

"All the same . . ."

"And no one in their right mind would give Crazy Larry the job. All this comes down to, Shiv, is Sol hassling Larry for money owed. It was probably when Sol said there'd be no more dope coming that Larry blew one of his last remaining fuses."

"Rewiring, that's what the guy needs," DC Bruce added, eyes still fixed on the game in front of him.

"If you want to go traipsing after Crazy Larry,"

Davidson said, "that's fine, but don't expect to get any-thing out of him. And I still don't see Sol Goodyear as the target of a hit."

"He must have enemies."

"But he's got friends, too."

Clarke narrowed her eyes. "Meaning?"

"Word is, he's back in Big Ger's employ. Well, not 'employ' exactly, but selling with Cafferty's blessing."

"Any proof of that?"

Davidson shook his head. "After we spoke on the phone, I made a few calls, and that's what I started to hear. Tell you something else, though . . ."

"What?"

"Birdies are saying Derek Starr's been brought back from Fettes to head *your* inquiry." At the next desk, Bruce started to make a little clucking sound. "Bit of a kick in the teeth, isn't it?" Davidson added.

"Stands to reason Derek would take over—he's a rank above me."

"Didn't seem to bother the bosses when it was you and a certain DI called Rebus . . ."

"I really am going to send Reynolds back here," Clarke warned him.

"You'll have to ask Derek Starr's permission."

She stared him out, and he burst into a laugh. "Have your fun while you can," she told him, heading for the door.

Back in her car, she wondered what else she could do to keep away from Gayfield Square. Answer: not much. Rebus had mentioned CCTV. Maybe she could make a detour by way of the City Chambers and put in that re-quest. Or she could call Megan Macfarlane and arrange another meeting, this time to talk about Charles Riordan and his taping of her committee. Then there was Jim Bakewell — Rebus wanted her to ask about the drink he'd had with Sergei Andropov and Big Ger Cafferty.

Cafferty . . .

He seemed to loom over the city, and yet very few of Edinburgh's citizens would even know of his existence. Rebus had spent half his career trying to bring the gangster down. With Rebus retired, the problem would become hers, not because *she* wanted it but because she doubted Rebus would let it go. He'd want her to finish what he couldn't. She thought again of the nights they'd been staying late at the office, Rebus running his most galling unsolveds past her. What was she supposed to do with them, these legacies? They felt to her like unwanted baggage. She had a pair of ugly pewter candlesticks at home, gifted to her in an aunt's will. Couldn't bring herself to throw them out, so they lay tucked away at the back of a drawer — also, she felt, the best place for Rebus's old case notes.

Her phone rang, 556 prefix: someone was calling from Gayfield Square. She thought she could guess who.

"Hello?"

Sure enough, it was Derek Starr. "You've snuck out on me," he said, trying to inject some surface levity into the accusation.

"Had to go talk to West End."

"What about?"

"Sol Goodyear."

There was a momentary silence. "Remind me," he said.

"Lives close to where Todorov was found. It was a friend of his who discovered the body."

"And?"

"Just wanted to confirm a few details."

He would know damned well she was holding something back, just as *she* knew there was nothing he could do about it.

"So when can we expect to see you back in the body of the kirk, DS Clarke?"

"I've got one more stop to make at the City Chambers."

"CCTV?" he guessed.

"That's right. I should only be half an hour or so."

"Heard anything from Rebus?"

"Not a dicky bird."

"DCI Macrae tells me he's been suspended."

"That's about the size of it."

"Not much of a swan song, is it?"

"Was there anything else, Derek?"

"You're my number two, Siobhan. That's how it stays unless I think you're playing away."

"Meaning what exactly?"

"Don't want you picking up any more bad habits from Rebus."

Unable to take anymore, she ended the call. "Pompous git," she muttered, turning the ignition.

"So what did you get up to last night, then?" Hawes asked. She was in the passenger seat, Colin Tibbet driving.

"Couple of drinks with some mates." He glanced in her direction. "You jealous, Phyl?"

"Jealous of you and your beery pals? Sure am, Col."

"Thought so," he said with a grin. They were heading for the southeast corner of the city, towards the bypass and the green belt. It hadn't surprised too many of the locals when FAB had been granted permission to construct its new HQ on what had previously been designated as protected land. A badger's sett had been relocated and a nine-hole golf course purchased for the exclusive use of employees. The huge glass building was just under a mile from the new Royal Infirmary, which Hawes guessed was handy for any bank employees suffering paper cuts from counting all those notes. On the other hand, it wouldn't surprise her if the FAB compound turned out to have its own sick bay.

"I stayed in, since you ask," she said now, watching Col slow to a halt as the lights ahead turned red. He did that thing they taught you in driving schools — not braking hard but changing back down through the gears. Up till now, everyone she'd met had started ignoring the maneuver as soon as they passed the test, but not Colin. She bet he ironed his underpants, too.

It was really starting to rile her that despite each deep-seated fault she located, she still fancied him. Maybe it was a case of any port in a storm. She hated the idea that she couldn't live her life perfectly adequately without a bloke in tow, but it was beginning to look that way.

"Anything good on the box?" he asked her.

"A documentary about how men are becoming women." He looked at her, trying to work out whether she was lying. "It's true," she insisted. "All that estrogen in the tap water. You lot gulp it down and then start growing breasts."

He concentrated for a moment. "How does estrogen get into the tap water?"

"Do I have to spell it out?" She mimed the action of flushing a toilet. "Then there's all the additives in meat. It's changing your chemical balance."

"I don't want my chemical balance changed."

She had to laugh at that. "Might explain something, though," she teased him.

"What?"

"Why you've started fancying Derek Starr." He scowled, and she laughed again. "Way you were watching him give that speech. . . . Might've been Russell Crowe in *Gladiator* or Mel Gibson in *Braveheart*."

"I saw *Braveheart* in the cinema," Tibbet told her. "The audience were on their feet, cheering and punching the air. Never seen anything like it."

"That's because Scots don't often get to feel good about themselves."

"You think we need independence?"

"Maybe," she conceded. "Just so long as people like First Albannach don't go scuttling south."

"What was their profit last year?"

"Eight billion, something like that."

"You mean eight million?"

"Eight *billion*," she repeated.

"That can't be right."

"You calling me a liar?" She was wondering how he'd managed to turn the conversation around without her noticing.

"Makes you wonder, doesn't it?" he asked now.

"Wonder what?"

"Where the real power is." He took his eyes off the road long enough to glance at her. "Want to do something later?"

"With you, you mean?"

He offered a shrug. "Christmas fair opens tonight. We could go take a look."

"We could."

"And a bite of supper after."

"I'll think about it."

They were signaling to turn in at the gates of First Albannach Bank's HQ. Ahead of them lay a glass and steel structure four stories high and as long as a street. A guard emerged from the gatehouse to take their names and the car's registration.

"Parking bay six-oh-eight," he told them. And though there were plenty of spaces closer to their destination, Hawes watched her colleague head obediently towards 608.

"Don't worry," she told him as he pulled on the hand brake, "I can walk from here."

And walk they did, passing serried ranks of sports cars, family saloons, and 4x4s. The grounds were still being landscaped, and just behind one corner of the main complex could be glimpsed gorse bushes and one of the golf course's fairways. When the doors slid open, they were in a triple-height atrium. There was an arcade of shops behind the reception desk: pharmacy, supermarket, café, newsagent. A notice board provided information about the crèche, gym, and swimming pool. Escalators led to the next level up, with glass-fronted lifts serving the floors above that. The receptionist beamed a smile at them.

"Welcome to FAB," she said. "If you'll just sign in and show me some photo ID . . ."

They did so, and she announced that Mr. Janney was in a meeting, but his secretary was expecting them.

"Third floor. She'll meet you at the lift." They were handed laminated passes and another smile. A security guard processed them through a metal detector, after which they scooped up keys, phones, and loose change.

"Expecting trouble?" Hawes asked the man.

"Code green," he intoned solemnly.

"A relief to us all."

The lift took them to the third floor, where a young woman in a black trouser suit was waiting. The A4-sized manila envelope was held out in front of her. As Hawes took it, the woman nodded once, then turned and marched back down a seemingly endless corridor. Tibbet hadn't even had a chance to exit the lift, and as Hawes stepped back into it the doors slid shut and they were on their way back down again. No more than three minutes after entering the building, they were out in the cold and wondering what had just happened.

"That's not a building," Hawes stated. "It's a machine."

Tibbet signaled his agreement by whistling through his teeth, then scanned the car park.

"Which bay are we in again?"

"The one at the end of the universe," Hawes told him, starting to cross the tarmac.

Back in the passenger seat, she pulled open the envelope and brought out a dozen sheets: photocopied bank statements. There was a yellow Post-it stuck to the front. The handwritten message speculated that Todorov had funds elsewhere, as indicated by the client when he opened his account. There was a single transfer involving a bank in Moscow. The note was signed "Stuart Janney."

"He was comfortable enough," Hawes announced. "Six grand in the current account and eighteen in savings." She checked the transaction dates: no significant deposits or withdrawals in the days leading up to his death, and no transactions at all thereafter. "Whoever took his cash card, they don't seem to be using it."

"They could have cleaned him out," Tibbet acknowledged. "Twenty-four K . . . so much for the starving artist."

"Garrets mustn't be as fashionable these days," Hawes agreed. She was punching a number into her phone. Clarke picked up, and Hawes relayed the highlights to her. "Took out a hundred the day he was killed."

"Where from?"

"Machine at Waverley Station." Hawes frowned suddenly. "Why did he leave Edinburgh from one station but come back to the other?"

"He was meeting Charles Riordan. I think Riordan frequented some curry house nearby."

"Can't really check with him, though, can we?"

"Not really," Clarke admitted. Hawes could hear voices in the background; all the same, it sounded a lot calmer than Gayfield Square.

"Where are you, Shiv?" she asked.

"City Chambers, asking about CCTV."

"How long till you're back at base?"

"An hour maybe."

"You sound inconsolable. Any word from our favorite DI?"

"Assuming you mean Rebus rather than Starr, the answer's no."

"Tell her," Tibbet said, "about the bank."

"Colin says to tell you we enjoyed our visit to First Albannach."

"Plush, was it?"

"I've stayed at worse resorts; they had everything in there but flumes."

"Did you see Stuart Janney?"

"He was in a meeting. To tell the truth, it was a real

production-line number. In and out and thank you very much."

"They've got shareholders to protect. When your profits are hitting ten billion, you don't want *any* bad publicity."

Hawes turned to Colin Tibbet. "Siobhan," she told him, "says the profit last year was *ten* billion."

"Give or take," Clarke added.

"Give or take," Hawes repeated for Tibbet's benefit.

"Makes you wonder," Tibbet repeated quietly, with a slow shake of the head.

Hawes stared at him. Kissable lips, she was thinking. Younger than her and less experienced. There was material there she could work with, maybe starting tonight.

"Talk to you later," she told Clarke, ending the call.

31

D r. Scarlett Colwell was waiting for Rebus at her office in George Square. She was on one of the upper floors, meaning the view would have been great if not for the buildup of condensation between the layers of double glazing.

"Depressing, isn't it?" she apologized. "Constructed forty years ago and fit for nothing but demolition."

Rebus turned his attention instead to the shelves of Russian textbooks. Plaster busts of Marx and Lenin were being used as bookends. On the wall opposite, posters and cards had been pinned up, including a photograph of President Yeltsin dancing. Colwell's desk was next to the window but facing into the room. Two tables had been pushed together, leaving just enough room for eight chairs to be arranged around them. There was a kettle on the floor, and she crouched down next to it, spooning coffee granules into two mugs.

"Milk?" she asked.

"Thanks," Rebus said, glancing towards her shock of hair. Her skirt was stretched tight, delineating the line of a hip.

"Sugar?"

"Just milk."

The kettle finished boiling, and she poured, handing him his cup before getting back to her feet. They stood very close to each other until she apologized again for the lack of space and retreated behind her desk, Rebus content to rest his backside against the table.

"Thanks for seeing me."

She blew on her coffee. "Not at all. I was devastated to hear about Mr. Riordan."

"You met him at the Poetry Library?" Rebus guessed.

She nodded, then had to push the hair away from her face. "And at Word Power."

It was Rebus's turn to nod. "That's the bookshop where Mr. Todorov did a reading?"

Colwell pointed towards the wall. This time when Rebus looked, he picked out the photograph of Alexander Todorov in full poetic flow, one arm dramatically raised, mouth agape.

"Doesn't look like a bookshop," Rebus declared.

"They moved it to a bigger venue — café on Nicolson Street. Even so, it was packed."

"He's in his element, isn't he?" Rebus was studying the picture more closely. "Did you take this, Dr. Colwell?"

"I'm not very good," she started to apologize.

"I'm the last one to judge." He turned and gave her a smile. "So Charles Riordan taped this session, too?"

"That's right." She paused. "In fact, it's a happy coincidence that you called me, Inspector . . ."

"Oh?"

"Because I was on the verge of phoning you, to ask a favor."

"What is it I can do for you, Dr. Colwell?"

"There's a magazine called the *London Review of Books*. They saw the obituary I wrote in the *Scotsman,* and they want to publish one of Alexander's poems."

"With you so far." Rebus lifted the cup to his lips.

"It's a new poem in Russian, one he recited at the Poetry Library." She gave a little laugh. "In fact, I think he'd only just finished it that day. Point being, I don't have a copy of it. I'm not sure anyone does."

"Have you had a look through his wastepaper bin?"

"Would it sound heartless if I said yes?"

"Not at all. But you didn't find it?"

"No . . . which is why I spoke to a nice man at Mr. Riordan's studio."

"That'll be Terry Grimm."

She nodded again, pushed her hair back again. "He said there was a recording."

Rebus thought of the hour he'd spent in Siobhan's car, the pair of them listening to a dead man. "You want to borrow it?" he guessed, remembering that Todorov had indeed recited some of the poems in Russian.

"Just long enough to write a translation. It would be my memorial to him, I suppose."

"I can't see a problem with that."

She beamed, and he got the feeling that if the desk hadn't been there, she might even have reached over and hugged him. Instead, she asked if she would have to listen to the CD at the station or would it be possible to take it away with her. The station . . . one place Rebus couldn't be seen.

"I can bring it to you," he said, and her smile widened before melting away.

"Deadline's next week," she suddenly realized.

"No problem," Rebus assured her. "And I'm sorry we haven't tracked down Mr. Todorov's killer yet."

Her face fell further. "I'm sure you're doing your utmost."

"Thanks for the vote of confidence." He paused. "You've still not asked me why I'm here."

"I was thinking you'd get round to telling me."

"I've been researching Mr. Todorov's life, looking for enemies."

"Alexander made an enemy of the *state*, Inspector."

"That much I believe. But one story I've been hearing is that he was dismissed from a lectureship for getting too friendly with his students. Thing is, I think the person who told me that was trying to sell me a pup."

But she was shaking her head. "Actually, it's true — Alexander told me about it himself. The charges were trumped up, of course — they just wanted him out, by fair means or foul." She sounded aggrieved on the poet's behalf.

"Do you mind if I ask . . . did he ever try anything with *you,* Dr. Colwell?"

"I have a partner, Inspector."

"With respect, Dr. Colwell, you're a beautiful woman, and I get the impression Alexander Todorov *liked* women. I'm not sure the existence of any partner short of a Ninja assassin would have deterred him."

She gave another perfect smile, lowering her lashes in feigned modesty.

"Well," she admitted, "you're right, of course. After a few drinks, Alexander's libido seemed always to be refreshed."

"A nice way of putting it. Are the words his?"

"All my own work, Inspector."

"He seems to have thought of you as a friend, though, or he wouldn't have taken you into his confidence."

"I'm not sure he had any *real* friends. Writers are like that sometimes — they see the rest of us as source material. Can you imagine being in bed with someone and knowing they're going to write about it afterwards? Knowing the whole world will be reading about that most intimate of moments?"

"I take your point." Rebus paused to clear his throat. "But he must have had some way of . . . 'quenching' that libido you mentioned?"

"Oh, he had women, Inspector."

"Students? Here in Edinburgh?"

"I couldn't say."

"Or how about Abigail Thomas at the Poetry Library? You seemed to think she had a crush on him."

"Probably not reciprocated," Colwell said dismissively. Then, after a moment's thought: "You really think Alexander was killed by a woman?"

Rebus shrugged. He was thinking of Todorov, more than a few drinks under his belt, weaving his way down King's Stables Road, a woman suddenly offering him no-strings sex. Would he have gone with a stranger? Probably. But even more likely with someone he'd known . . .

"Did Mr. Todorov ever mention a man called Andropov?" he asked.

She mouthed the name several times, deep in thought, then gave up. "Sorry," she said.

"Another long shot: how about someone called Cafferty?"

"I'm not really helping, am I?" she said as she shook her head.

"Sometimes the things we rule out are as important as the ones we rule in," he reassured her.

"Like in Sherlock Holmes?" she said. "When you've eliminated the—" She broke off with a frown. "I can never remember that quote, but you must know it?"

He nodded, not wanting her to think him ill-read. Every day on his way to work, he passed a statue of Sherlock Holmes by the roundabout on Leith Street. Turned out it was marking the spot where they'd knocked down Conan Doyle's childhood home.

"What is it, then?" she was asking.

He gave a shrug. "I'm like you, never seem to get it right . . ."

She rose from her chair and came around the desk, her skirt brushing against his legs as she squeezed past. She lifted a book from one of the shelves. From the spine, Rebus could tell it was a collection of quotations. She found the Doyle section and ran a finger down it, finding what she was looking for.

" 'When you have eliminated the impossible, whatever remains, however improbable, must be the truth.' " She frowned again. "That's not how I remember it. I thought it was to do with eliminating the possible rather than its opposite."

"Mmm," Rebus said, hoping she'd think he was agreeing with her. He placed his empty mug on the table. "Well, Dr. Colwell, seeing how I've done you a favor . . ."

"Quid pro quo?" She clapped the book shut. Dust rose from its pages.

"I was just wondering if I could have the key to Todorov's flat."

"As it happens, you're in luck. Someone from Building Services was supposed to stop by and get it, but so far no sign."

"What will they do with all his stuff?"

"The consulate said they'd take it. He must have *some* family back in Russia." She'd gone behind the desk again and opened a drawer, bringing out the key chain. Rebus took it from her with a nod of thanks. "There's a servitor on the ground floor here," she explained. "If I'm not around, you can always leave it with him." She paused. "And you won't forget that recording?"

"Trust me."

"It's just that the studio seemed pretty sure it's the only copy left. Poor Mr. Riordan — what a terrible way to die . . ."

Back outside again, Rebus descended the steps from George Square to Buccleuch Place. There were a few students around. They looked . . . the only word for it was "studious." He stopped at the bottom of the steps to light a cigarette, but the temperature was sinking, and he decided he might as well smoke it indoors.

Todorov's flat seemed unchanged from his first visit, except that the scraps of paper from the bin had been laid flat on the desk — Scarlett Colwell most probably, seeking the elusive poem. Rebus had forgotten about those six copies of *Astapovo Blues*. Had to find someone with an eBay account so he could shift them. Looking more closely at the room, he decided someone had removed some of the poet's book collection. Colwell again? Or some other member of the staff? Rebus wondered if he'd been beaten to it — a glut of Todorov memorabilia bringing prices down. He realized his phone was ringing and took it out. Didn't recognize the number, but it had the international code on the front.

"Detective Inspector Rebus speaking," he said.

"Hello, it's Roddy Denholm, returning your mysterious call." The voice was an educated Anglo-Scots drawl.

"Not too much of a mystery, Mr. Denholm, and I do appreciate you taking the trouble."

"You're lucky I'm a night owl, Inspector."

"It's the middle of the day here . . ."

"But not in Singapore."

"Mr. Blackman thought either Melbourne or Hong Kong."

Denholm laughed a smoker's throaty laugh. "I suppose I could be anywhere, actually, couldn't I? I could be around the next corner for all you know. Bloody wonderful things, mobile phones . . ."

"If you *are* around the next corner, sir, be cheaper to do this in person."

"You could always hop on a jet to Singapore."

"Trying to lower my carbon footprint, sir." Rebus blew cigarette smoke towards the living room ceiling.

"So where are you right now, Inspector?"

"Buccleuch Place."

"Ah yes, the university district."

"Standing in a dead man's flat."

"Not a sentence I think I've ever heard." The artist sounded duly impressed.

"He wasn't quite in your line of work, sir — poet called Alexander Todorov."

"I've heard of him."

"He was killed just over a week ago, and your name has cropped up in the inquiry."

"Do tell." It sounded as though Denholm was getting himself comfortable on a hotel bed. Rebus, likewise, sat down on the sofa, an elbow on one knee.

"You've been doing a project at the Parliament. There was a man making some sound recordings for you . . ."

"Charlie Riordan?"

"I'm afraid he's dead, too." Rebus heard low whistling on the line. "Someone torched his house."

"Are the tapes okay?"

"As far as we know, sir."

Denholm caught Rebus's tone. "I must sound an insensitive bastard," he admitted.

"Don't fret—it was the first thing your dealer asked, too."

Denholm chuckled. "Poor guy, though . . ."

"You knew him?"

"Not until the Parliament project. Seemed likable, capable . . . didn't really talk to him that much."

"Well, Mr. Riordan had also been doing some work with Alexander Todorov."

"Christ, does that mean I'm next?"

Rebus couldn't tell if he was joking or not. "I wouldn't have thought so, sir."

"You're not phoning to warn me?"

"I just thought it an interesting coincidence."

"Except that I didn't know Alexander Todorov from Adam."

"Maybe not, but one of your fans did—Sergei Andropov."

"I know the name . . ."

"He collects your work. Russian businessman, grew up with Mr. Todorov." Rebus heard another whistle. "You've never met him?"

"Not that I know of." There was silence for a moment. "You think this Andropov guy killed the poet?"

"We're keeping an open mind."

"Was it some obscure isotope like that guy in London?"

"He was beaten to a pulp before someone caved his skull in."

"Not exactly subtle, then."

"Not exactly. Tell me something, Mr. Denholm—how

did you come to choose the Urban Regeneration Committee for your project?"

"*They* chose me, Inspector — we asked if anyone would be interested in taking part, and their chairman said she was up for it."

"Megan Macfarlane?"

"No shortage of ego there, Inspector — I speak as one who knows."

"I'm sure you do, sir." Rebus heard something like a doorbell.

"That'll be room service," Denholm explained.

"I'll let you go, then," Rebus said. "Thanks for calling, Mr. Denholm."

"No problem."

"One last thing, though . . ." Rebus paused just long enough to ensure he had the artist's full attention. "Before you let them in, best check that it really *is* room service."

He snapped shut his phone and allowed himself a little smile.

32

"Can't be that much of it, if it fits onto one of these," Siobhan Clarke commented. She was back in the CID suite and, DCI Macrae being elsewhere, had commandeered his room, the better to accommodate Terry Grimm. Seated at her boss's desk, she held the clear plastic memory stick between thumb and forefinger, angling it in the light.

"You'd be surprised," Grimm said. "I'm guessing there's about sixteen hours on there. Could have squeezed more in if there had been anything usable. Unfortunately, the heat of the fire had done for most of it." He'd brought the evidence sacks with him. They were tied shut but still carried the faintest aroma of charcoal.

"Did anything catch your eye?" Clarke paused. "Or *ear*, I suppose I should say."

Grimm shook his head. "Tell you what I did do, though . . ." He reached into his inside pocket and drew out a CD in a plastic wallet. "Charlie taped the Russian poet at another event, few weeks back. Happened to come across it at the studio, so I burned you a copy." He handed it over.

"Thanks," she said.

"Some lecturer at the university was after the other show Charlie taped, but as far as I know *you've* got the only existing copy."

"Name of Colwell?"

"That's it." He stared at the backs of his hands. "Any nearer to finding out who killed him?"

She gestured in the direction of the main office. "You can see we're not exactly resting on our laurels."

He nodded, but his eyes never left hers. "Good way of avoiding an answer," he stated.

"It's a case of finding the 'why,' Mr. Grimm. If you can help shed some light, we'd be incredibly grateful."

"I've been turning it over in my head. Hazel and me have bounced it around, too. Still doesn't make any sense."

"Well, if you *do* think of anything . . ." She was rising to her feet, signaling that the meeting was over. Through the glass partition, she could see that there was a hubbub in the outer office. Out of it emerged Todd Goodyear. He knocked once and entered, closing the door after him.

"If I'm going to manage to actually *hear* what's on those committee recordings, I'm going to need to shift my stuff," he complained. "It's like the monkey house out there." He recognized Terry Grimm and gave a little nod of greeting.

"The Parliament tapes?" Grimm guessed. "You're still trawling through them?"

"Still trawling." Goodyear had a sheaf of paper under one arm.

He held the sheets out for Clarke to take. She saw that he had typed up his detailed notes on the contents of each tape. There were screeds of the stuff. In her early days as a detective, she, too, would have been this meticulous . . . back before Rebus showed her how to cut corners.

"Thanks," she said. "And this is for you . . ." Handing him the memory stick. "Mr. Grimm reckons there's about sixteen hours' worth."

Goodyear gave a protracted sigh and asked Terry Grimm how things were at the studio.

"Just about coping, thanks."

Clarke was sifting the typed sheets. "Did anything here jump out at you?" she asked Goodyear.

"Not one single thing," he informed her.

"Imagine how *we* felt," Grimm added, "sitting there for days on end, listening to politician after politician drone on . . ."

Goodyear just shook his head, unwilling to imagine himself in that role.

"What you got was the good stuff," Grimm assured him.

Clarke noticed that it had quieted down in the main office. "What was the noise about?" she asked Goodyear.

"Bit of a free-for-all at the mortuary," he explained casually, tossing the memory stick into the air and catching it. "Someone's trying to claim Todorov's body. DI Starr wanted to know who was the fastest driver." Another toss, another catch. "DC Reynolds claimed *he* was. Not everyone agreed . . ." He had been slow to notice that Clarke was glaring at him, but now his voice trailed off. "I should have told you straight off?" he guessed.

"That's right," she answered in a voice of quiet menace. And then, to Terry Grimm: "PC Goodyear will see you out. Thanks again for coming."

She marched downstairs to the car park and got into her car. Started the ignition and drove. She wanted to ask Starr why he hadn't said anything . . . why he hadn't asked *her*. Giving the job to one of his boys instead — Ray

Reynolds, at that! Was it because she'd gone off without telling him? Was it so she'd know her place in future?

She had plenty of questions for DI Derek Starr.

She turned right at the top of Leith Street, then hard left onto North Bridge. Straight across at the Tron and a right-hand turn, crossing oncoming traffic and onto Blair Street, passing Nancy Sievewright's flat again. If Talking Heads really did reckon London a small city, they should try Edinburgh. No more than eight minutes after leaving Gayfield Square, she was pulling into the mortuary car park, stopping alongside Reynolds's car, and wondering if she'd beaten his time. There was another car, a big old Mercedes Benz, parked between two of the mortuary's anonymous white transit vans. Clarke stalked past it to the door marked Staff Only, turned the handle, and went in. There was no one in the corridor, and no one in the staff room, though steam was rising from the spout of a recently boiled kettle. She moved through the holding area and opened another door into a further corridor, up some stairs to the next level. This was where the public entrance was. It was where relatives waited to identify their loved ones and where the subsequent paperwork was taken care of. Usually it was a place of low sobbing, quiet reflection, utter and ghastly silence. But not today.

She recognized Nikolai Stahov straight off. He wore the same long black coat as when they'd first met. Alongside him stood a man who also looked Russian, maybe five years younger but almost as many inches taller and broader. Stahov was remonstrating in English with Derek Starr, who stood with arms folded, legs apart, as if ready for a ruck. Next to him was Reynolds, and behind them the four mortuary staff.

"We have right," Stahov was saying. "Constitutional right . . . moral right."

"A murder inquiry is ongoing," Starr explained. "The body has to stay here in case further tests are required."

Stahov, glancing to his left, had noticed Clarke. "Help us, please," he implored her. She took a few steps forward.

"What seems to be the problem?"

Starr glared at her. "The consulate wants to repatriate Mr. Todorov's remains," he explained.

"Alexander needs to be buried in his homeland," Stahov stated.

"Is there anything in his will to that effect?" Clarke asked.

"Will or no will, his wife is buried in Moscow—"

"Something I've been meaning to ask," Clarke interrupted. Stahov had turned completely towards her, which seemed to annoy Starr. "What actually happened to his wife?"

"Cancer," Stahov told her. "They could have operated, but she would have lost the baby she was carrying. So she continued with the pregnancy." Stahov offered a shrug. "The baby was stillborn, and by then the mother only had a few days to live."

The story seemed to have calmed the whole room. Clarke nodded slowly. "Why the sudden urgency, Mr. Stahov? Alexander died eight days ago . . . why wait till now?"

"All we want is to return him home, with due respect to his international stature."

"I wasn't sure he had that much stature in Russia. Didn't you say that the Nobel Prize isn't such a big deal in Moscow these days?"

"Governments can have changes of heart."

"What you're saying is, you're under orders from the Kremlin?"

Stahov's eyes gave nothing away. "There being no next of kin, the state becomes responsible. I have the authority to request his body."

"But we have no authority to release it," Starr countered, having shuffled around towards Clarke, the better to meet Stahov's eye line. "You're a diplomat; you must be aware that there are *protocols*."

"Meaning what, exactly?"

"Meaning," Clarke explained, "we'll be hanging on to the body until instructed otherwise by judgment or decree."

"It is scandalous." Stahov busied himself tugging at the cuffs of his coat. "I'm not sure how such a situation can be kept from public view."

"Go crying to the papers," Starr taunted him. "See where it gets you . . ."

"Start the process," Clarke counseled the Russian. "That's all you can do."

Stahov met her eyes again and nodded slowly, then turned on his heels and headed for the exit, followed by his driver. As soon as both men had left, Starr grabbed Clarke by the arm.

"What are you doing here?" he spat.

She twisted out of his grip. "I'm where I should have been all along, Derek."

"I left you in charge at Gayfield."

"You left without so much as a word."

Perhaps Starr sensed that this was not an argument he could win. He glanced around at the onlookers—Reynolds, the mortuary staff—and allowed his face to soften. "A discussion for another time, perhaps," he offered.

Clarke, though she'd already decided not to push it, let him sweat for a moment as she pretended to think it over. "Fine," she said at last.

He nodded and turned to the mortuary attendants. "You did the right thing, calling us. If they try anything else, you know where we are."

"Think they'll sneak him out in the middle of the night?" one of the men speculated.

One of his colleagues gave a chuckle. "Been a while since we've had one of those, Davie," he commented.

Siobhan Clarke decided not to ask.

33

They gathered around a table in the back room of the Oxford Bar. Word had gone out that John Rebus needed a bit of privacy, meaning they had the space to themselves. Nevertheless, they kept their voices low. First thing Rebus had done was explain his suspension and admit that it was dangerous for them to be seen with him. Clarke had sipped her tonic water — no gin tonight. Colin Tibbet had looked to Phyllida Hawes for a lead.

"If I have to choose between Derek Starr and yourself . . . no contest," Hawes had decided.

"No contest," Tibbet had echoed, without sounding completely convinced.

"What's the worst they can do to me?" Todd Goodyear had added. "Send me back to uniform at West End? It's going to happen anyway," And he'd raised his half-pint of beer in Rebus's direction.

After which, they'd started detailing the day's events, Rebus careful to edit his own version — since he *was* supposed to be on suspension.

"You've still not talked to Megan Macfarlane or Jim Bakewell?" he asked Clarke.

"I've been a bit busy, John."

"Sorry," Goodyear said, almost choking on a mouthful of ale, "that reminds me — while you were at the mortuary, Bakewell's office called. There's a meeting with him penciled in for tomorrow."

"Thanks for the heads-up, Todd."

He winced visibly. Hawes was saying something about being thankful for any excuse to get out of the office.

"Isn't space to swing a cat," Tibbet concurred. "I opened my desk drawer this afternoon, somebody had left half a sandwich in it."

"Did they treat you to lunch at the bank?" Rebus asked.

"Just a couple of foie gras baps," Hawes informed him. "To be honest, the place reminded me of a very slick and upmarket production line, but a production line nonetheless."

"Ten billion in profits." Tibbet still couldn't take it in.

"More than some countries' GDPs," Goodyear added.

"Here's hoping they stick around if we get independence," Rebus said. "Put them and their nearest competitor together, well, it's not a bad start for a wee country."

Clarke was looking at him. "You think that's why Stuart Janney's staying close to Megan Macfarlane?"

Rebus shrugged. "Nationalists wouldn't want the likes of FAB packing up and shipping out. That gives the bank a bit of leverage."

"I didn't see any levers sticking out of Ms. Macfarlane."

"But she *is* the future, isn't she? Banks don't make profits without playing a long game — sometimes a very long game." He grew thoughtful. "Maybe they're not the only ones at that . . ."

His phone started to vibrate, so he checked the

number. Another mobile, one he didn't know. He flipped the phone open.

"Hello?"

"Strawman . . ." Cafferty's pet name for Rebus, its origins all but lost down the years. Rebus was on his feet, making for the front bar, down the couple of steps and then out into the night.

"You've changed your number," Rebus told the gangster.

"Every few weeks. But I don't mind friends knowing it."

"That's nice." Since he was outside, Rebus took the opportunity to get a cigarette going.

"They'll be the death of you, you know."

"We all have to go sometime." Rebus was remembering what Stone had said about taps on Cafferty's phones . . . could they listen in on a mobile? Maybe another reason Cafferty kept changing numbers.

"I want to see you," the gangster was saying.

"When?"

"Now, of course."

"Any particular reason?"

"Just come to the canal."

"Whereabouts on the canal?"

"You know," Cafferty drawled, ending the conversation. Rebus stared at the phone before snapping it shut. He had wandered out into the lane. No problem this time of night — no traffic. And if any cars did venture along Young Street, the noise they made was a giveaway. So he stood there in the middle of the road, smoking his cigarette and facing Charlotte Square. One of the regulars had told him awhile back that the Georgian building facing him at the far end of the street was the residence of the First Minister. He wondered what the country's leader made of the occasional motley crews to be found smoking outside the Oxford Bar . . .

The door opened and Siobhan Clarke emerged, sliding her arms into the sleeves of her coat. Todd Goodyear was right behind her, a single half-pint having provided ample sufficiency.

"That was Cafferty," Rebus told them. "He wants to see me. You two headed somewhere?"

"Got to meet my girlfriend," Goodyear explained. "Going to see the Christmas lights."

"It's still November," Rebus complained.

"They were switched on at six tonight."

"And I thought I'd start heading home," Clarke added.

Rebus wagged a finger. "Should never leave a pub together — people will talk."

"Why does Cafferty want to see you?" Clarke asked.

"He didn't say."

"Are you going to go?"

"Don't see why not."

"Where's the meeting — somewhere well lit, I hope?"

"The canal, near that bar at the Fountainbridge basin. . . . What are Phyl and Col up to?"

"Thinking about Princes Street Gardens," Goodyear said. "Ferris wheel and the ice rink are open for business."

Clarke's eyes were fixed on Rebus. "You after some backup?"

The look on his face was answer enough.

"Well . . ." Goodyear was turning up his collar as he examined the weather. "See you in the morning, eh?"

"Keep your nose clean, Todd," Rebus advised him,

watching as the young man headed towards Castle Street.

"He's all right, isn't he?" he offered. Clarke, however, was not to be deflected.

"You can't just go meeting Cafferty by yourself."

"It's not like it's the first time."

"But any one of them could be the *last*."

"If I'm found floating, at least you'll know who to pull in."

"Don't you *dare* joke about this!"

He rested the palm of his hand against her shoulder. "Siobhan, it's fine," he assured her. "But there is a fly of sorts in the ointment . . . SCD could be watching Cafferty."

"What?"

"I had a run-in with them last night." Seeing the look on her face, he withdrew his hand and held it up in a show of appeasement. "I'll explain later, but the thing is, they want me keeping my distance."

"Then that's what you should do."

"Absolutely," he said, making to hand her Stone's business card. "And what I want *you* to do is ring this guy Stone and tell him DI Rebus needs an urgent word."

"What?"

"Use the phone in the Ox — don't want him tracing your mobile. You stay anonymous, say Rebus wants a meet at the petrol station. Then hang up."

"Christ's sake, John . . ." She was staring at the card.

"Hey, another forty-eight hours, and I'll be out of your hair."

"You're suspended from duty and you're *still* in my hair."

"Like a brush through the tangles, eh?" Rebus said with a smile.

"More like malfunctioning curling tongs," Clarke told him, but she headed back into the bar anyway to make the call.

"Took your time" was Cafferty's opening line. He was on the same footbridge across the canal, hands in the pockets of his long camel hair coat.

"Where's your car?" Rebus asked, glancing back towards the deserted patch of wasteland.

"I walked. Only takes ten minutes."

"And no bodyguard?"

"No need," Cafferty stated.

Rebus lit another cigarette. "So you knew I was here the other night?"

"It was Sergei's driver who recognized you." The one who'd stared daggers at Rebus that night at the hotel. "Were you with us all the way to Granton?"

"It was a nice night for a drive." Rebus tried blowing smoke towards Cafferty's face, but the breeze whipped it away.

"It's all legit, you know. Follow us all you like."

"Thanks, I will."

"Sergei loves Scotland, that's what it comes down to. His dad used to read him *Treasure Island*. I had to take him to Queen Street Gardens. Pond there's supposed to be what gave Robert Louis Stevenson the idea."

"Fascinating." Rebus was staring at the canal's glassy surface. Might only be three or four feet deep, but he'd known men to drown in it.

"He's thinking of bringing his businesses here," Cafferty said.

"Didn't know we had a lot of tin and zinc mines."

"Well, maybe not *all* his businesses."

"I can't see the point really — it's not as if we don't have an extradition treaty with Russia."

"You sure about that?" Cafferty said with a teasing smile. "Anyway, we *do* have a policy on political asylum, don't we?"

"Not sure your pal fits the bill."

Cafferty just smiled again.

"That night in the hotel," Rebus pushed on, "you and Todorov, then you and Andropov, plus a government minister called Bakewell . . . what was that really all about?"

"I thought I'd already explained — I'd no idea who it was I bought a drink for."

"You didn't know that Todorov and Andropov grew up together?"

"No."

Rebus flicked ash into the air. "So what was it you were discussing with the Minister for Economic Development?"

"I'm betting you've asked Sergei the same question."

"How do you think he answered?"

"He probably told you they were talking about economic development — it happens to be true."

"You seem to be in the market for a lot of land, Cafferty. Andropov puts up the money, you act as his factor?"

"All aboveboard."

"Does he know about your history as a landlord? Flats stuffed with tenants, fire risks ignored, dole checks lifted and cashed . . ."

"You really are clutching at straws, aren't you? Anyone would think you were in *there*." Cafferty jabbed a finger towards the canal.

"You own a flat on Blair Street, it's let to Nancy Sieve-wright and Eddie Gentry." Just the two tenants, now Rebus thought of it; unusual for one of Cafferty's fire traps. "Nancy's friendly with Sol Goodyear," he went on, "so friendly, in fact, that she gets her gear from him. Same night Sol gets himself stabbed in Haymarket, Nancy trips over Todorov's body at the foot of Sol's lane." Rebus had brought his face close to the gangster's. "See what I'm getting at?"

"Not really."

"And now the consulate want to spirit Todorov's body away."

"Those straws I mentioned, Rebus, I'm losing count of them."

"They're not straws, Cafferty, they're chains, and guess who it is they seem to be winding themselves around?"

"Steady," Cafferty cautioned. "With language like that, you might want to start writing a bit of poetry your-self."

"Problem with that is, the only words I can find to rhyme with 'Cafferty' are 'evil' and 'bastard.' "

The gangster grinned, showing off expensive dental work. Then he sniffed the air and strolled to the far side of the bridge. "I grew up not too far from here, did you know that?"

"I thought it was Craigmillar."

"But I'd an aunt and uncle in Gorgie, they looked after me when my mum was working. Dad legged it a month before I was due." He turned towards Rebus. "You didn't grow up in the city, did you?"

"Fife," Rebus stated.

"You won't remember the abattoir then. Occasionally, you'd get a bull making a break for it. The alarm would sound and us kids would be kept indoors until the sharp-shooter arrived. I remember one time, I watched from the window. Bloody great beast it was, with snot and steam belching from it, kicking up its legs at the thought of all that bloody freedom." He paused. "Right up until the moment the gunman went down on one knee, got his aim right, and shot it in the head. Those legs buckled and the gleam left its eyes. For a time there, I used to think that was *me* — the last free bull."

"You're full of bull all right," Rebus retorted.

"Thing is," Cafferty said with a smile that was almost rueful, "nowadays, I think maybe it's you, Rebus. You're bucking and kicking and snorting, because you can't deal with the idea of me being legit."

"That's because 'idea' is as far as it gets." He paused, flicking the remains of his cigarette into the water. "Why the hell did you bring me here, Cafferty?"

The gangster shrugged. "Not too many chances left for these little tête-à-têtes. And when Sergei told me you'd followed us that night . . . well, maybe I was just looking for the opportunity."

"I'm touched."

"I heard on the news that DI Starr's been shipped in to head up the inquiry. They've already put you out to pasture, haven't they? Just as well the pension's healthy . . ."

"And all of it clean."

"Siobhan's got her chance to shine now."

"She's a match for you, Cafferty."

"Let's wait and see."

"Just so long as I've got a ringside seat."

Cafferty's attention had shifted to the high brick wall,

beyond which lay the development site. "Nice talking to you, Rebus. Enjoy that walk into the sunset."

But Rebus didn't budge. "Have you heard about the Russian guy in London? Got to be careful who you play with, Cafferty."

"No one's about to poison me, Rebus. Sergei and me, we see things the same way. Few years from now, Scotland's going to be independent—not a shred of doubt about that. Sitting on thirty years' worth of North Sea oil and God alone knows how much more in the Atlantic. Worst-case scenario, we do a deal with Westminster and end up with eighty or ninety percent of the cut." Cafferty gave a slow shrug. "And then we'll go and spend the money on our usual leisure pursuits—booze, drugs, and gambling. Put a supercasino in every city, and watch the profits stack up . . ."

"Another of your silent invasions, eh?"

"Soviets always did think there'd be revolution in Scotland. Won't matter to you, though, will it? You'll be out of the game for good." Cafferty gave a little wave of the hand and turned his back.

Rebus stood his ground a bit longer but knew there was little to be gained from sticking around. All the same, he hesitated. The Cafferty of the other evening had been an actor on a stage, with props, including the car and the driver. Tonight's Cafferty was different, more reflective. Lots of faces in Cafferty's wardrobe . . . a mask for every occasion. Rebus considered offering him a lift home, but why the hell would he want to do that? Instead he turned and headed back to his car, lighting another cigarette on the way. The gangster's story about the bull stayed with him. Was that how retirement would feel, all that strange and disconcerting freedom, but brutally short?

"No Leonard Cohen for you when we get home," he chided himself. "You're morbid enough as it is."

Instead, he played Rory Gallagher: "Big Guns" and "Bad Penny," "Kickback City" and "Sinnerboy." The whisky slipped down, just the three large ones with about as much water again. And after Rory came Jackie Leven, and Page and Plant after that. He thought about calling Siobhan, then decided against it. Let her have a bit of a break from John Rebus's worries. He hadn't eaten anything but didn't feel hungry.

When his phone rang, he'd probably been asleep for the best part of an hour. The whisky glass was still there on the arm of the chair, his hand gripped around it.

"Didn't spill a drop, John," he congratulated himself, hoisting his phone in his free hand.

"Hiya, Shiv," he said, having recognized her number. "Checking up on me?"

"John . . ." Her tone of voice said it all: something had happened, something bad.

"Spit it out," he told her, rising from the chair.

"Cafferty's in intensive care." She left it at that for a moment. Rebus clawed his free hand through his hair, then realized he shouldn't *have* a free hand. The glass had dropped to the carpet, meaning he now had splashes of whisky on his shoes.

"What happened?" he asked.

"Precisely the question I was about to ask you," she blurted out. "What the hell happened at the canal?"

"We just talked."

"Talked?"

"Cross my heart."

"Must've been a pretty robust exchange, then, seeing

how he's got a fractured skull. Plus broken bones, contusions . . ."

Rebus's eyes narrowed. "He was found by the canal?"

"Too right he was."

"Is that where you are now?"

"Shug Davidson took the trouble to call me."

"I'll be there in five minutes."

"No, you won't . . . you've been *drinking,* John. Your voice goes nasal after the first four or five."

"So send a car for me."

"John . . ."

"Just send a fucking car, Siobhan!" He ran the hand through his hair again, pulling at it. I'm being set up here, he told himself.

"John, how can Shug let you near? Far as he's concerned, you're going to be a suspect. If he lets a suspect walk into a crime scene . . ."

"Yes, fine, absolutely." Rebus was looking at his watch. "It's about three hours since I left him. When was the body found?"

"Two and a half hours ago."

"That's not good." His mind was whirling. He started towards the kitchen, thinking maybe a gallon of tap water would help. "Did you send Calum Stone on that wild goose chase?"

"Yes."

"Shit."

"He's here right now, along with his partner."

Rebus squeezed his eyes shut. "Don't speak to them."

"Bit late for that. I was talking to Shug when they arrived. Stone introduced himself, and guess what his first words to me were?"

"Something along the lines of 'Gosh, you sound just like the woman who sent me on a wild goose chase to a petrol station in Granton'?"

"That's about the size of it."

"All you can do is tell the truth, Shiv — I ordered you to make that call."

"And you were on suspension at the time — something *I* knew fine well."

"Christ, I'm sorry, Siobhan . . ." The tap was still running, the sink almost full. Maybe eight inches deep. He'd known men to drown in far, far less.

34

When the taxi dropped him at the Leamington Lift Bridge, she was waiting, arms folded, for all the world like the bouncer outside some exclusive club.

"You can't *be* here," she reiterated through gritted teeth.

"I know," he said. Plenty of onlookers: people who'd been heading home from a night out; locals from the neighboring tenements; even a couple from one of the canal boats. They stood on deck, holding mugs of steaming liquid.

"Why's your hair wet?" Clarke asked.

"Didn't have time to dry it," he answered. He could see everything; no need to get closer. SOCOs shining their torches against the surface of the opposite footpath. Arc lamps being plugged into some sort of mooring point—probably how the boats hooked up to electricity during their stay. Lots of quietly busy people. There was a huddle around one particular area of walkway.

"That where they found him?" he asked. Clarke nodded. "Pretty much where he was when I left him."

"Couple on their way home stumbled across him. One of the medics recognized the face. West End came running, and Shug thought maybe I'd want to know."

There were SOCOs up to their waists in the canal.

They wore the same sort of protection as anglers, complete with braces holding up their oilskin trousers.

"They'll find one of my cigarette butts," Rebus told Clarke. "Unless it's floated away or been eaten by a duck."

"That'll be nice when they trace the DNA."

He turned towards her, gripping one of her arms. "I'm not saying I wasn't here — I'm saying he was right as rain when I left him."

She couldn't meet his eyes, and he let her go. "Don't think what you're thinking," he said quietly.

"You don't *know* what I'm thinking!"

He turned away again and saw DI Shug Davidson giving orders to some of the uniforms from West End. Stone and Prosser were just behind him, deep in a discussion of their own.

"Any second now they'll see you," Clarke warned. Rebus nodded. He'd already taken a couple of steps back into the crowd of onlookers. She followed him until they were standing to the rear. This was where he'd parked his car the time he'd followed Cafferty. His head was thumping.

"Got any aspirin?" he asked.

"No."

"Never mind, I know where I can find some."

She caught his meaning. "You've got to be joking."

"Never more serious in my life."

She fixed her eyes on him, then glanced back towards the canal and made her mind up. "I'll drive you," she said. "My car's on Gilmore Place."

They didn't say much on the way to the Western General. Cafferty had been taken there not only because it was closer than the Infirmary but also because it specialized in head injuries.

"Did you see him?" Rebus asked as they reached the hospital car park.

Clarke shook her head. "When Shug called me, he thought he was the bearer of glad tidings."

"He knows there's history between us and Cafferty," Rebus agreed.

"But he could tell straightaway something was up."

"You told him I'd gone to meet Cafferty?"

She shook her head again. "I haven't told anyone."

"Well, you better had — only way to keep your head above the shit. Stone's going to work it out before long."

"Wait till they find out I've done a runner . . ." She pulled into a parking bay and turned off the ignition, then slid around to face him. "Okay," she said, "tell me."

He met her eyes. "I didn't touch him."

"So what did you talk about?"

"Andropov and Bakewell . . . Sievewright and Sol Goodyear . . ." He shrugged, deciding to omit the abattoir bull. "Funny thing is, I almost offered him a lift home."

"I wish you had." She sounded slightly more mollified.

"Does that mean you believe me?"

"I've got to, haven't I? All we've been through . . . if I can't believe *you*, what the hell else is there?"

"Thanks," he said quietly, squeezing her hand.

"You still owe me the story of your run-in with the SCDEA." She removed her hand from beneath his.

"They've had Cafferty under surveillance. Heard I'd been watching him and warned me off." He shrugged again. "That's about the size of it."

"And being bullheaded, you did exactly the opposite?"

Rebus had a sudden image: the bull with its legs buckling, a bullet between its eyes. . . . He shook himself free of it. "Let's go see what the damage is," he said.

Inside the hospital, the first question they were asked was: "Are you family?"

"He's my brother," Rebus stated. This seemed to oil the wheels, and they were shown to a waiting area, deserted this time of night. Rebus picked up a magazine. It was page after page of celebrity gossip, but as it was also six months out of date, chances were the celebrities had already been returned to obscurity. He offered it to Clarke, but she shook her head.

"Your brother?" she said.

Rebus just shrugged. His real brother had died a year and a half back. Over the past couple of decades, Rebus had paid him a lot less attention than Cafferty . . . probably spent less time with him, too.

You can't choose your family, he thought to himself, but you can choose your enemies.

"What if he dies?" Clarke asked, folding her arms. She had her legs stretched out, crossed at the ankles, and was slumped low in the chair.

"I'm not that lucky," Rebus told her. She glowered at him.

"So who do you reckon is behind it?"

"Can we make that a multiple-choice question?" he asked.

"How many names have you got?"

"Depends if he's gone upsetting his Russian friends."

"Andropov?"

"For starters. SCD reckoned they were close to having Cafferty in the bag. Might be a lot of people out there who couldn't let that happen." He broke off as an unfeasibly young doctor in the traditional white coat pushed through the swinging doors at the end of the corridor and, notes in one hand, pen between his teeth, marched up to them. He removed the pen and popped it into his top pocket.

"You're the patient's brother?" he asked. Rebus nodded. "Well, Mr. Cafferty, I don't have to tell you that Morris seems blessed with an unusually resistant skull."

"We call him Ger," Rebus said. "Sometimes Big Ger."

The young doctor nodded, consulting his notes.

"But is he okay?" Clarke asked.

"Far from it. We'll do another scan in the morning. He's still unconscious, but there's enough brain activity to be going on with." He paused, as if deciding how much more they needed to know. "When the skull is hit with tremendous force, the brain shuts down automatically so as to protect itself, or at least limit and assess the damage. The problem we sometimes have is getting it to restart."

"Like rebooting a computer?" Clarke offered. The doctor seemed to agree.

"And it's too early yet to say whether there's any damage to your uncle," he told her. "No blood clots that we could see, but we'll know more tomorrow."

"He's not my uncle," she said sternly. Rebus patted her arm.

"She's upset," he explained to the doctor. And then, as Clarke pulled her arm away: "So he was hit hard with something?"

"Two or three times probably," the doctor agreed.

"Attacked from behind?" The doctor was growing less comfortable with each new question.

"The blows were to the back of the skull, yes."

Rebus was looking at Siobhan Clarke. Alexander Todorov, too, had been hit hard from behind, hard enough to kill. "Can we see him, Doc?" Rebus asked.

"As I say, he's not awake at present."

"But all the same . . ." The doctor was looking worried now. "Is there a problem with that?" Rebus persisted.

"Look, I've been told who Mr. Cafferty is . . . I know he has a certain reputation in Edinburgh."

"And?" Rebus asked.

The doctor moistened his dry lips. "Well, you're his brother . . . asking all these questions. Please tell me you're not going to go after whoever did this." He decided some levity might help. "Wards are crowded enough as it is," he said with a weak smile.

"We'd just like to see him, that's all," Rebus assured him, patting the youngster's arm to reinforce the point.

"Then I'll see what I can do. You can wait here if you like."

Rebus answered by sitting down again. They watched the doctor depart through the swing doors. But as the doors came to rest, a face appeared at one of their porthole-shaped windows.

"Oh, Christ," Rebus said, alerting Clarke to the new arrivals— DI Calum Stone and DS Andy Prosser. "This is where you tell them the whole story, Shiv. And if you don't, I will." She nodded her understanding.

"Well, well," Stone said, sauntering forward, hands in pockets. "What brings you here, DI Rebus?"

"Same as you, I reckon," Rebus replied, standing up again.

"So here we all are," Stone continued, rocking back on his heels. "You to check if the victim still has a pulse, and us to start figuring out if we've just watched several thousand man-hours get flushed down the pan."

"Shame you pulled the surveillance," Rebus commented.

Stone's face grew red with rage. "Because *you* wanted a meet!" He pointed towards Clarke. "Got your girlfriend here to send us down to Granton."

"I'm not denying it," Rebus said quietly. "I ordered DS Clarke to make that call."

"And why would you do that?" Stone's eyes were drilling into Rebus's.

"Cafferty wanted to see me. Didn't say why, but I wasn't keen on having you lot in the vicinity."

"Why not?"

"Because I'd have been on the lookout for you, wondering where you were hiding—Cafferty might have noticed; he's got pretty good antennae."

"Not good enough to stop him getting whacked," Prosser added.

Rebus couldn't disagree. "I'm going to tell you what I told DS Clarke here," he continued. "If I was going to thump Cafferty, why would I tell anyone about the meeting? Either someone's setting me up, or we're talking about a coincidence."

"A coincidence?"

Rebus shrugged. "Someone planned to hit him anyway, just happened to coincide . . ."

Stone had turned to his partner. "You buying any of this, Andy?" Prosser shook his head slowly, and Stone turned back to Rebus. "Andy doesn't buy it, and neither do I. You wanted Cafferty for yourself, didn't like the thought of *us* nabbing him. Your gold watch is on the horizon, so you're pretty desperate. You go there to talk to him, and something happens . . . you lose it. Next thing he's sparked out and you're in trouble."

"Except it didn't happen like that."

"So what *did* happen?"

"We talked and I left him, went home and stayed there."

"What was so urgent that he needed to see you?"

"Not a lot really."

Prosser gave a little snort of disbelief, while Stone had a chuckle to himself. "You know, Rebus, that canal's not really a canal at all — not where you're concerned."

"So what is it?"

"Shit creek," Stone said triumphantly. Rebus turned his head towards Clarke.

"And they say vaudeville is dead."

"It's not dead," she replied, as he'd known she would. "Just smells funny."

Stone stabbed a finger in her direction. "Don't go thinking *you're* not in the swill, too, DS Clarke!"

"I've already told you," Rebus interrupted, "I take full responsibility —"

"Listen to yourself," Stone hissed. "Bailing out your girlfriend here is the last thing you should be focusing on right now."

"I'm not his girlfriend." The blood had risen up Clarke's neck.

"Then you're his patsy, which is almost as bad."

"Stone," Rebus growled, "I swear to God I'm going to . . ." Instead of finishing the sentence, he started balling both hands into fists.

"The only thing you're going to do, Rebus, is make a

statement and pray there's a lawyer out there desperate enough to want to represent you."

"Calum," Prosser offered as warning to his colleague, "the bastard's going to have a pop at you . . ." Prosser edged forward, eager to get his retaliation in first. All four of them froze for a moment as they watched the doors swinging closed. A nurse was standing there, looking bemused. Rebus willed her not to say anything, but she said it anyway.

"Mr. Cafferty?" Aiming the words at Rebus and no one else. "If you're quite finished here, we can let you see your brother now . . ."

DAY EIGHT

Friday 24 November 2006

35

When Rebus woke up next morning, it was to an insistent buzzing from the entryphone. He rolled over in bed and checked his watch—not yet 7:00. Still dark outside, and a few more minutes until the timer would kick the central heating into action. The room was cold, the hall floor sucking heat from his feet as he padded down it and picked up the phone next to the door.

"This better be good," he croaked.

"Depends on your point of view." Rebus recognized the voice but couldn't place it. "Come on, John," the man drawled. "It's Shug Davidson."

"Up with the lark, Shug."

"I've not been to bed yet."

"Bit early for a social call."

"Isn't it? Now how about letting me in?"

Rebus's finger hesitated above the entry button. He sensed that if he pressed it, his whole world would start to change—and probably not for the better. Problem was, what was the alternative?

He pressed the button.

DI Shug Davidson was one of the good guys. The force believed that human existence could be divided into two straightforward camps—good guys and bad. Davidson had made few enemies and many friends. He was conscientious and pragmatic, humane and sympathetic. But he had a serious look on his face this morning, only some of which could be attributed to lack of sleep. He also had a uniformed constable with him. Rebus had left the door ajar while he retreated to the bedroom to put some clothes on, yelling that Davidson could make tea if he liked. But Davidson and the uniform seemed content to stand in the hallway, so that Rebus had to squeeze past them to get to the bathroom. He brushed his teeth with more care than usual, staring at himself in the mirror above the sink. He was still staring at the reflection as he wiped his mouth dry. Back in the hall, he said the word "shoes" and made for the living room, finding them next to his chair.

"Do I take it," Rebus asked as he wrestled with the laces, "West End has need of my finely honed detective skills?"

"Stone's told us all about your rendezvous with Cafferty," Davidson stated. "And Siobhan mentioned the cigarette butt. Not the only thing we found floating in the canal, though . . ."

"Oh?"

"We found a polythene overshoe, John. Looks like there might be some blood on it."

"The sort of overshoes the SOCOs wear?"

"The SOCOs wear them, yes, but so do we."

Rebus nodded slowly. "I keep some in the boot of the Saab."

"Mine are in the VW's glove box."

"Just the place for them, when you think of it." Finally, Rebus seemed happy with the knots. He stood up and made eye contact with Davidson. "Am I a suspect, then, Shug?"

"Bit of questioning should put everyone's minds at rest."

"Glad to help, DI Davidson."

There was a bit more work to be done: finding keys and phone, picking out a coat to wear over his suit jacket. But then they were ready. Rebus locked the front door after him and followed Davidson downstairs, the constable bringing up the rear.

"Heard about the poor sod in London?" Davidson asked.

"Litvinenko?"

"Recently deceased. They've ruled out thallium, whatever that is . . ."

Turned out the two detectives were expected to sit in the back of the Passat while the uniform did the driving. Marchmont to Torphichen Place was a ten-minute ride. Melville Drive was quiet, the morning rush hour not yet begun. There were joggers busy on the Meadows, the car's headlights picking out the reflective strips on their shoes. They waited at the Tollcross junction for the light to change to green, drove round the one-way into Fountainbridge, and were soon passing the wine bar at the canal basin. This was where Rebus had waited for Cafferty and Andropov to come out, the night he'd followed them to Granton. Rebus was trying to remember if there was any CCTV on the canal itself. He didn't think so. But maybe there'd be cameras outside the wine bar. Just because he hadn't noticed any didn't mean they weren't there. Unlikely they'd have spotted him loitering in the vicinity, but you never knew. The Leamington Lift Bridge wasn't much used at night, but it *was* used. Drunks congregated with their bottles, youths walked to and fro, looking for action. Might someone have seen something?

A figure running away? The tenement on Leamington Road where he'd parked his car that first night . . . if a neighbor had been peering from their window at the right moment . . .

"I think I'm being fitted up, Shug," Rebus said as the car took a right at the roundabout, squeezing down the narrow arc of Gardner's Crescent and signaling left at the next lights, into Morrison Street. They were back into the one-way system and would have to take a couple more rights to bring them to C Division HQ.

"Lot of people," Davidson said, "are going to think he deserves a medal—the guy who clobbered Cafferty, I mean." He paused, fixing Rebus with a look. "Just for the record, I don't happen to be among them."

"I didn't do it, Shug."

"Then you'll be fine, won't you? We're cops, John, we *know* the innocent always go free . . ."

They were silent after that until the patrol car drew up outside the police station. No media, for which Rebus was thankful, but as they entered the lobby he saw Derek Starr having a whispered confab with Calum Stone.

"Nice day for a lynching," Rebus told them. Davidson just kept moving, so Rebus followed.

"Reminds me," Davidson was saying, "I think the Complaints are after a word, too."

The Complaints: Internal Affairs . . . cops who liked nothing more than dustbinning their own.

"Seems you were suspended a few days back," Davidson added, "but didn't take it to heart." He'd paused at the door to one of the interview rooms. "In here, John." The door opened outwards. Reason for that was a prisoner couldn't barricade himself in. Usual arrangement of table and chairs, with tape recorders and even a video camera bolted high up on the wall above the door, aimed at the table.

"The accommodation's fine," Rebus said, "but does it come with breakfast?"

"I can probably summon a bacon roll."

"With brown sauce," Rebus stated.

"Tea or coffee with that?"

"Milky tea, I think, *garçon*. No sugar."

"I'll see what I can do." Davidson closed the door after him, and Rebus sat down at the table, resting his head on his arms. So what if a SOCO had found an overshoe? Could be that one of the SOCOs themselves had left it there. Bloodstains might well turn out to be bits of bark or rust—plenty of both in the canal. Cops and SOCOs used overshoes, but who else? Some hospitals . . . maybe the mortuary . . . places that needed to be kept sterile. He thought of the lock on the Saab's boot and how he'd been meaning to get it fixed. It would close eventually, but only with persistence, and even then it would spring open with minimal effort. Cafferty knew Rebus's car. Stone and Prosser knew it, too. Had Andropov's driver clocked it that day outside the City Chambers? No, because they'd been in Siobhan's car, hadn't they? But Rebus had left the Saab curbside while he'd followed Cafferty and Andropov to the wine bar . . . an opportunity for either of the bodyguards to swipe anything they liked from the boot. Cafferty himself had said it: Andropov's driver had recognized Rebus. . . . A bloodstained overshoe—what were the chances of finding anything on it leading back to Rebus? He'd no way of knowing.

"Your last days as a cop, John," he told himself. "Savor them . . ."

The door opened and a woman constable appeared with a polystyrene beaker.

"Tea?" he speculated, sniffing the contents.

"If you say so," she responded, before making a tactical retreat. He took a sip and decided to be satisfied. When the door next opened, it was Shug Davidson, carrying in a third chair.

"Strangest bacon butty I've ever seen," Rebus told him.

"Rolls are coming." Davidson placed the chair next to his own, then sat down. He produced two cassette tapes from his pocket, unwrapped them, and slotted them into the machine.

"Do I need a lawyer, Shug?"

"You're the detective, you tell me," Davidson answered. And then the door opened once more and DI Calum Stone made his entry. He carried a case file with him and wore a grim look on his face.

"You've handed over control?" Rebus guessed, eyes on Davidson. But it was Stone who replied.

"SCD takes precedence."

"Feel free to help yourselves to some of my station's caseload, too," Rebus told him. Stone just smirked and opened the file. It was dog-eared and coffee-stained and bore the hallmarks of having been pored over many times in pursuit of a fresh angle on Cafferty. Funny thing was, Rebus kept a file much like it at home . . .

"Right, then, DI Davidson," Stone said, adjusting his jacket and shirt cuffs as he made himself comfortable, "switch that tape machine on and let's get down to business . . ."

Half an hour later, the rolls arrived. Stone rose to his feet and began pacing, not quite managing to look sanguine that he had not been included in the food order. Rebus's was cold, and the sauce was tomato rather than brown, but he attacked it with exaggerated zeal.

"This is delicious," he would say one minute, and "Proper butter, too," the next. Davidson had offered to split his own helping with Stone, but Stone had waved it aside. "Another cup of tea's what we need," Rebus suggested, and Davidson, finding his mouth full of stodgy dough, was forced to agree. So another round of teas arrived, and they washed down the last remnants of roll with them, Rebus daintily brushing bits of flour from the corners of his mouth before declaring himself "ready for round two."

The machine was switched on again and Rebus went back to defending Siobhan Clarke's role in the previous evening's events.

"She does whatever *you* tell her," Stone insisted.

"I'm sure DI Davidson here will vouch that DS Clarke is very much her own woman . . ." Rebus broke off and watched Davidson nod. "DI Davidson nods," he added for the benefit of the tapes. Then he rubbed a finger across the bridge of his nose. "Look, here's the bottom line—I've not tried to hide anything from you. I admit I saw Cafferty last night. I was there by the canal with him. But I didn't attack him."

"You admit you led an SCD surveillance unit away from the scene?"

"Stupid in retrospect," Rebus agreed.

"But that's all you did?"

"That's all I did."

Stone looked to Davidson and then back at Rebus. "In which case, Inspector, you won't mind if we go down to the processing area?"

Rebus stared at Stone. "Are you charging me?"

"We're asking you to volunteer your fingerprints," Davidson explained.

"And a DNA swab," Stone added.

"For purposes of elimination, John."

"And if I refuse?"

"Why would an innocent man refuse?" Stone asked. The smirk was back again.

36

Siobhan Clarke knew damned well she wouldn't find a space in the car park at Gayfield Square—all those new arrivals, driving in from all over the city. Her own flat was only a five-minute walk, her car parked curbside in a residents' bay. So she walked to work, taking with her a personal CD player. She'd found it under her bed, coated with dust. Replaced the batteries and found that the earphones from her iPod fitted the socket. On her way to work, she picked up coffee from the Broughton Street basement café. Seemed like an age since she'd met Todd Goodyear there. Derek Starr still didn't seem to have noticed her new recruit—plenty of bodies in the CID suite, meaning Todd might go undetected awhile longer.

When she arrived, there was someone at her desk. She flung her shoulder bag onto the floor next to the chair, hoping it might act as a hint. When it didn't, she flicked the officer's ear. He looked up from the call he was making, and she gestured for him to vamoose. He didn't seem happy about it, but got up anyway, continuing the conversation as he moved away. Todd Goodyear was standing in front of her with more sheets of transcript from the Urban Regeneration Committee.

"Doesn't seem quite as busy in here," Clarke commented, noting that Starr was in earnest conversation with Macrae in the DCI's office.

"We've requisitioned two of the interview rooms," he explained. "Numbers one and two—three's too cold, apparently." Then, after a meaningful pause: "What's this I hear about Cafferty?"

"Did your girlfriend tell you?" Clarke took a sip of cappuccino. Goodyear was nodding.

"She was summoned to the canal," he confirmed.

"That must have put a damper on your evening."

"Part and parcel of the job." He paused. "She saw you there, too. How do you want to play it?"

She didn't get his meaning at first, then realized that Todd had been present outside the pub. He, too, knew that Rebus had been on his way to a rendezvous with Cafferty.

"Anyone asks," she told him, "you tell them just as much as you know. For what it's worth, DI Rebus has already talked to the inquiry team."

Goodyear expelled some air. "Is he a suspect?"

Clarke shook her head. But she knew damned well the possibility was being discussed in Macrae's room. As soon as Goodyear had retreated, she reached into her bag for the CD player and took the disc from the top drawer of her desk. Todorov's recital for the benefit of the Word Power bookshop. She plugged herself in, cranked up the volume, and closed her eyes.

A café. The espresso machine was hissing somewhere in the distance. Charles Riordan had to be positioned near the front of the audience. She could hear Todorov clearing his throat. One of the booksellers gave the welcome and made some introductory remarks. Clarke knew the café. It was near the old Odeon cinema, popular with students. Big comfy sofas and mood music, the sort of place where you felt guilty ordering anything not fair-trade or organic. Didn't sound like there was amplification for the poet. Riordan's mic was good, though. When he changed its positioning, she could sense individuals in the audience: a cough here, a sniffle there. Murmurs and whispers. Riordan seemed almost as interested in these as in the main event. Figured: the man did like to eavesdrop.

When the poet started speaking, he covered almost identical ground to his recital at the Poetry Library—made the same icebreaking jokes, said how welcoming he found Scottish people. Clarke could imagine his eyes scanning the audience for any women who might like to take the welcome a little further. He veered a few times from the Poetry Library script, announcing at one point that he would next read a poem by Robert Burns. It was called "Farewell to All Our Scottish Fame." Todorov read it in heavily accented English, having apologized for "anglicizing" certain words:

> Farewell to all our Scottish fame,
> Farewell our ancient glory.
> Farewell even to the Scottish name,
> So famed in martial story.
> Now Sark runs over the Solway sands,
> And Tweed runs to the ocean,
> To mark where England's province stands—
> Such a parcel of rogues in a nation.

There were two further verses, each ending with the same last line. Applause and a couple of whoops when the poet had finished. Todorov then went back to poems from *Astapovo Blues* and ended by saying that copies were available for sale at the door. After the ovation had died down, Riordan's mic made another circuit of the room, catching reactions to the recital.

"Going to buy a copy, then?"

"Ten quid's a bit steep . . . anyway, we've heard most of them now."

"Which pub you headed for?"

"Pear Tree probably."

"What did you think?"

"Bit pompous."

"We on for Saturday?"

"Depends on the kids."

"Has it started raining?"

"I've got the dog in the car."

And then the ringing of a mobile phone, silenced when the recipient answered . . .

Answered in what sounded to Clarke suspiciously like Russian. Only a couple of words before the voice was muffled. Did the poet himself possess a mobile phone? Not as far as she knew. Meaning someone in the audience . . . ? Yes, because now the mic was sweeping back round again, catching Todorov being thanked by the bookseller.

"And if you'd be happy to sign some stock afterwards . . . ?" she was asking.

"Absolutely. My pleasure."

"Then a drink on us at the Pear Tree . . . You're sure we can't tempt you to supper?"

"I try to avoid temptation, my dear. It's not good for a poet of my advancing years." But then Todorov's attention was deflected. "Ah, Mr. Riordan, isn't it? How did the recording go?"

"It was great, thank you."

Dead men talking, Clarke couldn't help thinking.

The mic itself cut out after that. The timer on the player told her she'd been listening for the best part of an hour. Macrae's office was empty, no sign of Starr anywhere nearby. Clarke removed her earphones and checked her mobile for messages. There were none. She tried Rebus's home number but got his machine. He wasn't answering his mobile either. She was tapping the phone against her pursed lips when Todd Goodyear reappeared.

"Girlfriend's just given me a tip-off," he said.

"Remind me of her name."

"Sonia."

"And what does Sonia tell you?"

"When they were searching the canal, they came up with an overshoe. You know, the polythene sort with the elastic around the ankle?"

"Talk about contaminating the crime scene . . ."

He caught her meaning. "No," he clarified, "it wasn't dropped by a SOCO. There were spots of blood on it. Well, that's what they think, anyway."

"Meaning the assailant wore it?" Goodyear was nodding. Scene-of-crime clothing — protective overalls, hats, overshoes, and disposable gloves . . . the whole lot designed so as not to leave trace evidence. Yes, but that worked both ways, didn't it? Meant the investigators didn't leave anything that could be misconstrued; meant anyone wearing the getup could mount an attack without fear of getting the victim's blood or hair or fibers on them. Dump the overalls — or better still, burn them — and you had a good chance of getting away with it.

"Don't go thinking what you're thinking," Clarke warned Goodyear, the same words Rebus had used on her. "This had nothing to do with DI Rebus."

"Not saying it did." Goodyear seemed stung by the accusation.

"What else did Sonia say?"

He shrugged by way of an answer. Clarke made a flicking motion with her fingers, and he took the hint, turning and finding that the desk he'd been using had found a new owner in his absence. As he walked away, readying to remonstrate, Clarke picked up her bag and coat, headed downstairs and out into Gayfield Square. Rebus was parked by the curb. She gave the briefest of smiles and opened the passenger-side door, climbing in.

"Your phone's off," she told him.

"Haven't got round to switching it on."

"Have you heard? They've found an overshoe."

"Shug's already dragged me in for questioning," Rebus admitted, punching his PIN into his mobile. "Stone was there, too, enjoying every bastard minute."

"What did you tell them?"

"The truth, the whole truth, and nothing but the truth."

"This is serious, John!"

"Who knows that better than me?" he muttered. "But it only becomes problematic when they trace the overshoe to the boot of my car."

She stared at him. *"When?"* she echoed.

"Think about it, Shiv. Only reason to leave the shoe was to stick me more firmly in the frame. The Saab's boot hasn't shut properly for months, and there's nothing in there but crime-scene kit."

"And that old pair of hiking boots," she corrected him.

"Aye," he agreed, "and if a hiking boot would have

served the purpose, you can bet they'd have taken that instead."

"So who's the 'they'? You still think Andropov?"

He dragged his palms down his face, accentuating the bloodshot and dark-ringed eyes, the day's worth of gray stubble. "Proving it is going to be the killer," he replied at last.

Clarke nodded her agreement, and they sat in silence for a while, until Rebus asked how everything else was shaping up.

"Starr and Macrae started the day with a good old chin-wag."

"No doubt my name featured on the agenda."

"All I've been doing is listening to that other recording of Todorov."

"Nice to see you breaking a sweat."

"Riordan's mic picked up some of the audience. I think I heard a Russian voice."

"Oh?"

"Thought I might nip over to Word Power and ask them."

"Need a lift?"

"Sure."

"Do me a favor first, will you? I need the CD of Todorov's other performance."

"Why?" He explained about Scarlett Colwell and the new poem. "So you're keeping in her good books, eh?"

"Just go fetch it."

She opened the car door but then paused. "The show Todorov did for Word Power, he read out a poem by Burns — 'Farewell to All Our Scottish Fame.'"

Rebus nodded. "I know that one. It's about the English buying us off. Scotland lost all its money in a Panama landgrab. England suggested a union of the two countries."

"What was so bad about that?"

"I keep forgetting you're English. . . . We ceased to be a nation, Siobhan."

"And became a parcel of rogues instead?"

"According to Burns, yes."

"Sounds to me as if Todorov was a bit of a Scot Nat."

"Maybe he just looked at this country and saw a version of his own . . . bought and sold for gold, tin, zinc, gas . . ."

"Andropov again?"

Rebus offered a shrug. "Go get that CD," he told her.

37

The bookshop was small and cramped. Rebus feared that if he so much as turned around he would topple a display. The woman behind the till had her nose in a copy of something called *Labyrinth*. She worked there only part-time and hadn't been to the Todorov reading.

"We've got some of his books, though."

Rebus looked in the direction she was pointing. "Are they signed?" he asked. For his troubles, Clarke poked him in the ribs before asking the assistant if any photos had been taken on the night. She nodded and muttered something about the shop's Web site. Clarke looked to Rebus.

"Should've thought of that first," she told him. So they drove back to her flat, Rebus deciding to double-park rather than seek a space farther afield.

"A while since I've been here," he said as she led him down the narrow hallway. It was much the same layout as his own flat, but with meaner proportions.

"It's nothing personal," she apologized. "Just that I don't entertain much."

They were in the living room by now. Chocolate wrappers on the rug next to the sofa, alongside an empty wineglass. On the sofa itself sat a large, venerable-looking teddy bear. Rebus picked it up.

"It's a Steiff," Clarke told him. "Had him since I was a kid."

"Has he got a name?"

"Yes."

"Going to tell me what it is?"

"No." She'd gone over to the computer desk by the window and switched on the laptop, which rested there. She had one of those S-shaped stools that were supposed to be good for your back, but she sat with her feet on the bit that was meant for her knees. Within a matter of moments, she had found the Word Power Web site. Clicked on "Recent Events" and then "Photo Gallery" and started a slow scroll. And there was Todorov, being introduced to the crowd. They were seated on the floor and standing at the back, and all had about them the aura of the converted.

"How are we supposed to spot the Russians?" Rebus asked, leaning his hands against the edge of the desk. "Cossack hats? Ice picks in their ears?"

"We never did take a proper look at that list," Clarke said.

"What list?"

"The one Stahov made—Russian residents in Edinburgh. He even had his own name on it, remember? Wonder if his driver's on it, too." She was tapping the screen. Only his face was visible. He was seated on a brown leather sofa but with people crouched and seated on the floor in front of him. The photographer was no professional; everyone had been given red eyes. "Remember that fuss at the mortuary? Stahov wanted Todorov's remains repatriated. I'm pretty sure our friend here was with him." She tapped the screen again. Rebus leaned in farther for a better look.

"He's Andropov's driver," he said. "We went eyeball-to-eyeball in the lobby of the Caledonian Hotel."

"Must be working for two masters, then, because Stahov got into the back of his old Merc and this guy got behind the wheel." She turned her head and looked up at him. "Reckon he'll talk to us?"

Rebus shrugged. "Maybe he'll claim diplomatic immunity."

"Was he with Andropov that night in the bar?"

"No one's mentioned him."

"Might have been waiting outside with the car." She glanced at her watch.

"What now?" Rebus asked.

"I've got that appointment with Jim Bakewell MSP."

"Where are you meeting him?"

"The Parliament building."

"Tell him you need a coffee — I'll be at the next table over."

"Haven't you got anything better to do?"

"Like what?"

"Finding out who's behind the attack on Cafferty."

"You don't think there's a link?"

"We don't *know*."

"I could really use a shot of that parliamentary espresso," Rebus told her.

She couldn't help smiling. "All right, then," she said. "And I really will have you over to supper one night — promise."

"Best give me plenty of warning . . . diary's going to be bursting at the seams."

"Retirement's a whole new beginning for some people," she agreed.

"I don't plan on twiddling my thumbs," he assured her.

Clarke had risen from the stool. She stood in front of him, arms by her sides, eyes fixed on his. The silence lasted fifteen or twenty seconds, Rebus smiling at the end, feeling they'd shared a long conversation without the need for words.

"Let's go," he said, breaking the spell.

They called the Western General from the car, checking on Cafferty's progress.

"He's not woken up," Rebus said, relaying the message for Clarke's benefit. "Due another scan later today, and they've got him on drugs to prevent a blood clot."

"Think we should send him flowers?"

"Bit early for a wreath . . ."

They'd taken a shortcut down Calton Road, parked in one of the residential streets at Abbeyhill. Clarke told him to give her a five-minute start, which gave Rebus enough time for a cigarette. Tourists were milling around, a few interested in the Parliament building but the majority keener on the Palace of Holyrood across the street. One or two seemed to be puzzling over the vertical bamboo bars across some of the Parliament's windows.

"Join the club," Rebus muttered, stubbing the cigarette and heading inside. As he emptied his pockets and prepared for the metal detector at security, he asked one of the guards about the bamboo.

"Search me," the man said.

"Isn't that supposed to be *my* line?" Rebus replied. On the other side of the detector, he scooped up his stuff and made for the coffee bar. Clarke was in the queue, and he took his place directly behind her. "Where's Bakewell?" he asked.

"On his way down. He's not a 'coffee person' apparently, but I said it was for my benefit rather than his." She ordered her cappuccino and got out some money.

"Might as well add mine to the order," Rebus said. "And make it a double."

"Want me to drink it for you, too?"

"Could be the last espresso you ever buy me," he chided her.

They found two adjacent tables and settled at them. Rebus still wasn't sure about this vast, echoing interior. If someone had told him he was in an airport, he might have believed them. He couldn't tell what sort of statement it was supposed to be making. One newspaper report from a few years back had stuck in his mind, the journalist speculating that the building was too elaborate for its actual purpose and was, in fact, "an independent parliament in waiting." Made sense when you remembered that the architect was Catalan.

"Detective Sergeant Clarke?" Jim Bakewell shook Clarke's hand, and she asked him if he wanted anything. "We could take your drink to my office" was all he said.

"Yes, but now that we're here . . ."

Bakewell sighed and sat down, adjusting his glasses. He wore a tweed jacket and what looked like a tweed tie over a check shirt.

"Won't take long, sir," Clarke was telling him. "Wanted to ask you a couple of questions about Alexander Todorov."

"I was sorry to hear about him," Bakewell declared, but he was adjusting the creases in his trousers as he spoke.

"You shared a platform with him on *Question Time*?"

"That's correct."

"Can I ask for your general impression of him?"

Bakewell's eyes were milky blue. He nodded a greeting to a passing flunky before addressing the question. "I was late arriving, got held up in traffic. Barely had time to shake hands with him before we were ushered into the hall. He wouldn't wear any makeup, I remember that much." He removed his glasses and started polishing them with a handkerchief. "Seemed quite brusque with everybody, but he was fine in front of the cameras." He put his glasses back on and tucked the handkerchief into a trouser pocket.

"And afterwards?" Clarke asked.

"I seem to think he shot off. Nobody really hangs around. It would mean making small talk with each other."

"Fraternizing with the enemy?" Clarke offered.

"Along those lines, yes."

"So is that how you see Megan Macfarlane?"

"Megan's a lovely woman . . ."

"But you're not dropping round one another's houses for a chin-wag?"

"Not exactly," Bakewell said with a thin smile.

"Ms. Macfarlane seems to think the SNP will win May's election."

"Nonsense."

"You don't think Scotland's going to want to give Blair a bloody nose over Iraq?"

"There's no appetite for independence," Bakewell stated gruffly.

"No appetite for Trident either."

"Labour will do just fine come May, Sergeant. Please don't lose any sleep on our behalf."

Clarke seemed to be collecting her thoughts. "And what about the last time you saw him?"

"I don't think I understand."

"The night Mr. Todorov was killed, he'd just been having a drink in the Caledonian Hotel. You were there, too, Mr. Bakewell."

"Was I?" Bakewell furrowed his brow, as if trying to remember.

"You were seated in one of the booths with a business-man called Sergei Andropov."

"Was that the same night?" He watched Clarke nod slowly. "Well, I'll take your word for it."

"Mr. Andropov and Mr. Todorov grew up together."

"That's news to me."

"You didn't see Todorov in the bar?"

"I did not."

"He was bought a drink by a local gangster called Morris Gerald Cafferty."

"Mr. Cafferty did join us at the table, but he didn't have anyone with him."

"Had you met him before?"

"No."

"But you knew his reputation?"

"I knew he was . . . well, 'gangster' is maybe a bit strong, Sergeant. But he's a reformed character now." The politician paused. "Unless you have evidence to the contrary."

"What were the three of you talking about?"

"Trade . . . the commercial climate." Bakewell shrugged. "Nothing very riveting."

"And when Cafferty joined you, he didn't happen to mention Alexander Todorov?"

"Not that I remember."

"What time did you leave the bar, sir?"

Bakewell puffed out his cheeks with the effort of remembering. "Quarter past eleven . . . some time around then."

"Andropov and Cafferty were still there?"

"Yes."

Clarke paused for a moment's thought. "How well did Cafferty seem to know Mr. Andropov?"

"I couldn't say."

"But it wasn't the first time they'd met?"

"Mr. Cafferty's company is representing Mr. Andropov in some development projects."

"Why did he choose Cafferty?"

Bakewell gave an irritated laugh. "Go ask him yourself."

"I'm asking you, sir."

"I get the feeling you're fishing, Sergeant, and none too subtly at that. As development minister it's my job to discuss future planning potential with businesspersons of good standing."

"So you had your advisers with you?" Clarke watched Bakewell try to form an answer. "If you were there in your official capacity," she pressed, "I'm assuming you'd have a team backing you up . . . ?"

"It was an informal meeting," the politician snapped.

"Is that a regular occurrence, sir, in your line of work?" Bakewell was about to remonstrate, either that or retreat. He had his hands pressed to his knees, readying to rise to his feet. But there was a woman approaching, and she was already addressing him.

"Jim, where have you been hiding yourself?" Megan Macfarlane turned towards Clarke, and her face fell. "Oh, it's you."

"I'm being grilled about Alexander Todorov," Bakewell explained. "*And* Sergei Andropov."

Macfarlane glowered at Clarke and seemed ready to attack, but Clarke didn't give her the chance. "I'm glad I caught you, Ms. Macfarlane," she said. "I wanted to ask about Charles Riordan."

"Who?"

"He was recording your committee for an art installation."

"Roddy Denholm's project, you mean?" Macfarlane sounded interested. "What about it?"

"Mr. Riordan was friends with Alexander Todorov, and now both men are dead."

But if Clarke had hoped to divert Macfarlane's attention, she'd failed. The MSP stabbed a finger in Rebus's direction. "What's he doing skulking there?"

Bakewell turned towards Rebus but had no idea who he was. "I'm at a loss," he admitted.

"That's her boss," Macfarlane explained. "Looks to me like your private chat wasn't so private, Jim."

Bakewell stopped looking puzzled and started to look furious instead. "Is this true?" he asked Clarke. But Macfarlane, clearly enjoying every moment, was speaking again.

"What's more, I hear he's been suspended from duty, pending retirement."

"And how did you hear that, Ms. Macfarlane?" Rebus asked.

"I had a meeting with your Chief Constable yesterday

and happened to mention your name." She made a tutting sound. "He's not going to be pleased about this, is he?"

"It's an outrage," Bakewell spluttered, finally rising to his feet.

"I've James Corbyn's number if you need it," Macfarlane was telling her colleague as she waved her phone at him. Her assistant, Roddy Liddle, had arrived by her side, laden with files and folders.

"An outrage!" Bakewell repeated, causing heads to turn. Two security guards were looking particularly interested.

"Shall we?" Clarke suggested to Rebus. He still had half a shot of espresso left, but thought it only good manners to accompany her as she stalked towards the exit.

38

W hat now?" Rebus asked as he drove her back towards Gayfield Square.

"Talk to Stahov's driver, I suppose."

"Think the consulate will let you?"

"Have you got a better idea?"

He shrugged. "Just that it might be easier to grab him
on the street."

"What if he doesn't speak English?"

"I think he does," Rebus stated, remembering the cars
parked by the canal, Cafferty's bodyguard in conversation with Andropov's driver. "And if he doesn't, we both
know a friendly translator." Rebus gestured towards the
back seat, where he'd slung the CD. "And she's about to
owe us a favor."

"So I just grab the driver off the street and interro-
gate him?" She was staring at Rebus. "How much more
trouble do you want me to be in?"

The Saab crossed at the Regent Road lights and headed
into Royal Terrace. "How much can you take?" he eventually asked.

"Not much more," she admitted. "You think Bakewell
will talk to the Chief Constable?"

"He might."

"Then I'll probably be sharing that suspension
with you."

He glanced at her. "Won't that be fun?"

"I think you're getting demob-happy, John."

A patrol car was suddenly behind them, its lights flashing. "Christ, what now?" Rebus complained to no one in particular. He pulled over just short of the next roundabout and got out.

The patrolman took a bit of time adjusting the cap he'd just fixed to his head. He wasn't anyone Rebus knew.

"DI Rebus?" the officer checked. Rebus nodded his confirmation.

"Got orders to bring you in."

"Bring me where?"

"West End."

"Shug Davidson's throwing me a surprise party?"

"I wouldn't know about that."

Maybe not, but Rebus did: they had something to pin on him, and the bookies were giving a million to one on it being a medal. Rebus turned towards Clarke. She was out of the car now, resting her hands against its roof. Pedestrians had paused for a moment to watch the drama.

"Take the Saab," Rebus told her. "See that Dr. Colwell gets the CD."

"What about the chauffeur?"

"Some things you're going to have to decide for yourself."

He got into the back of the patrol car. "Blues and twos, lads," he said. "Can't keep Shug Davidson waiting."

But it wasn't Davidson waiting for him at Torphichen Place, it was DI Calum Stone, seated behind the interview room's only table while DS Prosser stood in the corner, hands in pockets.

"Seems I've got a fan club," Rebus commented, sitting down opposite Stone.

"Got a bit of news for you," Stone responded. "It was Cafferty's blood on that overshoe."

"DNA usually takes longer than that."

"All right, then—Cafferty's blood *type*."

"I sense a 'but' . . ."

"No usable prints," Stone admitted.

"Meaning you can't prove it came from the boot of my car?" Rebus clapped his hands together once and began getting to his feet. "Well, nice of you to let me know . . ."

"Sit down, Rebus."

Rebus considered for a few seconds, then sat.

"Cafferty's still unconscious," Stone explained. "They're not talking coma yet, but I know they're thinking it. Doctor says he could end his days a vegetable." His eyes narrowed. "So it looks like we might not get to steal your glory after all."

"You still think I did it?"

"I bloody well know you did."

"And I told DS Clarke all about it because I needed her to phone you and get you away from the stakeout?" Rebus watched Stone's slow, sustained nod.

"You used your crime-scene kit so you wouldn't get any blood on you," Prosser snapped from the corner. "Shoe blew into the canal, and you couldn't risk going in after it—"

"We've been through this!" Rebus spat back.

"No doubt we'll go over it again," Stone warned. "Soon as we've completed our inquiries."

"I can hardly wait." This time Rebus did rise to his feet. "That all you wanted me for?"

Stone just nodded again, then waited until Rebus reached the door before firing another question at him.

"Officers who brought you in say there was a woman in the car with you — DS Clarke, I presume?"

"Of course not."

"Liar," Prosser shot back at him.

"You're still on suspension, Rebus," Stone was saying. "Do you really want to take her down with you?"

"Funny, she asked me much the same thing not half an hour ago . . ." Rebus pushed open the door and made good his escape.

Dr. Scarlett Colwell was at her computer when Siobhan Clarke arrived. To Clarke's mind, the woman used a touch too much makeup and would look better without it. Nice hair, though, even if she suspected there might be a bit of dye in it.

"I've brought the CD of the poetry reading," Clarke said, placing it on the desk.

"Thank you so much." Colwell picked it up and studied it.

"Can I ask you to take a look at something?"

"Of course."

"I'll need to use your computer . . ." The academic gestured for Clarke to sit at the desk. Clarke squeezed past her, Colwell standing at her shoulder as she accessed the Word Power site and clicked the photo gallery option, bringing up the pictures from the café. "That picture," she said, nodding towards the wall and the shot of Todorov. "Did you happen to take any others?"

"They were so bad, I deleted them. I'm not great with cameras."

Clarke nodded and pressed a finger against the screen. "Remember him?" she asked.

Colwell peered at the chauffeur's face. "He was there, yes."

"But you don't know who he is?"

"Should I?"

"Did Todorov speak to him?"

"I couldn't say. Who is he?"

"A Russian . . . he works at the consulate."

Colwell stared more intently at the face. "You know," she said, "I think he was at the Poetry Library, too."

Clarke turned towards her. "Are you sure?"

"Him and another man . . ." But she started to shake her head. "Actually, I'm not certain."

"Take your time," Clarke invited, so Colwell ran both hands through her tresses and did some more thinking.

"I'm really not sure," she confessed after a pause, letting the hair fall around her face again. "I could be conflating the two readings—do you see what I mean?"

"Imagining the man into the one because you know he was at the other?"

"Exactly so. . . . Do you have any other photos of him?"

"No." But Clarke started typing again, entering the name Nikolai Stahov into the search engine. She drew a blank, so described the consular official to Colwell instead.

"Doesn't ring any bells," the academic apologized, so Clarke tried again, this time with a description of Andropov. When Colwell gave another shrug, Clarke tried the Web site for the *Evening News*. Skipping back through the days until she'd found the story about the Russians and their blowout meal. Tapping one of the faces in the on-screen photograph.

"He *does* look familiar," Colwell admitted.

"From the Poetry Library?"

The academic shrugged and gave a long sigh. Clarke told her not to worry and called the Poetry Library on her mobile.

"Ms. Thomas?" she asked when her call was answered.

"Not in today," another female voice reported. "Can I help?"

"My name's Detective Sergeant Clarke. I'm investigating Alexander Todorov's murder and I need to ask her something."

"She's at home today . . . do you have her number?"

Clarke jotted the number down, then made the call. She asked Abigail Thomas if she had easy access to the Web, then talked her through the links to Word Power and the newspaper.

"Mm, yes," Thomas eventually said, "both of them, I think. Seated near the front, second row maybe."

"You're sure of that?"

"Fairly sure."

"Just to check, Ms. Thomas . . . no one took photos that night?"

"The odd person could have used their camera phone, I suppose."

"And you've no CCTV in the library?"

"It's a *library*," Abigail Thomas stressed.

"Just a thought. . . . Thanks for your help." Clarke ended the call.

"Why is it so important?" Colwell asked, breaking Clarke's reverie.

"Might not be," the detective admitted. "But Todorov and Andropov had a drink in the same bar, the night the poet was killed."

"Judging by the news story, Mr. Andropov is some sort of businessman?"

"They grew up in the same part of Moscow. DI Rebus says they knew one another . . ."

"Oh."

Clarke saw that she'd struck a nerve. "What is it?" she asked.

"Might help to explain something," Colwell mused.

"And what's that, Dr. Colwell?"

The academic picked up the CD. "Alexander's extempore poem." She walked over to a set of shelves and crouched down in front of it. There was a portable hi-fi there, and she slotted home the recording, then pressed Play. The room was filled with the sounds of the audience finding their seats and clearing their throats. "About halfway through," Colwell added, holding down the skip button. But this took her directly to the end of the recording. "Forgot," she said, "there's only the one continuous track." So she went back to the start and this time used the fast-forward facility.

"First time I listened," Clarke said, "I noticed he performed some poems in English, some in Russian."

Colwell nodded. "The new poem was in Russian. Ah, here it is." She trotted back to her desk and brought out a pad of paper and a pen, concentrating hard as she started to write. Eventually, she told Clarke to press Rewind. They listened again, Clarke hitting Pause when she felt Colwell was falling behind. "I really need more time," the academic apologized. "This isn't the ideal way to translate a poem . . ."

"Call it a work in progress," Clarke cajoled her. Colwell pushed a hand through her mane of hair and started again. After twenty minutes, she tossed the pen back onto the desk. On the CD, Todorov was using English to tell the audience that the next poem was from *Astapovo Blues.*

"He didn't say anything about the new work," Clarke realized.

"Nothing," Colwell agreed.

"Didn't introduce it, either."

Colwell shook her head, then pushed her hair back into place again. "I'm not sure how many people would have realized it was a new piece."

"How can you be sure it *was* new?"

"There don't seem to be any drafts in his flat, and I know his published work rather well."

Clarke nodded her understanding and held her hand out. "May I?" The academic seemed reluctant, but eventually handed the pad over. "It's really very rough . . . I've no idea where the line breaks would go . . ."

Clarke ignored her and started reading.

Winter's tongue licks the children of Zhdanov. . . . The Devil's tongue licks Mother Russia, coating taste buds with precious metals. Heartless appetite. . . . The gut's greed knows no fullness, no still moment, no love. Desire ripens, but only to blight. There are morsels here for all in the heat of famine, penances for all as the winter's shadow falls . . . such a package of scoundrels in my country.

Clarke read it through twice more, then met Colwell's eyes. "It's not very good, is it?"

"It's a bit rough at the edges," the academic said defensively.

"I don't mean your translation," Clarke assured her.

Colwell nodded eventually. "But there's an anger to it."

Clarke remembered Professor Gates's words at the Todorov autopsy—*there's a fury here*. "Yes," she agreed. "And all that imagery of food . . ."

Colwell cottoned on. "The news story? But surely that appeared after Alexander died?"

"True, but the dinner itself was a few days earlier—maybe he'd found out about it."

"So you're saying this is a poem about the businessman?"

"Composed on the spot, just to get up his nose. Andropov made his fortune from those 'precious metals' Todorov mentions."

"Making him the Devil?"

"You don't sound wholly convinced."

"The translation is rough . . . I'm guessing at some of the phrases. I really need more time with it."

Clarke nodded slowly, then remembered something. "Can I try another CD with you?" She found what she was looking for in her bag and knelt down next to the hi-fi. Again, it took a little while to find the moment when, at the Word Power reading, Charles Riordan's roving mic picked up the Russian voice.

"There," Clarke said.

"It's only a couple of words," Colwell said. "He's answering a phone call. All he says is 'hello' and 'yes.'"

"Worth a try," Clarke said with a sigh, ejecting the disc and rising to her feet. She reached for the pad of paper again. "Can I take the poem with me meantime? Leave you to get on with something you feel is more accurate?"

"There was bad blood between Alexander and this businessman?"

"I'm not sure."

"But it's a motive, right? And if they met again in that bar . . ."

Clarke held up a hand in warning. "We've no evidence that they even *saw* one another in that bar, which is why I'd be grateful if you kept all of this to yourself, Dr. Colwell. Otherwise you could jeopardize the inquiry."

"I understand." The academic nodded her agreement. Clarke tore the sheet from the pad and folded it into four.

"One little piece of advice," Clarke said as she finished folding. "The final line of the poem, he's quoting from Robert Burns. It's not 'a package of scoundrels' . . . it's 'a parcel of rogues' . . ."

39

Rebus sat by the bedside of Morris Gerald Cafferty. He'd shown his warrant card and asked the day shift if Cafferty had had any other visitors. The nurse had shaken her head.

No, because — despite his goading of Rebus — Cafferty had no friends. His wife was dead, his son murdered years back. His trusted lieutenant of long standing had "disappeared" after a falling-out. There was just the one bodyguard at the house, and right now *his* main concern was probably where his next paycheck was coming from. Doubtless there would be accountants and lawyers — Stone would have the details — but these weren't the sort of men to pay respects. Cafferty was still in intensive care, but Rebus had heard two staff members discussing a looming bed crisis. Maybe they would move him back to an open ward. Or, if his finances could be unlocked, a private room. As of now, he seemed content with the tubes, machines, and flickering screens. There were wires attached to his skull, measuring brain activity. Fluids were being drip-fed into one arm. Cafferty seemed to be wearing some sort of gown with a front but, Rebus guessed, no back. His arms were bare, and the hairs covering them were like silver wires. Rebus stood up and leaned down over Cafferty's face, wondering if the machine might suddenly register awareness of his proximity, but there was no change in the readout. He traced the route from Cafferty's body to the machines and from there to the wall sockets. Cafferty wasn't dying; the doctor had confided that much. Another reason to move him from intensive care. How intensively did you have to tend a vegetable? Rebus looked at Cafferty's knuckles and fingernails, the thick wrists, the dry white skin on each elbow. He was a large man, yes, but not particularly muscular. There were lines around the neck, like the circles on a freshly felled tree. The jaw was slack, the mouth open to accommodate a tube. There was a single track down the side of the face where some saliva had dried to a crust. With eyes closed, Cafferty looked harmless enough. What little hair there was on his scalp needed a wash. The charts at the end of the bed had told Rebus nothing. They were just a way of reducing the patient's life to a series of numbers and graphs. Impossible to tell if a line angling upwards was a good sign or a bad . . .

"Wake up, you old bastard," Rebus whispered into the gangster's ear. "Playtime's over." Not a flicker. "No point you hiding there inside that thick skull of yours. I'm waiting for you out *here*."

Nothing apart from a gurgling in the throat, and Cafferty was making that same sound every thirty seconds or so. Rebus slumped back into his chair. When he'd arrived, a nurse had asked if he was the patient's brother.

"Does it matter?" he'd asked her.

"It's just that you do look like him," she'd said, waddling away. He decided that it was a story worth sharing with the patient, but before he could start there was a trembling in his shirt pocket. He took his mobile out, checking to left and right for anyone who might disapprove.

"What's up, Shiv?" he asked.

"Andropov and his driver were in the audience at the Poetry Library. Todorov made up a poem on the spot, and I think Andropov was its target."

"Interesting."

"Have they given you a break?"

It took a moment for Rebus to realize what she meant. "I'm not being grilled. Nothing on the overshoe but blood — same type as Cafferty."

"So where are you now?"

"Visiting the patient."

"Christ, John, how's that going to look?"

"I wasn't planning on sticking a pillow over his face."

"But say he snuffs it while you're there?"

"Not a bad point, DS Clarke."

"So walk away."

"Where do you want to meet?"

"I have to get back to Gayfield Square."

"I thought we were going to pick up the chauffeur?"

"*We* are doing no such thing."

"Meaning you're going to run it past Derek Starr?"

"Yes."

"He doesn't know this case like we do, Siobhan."

"John, as of now we've got precisely nothing."

"I disagree. The connections are beginning to come together . . . don't tell me you can't sense it?" He'd risen from his chair again, but only to bend over Cafferty's face. One of the machines gave a loud beep, to which Clarke added a voluble sigh.

"You're still by his bed," she stated.

"Thought I saw his eyelids flicker. So where is it we're going to meet?"

"Let me talk it through with Starr and Macrae."

"Give it to Stone instead."

She was silent for a moment. "I must have misheard."

"SCD has more clout than us. Give him the Todorov-Andropov connection."

"Why?"

"Because it might help Stone build his case against Cafferty. Andropov's a businessman . . . businessmen like to cut deals."

"You know that's not going to happen."

"Then why am I wasting my breath?"

"Because you think I need Stone to be my friend. He's got it in mind that I helped you get to Cafferty. Only way I can show him otherwise is to give him this."

"Sometimes you're too clever for your own good." He paused. "But you should still talk to him. If the consulate starts pleading diplomatic immunity, SCD's got a stronger hand than us."

"Meaning?"

"Meaning channels to Special Branch and the spooks."

"Are you going all James Bond on me?"

"There's only one James Bond, Shiv," he told her, hoping for a laugh, which didn't come.

"I'll mull it over," she conceded instead, "if you promise to be out of that hospital in the next five minutes."

"Already on my way," he lied, ending the call. His mouth was dry, and he didn't reckon the patient would mind if he borrowed some of the water on the bedside cabinet. There was a clear plastic jug with a tumbler next to it. Rebus drank two glasses, then decided to take a look inside the cabinet itself.

He wasn't expecting to find Cafferty's watch, wallet, and keys. But since they were there, he flipped open the wallet and found that it contained five ten-pound notes, a couple of credit cards, and some scraps of paper with phone numbers—none of them meaning anything to Rebus. The watch was a Rolex, naturally, and he weighed it in his hand to confirm that it was the real deal. Then he picked up the keys. There were half a dozen of them. They chinked and clinked as he rolled them between palm and fingers.

House keys.

Chinked them and clinked them and kept staring at Cafferty.

"Any objections?" he asked quietly. And then, after a further moment: "Didn't think so . . ."

His luck just kept getting better and better: no one had bothered to set the alarm, and Cafferty's bodyguard was elsewhere. Having entered by the front door, the first thing Rebus did was check the corners of the ceiling for security cameras. There weren't any, so he padded into the drawing room. The house was Victorian, the ceilings high with ornate cornicing. Cafferty had started collecting art, big splashy paintings that hurt Rebus's eyes. He wondered if any of them were by Roddy Denholm. The curtains were closed, and he left them that way, turning on the lights instead. TV and hi-fi and three sofas. Nothing on the marble-topped coffee table but a couple of old newspapers and a pair of spectacles—the gangster too vain to wear them anywhere outside the privacy of his home. There was a door to the right of the fireplace, and

Rebus opened it. Cafferty's booze cupboard, big enough to contain a double fridge and assorted wine racks, with bottles of spirits lining a shelf. Resisting temptation, he closed the door again and headed back into the hall. More doors off: a huge kitchen; a conservatory with a pool table; laundry room; bathroom; office; yet another, less formal, living room. He wondered if the gangster really enjoyed rattling around in a place this size.

"Course you do," he said, answering his own question. The stairs were wide and carpeted. Next floor up: two bedrooms with bathrooms attached; a home cinema, forty-two-inch plasma screen flush with the wall; and what seemed to be a storeroom, filled with boxes and tea chests, most of them empty. There was a woman's hat on the top of one box, photo albums and shoes beneath. This, Rebus guessed, was all that remained of the late Mrs. Cafferty. There was a dartboard on one wall, with puncture marks around its circumference, evidence that someone needed to improve his throwing. Rebus guessed that the dartboard would have fallen into disuse once the room changed identity.

The last door off the landing led to a narrow, winding stairwell. More rooms at the top of the house: one containing a full-size snooker table covered with a dust-sheet, the other a well-stocked library. Rebus recognized the shelves — he'd bought the same ones from Ikea. The books were mostly dusty paperbacks, thrillers for the gentleman and romances for the lady. There were also some children's books, which had probably belonged to Cafferty's son. The house felt little used, the floorboards creaking underfoot. He reckoned the gangster seldom took the trouble to climb this final set of stairs.

Heading back down, Rebus returned to Cafferty's office. It was a good-sized room with a window looking onto the back garden. Again, the curtains were closed, but Rebus risked easing them open so he could take a look at the coach house. Two cars parked in front of it — the Bentley and an Audi — and no sign of the bodyguard. Rebus closed the curtains again and switched on the light. There was an old bureau in the center of the room, covered with paperwork — domestic bills, by the look of it. Rebus sat in the leather chair and started opening drawers. The first thing he came across was a gun, a pistol of some kind with what looked like Russian lettering along the barrel.

"Little present from your pal?" Rebus guessed. There was, however, no ammo in the clip, and no sign of any bullets in the drawer. It had been a long time since Rebus had held a firearm. He tested it for weight and balance, then used his handkerchief to place it back where he'd found it. Financial statements in the next drawer down. Cafferty had sixteen grand in his current account and a further quarter of a million earning him interest on the money market. His portfolio of shares added another hundred thousand to the pot. Rebus saw no sign of any mortgage payments, meaning Cafferty probably owned the house outright. This part of town, it had to be worth a million and a half. Nor would this be the end of the gangster's wealth; Stone had hinted at various shell companies and offshore holdings. Cafferty owned bars, clubs, the lettings agency, and a snooker hall. He was rumored to hold a stake in a cab company. Rebus suddenly noticed something in the corner: a venerable safe with a tumbler lock. It was the color of verdigris and came from Kentucky. Walking over to it, he was unsurprised to find it locked. The only combination he could think of to try was Cafferty's birthday. Eighteen, ten, forty-six. Rebus pulled the handle, and the heavy door swung open.

He allowed himself a smile. Couldn't think why he had memorized that number, but it hadn't been wasted.

Inside the safe: two boxes of nine-mil ammo, four thick wads of notes, twenties and fifties, some business ledgers, computer disks, a jewelry box containing the late wife's necklaces and earrings. Rebus lifted out Cafferty's passport and flicked through it: no visits to Russia. Birth certificate for the man himself, birth and death for the wife and son. The wedding certificate showed that Cafferty had married in 1973 at the registry office in Edinburgh. He replaced each item and studied the disks — no labels, no writing. There wasn't even a computer in the office . . . point of fact, he hadn't seen one anywhere in the house. On the bottom shelf of the safe sat a small cardboard box. Rebus lifted it out and opened it. It contained two dozen shiny silver discs. CDs, he thought at first. But holding one up to the light, he saw that it was marked DVD-R, 4.7G. Rebus was no technophile, but he reckoned whatever this was, it would play on the system upstairs. There was no writing on any of the discs, but colored dots had been added to each one — some green, some blue, some red, some yellow.

Rebus closed the safe and spun the dial, then switched off the light and padded back upstairs, the box of discs in his hand. The home cinema boasted shuttered windows and a row of leather recliners, behind which was a further row comprising two double-seater sofas. He crouched down in front of the battery of machines and slotted the DVD home, then switched on the screen and retreated to one of the chairs. It took him three different remotes to get everything — screen, DVD player,

and loudspeakers — working. Seated on the edge of the
black leather chair, he began to watch what appeared to
be surveillance footage . . .

A room. A living room. Untidy, and with bodies
sprawled. Two of the bodies disentangled themselves
and headed elsewhere, holding hands. There was a sudden cut to a bedroom, the same two figures appearing,
peeling off their clothes as they started to kiss. Teenagers. Rebus recognized neither of them; didn't recognize
the setting either — somewhere a lot tattier than Cafferty's own house.

Okay, so the gangster got his jollies from amateur
porn . . . Rebus skipped ahead, but the action stayed
with the couple and their coupling. They were filmed
from above and from the side. Another skip and the girl
was in a bathroom, seated on the pan and then stripping
off again to take a shower. She was skinny, almost ema-
ciated, and had bruises on her arms. He skipped again,
but there was nothing else on the disc.

Next one — with a blue dot rather than a green. Different yet similar location, different yet all-too-familiar
action.

"Showing your pervy side, Cafferty," Rebus muttered,
ejecting the disc. He tried another green dot — back to
the characters from the first disc. Pattern emerging,
John. . . . Red dot: another flat, some communal dope-
smoking, a girl having a bath, a guy pleasuring himself
in his bedroom.

Rebus wasn't looking for any surprises from the yellow dot. Immediately, he was launched into the same
setups as previously, but with one important difference —
he knew both the flat and the actors.

Nancy Sievewright, Eddie Gentry. The flat on Blair Street. The flat that belonged to MGC Lettings.

"Well, well," Rebus said to himself. There was footage of a party in the living room. Dancing and booze and what looked to Rebus like a few lines of coke to go with the dope. A blow job in the bathroom, a punch-up in the hall. Next disc: Sol Goodyear had come to pay his respects, rewarded with a romp in Nancy's bedroom and some shared moments in the cramped shower cubicle. After he'd gone, she settled down with the hash he'd left and rolled herself a healthy joint. Living room, bathroom, her bedroom, the hallway.

"Everything but the kitchen." Rebus paused. "The kitchen," he repeated to himself, "and Eddie Gentry's bedroom . . ."

By the time he'd reached the final disc in the box he'd grown bored. It was like watching one of those TV reality shows, but with no adverts to break the monotony. This last disc was different, though: no little color-coded sticker. And it had sound. Rebus found himself watching the same room he was sitting in. The chairs and sofas had been filled by men. Cigar-smoking men. Men slurping wine from crystal glasses. Voluble, slurred, happy men, who were being shown a DVD.

"Wonderful meal that," one of them told the host. There were grunts of agreement, smoke billowing. The camera was pointing at the men, meaning it had to be . . . Rebus got to his feet and approached the plasma screen. There was a small hole drilled into the wall just above one corner of the TV. You'd never see it, or else you might take it for a bit of botched DIY. Rebus peered into it, but couldn't see anything. He exited the room and entered the one next door — en suite bathroom. Cabinet attached to a mirrored wall. Inside the cabinet: nothing . . . no camera, no wires. He put his eye to the peephole and was looking into the screening room. Back in the home cinema, the men's comments left Rebus in no doubt that they were watching some of the same footage he'd just viewed.

"Wish my wife was that dirty."

"Maybe if you plied her with class A rather than Chardonnay . . ."

"Worth a shot, I suppose."

"And they don't know you're watching them, Morris?"

Cafferty's voice, from the back of the room: "Not a clue," he growled happily.

"Didn't Chuck Berry get in trouble for something like this?"

"Getting a few ideas for the good lady, Roger?"

"Married twenty-odd years, Stuart."

"I'll take that as a no . . ."

Rebus found himself on his knees in front of the screen. Roger and Stuart, with their wine and cigars, stuffed to the gills by Cafferty and now enjoying this very different form of corporate hospitality.

Roger Anderson.

Stuart Janney.

First Albannach's brightest and best . . .

"Michael will be gutted he missed this," Janney added with a laugh. Meaning, no doubt, Sir Michael Addison. But Rebus reckoned Janney was dead wrong. He ejected the disc and went back to the one with the party on it. Bathroom blow job, the donor bearing an uncanny resemblance to Gill Morgan, aspiring actress and Sir Michael's pampered stepdaughter. Same head had been bent over one of the coke trails in the living room. Rebus went back to the footage of the home cinema, tried to work out which DVD the group was watching. Kept his eyes glued to the two bankers, wondering if either of them would exhibit signs of clocking their boss's step-kid. Grounds for a revenge attack on Cafferty? Maybe so. But what were they doing there in the first place? Rebus could think of several reasons. From the bank statements, Rebus now knew that Cafferty kept his various onshore accounts with FAB. Added to which, he was going to introduce a new and wealthy client to the bank — Sergei Andropov. And maybe the pair of them would be looking to do a deal with FAB, a vast commercial loan to help them buy up hundreds of acres of Edinburgh.

Andropov was relocating, ducking out of Russia altogether to escape prosecution. Maybe he thought the Scottish Parliament could be persuaded not to extradite him. Maybe he was buying his way into a forthcoming *independent* Scotland. Small country, easy to become a very big fish . . .

Cafferty oiling the wheels.

Hosting a memorable party . . . and secretly taping it. For his own satisfaction? Or to be used against the men themselves? Rebus couldn't see it having much effect on the likes of Janney and Anderson. But now another man was rising to his feet from one of the sofas. Looked to Rebus as if only Cafferty and this man had been occupying the back row.

"Bathroom?" he inquired.

"Across the hall," his host obliged. Yes, Cafferty wouldn't want him using the en suite through the wall; couldn't risk the camera being found.

"Won't ask why you need it, Jim," Stuart Janney commented to a few rugby-club guffaws.

"Nothing sordid, Stuart," the man called Jim responded, making his exit.

Jim Bakewell, Minister for Economic Development. Meaning Bakewell had lied at the Parliament, telling Siobhan he'd not met Cafferty until that night at the hotel.

"Try making a complaint to the Chief Constable now, Jimbo," Rebus muttered, stabbing a finger in Bakewell's direction.

There wasn't an awful lot more to the DVD. After half an hour, the spectators had wrung as much interest as possible from the show. There were three further members of the party who were new to Rebus. They looked like business types, ruddy-faced and big-bellied. Builders? Contractors? Maybe even councillors . . . Rebus knew he could probably find out, but that would mean taking the recording. Which was fine, so long as no one noticed it was missing. If anyone found out Rebus had been here, Cafferty's defense team would have a field day.

"Oh aye, John? What defense team is that then?"

Yes, because where was the crime? Bugging flats you were renting? Small beer — the magistrate would watch the DVDs with a good deal of interest, then stick the gangster with a pittance of a fine. Rebus made sure everything was switched off, no prints left behind, then headed downstairs and unlocked the safe again, replacing the box, keeping just the one disc for himself. Down the white marble hall and out into the sweet-smelling air, door secure behind him. He'd have to get Cafferty's keys back to him, but first he had some thinking to do.

He took a left out of the gate and another left at the top of the road, heading for Bruntsfield Place and the first available taxi.

Eddie Gentry, replete with eyeliner and the red bandanna, opened the door to him.

"Nancy's out," he said.

"Have you patched things up?"

"We had a frank exchange of views."

Rebus smiled. "Going to invite me in, Eddie? And by the way, I liked your CD."

Gentry considered his options, then turned and pushed open the living room door. Rebus followed him inside.

"Ever watch *Big Brother*, Eddie?" Rebus was making a circuit of the room, hands in pockets.

"Life's too short."

"It is that," Rebus seemed to agree. "Tell you something I didn't spot when I was here before."

"What?"

Rebus looked up. "Your ceilings have been lowered."

"Yeah?"

Rebus nodded. "Done before you moved in?"

"Suppose so."

"There might be original features — cornices, ceiling roses. . . . Why do you reckon the landlord would want them covered up?"

"Insulation?"

"How so?"

Gentry shrugged. "Makes the rooms smaller, meaning easier to heat."

"The rooms are all the same, then? Fake ceilings?"

"I'm not an architect."

Rebus locked eyes with the young man, saw the

slightest twitch at a corner of his mouth. Eddie Gentry was not feeling comfortable. The detective gave a low, drawn-out whistle.

"You know, don't you?" he asked. "You've known all along?"

"Known what?"

"Cafferty's got you wired — cameras in the ceiling, in the walls . . ." He pointed towards a corner of the room. "See that hole? Looks like someone's botched a bit of drilling?" Gentry's face gave nothing away. "There's a lens pointing at us. But you already know that. For all I know, maybe it's even your job to set the camera rolling." Gentry had folded his arms across his chest. "That session you did at CR Studios — I'm betting it didn't come cheap. Did Cafferty pay for it? Was that part of the deal? Bit of money in your pocket . . . cheap rent . . . no overcrowding . . . and all you had to do was throw a few parties." Rebus was thinking it through. "Dope provided by Sol Goodyear — and I'm betting it came cheap, too. Know why?"

"Why?"

"Because Sol works for Cafferty. He's the dealer, you're the pimp . . ."

"Fuck you."

"Careful, son." Rebus jabbed his forefinger towards the young man. "Have you heard what happened to Cafferty?"

"I heard."

"Maybe someone didn't like what he'd been doing. Remember that party with Gill Morgan?"

"What about it?"

"That the only footage of her you got?"

"I've no idea." Rebus looked disbelieving. "I never *watched* any of it."

"Just handed it over, eh?"

"No harm done, was there?"

"I don't think you're qualified to judge that, Eddie. Does Nancy know?"

Gentry shook his head.

"Just you, eh? Did he tell you he was doing the self-same thing in some of his other flats?"

"You mentioned *Big Brother* earlier — what's the difference?"

Rebus was standing close to the young man when he answered. "Difference is, they *know* they're being watched. I can't really decide who's the sleazier, you or Cafferty. *He* was watching complete strangers, but you, Eddie, were filming your mates."

"Is there a law against it?"

"Oh, I'm fairly sure there is. How often does the taping happen?"

"Three or four times — tops."

Because by then Cafferty was bored, and moved on to a new flat, new tenants, new faces and bodies . . . Rebus walked into the hallway, looked for the hole and found it. Nancy's bedroom: again, the false ceiling; again, the neatly drilled hole. The bathroom was the same. When Rebus emerged into the hallway, Gentry was leaning against the wall, arms still folded, jaw jutting defiantly.

"Where's the hardware?" Rebus asked.

"Mr. C took it."

"When?"

"Few weeks back. Like I told you, it was only three or four times . . ."

"Doesn't make it any less sordid. Let's take a look at

your room." Rebus didn't wait for an invitation, opened the door to Gentry's bedroom and asked where the cables were.

"They used to come down from the ceiling. Had them hooked up to a DVD recorder. If anything interesting was happening, I only had to press the Record button."

"And now the whole lot's been installed in some other flat so your landlord can show a fresh slice of grainy porn to his sweaty pals." Rebus was shaking his head slowly. "Wouldn't want to be in your shoes when Nancy finds out . . ."

Gentry didn't so much as flinch. "I think it's time you were leaving," he stated. "Show's over."

Rebus responded by getting right into the young man's face. "You couldn't be more wrong, Eddie — this particular show's only just getting started." He squeezed past, out into the hallway, pausing by the front door. "I lied by the way — that music of yours is going nowhere. You've just not got the talent, pal."

Closed the door after him and stood for a moment at the top of the stairs, reaching into his pocket for his cigarettes.

Job done.

40

The CID suite at Gayfield Square might as well have been a swimming pool — all they were doing was treading water. Derek Starr knew it and was having trouble motivating the group. There wasn't enough for them to do. No exciting new leads on either Todorov or Riordan. Forensics had produced a partial fingerprint from the small bottle of cleaning fluid, but all they knew so far was that it belonged neither to Riordan nor to anyone on the database. Terry Grimm had supplied information that Riordan's house was visited weekly by a team of cleaners from an agency, though they were usually told not to bother with the living-room-cum-studio. But any one of them could have left the print. No one was about to claim for certain that it belonged to the arsonist. It looked like another dead end. Same went for the e-fit of the hooded woman outside the multistory: officers had taken copies door-to-door, returning to the station with nothing but sore feet.

Having gone through the proper channels, Starr had at last secured CCTV footage from the few cameras in and around Portobello, but no one was very hopeful — all they showed was early-morning traffic. Again, without knowing how the attacker had reached Riordan's house, it was needle-in-a-haystack stuff. The way Starr himself kept looking at Siobhan Clarke, he knew she was holding back on him. Twice in the space of half an hour he'd asked her what she was working on.

"Going through the Riordan tapes," she'd explained. Not a word of truth in it—Todd Goodyear was typing up the last batch of transcripts, looking worn down by the whole experience. He kept staring into space, as if thinking himself into a better place. Clarke, meantime, was waiting for Stone to get back to her, having left a message on his mobile. She was still wondering if it was such a good idea. Stone and Starr seemed pretty pally; chances were, anything she said to the one would get back to the other. She had yet to mention to Starr the appearance of Sergei Andropov and his driver in the Poetry Library audience.

There were no longer any members of the media hanging about outside the station. The last mention of either death had been an inch-long paragraph on one of the *Evening News*'s inside pages. Starr was currently in another meeting with DCI Macrae. Maybe later today they would announce that the inquiry was being split into two, since no evidence had come to light connecting the Todorov murder to Riordan's fate. The team would be broken up; the Riordan case would go back to Leith CID.

Unless Clarke did something about it.

It took her a further ten minutes to decide. Starr was still in his meeting, so she grabbed her coat and wandered over to the desk where Goodyear was working.

"Going somewhere?" he asked, somewhat forlornly.

"We both are," she said, brightening his day.

The drive across town to the consulate took only ten minutes. It was housed on a grand Georgian terrace within sight of the Episcopalian Cathedral. The street was wide enough to accommodate a row of parking bays in the middle of the road, and a car was pulling out of one bay as they arrived. While Goodyear put money in the meter, Clarke studied the car next to hers—it looked very much like the one Andropov had been using at the City Chambers and Nikolai Stahov at the mortuary—an old black Merc with darkened rear windows. The license plate, however, wasn't the diplomatic kind, so Clarke called the station and asked for a check. The car was registered to Mr. Boris Aksanov, with an address in Cramond. Clarke jotted down the details and ended the call.

"You reckon they'll let us question him?" Goodyear asked on his return.

She gave a shrug. "Let's see, shall we?" She crossed to the consulate, climbed its three stone steps, and pressed the buzzer. The door was opened by a young woman with the fixed smile of the professional greeter. Clarke already had her warrant card open. "I'm here to see Mr. Aksanov," she stated.

"Mr. Aksanov?" The smile stayed fixed.

"Your driver." Clarke turned her head. "His car's over there."

"Well, he's not here."

Clarke stared at the woman. "You sure about that?"

"Of course."

"What about Mr. Stahov?"

"He's also not here at present."

"When's he due back?"

"Later today, I think."

Clarke was looking over the woman's shoulder. The entrance hall was large but barren, with peeling paintwork and faded wallpaper. A curving staircase led upwards, but she had no view of the landing. "And Mr. Aksanov?"

"I don't know."

"He's not driving Mr. Stahov, then?"

The smile was having a bit of trouble. "I'm afraid I can't help . . ."

"Aksanov's driving Sergei Andropov, is he?"

The young woman's hand was gripping the edge of the door. Clarke could tell she wanted to close it in their faces.

"I can't help," she repeated instead.

"Is Mr. Aksanov a consular employee?" But now the door really was being closed, slowly but determinedly. "We'll come back later," Clarke stressed. The door clicked shut, but she continued to stare at it.

"She had frightened eyes," Goodyear commented.

Clarke nodded her agreement.

"Waste of money, too — I put half an hour on the meter."

"Claim it back from the inquiry." Clarke turned and started towards the car, but paused at the Merc and checked her watch. When she got in behind the steering wheel, Goodyear asked if they were headed back to Gayfield Square. Clarke shook her head.

"Parking wardens round here are vicious," she said. "And that Merc goes into the red in exactly seven minutes."

"Meaning someone's going to have to feed the meter?" he guessed.

But Clarke shook her head again. "It's illegal to do that, Todd. If they don't want a ticket, they're going to have to move the car." She turned her key in the ignition.

"I thought embassies never paid their fines anyway."

"True enough . . . if they have diplomatic plates." Clarke put the car into gear and moved out of the parking bay, but only to stop again curbside a few dozen yards farther along. "Worth a bit of a wait, wouldn't you say?" she asked.

"If it keeps me away from those transcripts," Goodyear agreed.

"Detective work losing its allure, Todd?"

"I think I'm ready to go back into uniform." He drew back his shoulders, working the muscles. "Any news of DI Rebus?"

"They pulled him in again."

"Are they thinking of charging him?"

"Reason they pulled him in was to tell him there's no evidence."

"They didn't get a match from that overshoe?"

"No."

"Do they have anyone else in mind?"

"Christ, Todd, I don't know!" The silence in the car lasted half a dozen beats before Clarke expelled air noisily. "Look, I'm sorry . . ."

"I'm the one who should be apologizing," he assured her. "Couldn't help sticking my nose in."

"No, it's me . . . I could be in trouble."

"How?"

"SCDEA were watching Cafferty. John got me to send them elsewhere."

The young man's eyes had widened. "Bloody hell," he said.

"Language," she warned him.

"They had surveillance on Cafferty. . . . That has to look bad for DI Rebus."

Clarke gave a shrug.

"Surveillance on Cafferty . . ." Goodyear repeated to himself, shaking his head slowly. Clarke's attention had been diverted by movement along the street. A man was exiting the consulate.

"This looks promising," she said. Same man who'd been with Stahov at the mortuary, same man who'd been photographed at the Word Power event. Aksanov unlocked the car and got in. Clarke decided to let her engine idle, until she knew what he was going to do — move to a different bay, or head elsewhere. When he passed his third vacant bay, she had her answer.

"We're going to follow him?" Goodyear asked, fastening his seat belt.

"Well spotted."

"And then what?"

"I was thinking of pulling him over on some trumped-up charge . . ."

"Is that wise?"

"Dunno yet. Let's see what happens." The Merc had signaled left into Queensferry Street.

"Heading out of town?" Goodyear guessed.

"Aksanov lives in Cramond; maybe he's going home."

Queensferry Street became Queensferry Road. Looking at her speedometer, Clarke saw that he was staying within the limit. When the traffic lights ahead turned red, she watched his brake lights, but they were both in good working order. If Cramond was his destination, he'd probably keep going till the Barnton roundabout, then take a right. Question was, did she want him getting that far? Every few hundred yards on Queensferry Road, there seemed to be another set of lights. As the Merc stopped at the next red, Clarke brought her own car up close behind it.

"Reach over into the back seat, will you, Todd?" she asked. "On the floor there . . ." He had to undo his seat belt in order to twist his body around sufficiently.

"This what you want?" he asked.

"Plug it into the socket there," she told him. "Then put your window down."

"There's a magnet on the base?" he guessed.

"That's right."

The moment the flashing blue light was plugged in, it began working. Goodyear reached out of the window and attached it to the roof. The light ahead was still red. Clarke sounded her horn and watched the driver examine her in his rearview mirror. She signaled with her hand for him to pull over. When the light turned green, that was exactly what he did, crossing the junction and bumping his passenger-side tires up onto the pavement. Clarke passed him and then did the same with her car. Traffic slowed to watch but kept moving. The driver was out of the Merc. He wore sunglasses and a suit and tie. He was standing on the pavement when Clarke reached him. She had her ID open for inspection.

"Is there a problem?" he asked, his English heavily accented.

"Mr. Aksanov? We met at the mortuary . . ."

"I asked what the problem was."

"You're going to have to come to the station."

"What have I done wrong?" He had lifted a mobile phone from his pocket. "I will speak to the consulate."

"Won't do you any good," she warned him. "That's not an official car, which makes me think you're self-employed. No immunity, Mr. Aksanov."

"I am a driver for the consulate."

"But not *just* the consulate. Now get in the car." There was steel in her voice. He was still holding the phone, but had yet to do anything with it.

"And if I refuse?"

"You'll be charged with obstruction . . . and anything else I can think of."

"I've done nothing wrong."

"That's all we need to hear — but we need to hear it at the station."

"My car," he complained.

"It'll still be here. We'll bring you back afterwards." She managed a nice friendly smile. "Promise."

"How come you started driving Sergei Andropov around?" Clarke asked.

"I drive people for a living."

They were in an interview room at West End police station, Clarke not wanting to take the Russian to Gayfield Square. She'd sent Goodyear off to fetch coffee. There was a tape deck on the table, but she wasn't using it. No notebook either. Aksanov had asked to smoke, and she was letting him.

"Your English is good — there's even a trace of local accent."

"I'm married to a girl from Edinburgh. I've been here almost five years." He inhaled some smoke and blew it ceilingwards.

"Is she a poetry fan, too?" Aksanov stared at Clarke. "Well?" she prompted.

"She reads books . . . mostly novels."

"So it's just you that likes poetry?" He shrugged but

said nothing. "Read any Seamus Heaney lately? Or how about Robert Burns?"

"Why are you asking me this?"

"Just that you were spotted at poetry readings twice in as many weeks. Or maybe it's just that you *really* like Alexander Todorov?"

"People say he is Russia's greatest poet."

"Do you agree?" Aksanov gave another shrug and examined the tip of his cigarette. "Did you buy a copy of his latest book?"

"I don't see why this is any of your business."

"Can you remember what it's called?"

"I don't have to talk to you."

"I'm investigating two murders, Mr. Aksanov . . ."

"And what is that to me?" The Russian was growing angry. But then the door opened, and Goodyear came in with two drinks.

"Black, two sugars," he said, placing one in front of Aksanov. "White with none." The second Styrofoam cup was handed to Clarke. She nodded her thanks, then gave the slightest flick of the head. Goodyear took the hint and walked to the far wall, resting his back against it, hands clasped in front of him. Aksanov had stubbed out the cigarette and was readying to light another.

"Second time you went," she told him, "you took Sergei Andropov with you."

"Did I?"

"According to witnesses." Another mighty shrug, this time accompanied by downturned mouth. "Are you saying you didn't?" Clarke asked.

"I'm saying nothing."

"Makes me wonder what it is you're trying to hide. Were you on duty the night Mr. Todorov died?"

"I don't remember."

"I'm only asking you to think back a little over a week."

"Sometimes I work at night, sometimes not."

"Andropov was at his hotel. He had a meeting in the bar . . ."

"There's nothing I can tell you."

"Why did you go to those poetry readings, Mr. Aksanov?" Clarke asked quietly. "Did Andropov ask you to go? Did he ask you to take him?"

"If I have done anything wrong, go ahead and charge me!"

"Is that what you want?"

"I want to get away from here." The fingers that gripped the fresh cigarette were starting to shake a little.

"Do you remember the recital at the Poetry Library?" Clarke asked, keeping her voice low and level. "The man who was recording it? He's been murdered, too."

"I was at the hotel all night."

She hadn't quite understood. "The Caledonian?" she guessed.

"Gleneagles," he corrected her. "The night of that fire."

"It was early morning actually."

"Night . . . morning . . . I was at Gleneagles."

"All right," she said, wondering at his sudden increase in agitation. "Who was it you were driving — Andropov or Stahov?"

"Both. They traveled together. I was there all the time."

"So you keep saying."

"Because it is the truth."

"But the night Mr. Todorov died, you don't recall if you were working or not?"

"No."

"It's quite important, Mr. Aksanov. We think who-ever killed Todorov was driving a car . . ."

"I had nothing to do with it! I find these questions totally unacceptable!"

"Do you?"

"Unacceptable and unreasonable."

"Finished already?" she asked after fifteen seconds of silence. His brow furrowed. "Your cigarette," she pointed out. "You'd only just started it."

The Russian stared at the ashtray, where most of an entire cigarette smoldered, having just been stubbed out . . .

Having arranged for a patrol car to drop Aksanov at Queensferry Road, Clarke wandered back down the cor-ridor towards where Goodyear was sharing gossip with two other constables. Before she could reach him, how-ever, her mobile rang. She didn't recognize the caller's number.

"Hello?" she asked, turning so her back was to Good-year and his colleagues.

"Detective Sergeant Clarke?"

"Hello, Dr. Colwell. I had half a mind to call you my-self."

"Oh?"

"Thought I might need a translator; false alarm as it turned out. What can I do for you?"

"I've just been listening to that CD."

"Still wrestling with the new poem?"

"To start with, yes . . . but I ended up listening to the whole thing."

"Had the same effect on me," Clarke admitted, remembering back to when Rebus and she had spent the hour in her car . . .

"Right at the end," Colwell was saying. "In fact, after the recital and the Q and A have finished . . ."

"Yes?"

"The mic picks up some bits of conversation."

"I remember — doesn't the poet start muttering to himself?"

"That's just what *I* thought, and it was difficult to make out. But it's not Alexander's voice."

"Then whose is it?"

"No idea."

"But it's in Russian, right?"

"Oh, it's definitely Russian. And after a few plays, I think I've worked out what he's saying."

Clarke was thinking of Charles Riordan, pointing his all-hearing microphone towards various audience members, picking up their comments. "So what *is* he saying?" she asked.

"Something along the lines of — 'I wish he was dead.' "

Clarke froze. "Would you mind repeating that, please?"

41

Rebus rendezvoused with her at Colwell's office, and they listened to the CD together.

"Doesn't sound like Aksanov," Clarke stated. Her phone started to ring, and she gave a little growl as she answered. The voice in her ear identified the caller as DI Calum Stone.

"You wanted to speak to me?" he said.

"I'll have to phone you back later." She cut the connection and shook her head slowly, letting Rebus know it was nothing important. He'd asked for the relevant section of the recording to be played again.

"I'd lay money on it being Andropov," he muttered afterwards. He was leaning forward in his chair, elbows on knees, hands clasped, completely focused on the recording and seemingly immune to Scarlett Colwell, who was crouched not three feet away next to the CD player, face hidden by the curtain of hair.

"And you're sure you've got the words right?" Clarke asked the academic.

"Positive," Colwell said. She repeated the Russian. It was written on a pad, which Clarke was now holding—the same pad that had once held the translated poem.

"'I wish he was dead'?" Rebus checked. "Not 'I want him killed' or 'I'm going to kill him'?"

"Slightly less inflammatory," Colwell said.

"Pity." Rebus turned towards Clarke. "Plenty to be going on with, though."

"Plenty," she agreed. "Say it *is* Andropov . . . who's he talking to? Has to be Aksanov, hasn't it?"

"And you've just let him go."

She nodded slowly. "We can always pick him up again . . . he's pretty well settled here."

"Doesn't mean the consulate won't kick him onto a plane bound for Moscow." Rebus stared at her. "Know what I reckon? Andropov would love to have someone on the inside at the consulate. That way, he'd know how the land lies back home. If they planned to put him on trial, consulate would be among the first to know."

"Aksanov as his eyes and ears?" Clarke nodded her agreement. "Fair enough, but is he anything else?"

"Executioner, you mean?" Rebus pondered this for a moment, then realized that a tear was running down Scarlett Colwell's face.

"Sorry," he apologized to her. "I know this can't be easy."

"Just catch whoever did this to Alexander." She dabbed at her face with the back of her hand. "Just do that, please."

"Thanks to you," he assured her, "we've come a step closer." He picked up her translation of the poem. "Andropov would have been furious about this. Calling him greedy and a 'blight' and part of the whole 'parcel of rogues.'"

"Furious enough to want the poet dead," Clarke agreed. "But does that mean he did it?"

Rebus stared up at her again. "Maybe we should ask him," he said.

*   *   *

It had taken well over an hour for Siobhan Clarke to lead
DI Derek Starr through the story. Even then, he'd complained for a further fifteen minutes about being kept
"out of the loop" before agreeing that Sergei Andropov
should be brought in for questioning. They had to shoo
three detectives out of the interview room. The men had
set up base there and complained at having to move their
stuff.

"Smells like a prop forward's jockstrap in here," Starr
commented.

"I wouldn't know," Clarke replied with a thin smile.
She'd bumped into Goodyear in the CID suite, and he,
too, had voiced a complaint—about being abandoned at
the West End cop shop. True enough, Colwell's phone
call had led Clarke straight out to her car, Goodyear still
chatting to his pals in the corridor. Even so, she'd studied the young man's scowl and offered him four evenly
spaced words: *get used to it*. To which he'd replied that
he really was ready to go back to Torphichen and his
constable's uniform both.

They had dispatched a patrol car to the Caledonian
Hotel. Forty minutes later it was back and discharging its
unhappy human cargo. It was almost 8:00, the sky black
and the temperature falling.

"Do I have the right to a lawyer?" was Sergei Andropov's first question.

"Think you need one?" Starr shot back. He'd borrowed a CD player and was tapping it with one finger.

Andropov considered Starr's question, then took off
his coat, placed it over the back of the chair, and sat
down. Clarke was seated next to Starr, notebook and
mobile phone in front of her. She was hoping Rebus—

stationed outside in his car—would manage to keep quiet.

"When you're ready, DS Clarke," Starr said, pressing his hands together.

"Mr. Andropov," she began, "I spoke to Boris Aksanov earlier today."

"Yes?"

"We were talking about the recital at the Scottish Poetry Library . . . I believe you were there?"

"Did he tell you that?"

"There are plenty of witnesses, sir." She paused for a moment. "We already know that you knew Alexander Todorov in Moscow, and that the pair of you weren't exactly friends . . ."

"Again, who told you this?"

Clarke ignored the question. "You went to the reading with Mr. Aksanov and then had to sit and listen as the poet extemporized a new piece." Clarke unfolded the translation. *"Heartless appetite . . . The gut's greed knows no fullness. . . . such a parcel of rogues. . . .* Not exactly a love letter, is it?"

"It's only a poem."

"But directed at *you,* Mr. Andropov. Aren't you one of the 'children of Zhdanov'?"

"Like many thousands of others." Andropov gave a little laugh. His eyes were shining.

"By the way," Clarke said, "I should have offered commiserations at the start . . ."

"For what?" The eyes had narrowed and darkened.

"Your friend's injuries. Have you visited him in hospital?"

"You mean Cafferty?" He seemed dismissive of the tactic. "He'll survive."

"A cause for celebration, I'm sure."

"What the hell is she getting at?" Andropov directed the question at Starr, but it was Clarke who answered.

"Would you mind taking a listen to this?" On cue, Starr hit the Play button. The noise of the Todorov recital's conclusion filled the room. People rising from their seats, commenting on the evening, planning drinks and supper . . . and then the burst of Russian.

"Recognize it, Mr. Andropov?" Clarke asked as Starr paused the recording.

"No."

"Sure about that? Maybe if DI Starr plays it back . . . ?"

"Look, what are you getting at?"

"We have a forensics facility here in the city, Mr. Andropov. They have a pretty good track record when it comes to voice-pattern recognition . . ."

"What do I care?"

"You care because that's you on the recording, expressing to Boris Aksanov your desire to see the poet Alexander Todorov dead—the poet who had just humiliated you, the poet who opposed everything you stand for." She paused again. "And the very next night, that same man *was* dead."

"Meaning I killed him?" Andropov's laughter this time was louder and more sustained. "And when exactly did I do this? Did I spirit myself away from the hotel bar? Did I hypnotize your development minister so that he would not notice my disappearance?"

"Others could have acted on your behalf," Starr stated icily.

"Well, that's something you're going to have a great deal of trouble proving, since it happens to be untrue."

"Why did you go to the recital?" Clarke asked. Andropov stared at her and decided he had nothing to lose from answering.

"Boris told me he'd been to one a few weeks before. I was intrigued. I had never seen Alexander read in public."

"Mr. Aksanov didn't strike me as a poetry buff."

Andropov shrugged. "Maybe the consulate asked him to go."

"Why would they do that?"

"To ascertain how much of an irritant Alexander intended to be during his stay in the city." Andropov shifted in his seat. "Alexander Todorov was a professional dissident — it's how he made his living, picking the pockets of bleeding-heart liberals all over the Western world."

Clarke waited to see if Andropov had anything more to add. "And when you heard his latest poem?" she asked into the silence.

The shrug this time was conciliatory. "You're right, I was angry with him. What do poets give to the world? Do they provide jobs, energy, raw material? No . . . merely words. And often well remunerated in the process — certainly lionized above their due. Alexander Todorov had been suckled by the West *precisely* because he pandered to its need to see Russia as corrupt and corrosive." Andropov had made a fist of his right hand, but then decided against thumping the desk. Instead, he took a deep breath and exhaled noisily through his nostrils. "I did say that I wished he was dead, but those, too, were merely words."

"Nevertheless, could Boris Aksanov have acted on them?"

"Have you met Boris? He is no killer; he's a teddy bear."

"Bears have claws," Starr felt it necessary to comment. Andropov glowered at him.

"Thank you for that information—being a Russian, of course, I would not have known that."

Starr had started blushing. To deflect attention from the fact, he hit the Play button again and they eavesdropped once more. Pausing the recording, Starr tapped the machine again. "I'd say we've got grounds to charge you," he stated.

"Really? Well, let us see what one of your famed Edinburgh barristers will say about that."

"We don't *have* barristers in Scotland," Starr spat back.

"They're called advocates," Clarke explained. "But actually, at this point it's a solicitor you'd want—*if* we were charging you." Her words were aimed at Starr, appealing for him not to take it any further—not just yet.

"Well?" Andropov, taking her meaning, was asking the question of Derek Starr. Starr's mouth twitched, but he said nothing. "In other words, I am free to leave?" Andropov had moved his attention to Clarke, but it was Starr who barked out a response.

"Just don't leave the country!"

There was more laughter from the Russian. "I have no intention of departing your splendid country, Inspector."

"Nice warm gulag waiting for you back home?" Clarke couldn't help adding.

"That comment cheapens you." Andropov sounded disappointed in her.

"Going to drop by the hospital sometime?" she added. "Funny, isn't it, how people around you seem to end up either dead or in a coma?"

Andropov was rising to his feet, lifting his coat from

the chair. Starr and Clarke shared a look, but neither could think of any tactic to delay his departure. Good-year was just outside the door, ready to show the Russian out.

"We'll talk again," Starr assured Andropov.

"I look forward to it, Inspector."

"And we want you to surrender your passport" was Clarke's final salvo. Andropov gave a little bow of the head and was gone. Starr, who had risen to his feet, closed the door, walked around the desk, and sat down again, facing Clarke. Pretending to check for messages on her phone, she'd just broken the connection to Rebus.

"If it's anyone," Starr was telling her, "it's the driver. Even then, a bit of hard evidence might be useful."

Clarke had placed her notebook and mobile back in her bag. "Andropov's right about Aksanov — I don't see him as an assassin."

"Then we need to look at the hotel angle again, see if there's any way Andropov could have followed the poet."

"Cafferty was there, too, don't forget."

"One or the other, then."

"The problem," she sighed, "is that we've got a third man — Jim Bakewell's already said the three of them were in that booth till gone eleven . . . by which time Todorov was dead."

"So we're back to square one?" Starr didn't bother masking his exasperation.

"We're rattling the cage," Clarke corrected him. Then, after a moment's thought: "Thanks for sticking with it, Derek."

Starr thawed perceptibly. "You should have come to

me sooner, Siobhan. I want a break on this as much as you do."

"I know. But you're going to split the two investigations, aren't you?"

"DCI Macrae thinks it would help."

She nodded, as if agreeing with the analysis. "Do we work tomorrow?" she asked.

"Weekend overtime has been approved."

"John Rebus's last day," she stated quietly.

"Incidentally," Starr added, ignoring her, "the officer who showed Andropov out . . . is he new to the team?"

"West End sent him," she blithely lied.

Starr was shaking his head. "CID," he stated, "gets younger-looking every year."

"How did I do?" Clarke asked, sliding into the passenger seat.

"Three out of ten."

She stared at him. "Gee, thanks." Slammed shut the door. Rebus's car was parked directly outside the station. He was thrumming his fingers against the steering wheel, eyes straight ahead.

"I nearly came running in there," he went on. "How could you have missed it?"

"Missed what?"

Only now did he deign to turn his head towards her. "That night in the Poetry Library, Andropov was only a couple of rows from the front. No way he couldn't have seen the mic."

"So?"

"So you were asking the wrong questions. Todorov got him riled, he blurted out that he wanted him dead — no harm done at the time, the only other Russian speaker was his driver. But then Todorov *does* end up dead, and suddenly our friend Andropov has a problem . . ."

"The recording?"

Rebus nodded. "Because if we ever heard it and got it translated . . ."

"Hang on a second." Clarke pinched the skin either side of her nose and screwed shut her eyes. "Got any aspirin?"

"Glove box maybe."

She looked and found a strip with two tablets left. Rebus handed her a bottle of water, its seal broken. "If you don't mind a few germs," he said.

Her shake of the head told him she didn't. She swallowed the tablets and gave her neck a few rotations.

"I can hear the gristle from here," he commiserated.

"Never mind that — are you saying Andropov didn't kill Todorov?"

"Suppose he didn't — what would he be most afraid of?" He gave her a moment to answer, then plowed on. "He'd be afraid of *us* thinking he *had*."

"And we'd have his own words as evidence?"

"Bringing us to Charles Riordan."

Clarke's mind was moving now. "Aksanov got agitated about that when I questioned him — kept going on about how *he'd* been at Gleneagles all the time."

"Maybe afraid that we'd be putting him in the frame."

"You think Andropov . . . ?"

Rebus shrugged. "Rather depends on whether we can prove he left Gleneagles that night or early morning."

"Wouldn't he just have phoned Cafferty instead, got him to do something about it?"

"Possible," Rebus admitted, still tapping out a rhythm

on the steering wheel. They were silent for the best part of a minute, collecting their thoughts. "Remember the trouble we had getting the Caledonian Hotel to cough up details of their guests? Don't suppose Gleneagles will be any easier."

"But we've got a secret weapon," Clarke said. "Remember during the G8? DCI Macrae's pal was in charge of security at the hotel. Macrae even got a tour of the premises."

"Meaning he may have met the manager? Got to be worth a try." They fell back into silence.

"You know what this means?" Clarke finally asked.

Rebus nodded again. "We still don't know who killed Todorov."

"Whichever way you look at it, Andropov said he wanted him dead . . ."

"Doesn't mean he turned words into deeds. If I topped someone every time I cursed them, there'd be precious few students and cyclists left in Edinburgh — or anyone else for that matter."

"Would I still be here?" she asked.

"Probably," he allowed.

"Despite the three out of ten?"

"Don't push your luck, DS Clarke."

42

"Todd Goodyear not joining us?" Rebus asked.

"Has he grown on you?"

They were in Kay's Bar—a compromise. It did decent grub, but the beer was good, too. Slightly larger than the Oxford Bar, but managing to be cozy at the same time—the predominant color was red, extending to the pillars that separated the tables from the actual bar. Clarke had ordered chili, Rebus declaring that salted peanuts would be enough for him.

"You've managed to keep him below Derek Starr's radar?" Rebus asked, in place of an answer to her question.

"DI Starr thinks Todd is CID." She stole another of Rebus's peanuts.

"Do I get to dunk my fingers in your chili when it comes?"

"I'll buy you another packet."

He swallowed a mouthful of IPA. She was drinking a toxic-looking mix of lime juice and soda water.

"Anything planned for tomorrow?" he asked.

"The team's on duty all day."

"So no surprise party for the old guy?"

"You didn't want one."

"So you've just chipped in and bought me something nice?"

"Meant digging deep into the overdraft. . . . What time does your suspension end?"

"Around lunchtime, I suppose." Rebus thought back to the scene in Corbyn's office . . . Sir Michael Addison storming out. Sir Michael was Gill Morgan's stepfather. Gill knew Nancy Sievewright. Nancy and Gill and Eddie Gentry had been spied on, the recording watched by Roger Anderson, Stuart Janney, and Jim Bakewell. Everything in Edinburgh seemed connected. As a detective, Rebus had noticed time and again how true this was. Everything and everyone. Todorov and Andropov, Andropov and Cafferty, the overworld and the underworld. Sol Goodyear knew Nancy and her crew, too. Sol was Todd Goodyear's brother, and Todd led back to Siobhan and to Rebus himself. Shifting partners in one of those endurance dances. What was the film? Something about shooting horses. Dance and keep on dancing because nothing else matters.

Problem was, Rebus was about to bow out. Siobhan's chili had arrived, and he watched her unfold a paper napkin onto her lap. Day after tomorrow, he'd be seated at the edge of the dance floor. Give it a few weeks, and he'd be yet farther back, merging with the other spectators, no longer a participant. He'd seen it with other cops: they retired and promised to keep in touch, but each visit to the old gang merely underlined how far apart they'd grown. There would be an arrangement to share drinks and gossip one night a month. Then it'd be once every few months. Then not at all.

Clean break was the best thing, so he'd been told. Siobhan was asking if he wanted some of her food. "Grab a fork and tuck in."

"I'm fine," he assured her.

"You were in a world of your own there."

"It's the age I'm at."

"So you'll come to the station tomorrow lunchtime?"

"No parties, right?"

She shook her head in agreement. "And by end of play, we'll have closed all the cases."

"Of course we will." He gave a wry smile.

"I'll miss you, you know." She kept her eyes on the food as she scooped it up.

"For a little while maybe," he conceded, waving his empty glass at her. "Time for a refill."

"You're driving, remember."

"Thought you could give me a lift."

"In your car?"

"I'll get you a taxi home after."

"That's mighty generous."

"Didn't say I'd pay for it," Rebus told her, heading for the bar.

He did, though, pressing a ten-pound note into her hand and saying he'd see her tomorrow. She'd found a parking space for his Saab near the top of Arden Street. He'd been about to invite her in when a black cab rumbled into view, its roof light on. Siobhan Clarke had given the driver a wave, then handed Rebus his car keys.

"Bit of luck," she'd said, referring to the taxi. Rebus had held out the tenner, and she'd eventually taken it.

"Straight home, mind," he'd warned her. Watching the cab pull away, he wondered if he was going to take his own advice. It was almost 10:00, the temperature well above zero. He walked down the hill towards his door, staring up at the bay window of his living room. Darkness up there. No one waiting to welcome him. He thought about Cafferty, wondered what dreams the gangster would be having. Did you dream in a coma? Did you do anything else? Rebus knew he could visit him, sit with him. Maybe one of the nurses would bring a cup of tea. Maybe she'd be a good listener. Alexander Todorov's skull had been smashed from behind. Cafferty had been attacked from behind—but attacked cleanly while the poet had been roughed up first. Rebus kept trying to see the connection—Andropov was the obvious one. Andropov, with his friends in high places—Megan Macfarlane, Jim Bakewell. Cafferty hosting parties, wining and dining Bakewell and the bankers, all lads together . . . Andropov readying to bring his business to Scotland, where his new friends would cosset him, protect him. Business was business, after all: what did it matter if Andropov faced corruption charges back home? Rebus realized that he was still staring at his flat's unlit and unwelcoming windows.

"Nice night for a walk," he told himself, continuing downhill with hands in pockets. Marchmont itself was quiet, Melville Drive devoid of vehicles. Jawbone Walk, the path leading through the Meadows, boasted only a handful of pedestrians, students heading home from nights out. Rebus walked beneath the arches created from an actual whale's jawbone, and wondered—not for the first time—at its purpose. When his daughter was a kid, he would pretend they were being swallowed by the whale, like Jonah or Pinocchio. . . . There was some drunken singing in the distance from a couple of tramps on a bench, worldly goods stacked in bags by the side of them. The old infirmary compound was being transformed into new apartment blocks, changing the skyline. He kept walking, reaching Forrest Road. Instead of heading straight on in the direction of the Mound, he took a fork at Greyfriars Bobby and descended into the Grassmarket. Plenty of pubs still open, and people loitering outside the homeless hostels. When he'd first moved to Edinburgh, the Grassmarket had been a dump—much of the Old Town, in fact, had been in dire need of a face-lift. Hard now to remember just how bad it had all been. There were people who said that Edinburgh never changed, but this was patently untrue—it was changing all the time. Smokers were standing in clusters outside the Beehive and Last Drop pubs. The fish 'n' chip shop had a queue. A gust of fat-frying hit Rebus as he walked past, and he breathed deeply, savoring it. At one time, the Grassmarket had boasted a gallows, dozens upon dozens of Covenanters dying there. Maybe Todorov's ghost would bump into them. Another fork in the road was approaching. He took the right-hand option, into King's Stables Road. Passing the car park, he stopped for a moment. There was just the one vehicle on Level Zero, the ground floor. Driver would have to get a move on, the place was due to close in the next ten or so minutes. The car was parked in the bay next to where Todorov had been attacked. There was no sign of any hooded woman begging for sex. Rebus lit a cigarette and kept moving. He didn't know what his plan was. King's Stables Road would join Lothian Road in a minute, and he'd be facing the Caledonian Hotel. Was Sergei Andropov still there? Did Rebus really intend a further confrontation?

"Nice night for it," he repeated to himself.

But then he thought of those Grassmarket pubs. It would make more sense to retrace his steps, have a nightcap, and take a taxi home. He turned on his heels and started back. As he approached the car park again, he saw the last car leaving. It stopped curbside, and its driver got out, retreating to the exit. He unlocked some metal shutters, which started to creep downwards with an electric hum. The driver didn't wait to watch them drop. He was in the car and heading towards the Grassmarket.

The good-looking security guard, Gary Walsh. Parked on Level Zero. . . . Hadn't he told Rebus he always parked next to the security cabin on the next floor up? The shutters were closed now, but there was a little viewing window at chest height. Rebus crouched a little so he could peer inside. The lights were still on; maybe they stayed that way all night. Up in the corner, he could see the security camera. He remembered what Walsh's colleague had said: *camera used to point pretty much at that spot . . . but it gets moved around. . . .* Made sense to Rebus — if you worked in a multistory you'd want your car where the cameras could keep an eye on it. Sod anyone else, just so long as *your* car was safe . . .

Macrae's words: *less to this than meets the eye.* All those connections . . . Cath Mills, aka the Reaper, asking Rebus about one-night stands and flings with workmates . . . Alexander Todorov, on his way back from a day in Glasgow: a curry with Charles Riordan, one drink on Cafferty's tab, and semen on his underpants.

The woman in the hood.

Less to this than meets the eye . . .

Cherchez la femme . . .

The poet and his libido. There was a Leonard Cohen album called *Death of a Ladies' Man.* One of its tracks: "Don't Go Home with Your Hard-On." Another: "True Love Leaves No Traces."

Trace evidence: blood on the car park floor, oil on the dead man's clothes, semen stains . . .

Cherchez la femme.

The answer was so close, Rebus could almost taste it.

DAY NINE

Saturday 25 November 2006

43

Bright and early that morning, Rebus took his ticket from the machine and watched the barrier shudder upwards. He had entered by the car park's top level on Castle Terrace but followed the signs to the next level down. There were plenty of empty bays near the guardroom. Rebus walked over to the door and gave a knock before pushing it open.

"What's up?" Joe Wills asked, hands cupped around a mug of black tea. His eyes narrowed as he placed Rebus.

"Hello again, Mr. Wills — rough night, was it?" Wills hadn't shaved, his eyes were red-rimmed and bleary, and he hadn't got round to putting his tie on yet.

"Few drinks I was having," the man started to explain, "and the Reaper catches me on the mobile — Bill Prentice has gone and pulled a sickie and can I do his morning shift?"

"And despite everything, you were happy to oblige — that's what I call loyalty." Rebus saw the newspaper on the worktop. Polonium-210 was being blamed for Litvinenko's death; Rebus had never heard of it.

"What do you want anyway?" Joe Wills was asking. "Thought you lot had finished." Rebus noticed that Wills's mug was emblazoned with the name of a local radio station, Talk 107. "Don't suppose you've any milk on you?" the man asked. But Rebus's attention was on the CCTV screens.

"Do you drive to work, Mr. Wills?"

"Sometimes."

"I remember you saying you'd had a 'prang.' "

"Car still runs."

"Is it here just now?"

"No."

"Why's that, then?" But Rebus held up a finger. "You'd still not pass a Breathalyzer, am I right?" He watched Wills nod. "Very sensible of you, sir. But the times you *do* drive to work, I'm betting you keep the car where you can see it?"

"Sure." Wills took a sip of tea, squirming at its bitterness.

"Covered by one of the cameras, in other words?" Rebus nodded towards the bank of screens. "Always park in the same spot?"

"Depends."

"How about your colleague? Would I be right in thinking Mr. Walsh prefers the ground floor?"

"How do you know that?"

Again, Rebus ignored the question. "When I was here the first time," he said instead, "day after the murder, if you remember . . ."

"Yes?"

". . . the cameras downstairs weren't covering the spot where the attack took place." He gestured towards one of the screens. "You told me one camera used to, but it got moved around. But now I see it's been shifted again, so it's covering . . . here's another wild guess coming up — the bay where Mr. Walsh parks?"

"Is this going anywhere?"

Rebus managed a smile. "Just wondering this, Mr. Wills: when exactly did that camera get moved?" He was leaning over the figure of the guard. "Last shift you did before the murder, I'm betting it was pointing where it is now. Between times, someone tampered with it."

"I told you — it gets moved around."

Rebus wasn't six inches from Wills when he next spoke. "You know, don't you? You're not the sharpest tack in the carpet, but you worked it out before any of us. Have you told anyone, Mr. Wills? Or are you good at keeping secrets? Maybe you just want the quiet life, a few drinks at night and some milk to go with your tea. You're not about to grass up a mate, are you? But here's my advice, Mr. Wills, and it really would be in your interest to take it." Rebus paused, ensuring he had the man's undivided attention. "Don't say a fucking word to your workmate. Because if you do, and I get to hear about it, I'll have *you* in the cells rather than him, understood?"

Wills had stopped moving, the mug trembling slightly in his hands.

"Do we have an understanding?" Rebus persisted. The guard did no more than nod, but Rebus hadn't quite finished with him.

"An address," he said, placing his notebook on the worktop. "Write it down for me." He watched Joe Wills put down the mug and start to comply. Walsh's batch of CDs was in its usual place; Rebus doubted Wills would have much use for them. "And one last thing," he said, taking the notebook back. "When my Saab reaches the exit, I want you to override the barrier for me. Money you charge in this place is absolutely criminal."

*   *   *

Shandon was on the west side of the city, tucked in between the canal and Slateford Road. Not much more than a fifteen-minute drive, especially at the weekend. Rebus had switched on his CD player, only to find himself listening to Eddie Gentry. He ejected the disc and tossed it onto the back seat, replacing it with Tom Waits. But the patented gravel of Waits's voice was too obtrusive, so he settled for silence instead. Gary Walsh lived at number 28, a terraced house in a narrow street. There was a space next to Walsh's car, so Rebus parked the Saab and locked it. The upstairs window at number 2 was curtained. Stood to reason: when a man worked the late shift, he slept late, too. Rebus decided to leave the doorbell alone and knocked instead. When the door opened, a woman in full makeup stood there. Her hair was immaculate, and she was dressed for work, minus her shoes.

"Mrs. Walsh?" Rebus said.

"Yes."

"I'm Detective Inspector Rebus." As she studied his warrant card, he studied her. Late thirties or early forties, meaning maybe ten years older than her partner. Gary Walsh, it seemed, was a toyboy. But when Joe Wills had called Mrs. Walsh a "looker" he hadn't been kidding. She was well preserved and glowing with life. "Ripe" was the word Rebus found himself thinking. On the other hand, those looks wouldn't last much longer — nothing stayed ripe forever.

"Mind if I come in?" he asked.

"What's it about?"

"The murder, Mrs. Walsh." Her green eyes widened. "The one at your husband's place of work."

"Gary didn't say anything."

"The Russian poet? Found dead at the bottom of Raeburn Wynd?"

"It was in the papers . . ."

"The attack started in the car park." Her eyes were losing some of their focus. "It was last Wednesday night, just before your husband finished work . . ." He paused for a moment. "You really don't know, do you?"

"He didn't tell me." Some of the color had drained from her face. Rebus went into his notebook and pulled out a newspaper cutting. It showed a photo of the poet, taken from one of his book jackets.

"His name was Alexander Todorov, Mrs. Walsh." But she had dashed back into the house, not quite closing the door behind her. Rebus paused for a moment, then pushed it open again and followed her inside. The hallway was small, with half a dozen coats hanging on hooks next to the staircase. Two doors off: kitchen and living room. She was in the latter, seated on the edge of the settee as she tied a pair of high-heeled shoes around her ankles.

"I'm going to be late," she muttered.

"Where do you work?" Rebus was scanning the room. Big TV, big hi-fi, and shelves filled to the brim with CDs and tapes.

"Perfume counter," she was saying.

"I don't suppose five minutes will hurt . . ."

"Gary's sleeping—you can come back later. He's got to take the car to the garage, though, get the player fixed . . ." Her voice trailed off.

"What is it, Mrs. Walsh?"

She was rubbing her hands together as she got to her feet. Rebus doubted that her unsteadiness was due to the heels.

"Nice duffel coat, by the way," he told her. She looked at him as though he'd started using a foreign language. "In the hall," he explained. "The black one with the hood . . . looks right cozy." He smiled without humor. "Ready to tell me about it, Mrs. Walsh?"

"There's nothing to tell." She was looking around the room as if for an escape hatch. "We have to get the car fixed . . ."

"So you keep saying." Rebus narrowed his eyes and peered out of the window towards the Ford Escort. "What is it you've remembered, Mrs. Walsh? Maybe we should wake Gary, eh?"

"I have to get to work."

"There are some questions that need answering first." *Less than meets the eye:* those words kept bouncing around the inside of Rebus's skull. Todorov had led him to Cafferty and Andropov, and he'd latched onto both because *they* were the ones who interested him — because they were the ones he *wanted* to be guilty. Seeing conspiracies and cover-ups where none existed. Andropov had panicked because of that single outburst — didn't mean he'd killed the poet . . .

"How did you find out about Gary and Cath Mills?" Rebus asked quietly. Cath Mills . . . admitting to Rebus that night in the bar that she'd *almost* given up on one-night stands.

Walsh's wife gave a look of horror and slumped onto the sofa again, face in hands, smearing the perfect makeup. Started muttering the words "Oh God" over and over. Then, eventually: "He kept telling me it had just been that one time . . . just the once, and a mistake at that. A *huge* mistake."

"But you thought you knew better," Rebus added.

Yes, Gary Walsh would be tempted again, would stray again. He was young and chiseled and rock-star handsome, whereas his wife was getting older by the day, makeup doing only so much to cover the working of time. . . . "A pretty desperate measure," Rebus stated quietly. "Wearing that hood so he'd get the message. Hanging around the street, offering yourself to strangers . . ."

Smudgy tears were coursing down both cheeks, her shoulders heaving.

Alexander Todorov: wrong place, wrong time. A voluptuous woman offering no-strings sex, leading him into the car park where they'd be in full view of the camera. Gary Walsh's car their destination — not that Todorov was to know that. Screwing a man she'd only just met, so that her watching husband would know the price of further infidelity.

"Did you do it against the car?" he asked. "On the bonnet maybe?" He was still peering out at the Escort, thinking: fingerprints, blood, maybe even semen.

"Inside." Her voice wasn't much more than a whisper.

"Inside?"

"I had a set of keys."

"Is that where . . . ?" He didn't need to finish the sentence. She was nodding, meaning Walsh and the Reaper had enjoyed *their* tryst in the same place.

"Not my idea," she said, and Rebus had to strain to make out the words.

"The man you'd picked up," he realized. "He wanted to do it inside the car?"

She nodded again.

"Bit more comfortable, I suppose," he offered. But then

a thought hit him. The missing CD . . . Todorov's final performance, as recorded by Charles Riordan. . . . *Car to the garage . . . get the player fixed.* . . . "What's wrong with the CD player, Mrs. Walsh?" Rebus asked, keeping his voice level. "It's his CD, isn't it? He wanted to hear it while you were . . . ?"

She stared at him through a mess of mascara and eyeliner. "It's stuck in the machine. But I didn't know, I didn't know . . ."

"Didn't know he was dead?"

She shook her head wildly from side to side, and Rebus believed her. All she'd needed was a man, any man, and when it was over she'd pushed it from her mind. Hadn't asked his name or nationality, probably hadn't looked at his face. Maybe she'd taken a couple of strong drinks for courage.

And her husband hadn't wanted to talk about it afterwards . . . hadn't told her anything.

Rebus stood by the window, deep in thought. So many domestics down the years, partners abusing partners, lies and deceit, fury and festering resentment. *There's a fury here.* . . . Sudden or protracted violence, mind games, power struggles. Love turning sour or stale as the years passed . . .

And now here came sleepy-faced Gary Walsh, descending the staircase, calling out to his wife. "You still here?" Through the hall and into the living room, barefoot in faded denims and with his torso naked, rubbing one hand up and down his hairless chest as he wiped at his eyes with the other. Blinking as he realized there was a stranger in the room . . . looking to his wife for an explanation . . . her face creased in pain, tears dripping from her chin . . . then back to Rebus, placing him now, eyes turning towards the door in contemplation of flight.

"With no shoes on, Gary?" Rebus chided him.

"I could outrun you in diving boots, you fat bastard," Walsh sneered.

"And there's that sudden rage we've been looking forward to," Rebus said with just a hint of a smile. "Care to tell your wife what happened to Alexander Todorov when you got hold of him?"

"He fell asleep in the car," Mrs. Walsh was saying, playing the scene back in her mind, eyes stinging and red but fixed on her young husband. "I realized he was drunk, couldn't rouse him . . . so I left him." Gary had leaned his head against the door frame, arms behind him, hands pressed to the jamb.

"I don't know what she's talking about," he eventually drawled. "Really I don't."

Rebus had his mobile in his hand, punching in the necessary number. He kept his eyes on Walsh, Walsh staring back at him, still thinking about doing a runner. Rebus pressed the phone to his ear.

"Siobhan?" he said. "Bit of news to brighten your morning." He'd started giving the address when Gary Walsh spun round, hand snaking ahead of him, readying to unlock the front door. It was a few inches open, freedom shining in, when Rebus's weight smashed into him from behind, expelling all the air from Walsh's chest and the power from his legs. The door slammed shut again, and he slid onto his knees, coughing and spluttering and with blood dripping from his crumpled nose. His wife appeared not to have noticed, wrapped up in her own drama as she sat, head in hands, on the sofa's edge. Rebus picked his mobile up from the carpet, aware of the adrenaline pounding through him, his heart racing. One perk of the job he really was going to miss . . .

"Sorry about that," he told Clarke. "Just ran into someone . . ."

44

The Forensics team had come for the Ford Escort, their mechanic taking only a few minutes to extract the stuck CD. It played perfectly on the machine at Gayfield Square. There was nothing written on it but the single word "Riordan" — same as on the copy Riordan himself had made for Siobhan Clarke. More good news: looked like the toolbox in the boot would be helpful. Walsh had rinsed the blood from the claw hammer, but there were spots elsewhere. The rest of the car — in and out — would be dusted, tested, and checked by Ray Duff and his lab boys back at their Howdenhall HQ. It was, as even Derek Starr admitted, "a result." Starr hadn't been expecting much of anything from the day except overtime. Instead of which, he was bouncing on his toes, and had called the Chief Constable at home before anyone else had a chance — much to the annoyance of DCI Macrae (Starr's very next call).

Gary Walsh was in IR1 and Louisa Walsh in IR2, telling their separate stories. The husband's resistance crumbled only by degrees, as he was presented with one piece of evidence after another: the hammer, the blood, the moving of the camera afterwards to make it seem as though he could not have witnessed the attack. A search warrant was being issued. The detectives asked Walsh if they might conceivably find the items stolen from Alexander Todorov hidden somewhere in or around his home or place of work, but he'd shaken his head.

I didn't mean to murder him, just wanted him out of my car. . . . Sleeping like a baby after shagging my wife . . . stinking of booze and sweat and her perfume. . . . Smacked him around a bit, and he staggered off into the night. . . . I got in the car and started driving, then noticed he'd done something to the CD player, it wasn't working anymore. . . . The final fucking straw. . . . Saw him at the bottom of that alley and I just lost it . . . I lost it, that's all, and it's all her fault. . . . Thought if I took a few things away with me, it'd look like a mugging. . . . They're at the foot of Castle Rock, I chucked them over the wall . . .

"So," Siobhan Clarke said, "after everything we've gone through, it boils down to a domestic?" She sounded dazed and devastated, unwilling to believe. Rebus shrugged in sympathy. He was back inside Gayfield Square, DI Derek Starr himself having granted permission, saying he'd "deal with any and all repercussions."

"Big of you," Rebus had muttered.

"He has a fling," Clarke continued, for herself more than Rebus, "admits it to the wife, who acts out her revenge. Husband sees red, and the poor drunken sap she's cajoled into having sex with her ends up on a slab?" She started shaking her head slowly.

"A cold, cleansed death," Rebus commented.

"That's a line of Todorov's," Clarke told him. "And there was nothing 'cleansed' about it."

Rebus gave a slow shrug. "Andropov told me, '*Cherchez la femme*' — he was trying to muddy the water, but turns out he was right."

"The drink with Cafferty . . . Riordan recording

the recital . . . Andropov, Stahov, Macfarlane, and Bakewell . . . ?" She counted the names off on her fingers.

"Nothing to do with it," Rebus admitted. "In the end, it came down to a jammed CD and a man brought to the boil." They were standing in the corridor outside the interview rooms, keeping their voices low, aware of the presence behind the nearest doors of Walsh and his wife. Clarke was having a desolate little laugh to herself as one of the uniforms appeared around the corner. Rebus recognized Todd Goodyear.

"Back in the old woolly suit?" Rebus asked him.

Goodyear brushed his hands down the front of his uniform. "I'm pulling a weekend shift at West End — but when I heard, I had to make a detour. Is it true?"

"Seems to be." Clarke sighed.

"The car park attendant?" He watched her nod. "So all those hours I spent on the Riordan tapes . . . ?"

"Were part of the process," Rebus assured him, slapping a hand on the young man's shoulder. Goodyear stared at him.

"You're back from suspension," he realized.

"Not much escapes you, lad."

Goodyear held out a hand for Rebus to shake. "I'm glad they're looking elsewhere for whoever attacked Cafferty."

"Not sure I'm totally off the hook, but thanks anyway."

"Need to get the boot of your car fixed."

Rebus chuckled. "You're right about that, Todd. Soon as I get a minute . . ."

Goodyear had turned towards Clarke. Another handshake, and a thank-you for her help.

"You did okay, kid," she told him, affecting an American accent. The blood was creeping up his neck as he bowed his head a final time and headed back the way he'd come.

"God knows how much work he put into those Parliament tapes," Clarke said under her breath. "All of it redundant."

"Part of life's rich tapestry, Shiv."

"You really should get that car of yours fixed."

He made show of checking his watch. "Hardly matters, does it? Few hours from now I'll be binning the crime kit along with everything else."

"Well, before you do that . . ."

He looked at her. "Yes?"

"You've shown me yours, so I'm presuming you'll want to see mine."

He folded his arms, rocking on the balls of his feet. "Explain," he said.

"Last night, we said we wanted everything wrapped up by end of play today."

"Indeed we did."

"So let's go to the CID suite and see what that clever DCI Macrae has done."

Rebus, intrigued, was happy to follow. The empty room looked as if a bomb had hit it. The Todorov-Riordan team had left its mark.

"Not even anyone to crack a beer with," Rebus complained.

"Bit early," Clarke chided him. "Besides, I thought you didn't want a party."

"But to celebrate our success with the Todorov case . . ."

"Call that 'success'?"

"It's a result."

"And what do they add up to, all these results?"

He wagged a finger at her. "I'm leaving just in time — a few more weeks, and you'd be jaundiced beyond saving."

"Be nice to think we made a difference, though, wouldn't it?" she answered with another sigh.

"I thought that was what you were about to prove to me."

She gave a smile — eventually — and sat down at her computer. "I did it by the book — asked DCI Macrae to see if his pal would put in a word for us at Gleneagles. They promised they'd e-mail me the details first thing this morning."

"Details of what exactly?"

"Guests who left the hotel late at night or early morning, just before Riordan was killed. Ones who checked out, and ones who came back." She was making rapid clicks with her mouse. Rebus moved around the desk to stand behind her, so he could see what she was seeing.

"Who's your money on, Andropov or his driver?"

"Got to be one or the other." But then she opened the e-mail and her mouth fell open.

"Well, well" was all Rebus said.

It took them the rest of the morning and most of the afternoon to put everything together. They had the information from Gleneagles and had pushed their luck still further by asking for the guest's license plate. Armed with this, Graeme MacLeod at Central Monitoring — pulled from a golf game at Rebus's request — had gone back to the CCTV tapes from Joppa and Portobello, seeking a particular vehicle now, which made the task a whole lot easier. Meantime, Gary Walsh had been charged, his wife released. Rebus had studied both parties' statements while Clarke showed more interest in some rugby match on the radio — Scotland being tanked by Australia at Murrayfield.

It was 5:00 p.m. by the time they entered IR1, thanking the uniformed officer and telling him he could go. Rebus had stepped outside half an hour earlier for a cigarette, surprised to find it already dark — the day had sped past unnoticed. Just one more thing he'd miss about the job. . . . But there was still time for a bit of fun. As the door to IR1 started to close, Rebus whispered in Clarke's ear, asking for two minutes alone with the suspect, adding that he wasn't about to do anything daft. She hesitated, but then relented. Rebus made sure the door was closed, then walked over to the table and pulled out the metal-legged chair, making sure its feet scraped the floor with maximum discord.

"I've been trying to work out," he began, "what your connection with Sergei Andropov is, and I've decided it comes down to this — you want his money. Doesn't matter to you or your bank how he made it . . ."

"We're not in the business of dealing with crooks, Inspector," Stuart Janney stated. He was wearing a blue cashmere poloneck and pea green twilled trousers with brown leather slip-on shoes, yet this weekend attire was too studied and self-conscious to be truly casual.

"Feather in your cap, though," Rebus said, "bringing in a multimillionaire and all his chattels. Business has never been better at FAB, eh, Mr. Janney? Profits in the billions, but it's still a cutthroat world — dog eat dog, and all that. You always have to make sure your name's up there in lights . . ."

"I'm not exactly sure where all this is headed," Janney admitted, folding his arms impatiently.

"Sir Michael Addison probably thinks you're one of his golden boys. But not for much longer, Stuart—want to know why?"

Janney leaned back in his chair, seemingly unconcerned and not about to take the bait.

"I've seen the film," Rebus told him in a voice just above a whisper.

"What film?" Janney's eyes met Rebus's and stayed fixed on them.

"The film of *you* watching another film. Cafferty bugged his own screening room, if you can believe that. And there you are, getting your jollies watching amateur-hour porn." Rebus had lifted the DVD from his pocket.

"An indiscretion," Janney conceded.

"For most people, maybe, but not for you." Rebus gave the coldest of smiles, making sure the glint from the silver disc played across Janney's face, causing him to blink. "See, what you did, Stuart, goes *way* beyond 'indiscretion.'" Rebus pushed his elbows against the table, leaning farther across it. "That party? The scene in the bathroom? Know who the gobbler was, the drugged-up gobbler? Her name's Gill Morgan—ring any bells? You watched your chief's beloved stepdaughter snorting coke and doling out blow jobs. How's that going to play, next time you bump into Sir Mike at a corporate beanfeast?"

The blood was draining so rapidly from Janney's face, he might have had a tap attached to either foot. Rebus got up, tucking the disc back into his jacket, and walked to the door, opening it for Siobhan Clarke. She gave him a stare but saw she wasn't going to be enlightened. Instead, she replaced Rebus in the chair, placing a folder and some photographs on the table in front of her. Rebus watched as she took a moment to compose herself. She gave another look in his direction and offered a smile. He nodded his reply.

Your turn now, he was telling her.

"On the night of Monday, November the twentieth," Clarke began, "you were staying at Gleneagles Hotel in Perthshire. But you decided to leave early . . . why was that, Mr. Janney?"

"I wanted to get back to Edinburgh."

"And that's why you packed your things at three a.m. and asked for your bill to be made up?"

"There was a pile of work waiting for me in the office."

"But not so much," Rebus reminded him, "that you didn't have time to drop off Mr. Stahov's list of Russians to us."

"That's right," Janney said, still trying to take in some news Rebus had given him. Clarke could see that the banker had been shaken by whatever Rebus had said. Good, she thought, knocks him off balance . . .

"I think," she said, "you brought us that list precisely because you wanted to know what was happening about Charles Riordan."

"What?"

"Ever heard of the dog returning to its vomit?"

"It's Shakespeare, isn't it?"

"The Bible, actually," Rebus corrected him. "Book of Proverbs."

"Not quite the scene of the crime," Clarke continued, "but a chance for you to ask a few questions, see how things were going . . ."

"I'm still not sure what you're getting at."

Clarke gave a four-beat pause, then checked the contents of the folder. "You live in Barnton, Mr. Janney?"

"That's right."

"Handy for the Forth Road Bridge."

"I suppose so."

"And that's the way you came back from Gleneagles, is it?"

"I think so."

"Alternative would be Stirling and the M9," Clarke informed him.

"Or," Rebus added, "at a pinch you could do the Kincardine Bridge . . ."

"But whatever route you might happen to take," Clarke continued, "would bring you into town from the west or the north and leave you close to home." She paused again. "Which is why we're scratching our heads to comprehend what your silver Porsche Carrera might have been doing in Portobello High Street an hour and a half after you checked out of Gleneagles." She slid the CCTV image towards Janney. "You'll see that it's time-stamped and dated. Yours is pretty much the only car on the road, Mr. Janney. Care to tell us what you were up to?"

"There must be some mistake . . ." Janney was staring off to one side, concentrating on the floor rather than the evidence in front of his eyes.

"That's what you'll say in court, is it?" Rebus teased him. "That's what your ruinously expensive defense lawyer will stand up and tell judge and jury?"

"Maybe I just didn't feel like going home," Janney offered, causing Rebus to clap his hands together.

"That's more like it!" he said. "Car like that, you just

wanted to keep on driving down the coast. Maybe you wouldn't stop till the border—"

"But here's what we actually think happened, Mr. Janney," Clarke interrupted. "Sergei Andropov was fretting about a recording . . ." At the mention of "recording," Janney's eyes darted to Rebus, and Rebus offered a slow, exaggerated wink back. "Maybe he mentioned it to you," Clarke continued, "or it could have been his driver. The problem was, he'd made a remark about wanting Alexander Todorov dead—and now Todorov *was* dead. If the tape came to light, Mr. Andropov would be in the frame—might have to leave the country or end up being deported. Scotland's supposed to be his refuge, his safe haven. Only thing waiting for him in Moscow is a show trial. And if he leaves, all those potentially lucrative deals go with him. All his tens of millions go with him. That's why you decided to go have a word with Charles Riordan. The chat didn't work, and he ended up unconscious—"

"I didn't even *know* Charles Riordan!"

"Funny," Rebus said, mock-casually, "your bank's the main sponsor of an art installation he was doing at the Parliament. I reckon if we ask around, we'll find that you'd met him at some point . . ."

"I don't think you meant to kill him," Clarke added, trying to add some empathy to her voice. "You just wanted that recording destroyed. You knocked him out and looked for the tape, but it was hopeless . . . thousands upon thousands of tapes and CDs in that house of his. So then you set that little fire—not the kind that would consume a building and turn anyone inside into crispy strips. It was just the tapes you wanted—too many for you to cart them away, and not enough time to go through them all. So you stuck some paper into a bottle of cleaner, lit it, and walked away."

"This is nonsense," Janney said in a voice cracking with emotion.

"Problem was," Clarke went on, ignoring him, "all that acoustic baffling proved to be a fire hazard. . . . With Riordan dead, we were looking for a suspect in both killings—and Andropov still seemed to fit the bill. So all your hard work was in vain, Mr. Janney. Charles Riordan died—and died for nothing."

"I didn't do it."

"Is that the truth?"

Janney nodded, eyes everywhere but on either detective.

"Okay, then," Clarke told him. "You've nothing to worry about." She closed the folder and gathered together the photos. Janney could hardly believe it. Clarke was getting to her feet. "That pretty much takes care of it," she confirmed. "We'll just head along to processing, and then you'll be on your way."

Janney was standing, but with his hands pressing against the tabletop, helping him stay upright. "Processing?" he queried.

"Just a formality, sir," Rebus assured him. "We need to take your fingerprints."

Janney had made no attempt to move. "Whatever for?"

Clarke supplied the answer. "There was a print left on the bottle of solvent. It has to belong to whoever started the fire."

"But it can't be yours, Stuart, can it?" Rebus asked. "You were out enjoying a drive down our beautiful coastline in the crisp predawn air . . ."

"Fingerprint." The word slid out of Janney's mouth like a small, scuttling creature.

"I like to do a bit of motoring myself," Rebus was saying. "Today's my retirement—means I can do a lot more of it in the future. Maybe you'll show me the route you took. . . . Why are you sitting down again, Stuart?"

"Is there anything we can get you, Mr. Janney?" Clarke asked solicitously.

Stuart Janney looked at her and then at Rebus before deciding that the ceiling merited his full attention. When he spoke, his throat was so stretched that neither detective could quite make out the words.

"Mind repeating that?" Clarke asked politely.

"You can get me a lawyer," Janney duly obliged.

45

"Whenever anyone retires or resigns in the movies," Siobhan Clarke said, "they always seem to carry a box out of the building."

"That's true," Rebus agreed. He'd been through his desk and found precisely nothing of a personal nature. Turned out he didn't even have a mug of his own, just drank from whichever one was available at the time. In the end, he pocketed a couple of cheap ballpoint pens and a sachet of decongestant a full year past its sell-by.

"You had the flu last December," Clarke reminded him.

"Still dragged my sorry carcass into work, though."

"And sneezed and groaned for a full week," Phyllida Hawes added, hands on hips.

"Passing the germs to *me*," Colin Tibbet stated.

"Ah, the fun we've had," Rebus said with an affected sigh. There was no sign of DCI Macrae, though he'd left a note telling Rebus to leave his warrant card on the desk in his office. Derek Starr was absent, too. Gone 6:00, meaning he'd be in a club or wine bar, celebrating the day's results and trying the usual chat-up lines. Rebus looked around the CID suite. "You really didn't buy me anything, you miserable shower of bastards?"

"Have you seen the price of gold watches?" Clarke said with a smile. "On the other hand, the back room of the Ox has been reserved for the night, and there's a hundred quid's worth of a tab — what we don't get through tonight is yours for afterwards."

Rebus considered this. "So that's what it comes down to after all these years — you want me drinking myself to death?"

"And we've booked the Café St. Honoré for nine o'clock — staggering distance from the Ox."

"And staggering distance back again," Hawes added.

"Just the four of us?" Rebus asked.

"A few more faces might drop by — Macrae's promised to look in. Tam Banks and Ray Duff . . . Professor Gates and Dr. Curt . . . Todd and his girlfriend . . ."

"I hardly know them," Rebus complained.

Clarke folded her arms. "He needed a bit of persuading, so don't think I'm suddenly going to *un*invite them!"

"My party, but your rules, eh?"

"And Shug Davidson's coming, too," Hawes reminded Clarke.

Rebus rolled his eyes. "I'm still a bloody suspect for the assault on Cafferty!"

"Shug doesn't seem to think so," Clarke said.

"What about Calum Stone?"

"Didn't think he'd want to come."

"You know full well what I mean."

"Are we ready for the off?" Hawes asked. They all looked at Rebus, and he nodded. Really, he wanted five minutes on his own, to say a proper good-bye to the place. But he didn't suppose it mattered. Gayfield Square was just another cop shop. This old priest Rebus had known, dead several years back, had said that cops were like the priesthood, the world their confessional. Stuart

Janney had yet to confess. He would have a night in the cells to consider his options. Tomorrow or Monday, with a lawyer present and Siobhan Clarke seated opposite, he would lay out his version of the story. Rebus didn't suppose Siobhan saw herself as any kind of a priest. He watched her now as she slipped her arms into her coat and made sure everything she needed was in her shoulder bag. Their eyes met for a moment, and they shared a smile. Rebus walked into Macrae's office and placed his warrant card on the corner of the desk. He thought back to all the police stations he'd known: Great London Road, St. Leonard's, Craigmillar, Gayfield Square. Men and women he'd worked with, most retired, some of them long dead. Cases solved and left unresolved, days in court, hours spent waiting to give testimony. Paperwork and legal wrangling and cock-ups. Tear-stained evidence from victims and their families. Sneers and denials from the accused. Human folly exposed, all those biblical deadly sins laid bare, with a few more besides.

Monday morning, his alarm clock would be redundant. He could spend all day over breakfast, stick his suit back in the wardrobe, to be pulled out again only for funerals. He knew all the scare stories—people who left work one week and were in a wooden box by the next, loss of work equaling loss of purpose in the great scheme of things. He'd wondered often if the only thing for it was to clear out of the city altogether. His flat would buy him a fair-sized house elsewhere—the Fife coastline, or west to one of the distillery-strewn islands, or south into reiver country. But he couldn't see himself ever leaving Edinburgh. It was the oxygen in his bloodstream, but still with mysteries to be explored. He'd lived there for as long as he'd been a cop, the two—job and city—becoming intertwined. Each new crime had added to his under-standing, without that understanding ever coming near to completion. Bloodstained past mingling with blood-stained present; Covenanters and commerce; a city of banking and brothels, virtue and vitriol . . .

Underworld meeting overworld . . .

"Penny for them." It was Siobhan, standing in the doorway.

"You'd be wasting your money," he told her.

"Somehow I very much doubt that. Are you ready?" Hoisting her bag onto her shoulder.

"As I'll ever be."

He decided this much was true.

There were just the four of them at the Oxford Bar to start with. The back room had indeed been set aside for their use — with the help of strips of crime-scene tape.

"Nice touch," Rebus admitted, hoisting his first pint of the evening. After the best part of an hour, they headed to the restaurant. A bag of gifts was waiting there. From Siobhan, an iPod. Rebus protested that he would never master the technology.

"I've already loaded it," she told him. "The Stones, the Who, Wishbone Ash . . . you name it."

"John Martyn? Jackie Leven?"

"Even a bit of Hawkwind."

"My exit music," Rebus commented with a look close to contentment.

From Hawes and Tibbet, a bottle of twenty-five-year-old malt and a book of historical walks through Edin-burgh. Rebus kissed the bottle and patted the book, then insisted on wearing headphones for the first part of the meal.

"Listening to Jack Bruce beats you lot any day," he explained.

Just the two bottles of wine with dinner, then back to the Ox, where Gates, Curt, and Macrae had arrived, the bar providing a couple of bottles of champagne. Todd Goodyear and his girlfriend Sonia were the last to arrive. It was almost 11:00, and Rebus was on his fourth pint. Colin Tibbet was outside, taking gulps of fresh air while Phyllida Hawes rubbed his back encouragingly.

"Looks in a bad way," Goodyear commented.

"Seven double brandies will do that to a man."

There was no music, but then it wasn't needed. The various conversations were unforced and full of laughter. Anecdotes were recounted, with the two pathologists telling the best of them. Macrae shook Rebus's hand warmly and told him he had to get home.

"Remember to drop by and see us" were his parting words.

Derek Starr was standing in a corner, discussing work with a bored-looking Shug Davidson. The fact he'd come at all meant his wine bar chat-ups had failed yet again. Each time Davidson glanced over, Rebus offered him a winced commiseration. When a tray appeared with the next round of drinks, Rebus found himself next to Sonia.

"Todd tells me you work scene-of-crimes," he said.

"That's right."

"Sorry I don't recognize the face."

"I've usually got a hood over my head," she said with a shy smile. She was short, maybe five feet, with cropped blond hair and green eyes. The dress she was wearing looked Japanese and suited her slight, thin-boned figure.

"How long have you and Todd been an item?"

"A year and a bit."

Rebus looked over to where Goodyear was handing out drinks. "Must be doing something right," he commented.

"He's quite brilliant, you know. CID's got to be the next step."

"Might be a vacancy," Rebus conceded. "So how do you like scene-of-crimes?"

"It's all right."

"I heard you were at Raeburn Wynd the night Todorov was killed."

She nodded. "And at the canal, too. I was on call-out."

"Mucked up your plans with Todd," Rebus sympathized.

"How do you mean?" Her eyes had narrowed.

"Nothing," Rebus said, wondering if maybe he'd started slurring his words.

"It was me who found the overshoe," she added. Then her eyes widened, and she put her free hand to her mouth.

"Don't worry about it," Rebus assured her. "I'm no longer in the frame, apparently."

She relaxed and gave a little laugh. "But it says a lot about Todd's skills, don't you think?"

"Absolutely," Rebus agreed.

"Anything floating in that part of the canal, chances are it would end up getting stuck under the bridge — that's what he said."

"And he was right," Rebus admitted.

"Which is why CID would be mad not to take him."

"Our sanity's often been questioned," Rebus warned her.

"But you got a result on Todorov," she stated.

"Yes, we did," Rebus agreed with a tired smile. Good-year was chatting to Siobhan Clarke now. Whatever he said made her laugh. Rebus decided it was time for a cigarette break and reached out to take Sonia's hand, planting a kiss on the back of it.

"The perfect gentleman," she was saying as he moved towards the door.

"If only you knew, kid . . ."

Hawes and Tibbet were at the far end of the street, Tibbet with his back to the wall, Hawes in front of him, stroking the hair back from his forehead. A couple of other smokers were watching the show.

"A while since that happened to me," one said.

"Which?" his neighbor asked. "Feeling like spewing or having a woman run her fingers through your hair?"

Rebus joined in the laughter and then busied himself with the cigarette. At the other end of the street, the lights were on in the First Minister's residence. A Labour enclave since devolution, it was now under threat from the Nationalists. In fact, Rebus couldn't think of a time when Scotland hadn't returned a Labour majority. He had voted only three times in his life, each for a different party. By the time of the devolution referendum, he'd lost all interest. He'd met plenty of politicians since — Megan Macfarlane and Jim Bakewell were merely the latest examples — but reckoned half the regulars in the Ox would make better legislators. The likes of Bakewell and Macfarlane were a constant, and though Stuart Janney would go to prison, Rebus doubted it would have any real effect on First Albannach. They would continue to work with people like Sergei Andropov and Morris Gerald Cafferty, continue to rake in the bad money with the good.

Jobs and prosperity: the majority didn't care how they came into being or were sustained. Edinburgh had been built on the invisible industries of banking and insurance. Who cared if a few bribes oiled the wheels? What did it matter if some men got together to watch secretly filmed videos? Andropov had said something about poets seeing themselves as unacknowledged legislators, but surely that title belonged to the men in the pin-striped suits?

"Reckon she's trying to kiss it better?" one of the smokers asked.

Hawes and Tibbet were now in an embrace of sorts, faces pressed together. Good luck to them, Rebus thought to himself. Police work had wedged itself into his own marriage, cracking it wide open, but that didn't have to be the case — he knew plenty of cops who were still married, some of them even wedded to other cops. They seemed to make it work.

"She's doing a good job of it," the other smoker was answering his neighbor. The door was pulled open behind them, and Siobhan Clarke appeared.

"There you are," she said.

"Here I am," Rebus agreed.

"We were worried you'd sloped off."

"I'll just be a minute," he said, showing her the remaining inch of cigarette.

She had wrapped her arms around herself, protection against the cold. "Don't worry," she said, "we're not having speeches or anything."

"You've judged it just right, Shiv," he assured her. "Thanks."

She accepted the praise with a twitch of her mouth. "How's Colin doing?"

"I think Phyl's resuscitating him." Rebus nodded in

the direction of the two figures, who had now more or less merged into one.

"I hope they don't regret it in the morning," she muttered.

"What's life without a few regrets?" one of the smokers challenged her.

"They'll put that on my headstone," his companion stated.

Rebus and Clarke locked eyes again for a few silent moments. "Come back into the warm," she told him. He gave her a slow nod, stubbed out the remains of his cigarette, and did as he was told.

It was gone midnight when his taxi pulled up outside the Western General Hospital. He got as far as the corridor to Cafferty's ward before one of the nurses stopped him.

"You've been drinking," she scolded him.

"Since when did nurses start making diagnoses?"

"I'll have to call security."

"What for?"

"You can't go visiting a patient in the middle of the night. Not in that state."

"Why not?"

"Because people are sleeping."

"I'm not going to start playing the drums," he protested.

She pointed to the ceiling. Rebus looked, too, and saw that a camera was trained on them. "You're being monitored," she warned him. "A guard will be here any moment."

"Christ's sake . . ."

The doors behind her—the doors to Cafferty's ward—swung open. A man was standing there.

"I'll handle this," he said.

"Who are you?" she asked, turning to him. "Who gave you permission to . . . ?" But his warrant card silenced her.

"DI Stone," he explained. "This man's known to me. I'll see he doesn't cause further disturbance." Stone nodded towards a row of chairs, meant for visitors. Rebus decided he could do with a sit-down, so didn't argue. When he was seated, Stone nodded, letting the nurse know everything was under control. As she headed off, he sat beside Rebus, leaving one of the chairs empty between them. He started to tuck his ID back into his pocket.

"I used to have one of those," Rebus told him.

"What's in the bag?" Stone asked.

"My retirement."

"That explains a lot."

Rebus tried focusing on him. "Such as?"

"The amount you've put away, for one thing."

"Six pints, three shorts, and half a bottle of wine."

"And the man's still standing." Stone shook his head in disbelief. "So what brings you here? Bit of unfinished business still niggling you?"

Rebus had started opening his cigarettes, until he remembered where he was. "How do you mean?" he asked.

"Planning to unhook a few of Cafferty's plugs and tubes?"

"It wasn't me at the canal."

"A blood-spattered overshoe says otherwise."

"Didn't know inanimate objects could talk." Rebus was thinking back to his chat with Sonia.

"They've got a language all of their own, Rebus," Stone clarified, "and Forensics to do the translating."

Yes, Rebus thought, his mind clearing a little, and SOCOs to pick them up in the first place . . . SOCOs like little Sonia. "Can I assume," he said, "that you've been visiting the patient yourself?"

"Trying to change the subject?"

"Just wondering."

Stone nodded eventually. "The whole surveillance is in cold storage till he wakes up. Means I'm headed back home in the morning. DI Davidson will keep me informed of developments."

"I wouldn't try asking him any difficult questions tomorrow," Rebus gave warning. "He was last seen dancing his way down Young Street."

"I'll bear that in mind." Stone was rising to his feet. "Now come on, I'll give you a lift."

"My flat's the other end of town," Rebus stated. "I'll phone for a taxi."

"Then I'll wait with you till it comes."

"Not that you don't trust me, DI Stone."

Stone didn't bother answering. Rebus had taken a couple of steps towards the ward, but only to peer through one of the porthole-style windows. He couldn't figure out which bed was Cafferty's. Some of them had screens around them anyway.

"What if *you've* pulled the plug on him?" Rebus asked. "You've got yourself the perfect fall guy."

But Stone shook his head, and, like the nurse before him, gestured towards the security camera. "CCTV would prove you never crossed the threshold. Haven't you heard that old saying, 'The camera never lies'?"

"I've heard it," Rebus stated, "but I know better than to believe it." Having said which, he picked up his bag and preceded Stone back along the corridor towards the exit.

"You've known Cafferty a long time," Stone said.

"Nigh on twenty years."

"You first gave evidence against him in Glasgow High Court."

"That's right. Bloody lawyer got me mixed up with the previous witness, called me Mr. Stroman. After that, Cafferty's nickname for me was Strawman."

"Like in *The Wizard of Oz*?"

"Have I managed to tell you something that wasn't in your files?"

"You have, as a matter of fact."

"Nice to know I still have the odd trick up my sleeve."

"I get the feeling you're not going to let him go."

"Cafferty?" Rebus watched as Stone nodded.

"Or maybe you've readied DS Clarke to enter the fray on your behalf." Stone waited for a response, but Rebus didn't seem to have one. "Now you're leaving the force, you reckon there's a gap that'll never be filled?"

"I'm not quite that conceited."

"Maybe the same's true of Cafferty — when he pegs it, the vacancy won't stay open for long. Plenty small-timers out there, young and lean and hungry . . ."

"Not my problem," Rebus said.

"Then the only thing spoiling your party is Cafferty himself."

They had reached the main doors of the hospital. Rebus had his phone in his hand, readying to call for a cab.

"You really going to wait with me?" he asked.

"Nothing better to do," Stone answered. "But that

offer of a lift still stands. This time of night, taxis are bound to be thin on the ground."

It took Rebus half a minute to decide. Having nodded his agreement, he reached into the bag, pulling out the bottle of Speyside . . .

Monday 27 November 2006

EPILOGUE

There was a row of taxicabs parked outside Haymarket railway station, but Rebus managed to squeeze his Saab into a space next to them. He sounded the horn and rolled down the window. There were two uniformed officers standing by the station's exit doors. Monday morning, the day crisp and bright. The constables wore padded black jackets over their stab vests. They paid Rebus no heed whatsoever as he sounded the horn again. But then a parking warden homed in, having noted the double yellow line alongside the Saab. This drew the officers' attention. One of them said something to his companion and wandered over.

"I'll deal with this," he told the warden before crouching down so that his head was level with the window.

"I don't suppose I can call you DI Rebus anymore?" Todd Goodyear said.

"Not anymore," Rebus agreed.

"Sonia and me both enjoyed the party, if not the hangovers."

"Didn't actually notice you drinking, Todd. I mean, you had a drink in your hand, but it never quite made it as far as your lips."

"You don't miss much," Goodyear conceded with a smile.

"Actually, son, I miss all sorts of things."

"CID for one?" Goodyear guessed.

"Not quite what I was thinking of." Rebus peered over Goodyear's shoulder towards the young man's colleague. "Any chance I could borrow you for half an hour?"

Goodyear looked puzzled. "What for?"

"Something I want to talk to you about."

"I'm on duty."

"I know." But Rebus didn't look as if he'd take no for an answer. Goodyear straightened up, went and spoke to the other officer, then returned to the car, removing his cap before climbing into the passenger seat.

"Do *you* miss it?" Rebus asked.

"You mean CID? It was . . . interesting."

"I enjoyed my little chat with Sonia at the Ox."

"She's great."

"I can see that." Rebus paused as he maneuvered the car out of its space and into the traffic.

"Where are we headed?"

"Have you heard about Andropov?" Rebus asked, ignoring the question. "He's being sent home as an 'undesirable.' I got that from Siobhan yesterday — she was in work, giving Stuart Janney the chance to confess. The girl never switches off . . . tells me Stahov turns out to be one of the good guys. He'd been keeping a close eye on Andropov, didn't want him 'infecting' Scotland like he'd done Russia. Stahov was liaising with Stone . . ." Rebus paused. "But then you never knew DI Stone, did you?" He watched Goodyear shake his head. "He was the one who was watching Cafferty."

"Okay." Goodyear still seemed puzzled.

"Andropov," Rebus went on, "will face corruption charges in Moscow. He was planning on claiming political asylum, if you can credit that. Using all his useful contacts as referees. Might be true, of course — maybe his life *is* in danger back in Russia." Rebus sniffed loudly. "Not our problem, though."

"Where are we headed?" Goodyear asked again. Again, Rebus ignored him.

"Know what I did yesterday, while Siobhan was grafting? Went to Oxgangs and watched them demolish a couple of tower blocks. I could remember making a few arrests there down the years, but not the exact details. Guess that really does mean my time's past, Todd. There's a story in the paper this morning that more English voters than Scots think we should go independent." Rebus turned his head towards his passenger. "Makes you think, eh?"

"Makes me think you've yet to sober up from Saturday."

"Sorry, Todd, I'm rattling on, aren't I? Been doing a lot of mulling stuff over. Brought me back to a couple of things I should have spotted a lot sooner."

"What sorts of things?"

"I'm right in thinking you're a Christian, Todd?"

"You know I am."

"But then there are different types of Christian . . . and I'd say you tend towards the Old Testament variety — eye for an eye and all that."

"I've no idea what you mean."

"Can't say I blame you, of course — give me the Old Testament any time . . . good and evil, clear as day and night."

"I think you should drop me back at Haymarket."

But Rebus had no intention of doing that. "Saturday morning," he said, "in the corridor outside the interview rooms — do you remember? You were back in uniform and ready to say your good-byes."

"I remember."

"You told me I needed to get the Saab's boot fixed." Rebus looked at his passenger. "Haven't got round to it yet, by the way."

"Despite having time on your hands."

Rebus started to laugh, but then ceased abruptly. "Thing I was wondering is . . . how did you know?"

"Know what?"

"About that dodgy boot of mine — I've asked Siobhan and she doesn't recall saying anything to you about it. And I'm pretty sure it never cropped up when you and me had our various chats."

"That night at the Todorov murder scene," Goodyear explained.

Rebus nodded slowly. "The very conclusion I came to. You were already there at Raeburn Wynd when Shiv and me arrived. Meant you saw us getting the crime kit out of the car, saw me failing to shut the boot properly."

"So what?"

"Well, that's what I'm not sure of. But here's what I *am* sure of. Your granddad was put away with my help, and when he died it pulled your family apart. That sort of thing leaves a pain that can last for years, Todd. Your brother, Sol, went off the rails with the help of Big Ger Cafferty. You knew the rumors about me and Cafferty . . . Siobhan confirms that you were asking her about us. She feels bad about that actually . . ."

"Why?"

"She thinks maybe it was all because she told you I hated Cafferty's guts. To your way of thinking, that put me in the frame as Cafferty's assailant." He paused.

"Oh, and she also feels a bit guilty for bringing you into the team in the first place — feels she was suckered into it — because you managed to hide your ulterior motive."

"Where are we going?" Goodyear had a hand on his radio. It was attached to his shoulder by a clip and kept crackling with static noise.

"See, I've talked it through with her," Rebus was saying. "She says it makes sense."

"What does?"

"That night of the party, I got talking to Sonia . . ."

"So you've said."

"The night Cafferty was attacked, you said you were heading off to meet her." Rebus paused again. "She didn't seem to remember that. Besides which, she said it was *your* idea to look beneath the footbridge."

"What?"

"She found that overshoe because you told her where to look for it."

"Now hang on . . ."

"But here's the thing: you weren't even there at the scene, Todd. Way I see it, she maybe called to say she was headed to a job at the canal. That's when you told her to check the bridge — you knew there was a bridge and you knew what she'd find underneath it."

"Stop the car."

"Going to report me for abduction, Todd?" Rebus gave another cold smile. "DI John Rebus and Big Ger Cafferty — your family's biggest enemies, as far as you were concerned . . . and suddenly you saw a way to get revenge on one of them while implicating the other. You reckoned there was a chance my prints would be on the overshoe. Could have taken it from the boot any time you liked. There were three of us outside the Ox that night, Todd — you, me, and Siobhan. We all knew where I was headed . . . no one else did. You hoofed it after me, waited till Cafferty was alone, and crept up behind him. Siobhan tells me you were shocked to learn there'd been a surveillance on Cafferty. If I hadn't tricked Stone away from the scene, he'd have had you bang to rights."

"Rubbish," Todd Goodyear spat.

"Doesn't really matter one way or the other, since I can't prove a single bloody word." He turned towards the young man again. "Congratulations — you're getting away with it, Todd. Must mean the Big Man's looking out for you."

"I look out for myself, Rebus — me and my family both." The tone of voice had changed, hardening along with the look in Goodyear's eyes. "I'd been thinking about Cafferty for a long time. Then, when Sol got stabbed, it really started to rankle — thinking of how different things could've been for my folks. I knew you were close to Cafferty, so I had to get close to *you*." He was staring at the road ahead. "Then you told me you'd been the one in the witness box, the one who'd worked so hard to put my granddad away, and suddenly it all seemed to connect. I could take out you and Cafferty both."

"Like I say, an eye for an eye." Traffic ahead was thickening. Rebus eased his foot off the accelerator. "So you must be feeling pretty good now — cleansed, vindicated, avenged, all that sort of stuff . . ."

" 'I am pure from my sin.' "

"Another of your Bible quotes?" Rebus nodded to himself slowly. "That's all well and good, but it's not enough to save you — not by a long chalk."

"Red light," Goodyear stated. Meaning that they had

to stop at the junction ahead. With the car stationary, Goodyear pushed open his door.

"I was planning on visiting Cafferty," Rebus told him. "Thought maybe you'd want to see him again. Doctors say he's improving."

Goodyear was out of the car, but when Rebus yelled his name, he leaned down into it again.

"When Cafferty comes round," Rebus told him, "the first face he's going to see is mine . . . and guess what I'll be telling him? Better watch your back, Goodyear—and your front, if it comes to that. Cafferty may be a lot of things, but he's not the sort of coward who'll whack you from behind."

Goodyear slammed the door shut just as the lights turned green. Rebus pushed his foot down on the accelerator, watching in his rearview as Goodyear fixed his cap back on to his head. He was staring at the car as the distance between them grew. Rebus exhaled noisily and wound the window down a little. He'd got the garage to connect his new iPod to the stereo. He pressed Play and turned up the volume.

Rory Gallagher: "Sinner Boy," all the way to Cafferty's hospital bed.

Siobhan Clarke was waiting for him there. "Did you talk to him?" she asked. He nodded, eyes on Cafferty's seemingly lifeless form, the regular bleeping and blinking from the machines providing slivers of reassurance. The gangster had been moved from intensive care, but bringing all the peripheral equipment with him.

"I hear your team drew," Rebus commented to Clarke.

"Two up till the seventieth sodding minute . . . not that I was taking much of it in."

"Well, you were a bit busy with Stuart Janney—no confession yet?"

"It'll come." She paused. "How about Goodyear? Is he going to own up?"

"Todd knows better than that."

"I still can't believe I—"

"Hell with it, Shiv, how were you supposed to know?" Rebus seated himself on the chair next to hers. "If it's anybody's fault, it's mine."

She stared at him. "Want any more weight on those shoulders?"

"I'm serious—things went wrong for Todd and his family from the minute the granddad was sent down, and I helped that happen."

"That doesn't—" But she broke off as he turned towards her.

"They found class A in that pub, Shiv, but Todd's granddad wasn't shifting anything half that serious."

"What are you saying?"

Rebus gazed at the wall opposite. "Back then, Cafferty had cops on his payroll, guys in CID who'd plant whatever he told them to."

"You . . . ?"

Rebus shook his head. "Thanks for the vote of confidence, though."

"But you knew it had happened?"

He nodded slowly. "And did nothing about it—that's the way things were back then. Cafferty would've been dealing and not liking it that he was being undercut in Harry Goodyear's pub." He puffed out his cheeks and let the air burst from them before continuing. "Awhile back, you asked me about my first day in CID. I lied and said I couldn't remember. What really happened was I walked out of police college and into the station canteen — and the first thing I was told was: forget everything you've just had drilled into you. 'This is where the game begins, son, and there's only two teams — us and them.'" He risked another glance towards her. "You covered for mates who'd had too many whiskies with lunch . . . or gone a bit too far on an arrest . . . prisoners falling downstairs or stumbling into walls . . . you covered for *every*body on your team. I stood in that witness box knowing damned well I was covering for a colleague who'd set the old guy up."

She was still staring at him. "So why tell me? What the hell am I supposed to do with this?"

"You'll think of something."

"That's so bloody typical of you, John! It's ancient history, but you couldn't just keep it to yourself — you had to dump it on me."

"Hoping for absolution."

"You're in the wrong place for that!" She fell silent for a moment, shoulders slumped. Then, after a deep breath: "Nurse tells me you came straight here after the party, reeking of booze."

"So?"

"There was another detective . . ."

"Stone," Rebus acknowledged. "He wanted to make sure I wasn't going to pull the plug on the patient."

"There's not a shred of subtlety in your whole damned body, is there?"

"Are you saying I'm like a bull in a china shop?"

"What do you think?"

He considered the question for all of five seconds. "Maybe the bull's just running from the abattoir," he told her, readying to get to his feet. Clarke got up, too, looking bemused and watching as he leaned over the bed, willing Cafferty to wake up.

"You're really going to tell him what Goodyear did?" she asked.

"What's the alternative?"

"The alternative is, you leave it to me." They'd started heading for the exit. "Little turd's not going to get away with this. Things have changed, John — no cover-ups, no turning a blind eye . . ."

"That reminds me," he said. "I paid a visit to the Andersons yesterday."

She stared at him. "Having fully apprised them of your noncombat status?"

"Their daughter was home from college. She really does look a lot like Nancy."

"What are you saying?"

"I took Roger Anderson outside and told him I reckoned he'd recognized Nancy that night. Recognized her from the DVD, I mean. He liked the feeling of power it gave him, knowing something she didn't. That's why he kept pestering her. He didn't like it when I added that maybe it also had something to do with her resemblance to his daughter." He allowed himself a smile at the memory. "That's when I told him who the girl in the bathroom was . . ."

His eyes met Clarke's, and he broke off abruptly, knowing what she was about to say. She said it anyway:

"What DVD?"

He made show of clearing his throat. "Forgot I hadn't told you." He was holding the door open for her, but she was standing her ground.

"Tell me now," she demanded.

"It would just be more baggage, Shiv. Trust me, you're better off without it."

"Tell me anyway."

Rebus had just started to open his mouth when a high-pitched alarm sounded from inside the ward. No expert in medical equipment, he reckoned he still knew a flatline when he heard one—and coming from the equipment next to Cafferty's bed. He stormed back in, hauling himself up onto the bed, straddling the prone figure. Started pumping both hands down on Cafferty's chest.

"Kiss of life," he yelled at Clarke, "every third beat!"

"Staff are coming," she told him. "We should leave it to them."

"Damned if this bastard's going to give up the ghost on me now." Flecks of Rebus's saliva hit Cafferty's forehead. He pumped his hands again, one palm on top of the other. Counted it out. One, two, three. One, two, three. One, two, three. Knew people who'd recovered from CPR but with a rib or two broken from the effort.

Push hard, he told himself.

"Don't you bloody well dare!" he hissed from between gritted teeth.

Saw the first nurse on the scene draw back, thinking the words were meant for her.

Blood rushing through Rebus's ears, almost deafening him. No cold, cleansed death for you, he was thinking.

One, two, three. One, two, three.

After all we've been through . . . can't end with a couple of whacks from Todd Goodyear . . .

One, two, three. One, two, three.

There should be mess . . . and fuss . . . and blood.

One, two, three.

"John?"

One, two, three.

"John?" Siobhan's voice seemed to be coming to him from some far-distant place. "That's enough now. You can let go now."

The machines were making noises. Sweat in his eyes and the hissing in his ears — couldn't tell if they were good news or not. In the end, it took two doctors, an attendant, and a nurse to drag him off the bed.

"Is he going to be all right?" he heard himself ask. "Tell me he's going to be all right . . ."

In January 2010, Reagan Arthur Books / Little, Brown and Company will publish Ian Rankin's new novel, **Doors Open**. *Following is an excerpt from the novel's opening pages.*

Mike saw it happen. There were two doors next to one another. One of them seemed to be permanently ajar by about an inch, except when someone pushed at its neighbor. As each liveried waiter brought trays of canapés into the saleroom, the effect was the same. One door would swing open, and the other would slowly close. It said a lot about the quality of the paintings, Mike thought, that he was paying more attention to a pair of doors. But he knew he was wrong: it was saying nothing about the actual artworks on display, and *everything* about him.

Mike Mackenzie was thirty-seven years old, rich and bored. According to the business pages of various newspapers, he remained a "self-made software mogul," except that he was no longer a mogul of anything. His company had been sold outright to a venture capital consortium. Rumor had it that he was a burn-out, and maybe he was. He'd started the software business fresh from university with a friend called Gerry Pearson. Gerry had been the real brains of the operation, a genius programmer, but shy with it, so that Mike quickly became the public face of the company. After the sale, they'd split the proceeds fifty-fifty and Gerry then surprised Mike by announcing that he was off to start a new life in Sydney. His emails from Australia extolled the virtues of nightclubs, city life and surfing (and not, for once, the computer kind). He would also send Mike JPEGs and mobile-phone snaps of the ladies he encountered along the way. The quiet, reserved Gerry of old had disappeared, replaced by a rambunctious playboy—which didn't stop Mike from feeling like a bit of a fraud. He knew that without Gerry, he'd have failed to make the grade in his chosen field.

Building the business had been exciting and nerve-racking—existing on three or four hours' sleep a night, often in hotel rooms far away from home, while Gerry preferred to pore over circuit boards and programming issues back in Edinburgh. Ironing the glitches out of their best-known software application had given both of them a buzz that had lasted for weeks. But as for the money . . . well, the money had come flooding in, bringing with it lawyers and accountants, advisers and planners, assistants, diary secretaries, media interest, social invites from bankers and portfolio managers . . . and not much else. Mike had grown tired of supercars (the Lambo had lasted barely a fortnight; the Ferrari not much longer—he drove a second-hand Maserati these days, bought on impulse from the small ads). Tired, too, of jet travel, five-star suites, gadgets and gizmos. His penthouse apartment had featured in a style magazine, much being made of its view—the city skyline, all chimneypots and church spires until you reached the volcanic plug on top of which sat Edinburgh Castle. But occasional visitors could tell that Mike hadn't made much of an effort to adjust his life to fit his new surroundings: the sofa was the same one he'd brought from his previous home; ditto the dining table and chairs. Old magazines and newspapers sat in piles either side of the fireplace, and there was little evidence that the vast flat-screen television with its surround-sound speakers ever got much use. Instead, guests would fix their attention on the paintings.

Art, one of Mike's advisers had advised, was a canny investment. He'd then gone on to suggest the name of a broker who would ensure that Mike bought wisely; "wisely and well" had been his exact words. But Mike learned that this would mean buying paintings he didn't necessarily like by feted artists whose coffers he didn't really feel like filling. It would also mean being prepared to part with paintings he might admire, solely to comply with the fluctuations of the market. Instead of which, he had gone his own way, attending his first sale and finding a seat right at the front—surprised that a few chairs were still vacant while people seemed content to stand in a crush at the back of the room. Of course, he had soon learned the reason—those at the back had a clear view of all the bidders, and could revise their own bids accordingly. As his friend Allan confided afterwards, Mike had paid about three grand too much for a Bossun still life because a dealer had spotted him as a tyro and had toyed with him, edging the price upwards in the knowledge that the arm at the front of the room would be hoisted again.

"But why the hell would he do that?" Mike had asked, appalled.

"He's probably got a few Bossuns tucked away in storage," Allan had explained. "If prices for the artist look like they're on the way up, he'll get more interest when he dusts them off."

"But if I'd pulled out, he'd've been stuck with the one I bought."

To which Allan had just shrugged and given a smile.

Allan was somewhere in the saleroom right now, catalog open as he perused potential purchases. Not that he could afford much—not on a banking salary. But he had a passion for art and a good eye, and would become wistful on the day of the actual auction as he watched paintings he coveted being bought by people he didn't know. Those paintings, he'd told Mike, might disappear from public view for a generation or more.

"Worst case, they're bought as investments and placed in a vault for safe keeping—no more meaning to their buyer than compound interest."

"You're saying I shouldn't buy anything?"

"Not as an investment—you should buy whatever *pleases* you . . ."

As a result of which, the walls of Mike's apartment were replete with art from the nineteenth and twentieth centuries—most of it Scottish. He had eclectic tastes, so that cubism sat alongside pastoral, portraiture beside collage. For the most part, Allan approved. The two had first met a year ago at a party at the bank's investment arm HQ on George Street. The First Caledonian Bank—"First Caly" as it was more usually called—owned an impressive corporate art collection. Large Fairbairn abstracts flanked the entrance lobby, with a Coulton triptych behind the reception desk. First Caly employed its own curator, whose job it was to discover new talent—often from degree shows—then sell when the price was right and replenish the collection. Mike had mistaken Allan for the curator, and they'd struck up a conversation.

"Allan Cruikshank," Allan had said, shaking Mike's hand. "And of course I already know who *you* are."

"Sorry about the mix-up," Mike had apologized with an embarassed grin. "It's just that we seem to be the only people interested in what's on the walls . . ."

Allan Cruikshank was in his late forties and, as he put it, "expensively divorced," with two teenage sons and a daughter in her twenties. He dealt with HNWs—High Net Worth individuals—but had assured Mike that he wasn't angling for business. Instead, in the absence of the curator, he'd shown Mike as much of the collection as was open for general viewing.

"MD's office will be locked. He's got a Wilkie and a couple of Raeburns . . ."

In the weeks after the party, they'd exchanged emails, gone out for drinks a few times, and become friends. Mike had come to the viewing this evening only because Allan had persuaded him that it might be fun. But so far he had seen nothing to whet his jaded appetite, other than a charcoal study by one of the major Scottish Colorists—and he already had three at home much the same, probably torn from the self-same sketchbook.

"You look bored," Allan said with a smile. He held his dog-eared catalog in one hand, and a drained champagne flute in the other. Tiny flakes of pastry on his striped tie showed that he had sampled the canapés.

"I *am* bored."

"No gold-digging blondes sidling up to you with offers you'd be hard pressed to refuse?"

"Not so far."

"Well, this *is* Edinburgh after all; more chance of being asked to make up a four for bridge . . ." Allan looked around him. "Busy old night, all the same. Usual mix of freeloaders, dealers and the privileged."

"And which are we?"

"We're art lovers, Michael—pure and simple."

"So is there anything you'll be bidding on come auction day?"

"Probably not." Allan gave a sigh, staring into the depths of his parched glass. "The next lot of school fees are still on my desk, awaiting checkbook. And I know what you're going to say: plenty of good schools in the city without needing to pay for one. You yourself attended a rough-hewn comprehensive and it didn't do you any harm, but this is *tradition* we're talking about. Three generations, all schooled at the same fusty establishment. My father would curdle in his grave if I put the boys elsewhere."

"I'm sure Margot would have something to say about it, too."

At mention of his ex-wife, Allan gave an exaggerated shudder. Mike smiled, playing his part. He knew better than to offer financial assistance—he'd made that mistake once before. A banker, a man whose daily dealings involved some of the wealthiest individuals in Scotland, couldn't be seen to accept handouts.

"You should get Margot to pay her share," Mike teased. "You're always saying she earns as much as you do."

"And used that purchasing power to good effect when she chose her lawyers." Another tray of undercooked pastry was coming past. Mike shook his head while Allan asked if the fizz could be pointed in their direction. "Not that it's worth the effort," he muttered to Mike. "Ersatz, if you ask me. That's why they've wrapped those white cotton napkins around the bottles. Means we can't read the label." He took another look around the chatter-filled room. "Have you pressed the flesh with Laura yet?"

"A glance and a smile," Mike replied. "She seems popular tonight."

"The winter auction was the first one she'd fronted," Allan reminded him, "and it didn't exactly catch fire. She needs to woo potential buyers."

"And we don't fit the bill?"

"With due respect, Mike, you're fairly transparent—you lack what gamblers would call the 'poker face.' That little glance you say you exchanged probably told her all she needed to know. When you see a painting you like, you stand in front of it for minutes on end, and then you go up on your tiptoes when you've made up your mind to buy it." Allan attempted the movement, rocking on his heels and his toes, while holding out his glass towards the arriving champagne.

"You're good at reading people, aren't you?" Mike said with a laugh.

"Comes with the job. A lot of HNWs want you to know what they're thinking without them having to spell it out."

"So what am I thinking now?" Mike held a hand over his own glass and the waiter gave a little bow before moving on.

Allan made a show of screwing shut his eyes in thought. "You're thinking you can do without my smart-assed remarks," he said, opening his eyes again. "You're wishing you could stand in front of our charming hostess for minutes on end—tiptoes or no tiptoes." He paused. "And you're just about to suggest a bar where we can get ourselves a *real* drink."

"That's uncanny," Mike pretended to admit.

"What's more," Allan added, raising his glass in a toast, "one of your wishes is about to be granted . . ."

Yes, because Mike had seen her, too: Laura Stanton, squeezing her way through the throng, heading straight towards them. Almost six feet tall in her heels, auburn hair pulled back into a simple ponytail. She wore a sleeveless knee-length black dress, cut low to show the opal pendant hanging at her throat.

"Laura," Allan drawled, pecking her on both cheeks. "Congratulations, you've put together quite a sale."

"Better tell your employers at First Caly—I've got at least two brokers in the room scouting on behalf of rival banks. Everyone seems to want something for the boardroom." She had already turned her attention towards Mike. "Hello, you," she said, leaning forward for another exchange of kisses. "I get the feeling nothing's quite caught your fancy tonight."

"Not strictly true," Mike corrected her, causing her cheeks to redden.